A CURSE OF BREATH AND BLOOD

K.W. FOSTER

aethonbooks.com

A CURSE OF BREATH AND BLOOD
©2024 K.W. FOSTER

This book is protected under the copyright laws of the United States of America. No part of this publication may be reproduced, stored in a retrieval system, or transmitted, in any form or by any means, without the prior permission in writing of the publisher, nor be otherwise circulated in any form of binding or cover other than that in which it is published and without a similar condition including this condition being imposed on the subsequent purchaser. Any reproduction or unauthorized use of the material or artwork contained herein is prohibited without the express written permission of the authors.

Aethon Books supports the right to free expression and the value of copyright. The purpose of copyright is to encourage writers and artists to produce the creative works that enrich our culture.

The scanning, uploading, and distribution of this book without permission is a theft of the author's intellectual property. If you would like to use material from the book (other than for review purposes), please contact editor@aethonbooks.com. Thank you for your support of the author's rights.

Aethon Books
www.aethonbooks.com

Published by Aethon Books LLC.

Aethon Books is not responsible for websites (or their content) that are not owned by the publisher.

This book is a work of fiction. Names, characters, places, and incidents are the product of the author's imagination or are used fictitiously. Any resemblance to actual events, locales, or persons, living or dead is coincidental.

All rights reserved.

AUTHOR'S NOTE

This book features depictions of abuse, addiction, and violence that are not suitable for readers under the age of 18. If you or a loved one is trying to escape a domestic violence situation, please call **1-800-799-7233** or text **BEGIN** to **88788**.

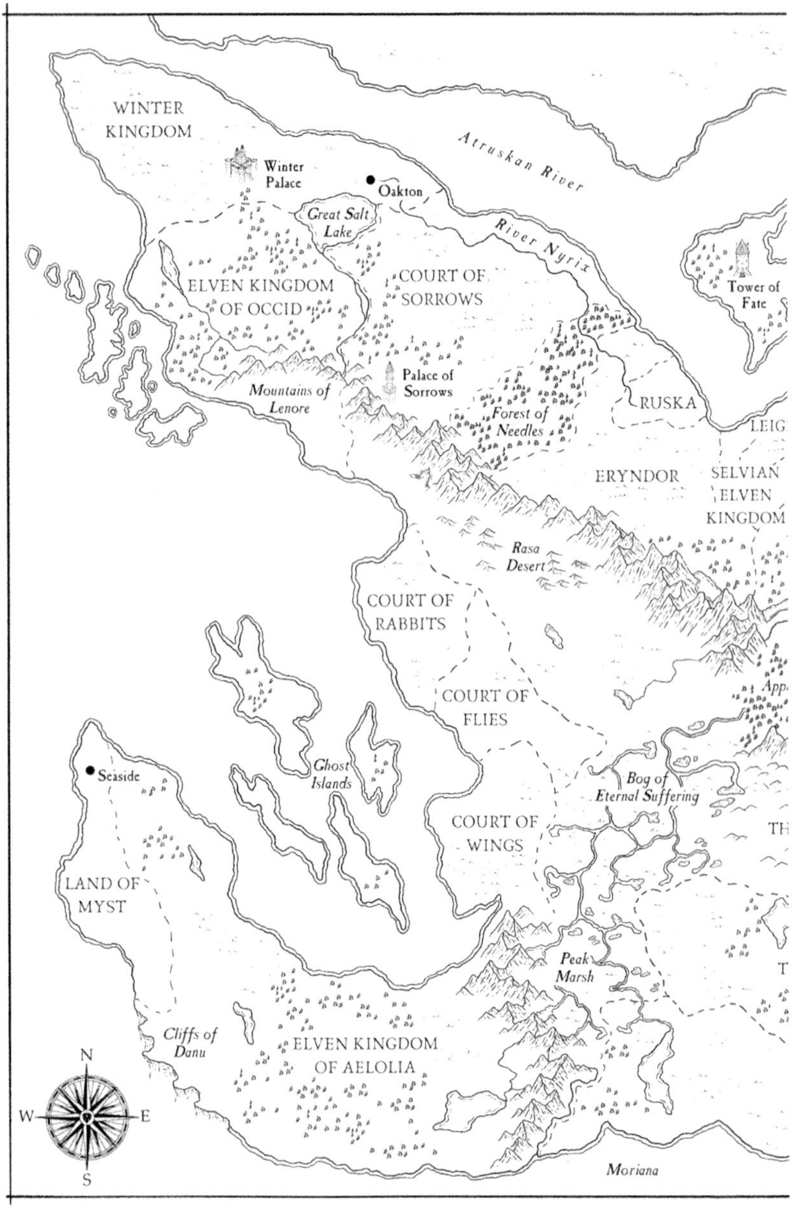
WINTER KINGDOM
Winter Palace
Oakton
Atruskan River
Great Salt Lake
River Nyrix
Tower of Fate
ELVEN KINGDOM OF OCCID
COURT OF SORROWS
Palace of Sorrows
Mountains of Lenore
Forest of Needles
RUSKA
LEIG
ERYNDOR
SELVIAN ELVEN KINGDOM
Rasa Desert
COURT OF RABBITS
COURT OF FLIES
App
Ghost Islands
Seaside
Bog of Eternal Suffering
COURT OF WINGS
TH
LAND OF MYST
Peak Marsh
T
Cliffs of Danu
N
W
E
S
ELVEN KINGDOM OF AELOLIA
Moriana

COURT OF SCREAMS

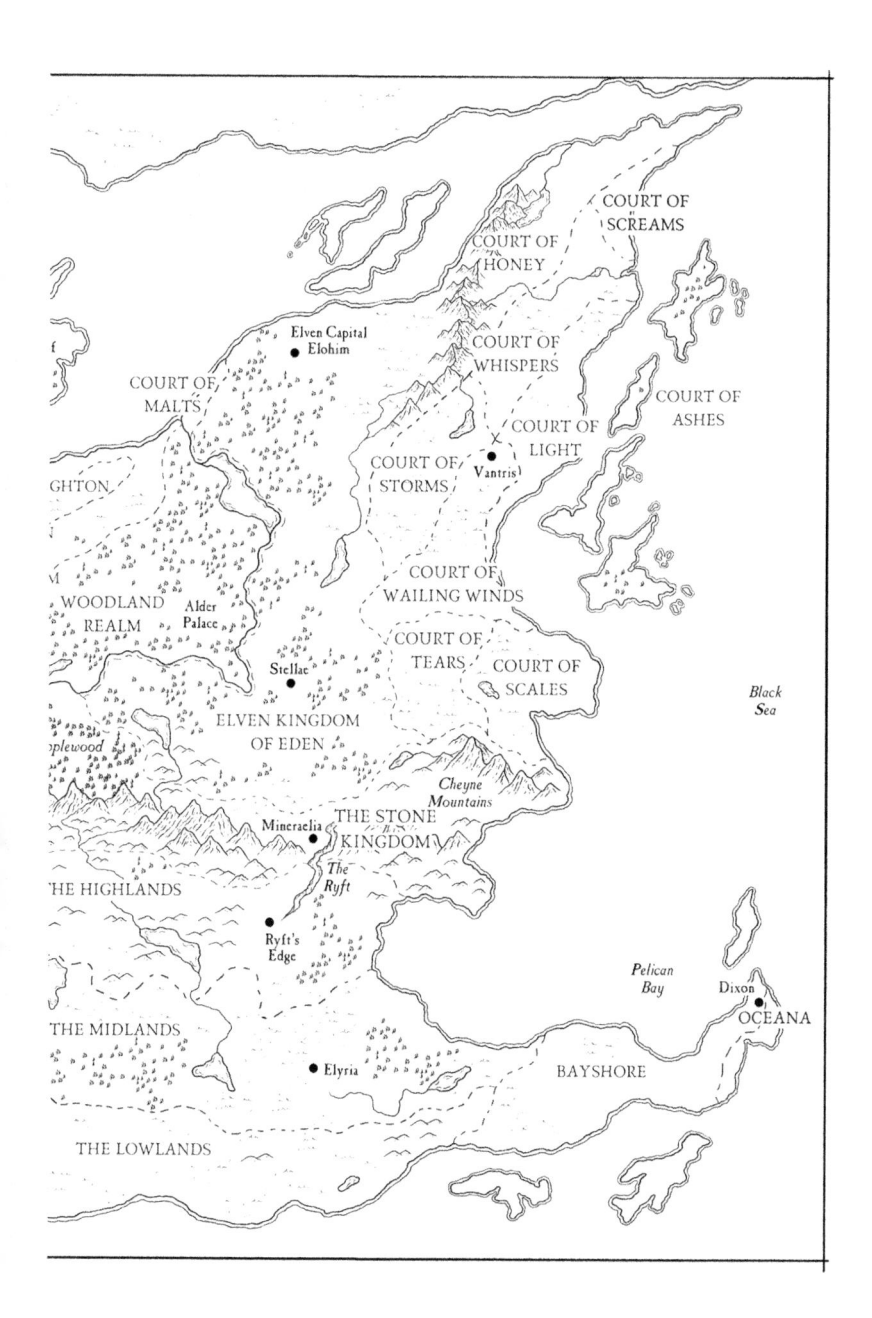

COURT OF HONEY

COURT OF WHISPERS

Elven Capital
Elohim

COURT OF MALTS

COURT OF ASHES

COURT OF LIGHT

GHTON

COURT OF STORMS

Vantris

WOODLAND REALM

Alder Palace

COURT OF WAILING WINDS

Stellac

COURT OF TEARS

COURT OF SCALES

Black Sea

ELVEN KINGDOM OF EDEN

plewood

Cheyne Mountains

Mineralia

THE STONE KINGDOM

HE HIGHLANDS

The Ryft

Ryft's Edge

Pelican Bay

Dixon

OCEANA

THE MIDLANDS

Elyria

BAYSHORE

THE LOWLANDS

DEDICATION

To those lost in darkness, you are not alone.

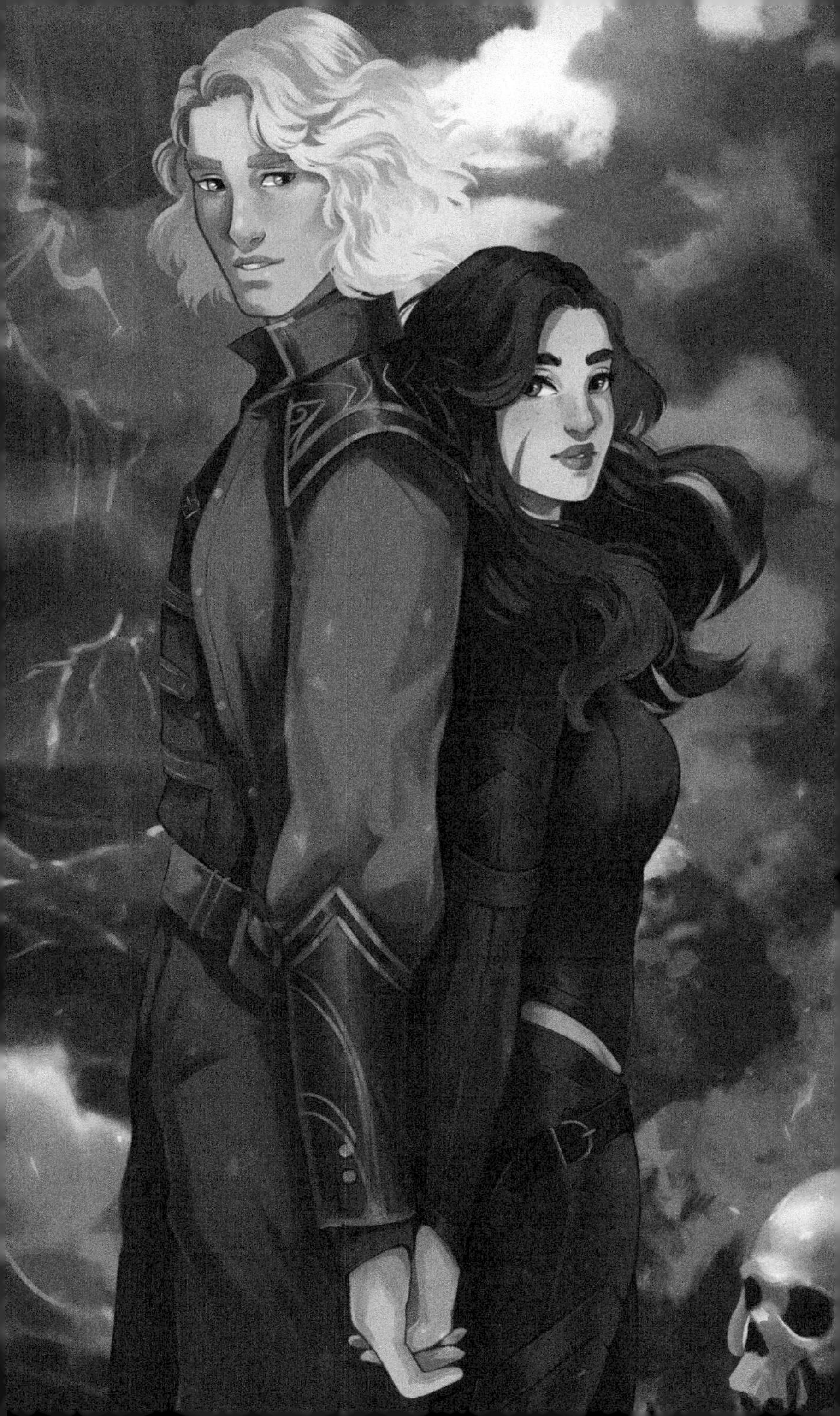

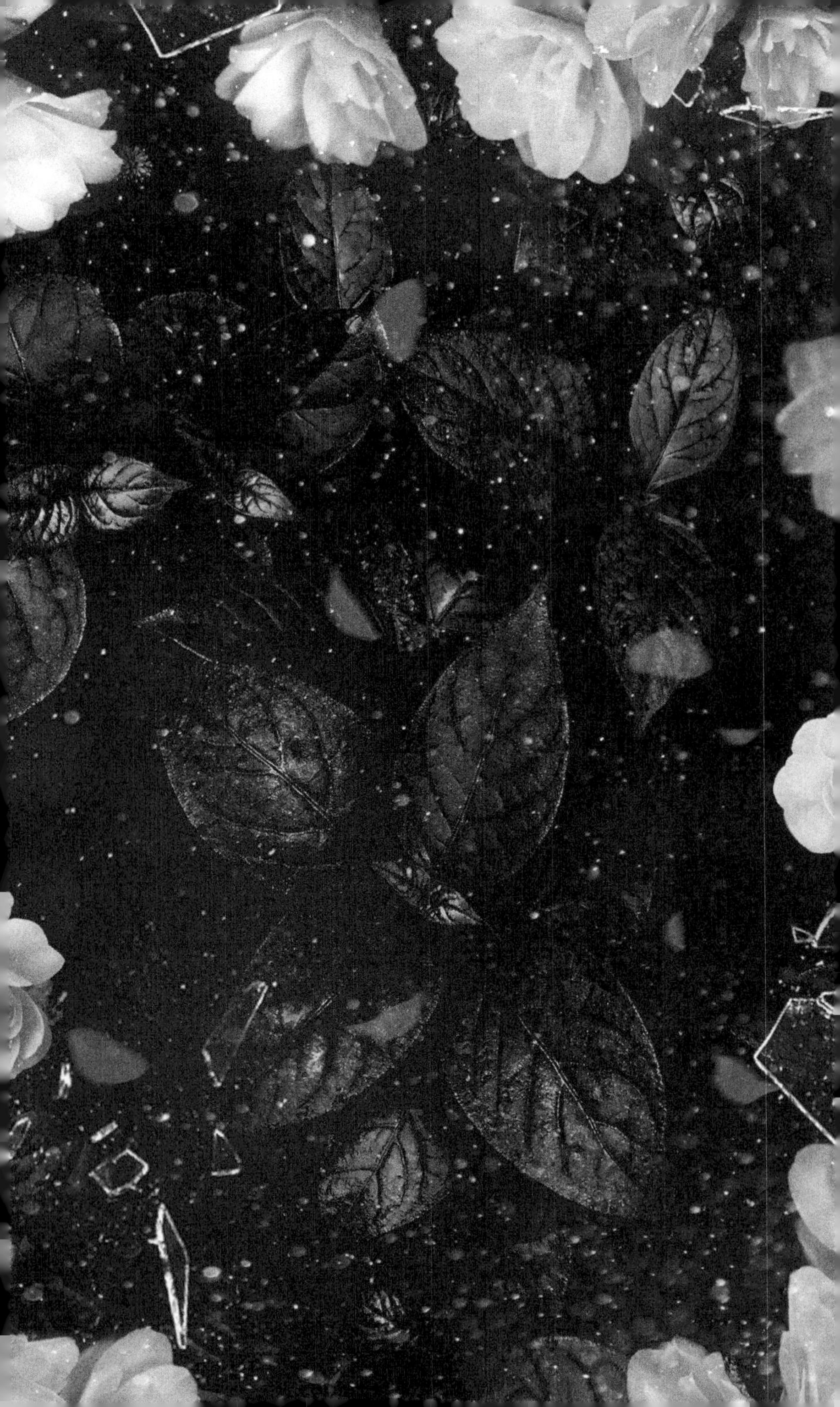

A History of Moriana and the World of the Mind Breaker Series

Moriana is a diverse continent, home to many different races and cultures.

The Beginning

Before the Trinity culled the land and tamed the magic, the Gods of Old roamed freely, wreaking havoc. It was a brutal and bloody time. The people of Moriana called out for a hero, and they received three. Upon hearing their cries, the Trinity ascended from the heavens, smiting the Gods of Old and creating the three major races—the Elves, to which **Eris** gave her Breath and, with it, eternal life. They were meant to be the keepers of knowledge so that evil could not slink back into the world. **Illya** created the **Sylph** from her blood, instilling each of the founding families with a magical gift. The Sylph were created to protect the continent in case the evil ever arose again. With her golden apple, the goddess **Ammena** created the **Humans** to cultivate and care for the earth. She instilled in them a deep understanding of the importance of balance in nature and hoped that by making them mortal, they would value the time given to them.

War of Three Faces

Peace reigned over the land, but in secret, an orphan-turned-god was building a cult that would eventually consume the continent. His name was Crom Cruach. A half-elf, half-sylph magus (magic wielder) raised in a primitive sect of humans who feared magic. Once his magic was discovered, he was an outcast from the only family he'd ever known. Angry and alone, he made his way to the Rasa desert, where he unknowingly fulfilled an ancient prophecy of the Rasa Tribe. Made a living god, he used the Rasa to spread his influence by both diplomatic and violent means. When his powers had grown, as well as his influence, he left the desert, returning to his home in the mountains, where he took control of his old tribe and their fierce warriors. Crom used these warriors, combined with his political influence, to conquer the continent, wiping out all those who crossed him. Humans, Sylph, and Elves band together to fight Crom's influence, resulting in a brutal war that lasted a hundred years. In the end, Crom was defeated, and his followers fled the continent. Crom's body was burned and placed in an unmarked tomb. Only the Elven King, Arendir knows where he is entombed to this day.

Peace reigned once again, but many of the cities of the continent had been destroyed.

To celebrate their victory over Crom Cruach, the Elves invited the sylph and humans to a month-long victory celebration in the elven capital of Elohim. Jealous of the sylph's gifts and inherent strength, they hatched a plan to take their powers for their own. After the sylph leaders had been thoroughly plied with enchanted wine, the elves slipped into the sylph leaders' chambers, slit their wrists, and drank their blood, gaining the gifts Illya had instilled in them. But the effects were only temporary. Now that the elves had gotten a taste for The Blood, their lust for power was insatiable. Using these new gifts and gaining allies across the continent, the elves enslaved the sylph for nearly five hundred years.

The Sylph and Elven War

What started as a small rebellion grew into a full-blown war, raging for nearly fifty years and tearing the continent apart again. Most humans allied with the sylph, but some allied with the elves. Eventually, the Treaty of Three Kings was signed, freeing the sylph from their bondage. Torn between the old and new, the sylph split into two sets of Courts: The Wild, which upheld the old traditions, and the Council Courts, who considered themselves more civilized.

An uneasy peace has existed on the continent since.

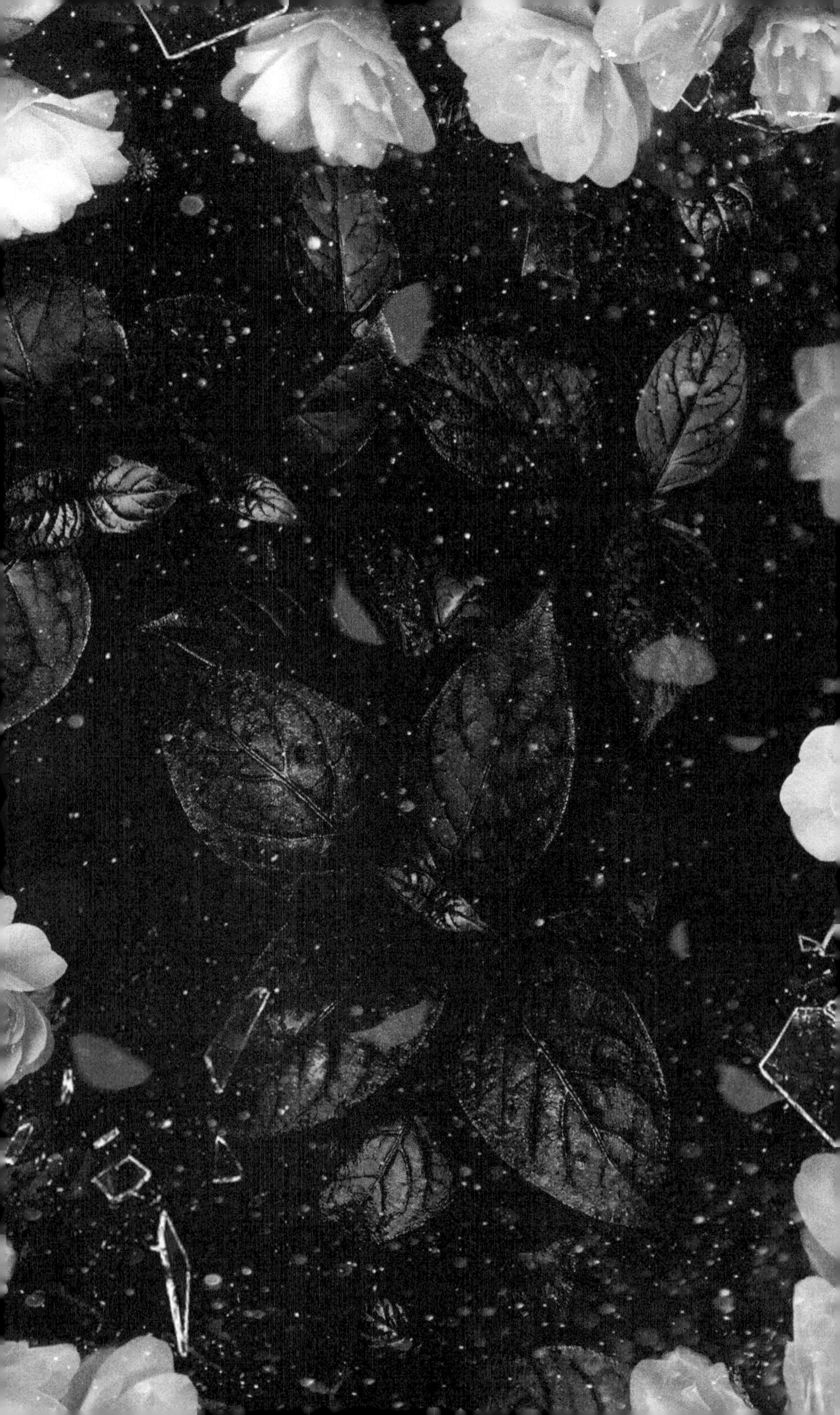

PROLOGUE
AELIA

Before

TEARS STAINED MY CHEEKS AS CAIDEN PULLED ME IN CLOSER. Silver streaks of moon danced across his chiseled face. His golden hair, like a halo, illuminated piercing blue eyes.

"I don't want to go," I sniffled. "I don't want to leave you." I dug my fingers into his back, hoping to somehow convince him to take me away from here.

Music and laughter trickled in through the walls of the cabin. A reminder this was to be a happy day. The people of Elyria hadn't seen a Promised Day celebration in decades. This was a time for them to celebrate. To rejoice in the union of two kingdoms.

"I know, Aelia. I know." He brushed an unruly piece of my hair behind my ear. "But we knew our love was doomed before it began. A sylph and a human could never marry."

A hot cry grew in my chest, working its way up my throat. I buried my face in Caiden's neck, letting out a wail of pain. Primal and fierce. Our love died before it ever had a chance to live.

"I know, but I hoped—"

His finger pressed against my lips.

"Hope is a dangerous thing. It blinds us to reality."

Shaking, I nodded. How many times had I let hope get the better of me? I needed to grow up. I would be a queen soon, ruling over a kingdom on my own. I needed to give up these silly notions. Caiden and I were over.

"Gideon is an up-and-coming royal. He will treat you fairly. At least from the time I've spent in his court."

"Promise me you'll visit?" I asked, knowing the pain it would cause me.

Caiden kissed my forehead. "I'm not that strong, Aelia. I love you too much."

My chest tightened. Words escaped me. There was nothing left to say besides goodbye. Tomorrow, I would be loaded into a golden carriage and whisked away to the Highlands, where my betrothed, Gideon Ironheart, waited for me. Tomorrow, I would no longer be a princess but a queen-in-waiting. Tomorrow, the life I've known for twenty-five years would be over.

"I don't want to love anyone else but you."

Caiden gently stoked my back with his callous hands. "You'll always have a place in my heart."

"I'm afraid you'll forget me."

Caiden's chest swelled with a breath. "There's something I have to tell you."

Pulling myself from his embrace, I met his gaze. "What is it?"

"I promised your mother I'd protect you with my life, and I mean that. If you are in danger, real danger, send a raven to me. I will come for you." His hand was on my face and our eyes locked.

"I love you, Caiden."

"I love you too, Aelia."

Our lips locked, bodies entwining for one final union.

The ride to the Highlands took ages. Alone with my thoughts, I dreamt of Caiden rescuing me, but no rescue would ever come. The smell of wheat turned into the sweet smell of pine as we climbed farther into the Highlands. Even the air here was thinner, making my head light.

Cresting over the top of the trees, a castle came into view. Spindled towers rose high into the sky, each one capped in gold. A thriving city of brick splayed out before it. The Cheyne Mountains rose like a protective shield in the distance.

I swallowed hard at the sight of my new home. Ryft's Edge, the jewel of the Highlands.

Gideon waited for me, dressed in his finest attire, a black velvet coat with the hawk of the Highlands embroidered onto the chest. A diadem of golden leaves encircled his dark hair.

Tall and broad-shouldered, with a muscular build that only came with time in the sparring ring. I'd heard tales of his prowess in battle, and his rigid stance confirmed it.

The carriage stopped in front of him. I tried not to stare at my future husband. A strong jaw and high cheekbones gave him the appearance of elegant masculinity, while his crooked nose added a bit of character.

I covered my face with the ceremonial veil, trying my best to calm my nerves. Visions of Caiden's smiling face flashed before my eyes.

I took a deep breath.

The handle clicked open.

A jeweled hand extended toward me. Hesitantly, I took it.

Gideon smiled back at me.

"Princess Aelia, Springborn, I presume?" His voice was warm, like a loving caress.

My skin pricked at his touch.

"Prince Gideon, I presume?"

"Your presumption is correct."

Fingers clasped around mine, he pulled me out of the carriage where a fleet of servants waited to attend to me.

Looking for support, I gripped his hand tighter.

Leaning in, he whispered, "It's alright, I've got you now."

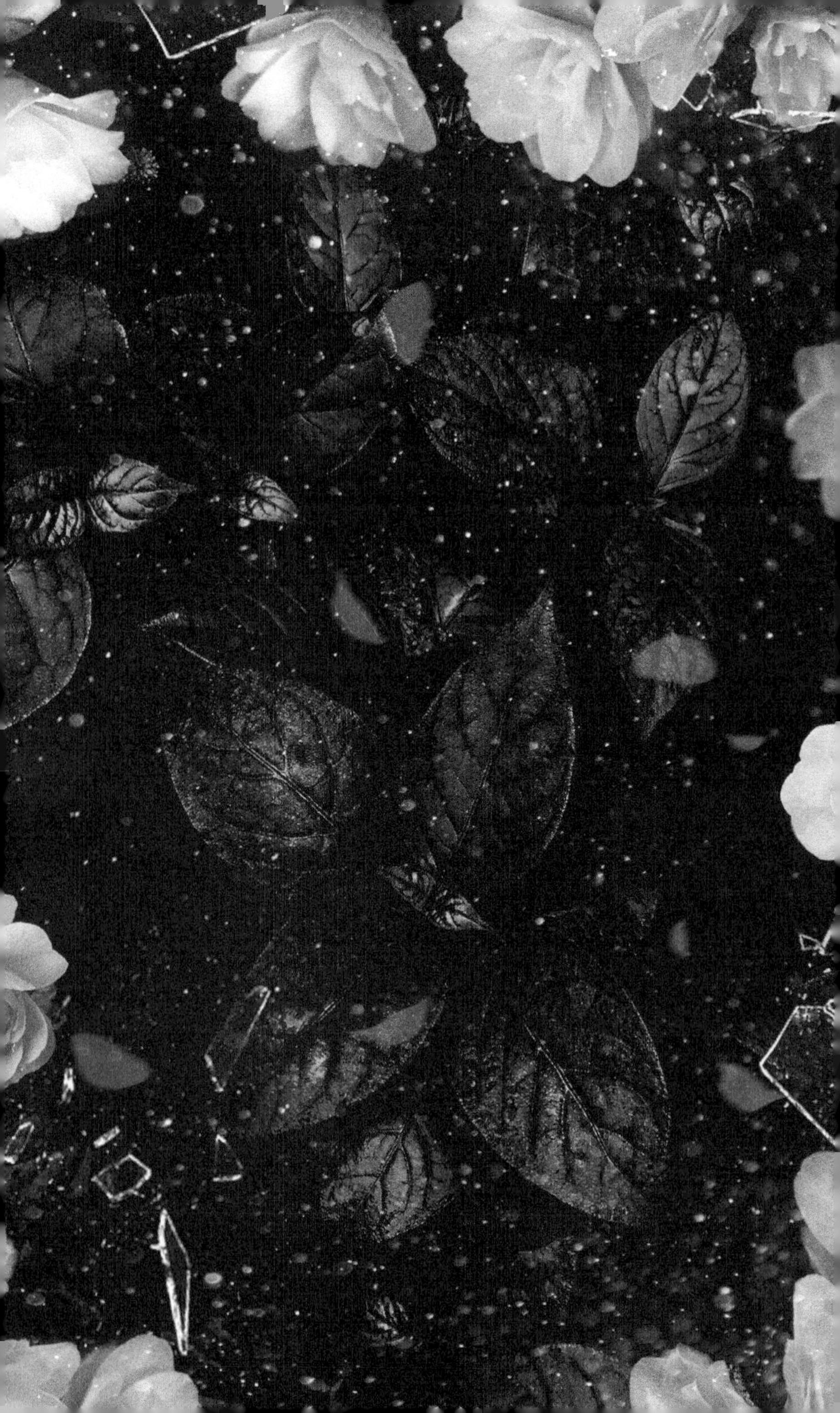

1 AELIA
FIVE YEARS LATER

The guards beat him to a pulp before I arrived.

I stood with my hands crossed over my chest, drumming my fingers on my arm. Usually, I knew the full details of a job when an employer came looking for me, but kings don't send forewarning, the Winter King least of all.

The uneasiness pricking at the back of my neck made the raging winter storm outside seem more welcoming than any tavern room gold could provide. A fireplace at the end of the hall crackled as it fought the cold. Shreds of firelight peered from behind the broad frame of the Winter King. Though his body blocked the heat, it did not stop the bits of shadows dancing on the young boy's beaten face.

"Destroy him," the king's voice shattered through my ears.

I gazed at the soldier, no older than seventeen, with a bloodied lip and an eye so swollen, I wondered if it would ever heal. Still, he stared back at me. A slick sweat coated his brow.

"Will it hurt, Miss?" His brown eyes full of fear.

I crouched down. "Only if you resist me."

I did not break bodies; I broke minds.

Acne still dotted the soldier's face. His youth made me flinch, and I hoped the king didn't notice. Why did he want this boy to suffer?

As if answering my question, the king's daughter burst in, flooding the room with a bone-chilling cold.

"Please, Father..." With clenched fists, her eyes darted between her father and the boy. "Please spare him." Head held high, she threw herself between them.

My eyes snapped to the king. Grinding his jaw, he reached for his daughter, yanking her away.

I ran my hand through my hair—a nervous tick I picked up to ease the tension building in my chest. *Breathe, Aelia, do not let your affinity for young love get the better of you.*

The king stared at his daughter. His mouth bracketed tight. A spasm hooked the corner of his eye. In an instant, his long years of diplomatic training erased every trace of emotion from his face, hiding it away—but even the best liars have a tell. Hidden in the loose curl of a fist, the tip of his thumb worries an incongruously simple gold band on his ring finger. Thinking of his dead queen, perhaps? I could work with that.

Bowing my head, I pleaded with his more sentimental side, "May I make a suggestion, Your Majesty?"

"I am not paying you for your opinion, mercenary," he snapped at me.

Mercenary—he spat the name at me. A knot twisted in my stomach. Once, I was a queen. Now, I'd break the mind of whomever they put before me so long as they had enough gold to pay.

"Perhaps I might suggest a compromise?"

The princess's youthful face brightened with hope.

"Go on..." The king crossed his arms over his chest.

Biting the inside of my cheek, I stalled for time, choosing my

A CURSE OF BREATH AND BLOOD

words wisely. "Let me erase the princess from this boy's mind and replace it with a life of celibacy. He will serve you faithfully until his death. I guarantee it."

The young man's shoulders stiffened as his eyes bounced back and forth between the king and me. He did not dare to look at the princess.

"Yes, please, Father. Please let her erase his mind." Tears streamed down the girl's face. "And... mine too," she said through sniffles, daring to approach the boy. "I don't want to live without him." She ran a dainty hand down the boy's still-round face.

A fragment of a memory flashed through my mind of hands entwined, a breath on my neck, stolen glances from across a crowded room.

I swallowed the thickness growing in my throat, pushing back the memories of my youth, of the love I lost.

"Out of the question!" he snarled. His brow furrowed in brief regret before he hid the weakness away. He tried again, softer, "We have a responsibility, my darling. As regents, we must never compromise the secrets or security of our kingdom. Certainly, we must never let a magus go digging through their mind."

"No." The princess rushed to her father, yanking on his crossed arms, hoping her touch would make him understand. "This is what you wanted. I don't want to live every day knowing he'll never remember what we had." She wiped the tears from her eyes. "Please give me this mercy."

The king softened. "Very well. Erase both their memories."

"Thank you, Father." The princess embraced the king, turning his once stern face red.

The young man relaxed, his shoulders drooping.

I took a deep breath, steadying myself. To enter another's mind is to enter a maze. You don't know where it leads, and you don't know if you can escape before the hedges close in on you.

Slowing my heart rate, I focused on calming memories—the smell of my horse, Arion, the sun kissing my face. Going into a mind without stilling your own could trigger defenses.

I closed my eyes, reaching deep inside myself for my power. I knocked on the simple peasant door leading to the boy's mind.

Click, the door swung open.

Show me the love you shared with the princess. Start at the beginning.

He took me to where he first met the princess—the palace's great hall. Garlands of flowers hung from the rafters, filling the room with the scent of lilac and jasmine—an Ostara celebration. From across the room, the princess and the soldier locked eyes. She gave him a coy smile, sending his pulse racing.

A sharp pain clawed at my heart. Fragments of my past invaded my mind. A stolen smile, a kiss under the cover of darkness, this could have been me—had been me.

Slamming the door on my nostalgia, I focused on the task at hand; sweat dripped down my temples. One by one, I erased every kiss, every glance, every loving embrace. I took every memory until his unyielding allegiance belonged to the Winter King rather than his former beloved.

A slow breath escaped my lips. I worked through his mind, trying to keep the parts of him I could. I worked with a surgeon's precision, clipping the princess's lacy outline from every memory. Were I to take too much, his entire personality could change. Too little, and her face disappears but the absence remains, little fragments worming through the brain like an unscratchable itch.

The boy's dark head hung low. His shoulders rising and falling with shallow breaths. The smell of sweat replaced the smell of fear.

"It is done."

"Is he… alive?" The king leaned in to get a closer look.

Raising his head, the boy's eyes shone with the vigor of a hunter eager for the kill. "My King, my life is yours."

The cracking of my knees echoed through the lavish chamber as I stood. "He is your acolyte now. He will follow you until his bitter end, and perhaps even in death, he will remain loyal."

The silver-haired king's face lit with pleasure. "Very well." The king motioned to two guards who led the boy out while the princess looked on, tears streaming down her face.

My fingers itched to light the cigarette in my pocket—a ritual I saved for after a completed job. Thinking about smoke burning in my lungs set me at ease. Even now I could taste the spice of clove on my tongue.

"Are you ready?" I asked the princess. Breaking one mind exhausted me; breaking two would deplete me. Already, my arms hung heavy at my sides, and my eyes begged for sleep.

The princess nodded, although her body trembled with fear.

"Give me a moment." I crouched down once more to collect myself. My hair escaped its leather tie, swinging down to curtain off my face, hiding my exhaustion. *Do this, and you can charge twice as much, Aelia. Do this, and you can drink yourself stupid later.* Wiping my sweaty palms on my pants, I inhaled the dry air of the overheated throne room. "Alright, let's get this over with."

The king signaled for a seat for the princess, and two attendants eagerly carried a plush chair over.

Gripping the arms of the chair tightly, her knuckles turned white. The princess steadied herself.

"I promise it won't hurt. But you must show me everything. I cannot leave a memory to fester."

She nodded, her shoulders slumping.

I chewed on the sandy taste filling my mouth—an unfortunate side effect of telepathy. "Close your eyes and show me the love you shared with the soldier," I said, reaching out my mind once again.

A large iron door engraved with the sigils of the Winter Kingdom—two giant white bears fighting, greeted me. Their teeth bared in a sign of strength.

I pushed the doors open, but instead of the Ostara celebration, I entered her bed chambers. The princess stared down at a field of frost tipped wheat. Below, the young soldier laughed with his friends. My pulse quickened. Had he seen her too? Was there more left in his mind I did not take? Hurriedly, I erased the memory, hoping there weren't any others.

With exhaustion biting at the corners of my vision, I cut precisely and with haste. In my tired state, the princess's psyche could sense me. Whereas on a full night's rest I was invisible; tired, I became a thorn in the girl's mind, hacking away at her precious memories.

I had to get out.

The psyche wanted me gone. Members of the crowd turned their heads to face me.

I erased them as fast as I could.

Another memory. A stolen kiss. A stranger with their hand over my mouth. Jamming my elbow into soft flesh, I took what I could. I hated sloppy work, but I did not have the luxury of time on my side.

Cutting more like a butcher than a surgeon, I wiped the rest of the girl's memories. Sweet and innocent. Their love faded to nothingness in her mind.

The princess opened her eyes. "Who are you?" she asked, blinking at me.

I pushed down the bile rising in the back of my throat.

"No one." I slowly backed away. The chill of winter clinging all at once to my back.

"Your payment," the king said, motioning for an attendant, who presented me with a sack of gold and a ruby the size of a goose egg.

I packed both away in my satchel. "Pleasure doing business with you."

On my way out of the throne room, I caught a glimpse of the king and his daughter embracing. Jealousy tugged at my heart. No warm embrace waited for me tonight. Only the bite of a stiff drink and a pinch of dust lull Aelia Springborn, Queen of the Highlands, to sleep.

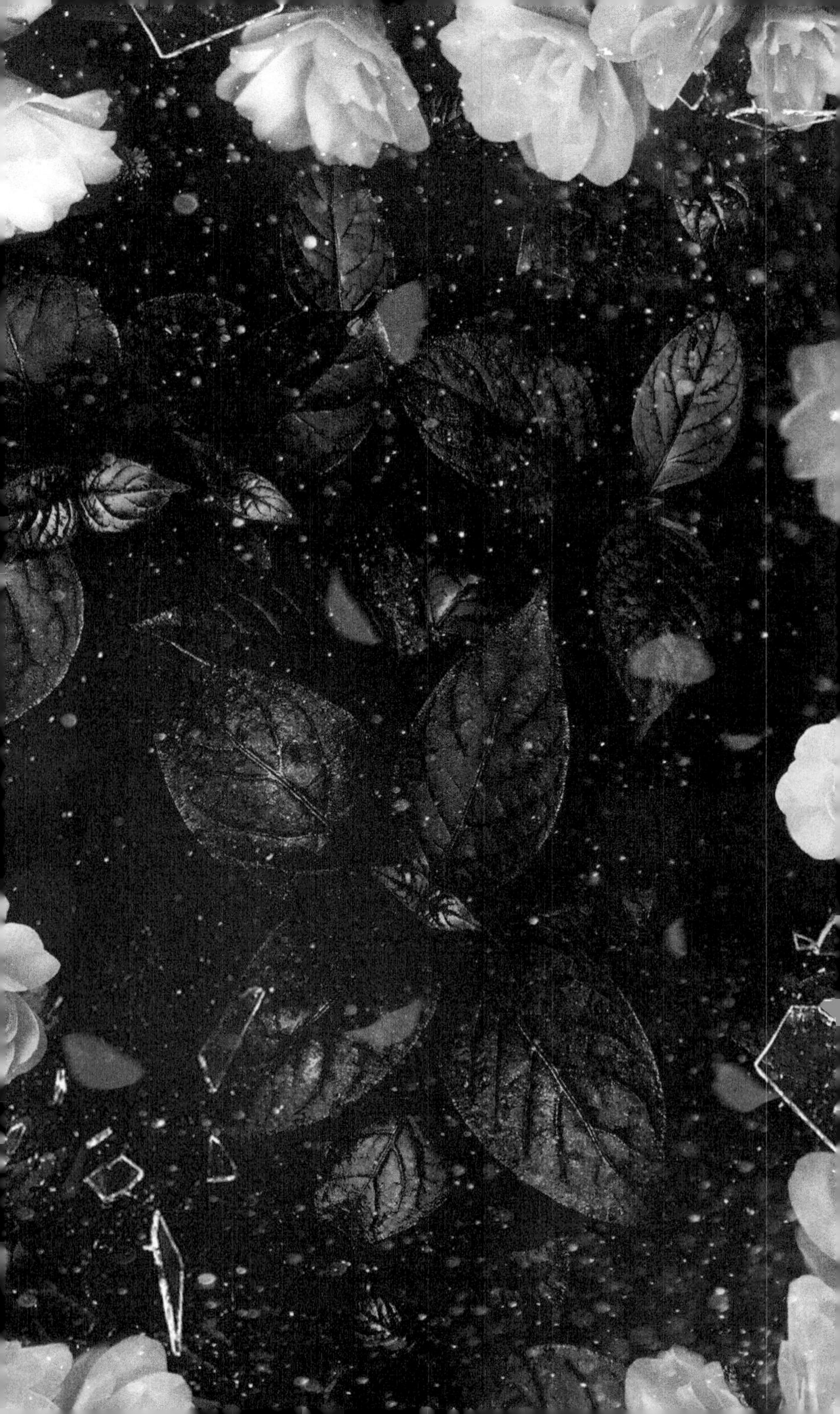

2 AELIA

While the barkeep poured me a drink, I surveyed the dingy pub. Low-lit candles struggled against the darkness, casting the room in shadow. Ripped wallpaper adorned the decrepit walls. The stench of old ale and sweat hung heavy in the air.

Downing the shot of brown liquid, I let the alcohol burn away the stress of the day. Warmth spread through my body.

Patrons huddled near a massive fireplace, trying to stay warm as a winter wind rattled the windows. At the other end of the bar, a group of soldiers cheered, clinking their mugs together. A tall, broad-shouldered young commander with dusty brown hair caught my eye. I flashed him a flirtatious smile. He returned it with a smile.

"Well, well, well, if it isn't the Traitorous Queen herself..." A voice as cold as frost-covered glass sent a shiver down my spine.

I dug my nails into the grease-laden bar, turning to face a ghost from my past. He hadn't changed a bit since last I'd seen him—still as tall and thin as always. A shock of white cascaded down the center of his pale head. Why had he come back to haunt me?

I stilled my face into a stoic look, hoping it hid my churning stomach.

"What do you want, Lucius?" I picked at my nails carelessly. His lord could not be far away.

"You know why I'm here, Aelia." He cocked his head. Disdain clouded his black eyes.

I arched an eyebrow. "You can tell your lord I'm busy." Taking another drink of liquor, I hoped it would give me the courage to face the man whose heart I shattered into a million pieces. My fingers tingled as the alcohol worked its way through my system.

"It's serious, Aelia." He leaned in, the scent of his beloved mint leaves heavy on his breath. "He's found something."

I paused; my thumbnail still wedged under my ring finger. "Bullshit."

"Read my mind and see if I'm lying." He tapped his temple with an immaculately manicured finger.

"I don't work for free." I signaled for the barkeep to pour me another drink.

Lucius caught my hand before I could down the shot, spilling some of the chestnut liquid onto the bar. "I did not travel to the end of the world to play games with you." A muscle ticked in his jaw as he tried to contain his ire for me.

"Pity. I love games. Especially ones where I get to upset the infamous Spy Master of the Stormlands." I ran my free hand through his long, silken hair. Exhilaration rushed through my veins at the sight of his cold eyes and pinched mouth.

"We don't have time for this nonsense." Lucius carried an air of intensity about him, but the fact they were here at the edge of the continent told me they found something tangible. His lord wouldn't have traveled to the edge of the world for nothing.

I pouted my bottom lip. "But we're having so much fun here."

"Grow up, Aelia." His words soaked in disdain.

A CURSE OF BREATH AND BLOOD

"Fine," I huffed, rolling my eyes.

He released me, and I tipped my head back, letting the dark liquor burn my throat. My head buzzed.

"He's waiting upstairs," Lucius said through gritted teeth.

"Lead the way." I pulled out a cigarette to calm my nerves, making him wait until I lit it.

Lucius turned and parted the crowd. I followed him up the creaky stairs to a small suite. He knocked four times.

Pushing my hair behind my ears, I took a deep breath.

A mammoth, sylph man with umber skin and pale green eyes answered the door. The sigil of the Stormlands, a bolt of lightning striking an oak tree, embossed in his armor—Roderick Bonecleaver, general of the Court of Storm's armies.

I strained my neck to see the room behind him, but he took up most of the doorway.

"Took you long enough," he said to Lucius. His deep voice commanded attention.

"I told you she wouldn't come easily," Lucius replied, pushing his way past Roderick.

Taking a drag from my cigarette, I lingered in the curling smoke before stepping into the light cutting through the dark hallway.

"Aelia! It's been a long time." Roderick's perfectly shaped lips curved into a disarming smile. My chest lightened as he squeezed me tight.

His sylph fangs gleamed like pearls in the flickering candlelight. A reminder of the creatures they were before their goddess, Illya, blessed them with her blood. Turning them into something resembling a human but with the strength of one hundred men.

"It's nice to see you too, Roderick," I squeaked out.

He set me down.

Lucius glowered at us.

"Let's get this over with." Running my fingers through my

hair, I prepared to see the man who had owned my heart for nearly ten years.

"After you." Roderick stepped aside, creating a path for me.

A mix of fear and anticipation coiled in my stomach. Part of me wanted to puke, part of me wanted to run. *No, Aelia. Face your fears.* I straightened and stepped into the dingy room.

Time stopped at the sight of Caiden Stormweaver, Lord of the Court of Storms, sitting at a small table in the dim room. Golden hair cascaded in waves over his sculpted brow. His square jaw pebbled with stubble. Blue eyes fixed on mine.

My fingers twitched with the memories of summer days spent lying on the grass, exploring each other's bodies. Memories I wish I could erase. The irony in being one of the last telepaths on the continent—I could erase anyone's mind but my own.

Regret rotted in my stomach, but somehow, I willed my feet to move.

"Please take a seat." He motioned to the worn chair in front of him.

Chewing the side of my lip, I wiped my sweating palms on my pants in hesitation.

He held up his hands. "No tricks, I promise." His voice was as smooth as aged brandy.

I took the seat, noting all the exits. A small window I could easily break through to my left and the door behind me. "I assume you're here about the oath, Caiden," I said, crossing my arms over my chest.

He nodded. "Yes, blood oaths are not easily undone. I promised I'd protect you and your sister. So here I am, at the edge of the world, making good on my promise."

The gold in his hair caught in the flickering candlelight.

My anger did not stop my breath from hitching when I peered into his soft eyes. The same eyes I remember staring back at me all those years ago when our flesh and souls had become one.

Caiden pushed an unruly piece of hair out of his face. "I have located Baylis."

"Bullshit. Have you come here to taunt me?" Hope flickered in my chest, but I dared not give it air.

Caiden examined the shabby room while a winter wind battered the windows. "Do you think I traveled all this way for a joke?"

"I think you've traveled further for less." I gave him a snarky look.

A flame crackled in the hearth.

He held up his hand. A ring of gold encircled his fourth finger. "I'm not here to win you back, Aelia."

Thorns grew in my throat. He'd moved on.

Caiden's eyes would not meet mine, making me squirm in my chair. "It gets worse."

I ground my teeth together. A pressure building inside me.

"Gideon has her."

A breath escaped my chest at the name. Gideon Ironheart, King of the Highlands, my husband. "No shit. I've suspected that for five years. What proof do you have? I know every inch of his palace. Every place he would hide her. Every secret he keeps. And I haven't found so much as a whiff of Baylis."

"My scouts saw her in Gideon's traveling party, making their way towards the Woodland Realm." Lucius's eyes told me I should be worried, but I had become ignorant of the politics of men and magus since I fled Ryft Edge.

"Are you sure it was her? Could have been a body double? Could have been a glamour to lure me out of hiding. Could have been a coincidence."

"Trust me. My men are very good at what they do." He leaned back in his chair.

Matching his stance, I bit my lower lip. "I trust you and your men about as far as I can throw them."

Caiden let out an exasperated sigh. "I knew this was a waste of time. I should have known you'd never believe me. Guess I'll save Baylis myself."

My chest tightened. I compressed my insides. He had my goat, and he knew it. "Fine, I'll bite. What else do you know?"

A smile tugged at the corner of Caiden's mouth. "We think he's planning to offer her as a gift to the Alder King."

"Why would the Alder King want my sister?"

Caiden mulled over his words, rubbing his jaw. "We think Gideon will claim she has your mother's gift of sight."

"Psh. Neither my sister nor I can see into the future."

Caiden shrugged his broad shoulders. "It's been years since any of us have seen Baylis. Perhaps her powers manifested, after all."

The last time I saw Baylis, we were lowering our father into the ground.

"If Baylis had powers, I would know."

"We all know Gideon has ways of manifesting powers," Roderick said, tapping his temple.

"You don't have to tell me how Gideon can manifest powers." I traced my finger down the side of my face where a glamour now covered a jagged scar. "Great, tell me where she is, and I'll go rescue her."

"I know you've been on your own for a while, but I need your help with this. I have an oath to fulfill, too, if you remember," Caiden said.

"Oh, the oath you took before you sent my sister into the wild by herself?" I took a drag off my cigarette, letting the smoke fizzle in my lungs.

Rubbing the bridge of his nose with his fingers, Caiden sighed. "If we're pointing fingers, why don't we talk about who leaked the information to Highlands leading to the downfall of your kingdom."

A challenge. I let out a long, billowing plume of smoke.

Pressing my palms onto the table, I pushed myself up. "You don't know what it was like in that palace. Under Gideon's thumb. I didn't have a choice. I didn't even know what I was doing."

"Oh, don't give me that excuse. We always have a choice." He shook his head, dismissing my pain.

He thought he had me, but I knew where to twist the knife.

"Just like you had the choice to save me, and you didn't."

His face went pale.

That's right, I know which scars to reopen.

"I've apologized for that a million times. I can't go back in time, Aelia. What do you want me to do?"

A wave of emotion washed over me at the thought of our final goodbye all those years ago. Why was this happening now? Why did I let him affect me after all these years? I took another drag off my cigarette. Anything to distract me from the emotions bubbling in my stomach. The events of the day, combined with the alcohol coursing through my veins, made me emotional. Exhausted, I gave in. "Fine, tell me what you know."

He narrowed his eyes at me. "We believe she will be offered at the Alder King's Yule Revelry. Though there's one tiny hiccup." Caiden scrunched his fingers together. "We don't have an invitation... yet."

I leaned back in my chair, praying for something stronger than a cigarette to ease my nerves.

"Yet?" I asked. "The son of a high lord can't get any invitation he wants? I have not been an emissary in a long time, but I remember you can't go anywhere near the Alder Palace without an invitation."

Mischief gleamed in his blue eyes. "That's why we're going to have to steal one."

"Ah, no. I'm a telepath. I'll find a way into the Alder Palace by myself. Thanks." I headed toward the hallway.

A hand grabbed mine. I turned to see a curvy witch with curly brown hair and a face full of freckles bound through the door.

My heart lightened at the sight of Amolie, my trusted friend and confidant.

"What are you doing here?" I said, half-mad, half-relieved to see my friend.

"Caiden invited me. He thought you would need someone with my set of skills." She wiggled her fingers at me.

Turning to Caiden, I said, "I'm assuming this is how you found me." I noted they hadn't sent Amolie to confront me. Lucius must have wanted the pleasure of that all for himself.

Caiden would not meet my gaze. "It's not important *how* I found you. What's important is we leave at dawn, and you need to be ready." Caiden stood, straightening his embroidered tunic.

"You're not going to tell me the plan?" I tried not to wobble, but the liquor poisoning my blood made the room spin.

Caiden moved closer to me. The smell of leather and horses still clung to his skin. "You're drunk, Aelia. Sober up, and we'll talk in the morning."

"Do not get me killed, Lord Stormweaver," I said through gritted teeth.

Caiden paused by the door. "It's a good thing you're hard to kill, Springborn." Lightning flashed in his eyes.

I couldn't help but remember the young man I had fallen for all those years ago. The one who waited for me in darkened alleyways. The one who held me close when the world fell apart. I snapped my fingers nervously, trying to distract myself from the ache in my heart.

"We leave at dawn, Aelia. Don't be late," Caiden said as he headed out, his entourage in tow.

"I didn't say I was coming," I yelled after them.

"Dawn!" Caiden's voice echoed through the old halls.

I huffed, blowing a stray strand of dark hair out of my face. Exhausted, I didn't want to feel anymore. I didn't want to think. I wanted to sink into a warm bath and hold my breath until my lungs begged for air. Scream until I had no voice left.

I lingered in the empty room, pouring pink dust in small lines onto the table. Once used for battlefield pain, pixie dust, or "dust," the product of the elusive pixie faerie. Their magic dust had no effect on the magus, fully magical creatures like the elves and sylph, but for humans and half-breeds, the cravings were insatiable.

An expert at dosing, my usage became scientific. A pinch to take the edge off, one line to numb me. The color affected the potency. I examined the dust—a solid shade of fuchsia—incredibly potent. Just a pinch would do. I looked at my use medicinally, only using what I needed to get through the long nights.

I didn't want to think anymore. Snorting the drug, I let it fizzle in my brain. My eyelids drooped, and my head felt heavy on a wobbly neck. In a matter of moments, my life had been turned upside down. A chill ran down my spine at the thought of Gideon doing to Baylis what he had done to me all those years ago.

I made my way back downstairs, gripping the handrail for balance, and signaled to the bartender for another drink. He obliged when I put a gold coin down on the counter.

Lazily sipping a glass of whiskey, I tried not to think about what lay ahead of me when the sun rose. The young captain sidled beside me at the bar.

He gave me a wide smile. "I thought you left."

My chest tingled at the nearness of his body to mine. I moved closer. The scent of sweat from a day of training lingered on his skin. Twining my arms around his neck, I took in his appearance.

A muscular build with brown bedroom eyes and a thick mop of wavy brown hair—not bad for a human.

"How could I leave someone as handsome as you behind?" I whispered into his ear. His pulse quickened as he ran his hands over my body.

Gideon took everything from me—my home, my family, my lover, my looks, but he couldn't take my body. I learned sex could be a way to both bury my feelings and feel good about myself.

I ran my tongue up his neck. The salty taste of sweat filled my mouth. "Let me take you home," I whispered.

He didn't resist when I pulled him toward the door.

I needed to forget Caiden, to forget the ring on his finger, to forget the anxiety welling in my chest.

Tonight, I would pour all my feelings into this young man as if he could fill the emptiness in my soul.

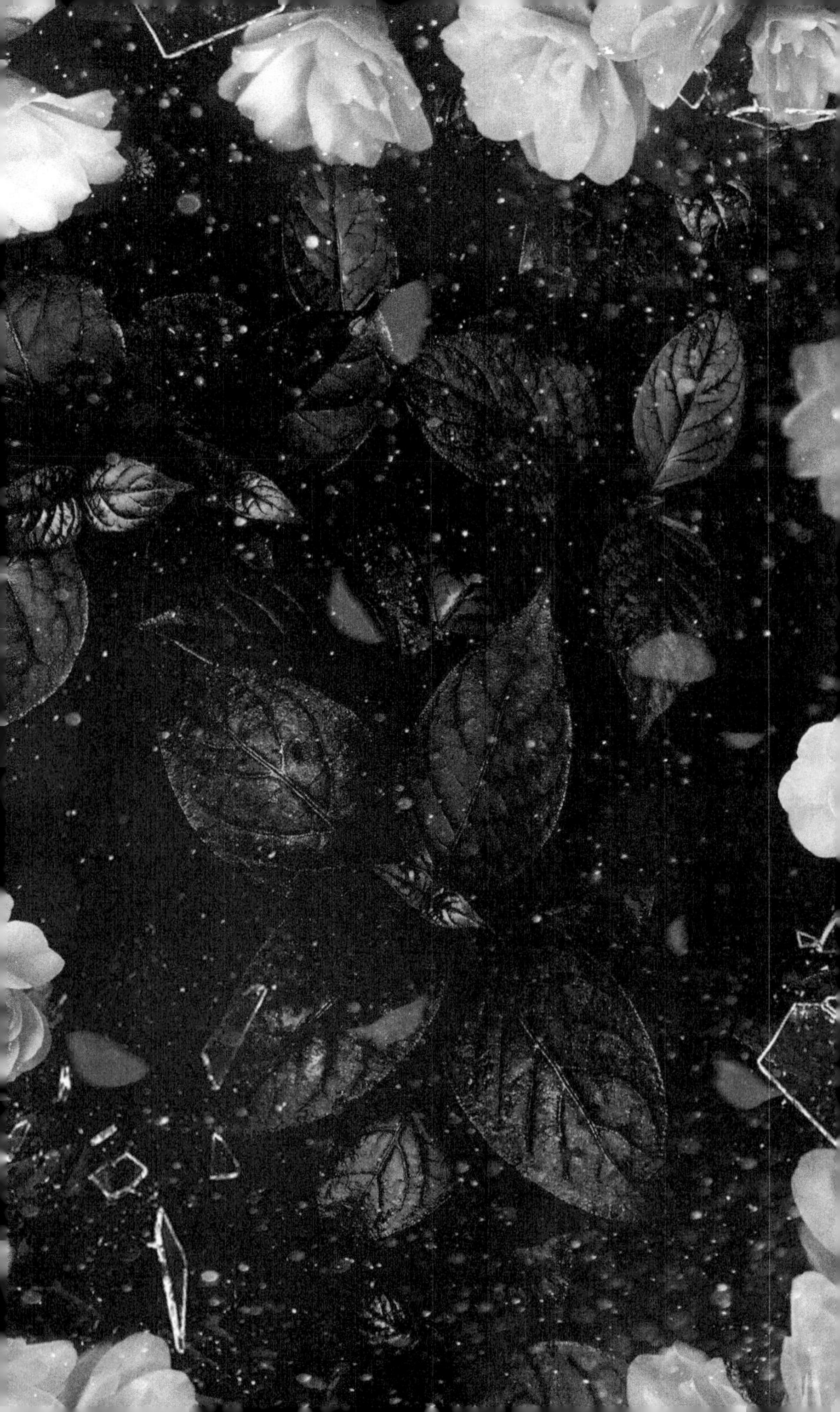

3 CAIDEN

"Well, that went well," Lucius said as the group trudged to the inn. Wet snow seeped into their boots, freezing their toes.

Caiden pulled his cloak tightly around his face—partly to fend off the cold, partly to diminish the tingling in his chest. Seeing Aelia tonight, he couldn't help but think of the girl he had fallen in love with all those years ago. Hazel eyes, more yellow than green, still gave glances of the woman she used to be.

"Aelia has been through a lot. Give her a break," Amolie chimed in.

Caiden sighed. His breath turned to vapor in the cold night air. He pushed the memories away.

They settled into the parlor of the quaint inn. Bookshelves lined the walls, and plush couches dotted the room. An aroma of cloves and cedar filled the air.

"What are you thinking?" Lucius took a seat next to the fire. "It must be hard to see her after all of this time."

Rocks piled in Caiden's stomach. "I wish I had never made that oath to her mother." He brushed his hair behind his ears.

"You and me both." Lucius stoked the fire, gazing into the flames.

Caiden collapsed onto one of the plush couches. "Young love is a powerful drug. I only wanted the best for Aelia. I didn't know what her mother was."

Lucius clicked his tongue. "The blood binding should have given you a clue."

Roderick entered the room carrying three mugs of mulled wine. "Your honor gets you in trouble, my friend."

"I can't change. It's been ingrained into me since birth. You know my father. His honor is his life. Besides, it's my fault we're in this situation in the first place. I'm the one who sent Baylis out into the wilderness. I'm the one who should rescue her."

Caiden fiddled anxiously with the rings on his fingers.

Both men fell silent. Five years ago, Caiden put Baylis on a horse and sent her into the night—never to be seen again until now.

"You did what you had to," Lucius said, "She would've been killed, and Aelia would have never forgiven you."

Caiden braced his elbows on his knees, staring into the fire. "She hasn't forgiven me now."

Lucius shrugged. "True, but at least her sister is alive."

"I guess the Fates wanted us to end up here."

Roderick handed Caiden a mug, and he gratefully slugged it down. The acidic taste of the wine and spices sent a fuzzy feeling through his body.

"Or maybe we upset their plans." Roderick drained the mug of mulled wine. Not even a blush reddening his face.

Caiden rolled his eyes. "Let's get back to the task at hand. Baylis Springborn rides with Gideon. There's no telling what kind of monster he's made her."

"Yeah, look what he did to Aelia," Lucius mumbled under his breath, not bothering to look up from the book he was pretending to read.

"Bite your tongue, Lucius. We may have our differences, but she's one of us."

Fire burned in Caiden's chest.

"She lost that privilege when she burned her kingdom to the ground and abandoned us... abandoned you."

Lucius pointed at Caiden, shoulders rigid with anger.

Blood boiled in Caiden's veins. Despite their history, Caiden did not hate Aelia. Life took her down a different path. True, he could not forgive her for some of the things she did, but she could be redeemed. "That was a long time ago, Lucius. Let it go. We just need to get Baylis back, and then we can all go our separate ways." His heart ached at the thought of their last meeting.

I never loved you, Caiden. Leaning back on the couch, he swallowed the lump in his throat.

Pushing his round spectacles up his nose, Lucius gave Caiden a knowing look. "Promise me you will not fall in love with her again."

Caiden choked out a laugh. "I'm married."

"Your wife would understand. People fall in love with people who aren't their partners all the time. Especially lords."

"Yeah, I used to fall in love with every man and woman I met," Roderick chimed in.

"We're not all honey tongues, Roderick," Lucius snipped at him.

Roderick shrugged. "Maybe I'll woo Gideon into giving us Baylis back."

Raising his mug of mulled wine, Caiden said, "Now, that would be a sight."

The men clinked their drinks.

As the evening progressed, the three friends gradually fragmented their separate ways. Caiden retreated to his shared room with Lucius only to lay awake.

Tapping his hands on his chest, he thought about how his life had come to this point. Once in line to command all the sylph armies, a fateful arrow ended his career. Now, he spent his days managing the Stromland kingdom with his brother while their father sat on the High Council in the capital city of Vantris. An honorable life, but not the one he dreamed of.

His thoughts drifted to his wife, with her golden hair like bottled sunlight. A daughter of the Court of Scales, magic weaved through her voice. How he wished to hold her, feel her warmth. A smile crossed his face at the thought of her. What would she think of him now? Traveling across the continent for a woman who caused him so much pain. Would she understand?

He couldn't think about such things now. Not when they were headed out on a dangerous mission in the morning. Through the darkness, Caiden whispered a prayer to Illya. "Guide me with your light, goddess. Protect us on this journey and bring us home safely."

Only silence answered his prayer.

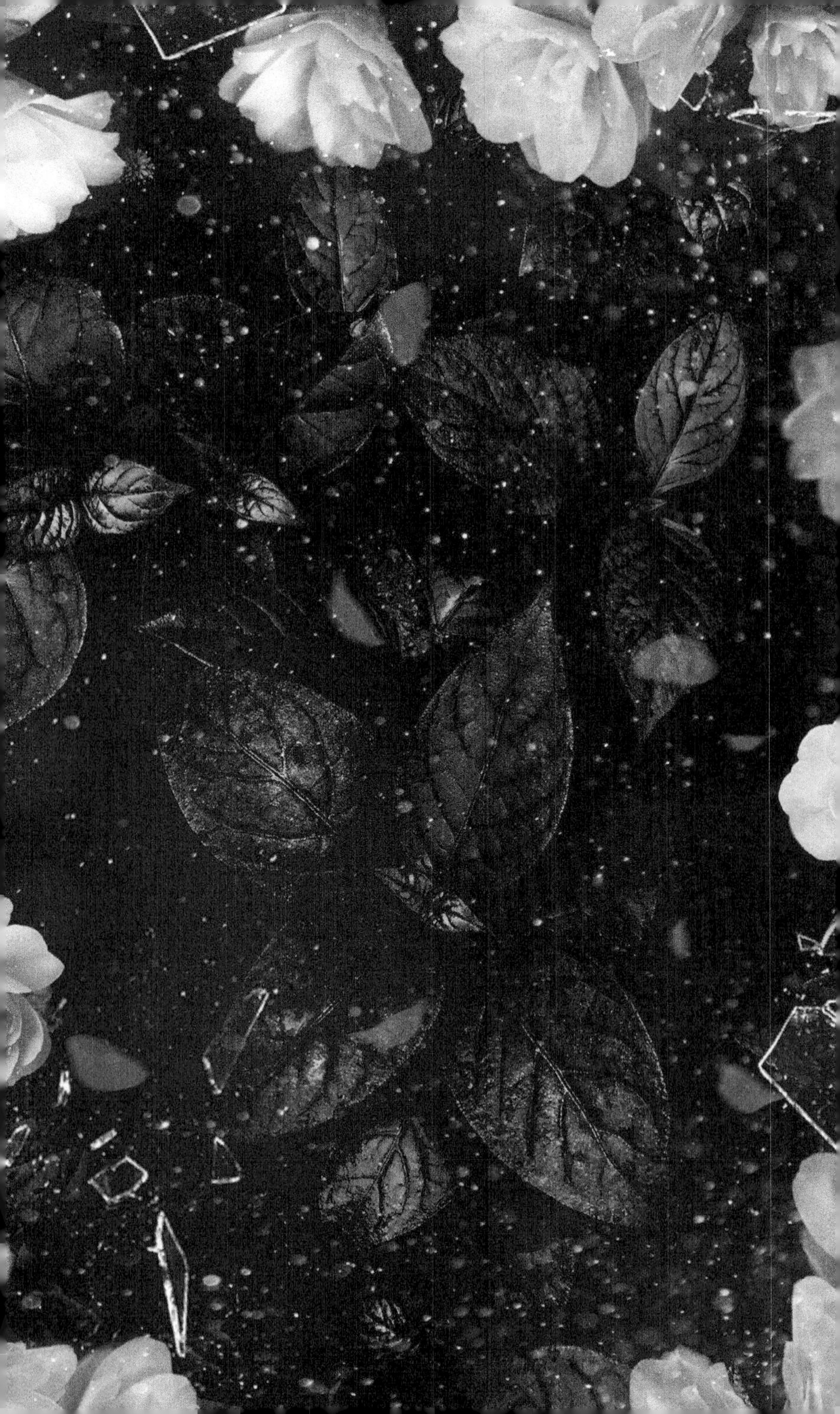

4 AELIA

A POUNDING AT MY DOOR PULLED ME FROM MY SLUMBER. My head throbbed. The young commander stirred in his sleep next to me. The sight of his lush lips and bare chest brought flashes of the night we shared. I ran my hands over my face, rubbing the sleep from my eyes. *Fuck.* Why did I do this again? I shouldn't have let my emotions get the better of me.

"Aelia! C'mon!" Roderick's deep voice overflowed with annoyance.

Pulling myself from the warm bed, I donned my fur-lined cloak. Hands shaking and head throbbing. I needed something to take the edge off. A little willow bark should do the trick. I pulled some from the tiny box next to my bed. The sweet, earthy taste calmed my aching head.

I heaved open the heavy door. Cold air blasted me in the face.

"Don't you know rest is important for a lady's beauty?"

Roderick looked around. "I don't see any ladies here."

I scrunched my nose at him.

"We need to go before the sun gets too high," Lucius said.

Roderick peered over my shoulder at the commander in my bed. "Late night?"

"That's none of your business." Leaning against the door, I blocked his eyeline. Both women and men fell at Roderick's feet. Although I couldn't deny... in a past life, I would have invited him to join us.

"I don't need your dregs, Aelia." A small smile pierced his lips. His teeth gleamed like pearls against his ebony skin.

Lucius broke the silent staring contest between Roderick and me. "Enough, you two, let's get going."

"What about breakfast?" I said, my head already feeling lighter.

"Some of us rose at dawn and ate then." Lucius scoffed.

"Some of us were busy then." Motioning to the sleeping man in my bed. "You can't expect me to ride with an empty stomach."

I wanted to make them work for me.

"You'll be fine, Aelia. It doesn't look like eating has been a priority for you in some time."

Running my hands over the sharp edges of my hips reminded me of the woman I used to be. "Look, you can either get some breakfast or spend the morning hearing me complain about how hungry I am."

"Trinity be," Lucius huffed, pointing a long finger at me. "I'll get something from the pub. But when I get back, you better be ready to go."

"Oh, I'll be ready," I said, shutting the door in his face.

Across the room, the commander stirred in his sleep, reaching for a body but finding none. His eyes fluttered open upon feeling the hollowness beside him.

"I have to go," I whispered. I hated to admit it, but this young man had wormed his way under my skin. Maybe it was his naivety or the fact I was avoiding meeting Caiden, but for some reason, I wanted to stay with him.

"Don't go," he murmured into my neck. The heat of his breath harsh against my cold skin.

"I wish I could." I peeled myself from his arms. Something made me want to linger longer. Perhaps because of the night we shared? Or the ghost from my past who waited outside my door?

Emotions swirled through my heart as I dressed. Rage, lust, and jealousy all mixing to create a perfect storm of confusion.

I closed my eyes and breathed deep, settling my mind, before laying one last kiss on the commander's supple lips. "It's time for you to go."

He dressed without a fuss. "It was nice to meet you." His brown eyes showed an earnest longing.

An ache clawed at my heart. *Get a hold of yourself, Aelia.*

"Goodbye," I said, running a gloved finger down the commander's stubbled jaw.

He reached for me longingly, but our love story had come to an end. I watched from my window as he disappeared into the crowd buying their daily bread. What must it be like to live such a simple life?

I gathered my things, braided my hair, and applied black kohl around my eyes to keep the winter sun from blinding me. By the time Lucius and Roderick returned, I donned my fur-lined leather cuirass.

"Mercenary work pays well," Roderick said, picking up one of my expertly crafted weapons.

"Business has been good." I laced up my knee-high boots.

Lucius handed me a sausage roll. The greasy smell made my mouth water. I devoured the savory treat.

A bitter wind spilled in through the door as Roderick carried my saddle bags out. I tightened my cloak around my neck and headed into the snowy street behind him, taking one last look at the bed the commander and I shared, wanting to stay in this moment forever. Afraid to move forward but not wanting to look back. As soon as I stepped outside the door, my life would change. No longer hiding in shadows but forced into the light.

We rode in tense silence until the sun sank low in the sky, casting its pink and gold light across the snowy planes.

A terse silence hung in the air until I could not bear it any longer. "So, tell me about this wife of yours?" Ever the glutton for punishment—part of me hoped she proved awful. Part of me hoped she embodied everything Caiden deserved. Everything I wasn't.

"Why do you care?" he mumbled under his breath.

"I don't. But I can't stand this silence," I lied while my heart flipped in my stomach.

Caiden's body stiffened. "Why don't we make a deal? I don't tell you about my life, and you don't tell me about yours."

"Fine by me." I shifted nervously in my saddle. "So, what's the plan for getting the invitation?"

Caiden's gray mare bobbed her head happily as we made our way down the snow-covered road. A wind blew from the west. Caiden fiddled with the reins. "The Court of Sorrows is near. I've already sent word we're coming for a state dinner."

I took a deep breath.

"I wrote to Queen Nysemia to inform her we are on an emissary trip from the capital. She has agreed to host us. I will seduce her while you extract the location of the invite from the mind of Theon, her consort. Then you will give the information to Lucius, who will steal the invitation."

I barked out a laugh. "Tell me you're joking. She's never going to be alone. Nysemia is smart. Smarter than you, Caiden. She's going to know something's off."

"Do you have a better plan?" Caiden snapped.

"Well, I used to be a diplomat. I know Nysemia is a member of the Wild Courts, beholden to the Alder King. She'll want to impress him. She's likely to invite him to her party.

And since he's a recluse who hasn't left his forest in five hundred years, he'll probably send an emissary. That's who we'll want to target..." I straightened my back to my full height. "That's who *I* will target. I'm sure you can figure out who that is."

"The Alder King holds the reins to the continent's deadliest army, and you want to go poking around in one of their minds?" Lucius glowered at me through darkened eyes.

"I'm sure that's Gideon's plan. We're the last two telepaths on the continent, as far as I know. My sister could just be an excuse to get close to the Alder King. He's charming, and someone with my sister's alleged gift is hard to resist."

Caiden rubbed his temple while his mare plodded along. "Lucius, see what you can find out. See who their emissary is."

Lucius nodded.

Night descended upon us as we continued our journey. Desolate trees rose from snow-covered copses, concealing malevolent creatures within.

A prickling at the nape of my neck put me on guard.

If the others noticed, they did not say.

I pushed it out of my mind. *You're losing it, Aelia.*

A twig snapped in the woods.

"Did you hear that?" My eyes searched for the source of the sound.

"Probably just a deer," Roderick said.

"I think—"

A supernatural scream ripped through the silent night.

I sucked in a breath.

Caiden and his men unsheathed their swords. In woods such as these, banshees lurked, enticing travelers toward their demise, exploiting their most profound fears.

"Keep moving. They won't leave the woods," Roderick said, scanning the trees for anything suspicious.

Night closed in on us, darkness emboldening the creatures lurking at the edge of the forest.

I gripped my sword.

Eyes settled on us, waiting to strike.

"We need to make a run for it," Caiden gathered the reins of his horse. "The nearest town is a few miles up the road. When I say so, we run."

Frigid air burned my lungs as I braced for Arion's gallop.

"*Aelia*," a familiar voice whispered in my ear.

Baylis's voice. But was it real?

Holding up a shaking hand, I couldn't be sure this voice wasn't from the withdrawal.

My heart leapt into my throat.

"Did you hear that?" My voice trembled. Arion danced in circles beneath my seat. The horses' eyes rolled white with fear.

"Whatever it said. Don't listen to it." Caiden's words were firm as iron, yet the voice endured.

"*Help me! Help me! I'm here.*"

"Shut it out. It's not real." Lucius reached for my hand from his horse.

I built a wall of stone in my mind.

Razor-sharp claws tore at my defenses.

I shut my eyes and shot back at the creature with my power, crushing its mind in a vice of my own making.

It hissed and wailed, letting out a deafening shriek. The horses reared, throwing us to the ground. The impact knocked the wind out of me. Gasping for breath, the world spun around me.

Another deafening wail came from the forest.

We cowered in pain.

"Make it stop!" Roderick yelled.

Out of the woods crawled the husk of a woman. Ghostly white with black hair, tattered rags hung limp from her skeletal body.

No eyes, just two black holes, stared back at me. Her erratic movements made my skin crawl as my soul tried to escape its mortal coil—banshee.

She crept on all fours like a spider, contorting her frail body in unnatural ways.

With a shaking hand, I reached for my sword. But I was too slow.

The banshee seized the opportunity.

Scuttling toward me, her jagged fingers gripped my hair.

A hot scream ripped through my lungs.

Tugging me backward, I fell to the ground.

Pain rattled through my mind, hardening the breath in my chest. I gasped for air.

"Help!" I called out, but the banshee ran at a pace the men had trouble keeping up with. Rocks and branches bruised my body as she dragged me deeper into the thick forest, ripping my hair from my head. The pain blinded me more than the darkness.

I grasped at anything to slow her down, but the small brush slipped through my wet fingers. Deep snow made it impossible for me to dig my heels in. Her rotting flesh brought acid to my throat. Gripping the hilt of my dagger, I thrust it into her abdomen, twisting through the aged flesh and bone. Howls of pain mixed with the sound of metal on bone echoed through the silent forest.

She released my hair and I scrambled to my feet.

Baring her rotting teeth, she sat back on her haunches, preparing to launch her decaying body at me.

A guttural screech rippled through my lungs, unleashing a rage long dormant—monsters didn't scare me.

Just try to kill me, you bitch. I know you can hear me.

She lunged with all of her might, knocking me to the ground, jagged nails clawing at my face. I held her wrists to block her attacks, but the tips of her nails still scraped against my lips, drawing blood.

Thrusting my boot into her abdomen, she tumbled backward, hitting her empty head on a rock.

Pinning her down with my mind, I searched for any humanity left in her, but found none. No kernel of the person she had been. Not even an ancient memory of a life long gone.

Writhing in pain, she tried to free herself—scraping her claws wildly at my face. But decades of decay weakened her addled mind.

The hate in her hollow eyes dimmed as I slid my dagger into her side once more. Brittle bone cracking against cold hard dragon steel.

Her body spasmed as the last bit of life faded into oblivion.

Sinking to my knees, I let out a breath. My muscles still twitching. Whether it was from the withdrawal or the fight I did not know.

Caiden and Roderick trampled through the woods after me.

"Thanks for the help," I said sarcastically, pointing my dagger coated in the banshee's black blood at them—my chest heaving from the ordeal.

"You managed on your own." Caiden leaned over to catch his breath.

Weary from the attack and the dust thinning in my blood, I hung my head between my knees. The cold earth sent a chill up my back.

Roderick handed me a handkerchief.

I wiped the dirt and blood away. Scratches seared my face. The sting of my screams still burned in my lungs. "We should bury her," I said, tonguing the cut on my lip. The banshee had been human once. It seemed like the right thing to do.

"The longer we stay here, the more unwanted attention we'll

attract. Digging a grave will only make it easier for others to track us," Roderick said, touching the banshee with his boot.

I leaned down, saying a silent prayer in my mind. "Ammena, keep you," I whispered to the body whose soul had left eons ago.

Another branch snapped deeper in the wood. My skin twitched with the urge to flee.

"It's time to go," Caiden said, hurrying me along.

Deep roots spread like veins underneath the snow, making our path treacherous as we trudged toward the road.

"Thank the Trinity you're okay." Amolie brightened at the sight of my bloodied face. Mixing a lightning bug potion, she hung them around our horses' necks, lighting our way to the nearest village.

A clammy sweat dampened my brow. While the others rode ahead, I snorted a pinch of dust to keep myself from withdrawal. An instant high buzzed through my head. Only a little dust remained in the bag. I'd need more soon.

We stopped at a small inn on the outskirts of Oakton, a mid-sized city on the border of the Winter Kingdom. The men stayed in one room while Amolie and I bunked together.

"Banshees," Amolie said, changing into her nightshirt. The raven tattoo on her shoulder glistened in the candlelight. "I should have given you this earlier." She tossed a pendant of pink salt toward me. Salts had special uses in magic. Pink salt for protection, white salt for pulling a clarifying spell, and black salt for summoning. The magus never used salt for food, only for magic. Choosing to enchant their food for taste.

"Thanks," I said, putting the pendant on. A light pulse vibrated through my chest—the salt pulling the negative energy from my body.

"How are you feeling?" Amolie asked as we settled in for the night.

My hand quivered as I undid the laces on my boots. "Do I look *well*, Amolie?"

She shrugged, her curls forming a halo around her round face. "No, that's why I asked."

I slid into bed. The cool sheets and plush mattress calmed my ravaged body. "I haven't been well in a very long time."

"I had to tell them, Aelia. I knew you would want to know about Baylis."

Staring at the ceiling, I let my anger fade. "I know, Am. You always mean well." I rubbed my tired eyes. "I'm so foolish. I should have known Gideon would go after her." A single tear trickled down my cheek.

Had I overlooked the obvious because I'd been too high to realize it or had I been willfully ignorant the entire time? Not wanting to see what was right in front me. A pit opened in my stomach. I knew the answer, but I didn't have the guts to face it.

"We all thought she was dead," Amolie said.

"That might have been better than whatever is happening to her now." My chest tightened at the thought of my time in Ryft's Edge. How Gideon had charmed me—wormed his way into my heart—into my mind. And now he was doing the same to my sister.

"I know you're scared, Aelia. But we'll save her."

I sobbed silently to myself. "Why is my life like this? What did I do to offend the Trinity in such a way they sought to seek revenge on me like this?"

"I don't think Ammena meant for any of us to lead an easily life." She twiddled her short fingers anxiously. "I never dreamed when I crossed the black sea ten years ago to marry the high wizard, that I'd be back here again."

"I know what you mean." I messaged my temples.

"I know you do… That's why we get along so well, you and me. We are cut from the same cloth."

"Bonded through trauma," I snickered.

"It's true, though. I never thought I'd find a friend again—and then slowly, I got to know you. I learned all your weaknesses, your triumphs, your joy… and your sadness. I saw a reflection of my own pain."

A lump grew in my throat at Amolie's vulnerability. "You're too good to me, Am. I don't deserve a friend like you."

"You deserve more than you think you do, Aelia."

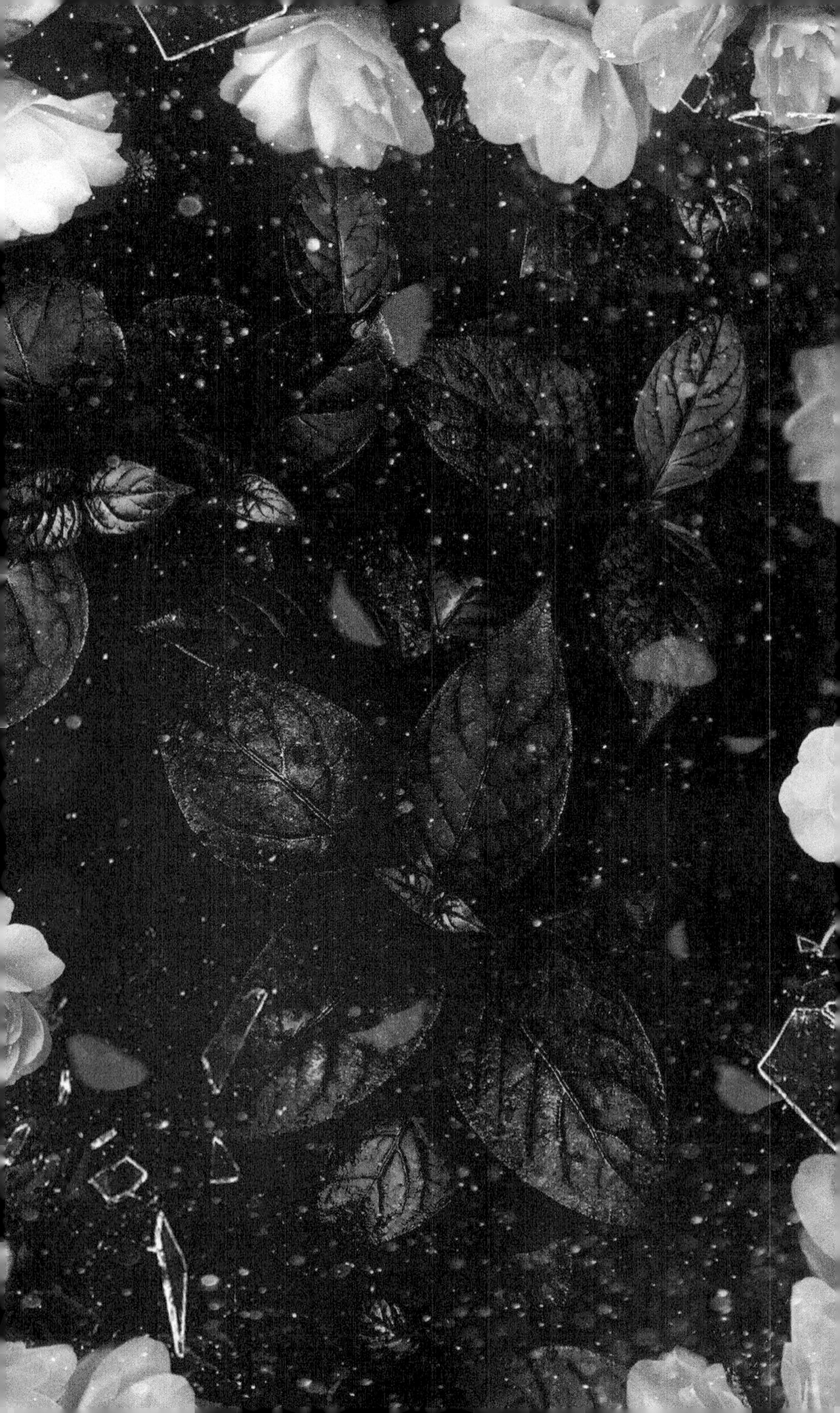

5 AELIA

Two brown eyes peered into my soul. My mind brought the face into focus.

My heart twisted in my chest.

A devious smile cut the handsome face in two.

I squirmed to escape his glance, but my body wouldn't move.

White light surrounded us, illuminating the edges of his face. I screamed, but no sound left my lungs.

"Shh…" His lips graced my cheek. "I've been looking for you, my love."

Another silent scream. I grasped at any shred of reality I could. "You're not real. You're not real. I am safe. I am protected."

"Oh, my little queen. I am real." The words dripped like poison from his lips.

"Fuck you, Gideon."

"Aelia!" A familiar voice pulled me back to reality. "Wake up, Aelia."

My eyes fluttered open to find Caiden gripping my shoulders. Sweat drenched my body. Tiny bruises formed on my palms where my finders had been embedded.

"I could hear you screaming through the walls."

The light from a single candle illuminated his sculpted physique.

His heat radiated through me, causing my cheeks to flush red.

I gasped for air. I wanted him closer. My fingers itched to feel his skin just a moment longer.

Any flame burning inside me went cold at the sight of his wedding ring glinting in the candlelight. Once, long ago, that ring could have been mine. Nausea bubbled in my stomach, bringing up the hurt and humiliation I thought I'd gotten over.

"Thank… you," I said through ragged breaths.

Caiden scoffed. "I need my rest. It's hard to sleep through your screams." He released me, though his touch lingered on my skin.

I deserved every ounce of disdain Caiden directed at me. He remained as guarded as I, and rightly so.

After I escaped from Ryft's Edge, Caiden tried to put me back together. To mend my broken soul, but I couldn't be fixed. There was nothing left of the girl he had fallen in love with. Carved into a thousand tiny shards, I couldn't be put back together again.

Broken, I wanted Caiden to hurt the way I did.

"*I never loved you. You are nothing to me. I never want to see you again.*" My words still haunted me to this day.

Tossing and turning, I tried to convince myself it had all been a dream. Gideon couldn't be here. But he seemed so close. So real. My skin crawled from his lips on my cheek. I needed to get far away from here.

Instinctively, I reached for my satchel. Rummaging through it, I pulled out the small bag where I kept my stash of dust. Tipping it over, my heart sank. Only a few flecks poured out. *Shit*. I'd need more.

Fresh air would help. Throwing the covers off the bed, I pulled on my leathers and wool cloak.

Amolie's bed lay empty. Sometimes, when she couldn't sleep, she prayed at the temple of Ammena—the human goddess of the Trinity.

I tucked my dagger, Little Death, into my leather pants and slipped out into the night, pulling my hood up over my head.

Cold night air whipped at my face as I traversed the city's snow-covered streets. Wooden buildings sagged with the weight of water, and the taste of salt lingered in the air. I raised my mental barriers like a thick wall of stone in my mind. Gideon sought my thoughts like a shark searching for blood in the water. I needed to protect myself. If what I had dreamed was real, he wouldn't be far off. Our blood mixed, our thoughts eternally linked.

I snapped my fingers nervously, trying to distract myself from the craving clawing at my mind. Without a medicinal dose, my thoughts would consume me. My chest refused to unknot. I needed to find dust soon before I curbed my need in other ways.

Shops run by both humans and magus lined the docks. I canned each one, looking for any sign they carried what I sought.

Even this late in the evening, salt mongers raked the terraced bay of the lake.

My eyes searched frantically for anyone peddling more than just salt and fish.

I hurried through the stalls, desperate to find a hit, before I did something rash. Champing on the willow bark I used as a placebo, its effects would only last so long.

I dug my nails into my palms, the pain a welcomed relief.

Down back alleys I marched, feet slipping on wet snow. Pain radiated through my mind. I needed dust and I needed it soon, or else I would be a puddle of nothing in the streets of a strange city.

I rounded the corner of the seedier part of town. Questionable characters lingered in darkened alcoves. The sound of glass breaking and fists shattering bone echoed through the streets.

A brothel nestled between two saloons shone like a beacon of hope. If the women didn't have dust, they could provide me with other distractions.

Dark wood and mirrors paneled the walls. The smell of smoke and incense hung heavy in the air. All around me, courtesans flirted with their customers.

I sauntered up to a black-haired nymph sitting at the bar.

She gave me a smile full of razor-sharp teeth. "Trouble's here."

She slid me a shot of amber liquid.

I let it burn in my throat before asking, "How much for dust?"

She downed her own drink. Her iridescent skin glowed in the soft light of candles.

"How much are you looking for?"

I drummed my fingers on the shabby wooden bar.

"Enough for me to forget my name."

The nymph raised an eyebrow at me. "Ah, it's *that* kind of night, is it?"

"It's *that* kind of life."

She pulled a glass vile filled with pink dust from between her ample breasts.

"Be careful. This is new. Folk are saying it's stronger than usual."

"Perfect." I placed three gold coins on the bar.

"Come back anytime." She flicked her hair behind her back.

I left the nymph and headed for the nearest darkened alleyway.

Exhilaration raced through my veins at the thought of the dust tingling my senses. My fingers twitched at the promised sweet relief.

I snorted a pinch of the dust off my pinky finger and rubbed the rest on my gums. My body relaxed. Bleary-eyed and light-headed, something like happiness filled my belly. A moment's rest from the perpetual state of hyper-vigilance I lived in.

Lighting a cigarette, I strolled down the docks. Magus flocked to Oakton for the precious salts they harvested from the lake. The scent of salt water and brine heavier here.

A euphoric feeling blanketed my mind, dulling my senses. I sat on the shoreline contemplating how I ended up traveling with my former lover to thwart my husband.

The point of an iron knife seared into my chin.

Fuck. I jolted my head back, slamming it against the crate I had been leaning against.

Stars dotted my vision.

"You're off your game, Springborn," a seductive female voice said.

I winced. "You are far from the Undersea, Ursula."

She let out a cackle. "Even salt-lake Nymphs bow to my queen."

Shit. I should've known better. Of course, the Queen of the Undersea would send her best assassin. Once lovers, our paths crossed when I was on a mission to steal her queen's pearl. She never forgave me for the betrayal.

I lifted my neck to avoid the dagger's searing heat. "What do you want, Ursula? I said I was sorry for the pearl. You know how business is."

"Breaking my heart is *just business*?" Her words came out in a hiss as she moved before me in the smooth way only a creature accustomed to moving in water could. Her long blue hair, the color of the tides, glistened in the moonlight. Hate danced in her sea-glass eyes. She wore a skintight blue dress resembling her fin.

Something about the curve of her body made me want to put my hands on it. I didn't know if this was a side effect of the dust or something more. "I didn't—"

"Enough." She cut me off before I could come up with an excuse. The tip of her dagger burned my skin. "It's time for me to repay the favor." A smile of razors crossed her fish-like face. "Get up. There's someone who wants to see you."

She wrapped a rope of seaweed around my wrists. The sliminess turned my stomach.

We walked through the docks to a warehouse on stilts. Waves slapped the shore beneath as the tide rose. Once inside, she escorted me to a small room in the back, where a single candle sat on a bare table next to a wooden chair. What was she planning? What other ghost would be haunting me tonight?

Bile rose in my throat at the stench of dead fish permeating every pore of the place.

"Sit. And don't you dare try to run away," Ursula said, pointing her dagger at the empty chair.

I took a seat, focusing my mind on hers. *Let me in, Ursula.*

"Get out of my head."

You don't have to do this. Whatever this is about. We can fix it.

"I said, get out of my head."

She clasped iron manacles around my wrists. Iron negated magic in the blood. I sucked in a shallow breath. The cold metal seared my skin.

I tried to push further, but it was no use. The iron, combined with dust, left my head spinning. Every strand of her mind I grasped slipped through my fingers. I gave up.

"Sit here. I'll be right back."

Head heavy, I slumped in my chair, waiting for her to leave.

Dampness chilled my bones. I surveyed the room for potential escape routes. One door leading to the dock, and a tiny window too small for me to fit through, were my only options.

Hushed whispers debated outside the door—Ursula's smooth, sultry voice and another harsher, more cracked one.

My eyes flitted from the window to the door. Could I fit through it? Maybe if I wriggled just right.

"Right this way," Ursula said, unlocking the door. I focused on the rhythm of the waves through the slits in the warped floor.

My heart leapt into my throat at the sight of the tall, broad-shouldered, graying man. Brutus Strong, Chief Commander of the Highland army, his face full of scars from a lifetime of battles. The years of a mortal life left his once handsome face cracked and frayed.

Breaths rattled in my chest. I had to get out of here.

"Hello, Aelia. You're looking…" His brows knitted in disgust. "Well, you've looked better."

I cringed at his voice, remembering all the times he'd laughed while Gideon let him beat me.

"Always the gentleman, Brutus. Why are you here?"

A smile crossed his lined face. "King Gideon doesn't appreciate his belongings disappearing."

"It's almost like I didn't want to be found," I practically spat the words at him.

The sound of an empty glove hitting my face rang in my ears before the sharp pain of the slap stung my cheek. Stars clouded my vision, and pain shot through my lip as the freshly healed scrape ripped anew, filling my mouth with the metallic taste of blood.

Launching myself into his mind, I hit a wall of steel, shooting me out as quickly as I had come in.

Brutus barked out a laugh. "I've been trained, little bird. You won't get in here." He tapped his temple with a bulbus finger.

Rage burned in my veins.

"Hey—" Ursula stepped in between us. "You said she wouldn't be harmed."

A backhand to the face sent Ursula crashing to the floor.

She bared her teeth at him.

Brutus clicked his tongue at her. "Not so fast, little mermaid. Remember our deal."

Wiping the blood from her mouth, Ursula picked herself up from the floor. "You're an asshole. I should kill you for that." Her nostrils flared, their faces nearly touching.

"Oh, little fish, if you kill me, who will pay you?" He dangled a pouch of gold in front of her.

Snatching the pouch, she stomped out of the room.

"Alright, where is he?" I asked once Ursula left. My head buzzed, and my vision blurred.

"He's busy." A deviant smile crossed his face, sending a shiver down my spine.

I braced for the impact of his fist. Years of pent-up anger were released in one swing, and it landed like a hammer. Spitting blood onto the decaying wood floor, I tried to focus my vision, but the room spun around me.

"That was for making me look foolish."

"You didn't need my help with that." A bloody smile tugged at the corners of my mouth.

Hatred burned in his blue eyes.

"Where is my sister?"

"Oh, she is a fair thing, isn't she? My king has a special place in his heart for her." His dialect resembled the royalty of the Highlands, but if you listened closely, you could hear the slums in his words.

A pit opened in my stomach. "If you've laid a finger on her, I will—"

"Shh—I promise she's in excellent hands." He leaned in close to me. The acrid smell of mead seeped from his lips.

Bile bubbled in my throat.

"Let's go, little bird." Hauling me to my feet, he pulled me along behind him. I rattled the chains.

I needed to get out of here.

Three of them versus one of me, and I had no magic.

The iron mixed with the dust in my veins, making my feet clumsy. Why did I have to take dust? Why was I such a colossal fuck up? Why did I do this to myself?

We wove our way through the docks. Brutus's torch cast a pitiful glow. Two of Gideon's guards flanked me. Their swords clinked at their sides. At this time of night, the docks were empty. Even the salt traders had gone to bed. No one would hear me scream.

Frantically, I searched for some way to escape. Massive crates filled with salt and fish lined the docks—an idea formed in my mind. Brutus may have had training against telepaths, but the other men didn't. If I could get inside one of their minds, I could possibly get him to free me. Damn, these iron cuffs.

Dead-eyed, the men plodded along with stoic faces. Something was off about them, but I couldn't put my finger on it. Glassy eyes usually indicated a glamour, but these were soldiers. What reason could he have for glamouring them?

Brutus rounded the corner ahead, leaving me a millisecond to enact my plan.

I ducked left down a row of cargo crates. Then right down another, hoping to lose them.

"Hey, stop," the soldiers yelled.

"Get her!" The sound of Brutus's heavy footsteps scrapped across the frozen snow.

I ran down another aisle. They were stronger and faster than me, but I had the element of surprise on my side.

Concealed in shadow, I wedged between two crates and listened for the men's footsteps.

Crunch, crunch, crunch, one of them drew near. I tightened the chains of my manacles and held my breath.

"Tracks! Here!" the man yelled to the others. "I found—"

My chains were around his neck before he could finish his sentence.

He clawed at his neck, tossing me back and forth, but I held steady.

He gasped for air, sinking into the snow.

Brutus's footsteps grew louder with each passing second.

C'mon. The iron burned into my skin. Tears welled in my eyes. The soldier flailed, trying to save his own life, but slowly, his windpipe collapsed. He slunk into a heap on the ground.

Pausing for a moment, I contemplated the intimacy of the kill. I had held his life in my hands and snapped his neck. Maybe I was the monster after all.

I searched his body for a key.

Please, please, please.

Precious seconds ticked by.

I padded the soldier's armor.

No key.

Fuck.

Brutus stood at the end of the row. "Now, little bird, don't make this difficult."

His head swiveled as he searched for me.

My chest loosened a bit.

He couldn't see me. He followed my footprints here.

I grabbed the sword from the soldier's sheath and ducked between the crates again.

"Oh, little bird. Come out and play."

The flickering light grew brighter with each step he took.

Sucking in a breath, I crouched low. *Please let this work, please let this work.*

Brutus stopped at the body of the soldier, clicking his tongue in disgust. "Pathetic."

I gathered every ounce of courage I could muster, biting my lip so hard it bled.

I struck hard and fast, stabbing my sword through his thigh.

Brutus let out a cry of pain. Slipping on the ice, he tumbled to the ground. Blood pooled around him.

I ran.

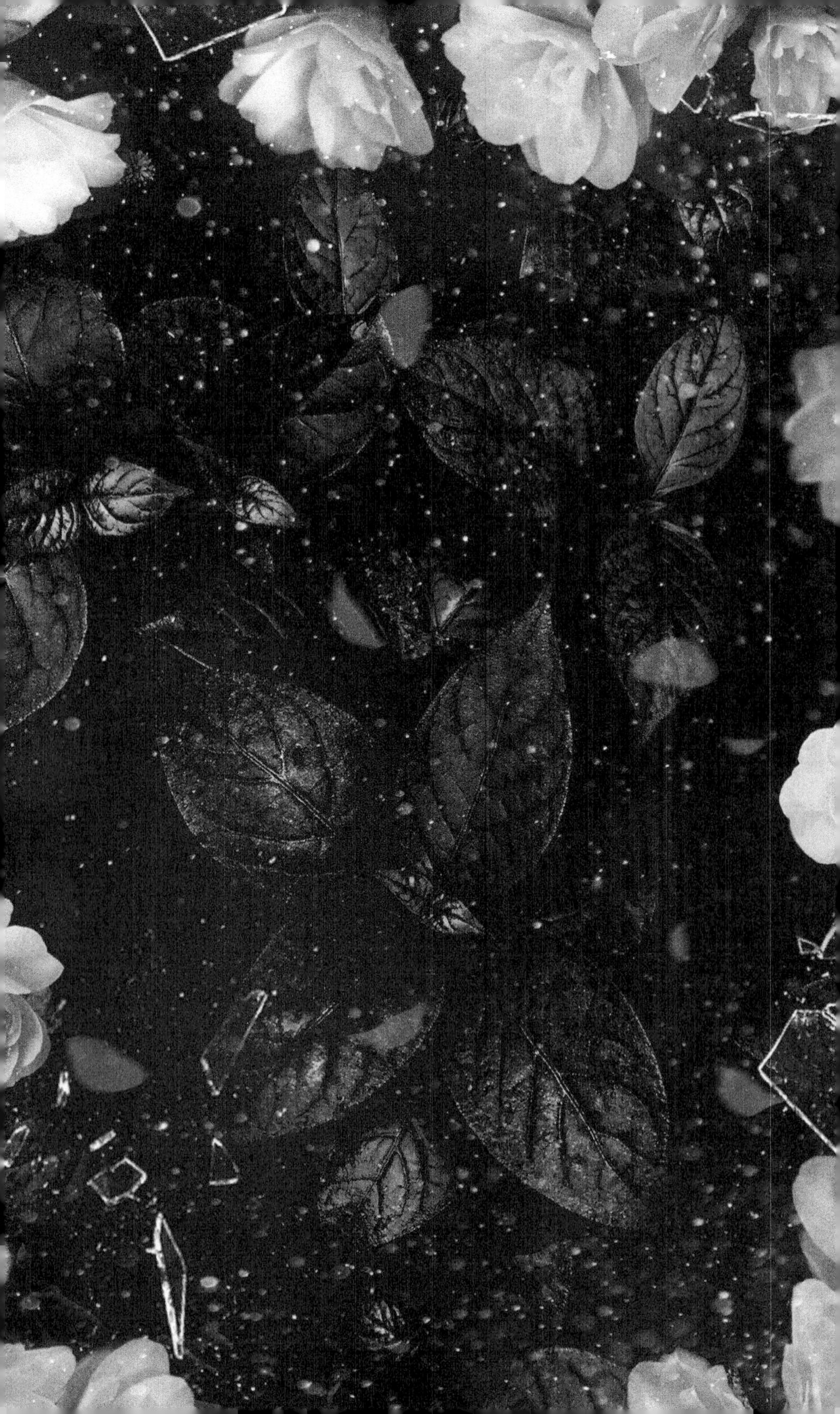

6 CAIDEN

Before

"Do you love my daughter, Caiden?" Queen Isadora gazed out the window. Her dark hair fell in soft waves over her narrow shoulders.

"Yes," Caiden answered.

The queen did not look back at him. "Good. She will need you in the future."

Caiden kicked the air aimlessly. "She has a king to take care of her now."

"She still loves you, and you love her more purely than I could have hoped for." Isadora faced him then. Her heavy ballgown dragged on the stone floors.

"What are you playing at, queen?" Caiden arched a brow.

Isadora sighed, rubbing her head. "I need you to promise me something."

Caiden swallowed hard. "Anything for Aelia."

"Good." Isadora pulled a dagger from the folds of her dress. "I want you to swear you'll protect my daughters." Dragging the blade across her palm, blood dotted her pale skin.

"The laws of this land bind me to my word. Why all this?"

"Because the laws of this land can be broken, but blood is forever."

Caiden pulled a dagger from his bandolier and slit his palm.

Magic buzzed between them, heating their palms and fizzling out.

"What are you?" Caiden looked at his palm where a scar had already formed.

Isadora ran a hand through her silken hair, twisting the end around her dainty finger. "A mother who loves her children."

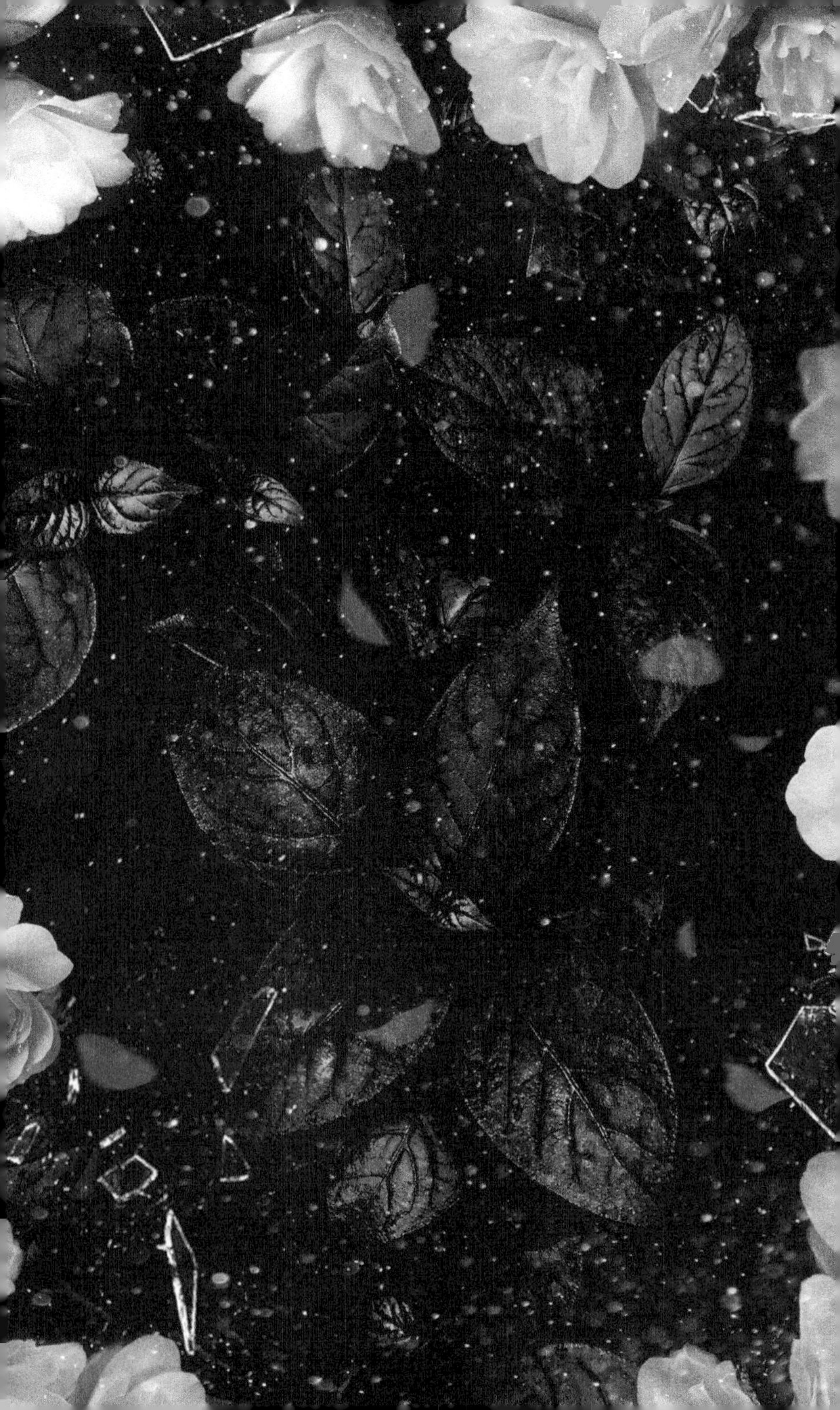

7 AELIA

Burning pain seared into every inch of my body as I headed back to the inn. The manacles still bound my hands. One soldier remained unaccounted for. More would come.

I had to get back to the inn and warn the others.

Dawn's first light peeked over the horizon, casting the city in pink and yellow. Fisherman and salt sellers made their way to the lake for another day of hard labor.

I kept to the alleys, hoping no one would look my way, always looking behind me. Gideon's men were quick, but it would be hard to track me with all the foot traffic heading toward the lake.

My head ached as the dust wore off. This would not be pleasant.

I pushed the door open to find Amolie still asleep in her bed.

"Amolie, wake up. I don't want to alarm you, but we have to go now."

Amolie's hazel eyes blinked awake. "What are you talking about?"

"I fucked up. I fucked up big time." I paced back and forth, body shaking.

Amolie popped out of bed, her messy curls flying everywhere. "Oh, Aelia. What did you do?"

"Pack, and I'll get Caiden. We need to leave. Now."

The door to the men's room opened before I could knock. Lucius answered, wearing his padded riding attire, his hair pulled back into a white bun. "What did you do this time, Springborn?"

"I need to talk to Caiden, and I need you to take care of these." I held up my manacled hands.

Lucius clicked his tongue. "I can't decide if I want to know or if I should just pick the lock and let it be."

"It's not what you think it is."

Lucius drew a lockpick from his pocket and got to work on my handcuffs. His face contorted as he waited for the click of freedom.

"What is it now, Aelia?" Caiden didn't bother to look up from where he was lacing his boots.

Click. The manacles thudded on the floor. I rubbed the soreness from my wrists.

"We need to go now. Gideon is here. Or, at least, his men are. I went out last night for..." Lie, lie, lie, you can't let him know about your weakness. "For a smoke, and they found me." I danced from foot to foot like a child waiting for their scolding.

Caiden stood, balling his hands into fists.

"How could you be so foolish as to go out alone?"

I crossed my arms over my chest in defiance. "I needed to clear my head—"

"And buy some dust." The judgment in his voice made my heart sink.

Had I been that obvious? I thought I had control of myself around him. Unless Amolie told him.

"Go fuck yourself, Caiden." I spit the words at him.

"You're pathetic, you know that, Aelia? I can't believe I ever

—" He caught himself. Those words were too cruel to utter, but I wanted to push him to see how far he'd go.

"You know what? If you're so desperate to be free of me, I'll grant your wish, Caiden."

Our noses nearly touched, and his warm breath made my wet skin dimple with goosebumps.

"You're high as a kite."

"I'm sober enough to grant you your wish right now. I'll erase your entire mind if you ask me to." I glowered at him, hoping to spark his ire.

"Enough, you two," Amolie interrupted. "You're both acting like children. Gideon is coming for us. We need to go now."

A ball of fire ripped through the window, setting the floor ablaze.

"Out the back window." Lucius sprinted across the room before a breath left my chest. He opened the window and motioned for us to climb out. Flames crept up the dingy curtains. Smoke filled the air. A jagged cough escaped my lungs.

Escaping onto the roof, my feet skidded across the thatches. Below, merchants lined the streets, setting up their stalls for the day.

"We're going to have to jump," Roderick said.

Flames shattered the windows behind us.

"Where?"

"There." He pointed to a fruit stand below.

Screams erupted as flames burst from the inn.

"Now!"

We all jumped, landing in the fruit stand below. Pulp covered us from head to toe. We didn't have time to think.

My head throbbed, and my body ached. Each breath stung like a thousand bees. I didn't know if I could run. I didn't know if I could get up.

"The stables, we need the horses." Caiden sprung to his feet.

The sound of clinking armor echoed through the morning streets. People hurried to avoid being trampled.

Caiden pulled me from the cart, and together, we ran toward the stables.

With no time to spare, we mounted our horses bareback before bursting out the back of the barn. "Ride swift and true, boy," I said, jamming my heels into Arion's sides.

Our horses' hooves skidded on the cobblestones as we fled Brutus's men, taking sharp turns, hoping to lose them.

"The rooftops," Roderick shouted as an arrow whizzed past my head. We turned down a covered market street. The echoes of the horses' hooves pounded in my ears. My heart beat faster with every step Arion took. I would not go back to Gideon. I would not be his caged bird again.

We escaped the city and hit an open field of snow. I let Arion loose. As we led the others towards the forest, the ebony stallion lengthened his stride. We were on the edge of the Winter Kingdom and the Court of Sorrows. Gideon did not have a treaty with Queen Nysemia and lacked the boldness to cross the barrier between humans and sylph's lands.

"A little further," I whispered to Arion, urging him onward. Riders appeared behind us. Their horses' breaths turned to mist in the morning sun. I'd recognize their red eyes anywhere. Blood Riders—born and bred to end lives. Death gleamed in their fanged smiles.

"Don't look back!" Caiden called. "Keep going."

They needed a chance. Gideon wanted me. "Head for the woods. I'll meet you there." I turned Arion violently. He whinnied with displeasure but kept moving. The others split off, heading into the forest.

The Blood Riders followed me, urging their water horses forward. Sharp fangs protruded from the creatures' mouths as they chased us through open snowy fields. Dread coiled like a snake in my stomach. Arion could not run forever. Eventually, we would hit the great Atruskan River.

The ground quaked under the water horses' hooves as they gained on us. Still, I urged Arion forward. The stallion gave me everything he had in him. His feet barely touched the ground as we sped through the snow.

A blinding pain seared into my back, hitching the breath in my lungs—an arrow.

My lungs slowly filled with blood, but removing the arrow meant certain death. A river of fire flowed through my veins. Wincing in pain, I reached to feel the weapon. *Shit.*

The Blood Riders were so close I could smell the rotting flesh on their breaths. I pulled Little Death from its sheath. Dragon steel slayed gods; surely, it could kill a Blood Rider.

I needed to put the dagger where it would do the most damage.

One rider broke away from the pack, surging toward us.

I jumped from Arion, planting my feet into the fresh snow.

Pleasure filled the rider's dead eyes—he thought he had me now.

I gave him a smile before hurling my dagger with all my might into the horse's chest.

The creature screamed in pain, slamming its rider into the snow. I held out my hand, calling Little Death back.

The rider lay lifeless, steam rising off the still-warm beast. I scrambled to him, not checking his pulse before I slit his throat. Hot blood spilled from his neck, staining the pristine snow.

A small crossbow dangled from his bandelier. I hastily snatched it before crouching down, using the horse's body as cover. The rancid stench of the creature brought bile to my throat. With the arrow still lodged in my back and my breathing labored, I waited for the others.

Three more riders approached. Their gray skin identical to the overcast sky. Drool dripped from their long incisors. Where lips should have been, only skin met teeth—monsters just like me.

Firing a bolt, I hit one in the chest. His limp body plunked into the snow like a sack of potatoes.

"Got you now, little lamb," a deep voice echoed as the other two riders approached. Their water horses strained against the bits, begging to taste the blood on the snow.

Laying perfectly still, my breath barely a whisper, I waited for them.

Their boots crunched in the hardened snow as they dismounted.

One bolt left.

The crunching grew louder with each step, scraping against my eardrums. I gritted my teeth to withstand the pain. The iron flowing through my veins made it impossible to use my telepathy.

"Ah, Aelia, always the troublemaker."

I grimaced at the voice of one of my guards in Ryft's Edge.

My spine screamed in pain as he yanked my hair, but I wouldn't give them the satisfaction of hearing me cry. Clenching my jaw, I dug my bare hands into the snow. The burning cold distracted me from the arrow in my back.

He leaned down so his lips were practically on my ear. "You could've made this easy. Now I have to explain to the king how you got an arrow in your back."

"Fuck you," I said, spitting blood onto the ground.

He released my hair, slamming my face into the hardened snow, reopening my wounds. Blood poured from my nose.

"Put her on the horse," the man said.

Next to me, a water horse devoured the dead body of a Blood Rider.

A pair of powerful hands hauled me upward, forcing me to face the leader of the Riders, a muscled man no older than thirty with pale skin and eyes the color of dried blood. He looked through me, reducing me to a state of utter insignificance. I made sure to conceal the crossbow under my cloak. There would be no second chances.

"Make sure she doesn't have any weapons," he barked at the rider holding me.

A smile graced my lips.

"What are you smilin' at?" His brows knitted in confusion.

"Too late," I said, firing my last bolt straight into his neck.

A look of shock crossed his round face, and blood seeped from the wound.

The bolt had hit an artery.

He sank to his knees, taking his last gasps of air. Blood flowed like a river around his lifeless body. The water horses seized the opportunity to lap up the fresh sanguine.

"I should kill you for what you did." The Blood Rider pressed a blade into my neck.

I fought as best I could against his grip. "I don't think your king would be too happy with you."

"Drop the weapon." He dug the tip of the knife into my skin.

I sucked in a breath, dropping Little Death and the crossbow into the snow.

Blood filled my lungs as death closed in upon me.

My healing powers lacked the strength for a wound this severe. Knees going limp, I sank into the snow.

"Shit." The soldier said as my body hung lifeless in his arms. "Shit. We weren't supposed to kill her." He laid me down. The cold proved a brief respite from the pain.

My vision tunneled. I could hear the soldier's frantic footsteps dancing around my head. A smile tugged at the corner of my lips, finding solace as I imagined the look on Gideon's face when they brought him my lifeless body.

Darkness encroached upon me.

A man no older than fifty appeared before me, dressed in

cream robes with hair as white as fresh snow. The corners of his eyes wrinkled as he smiled at me. "Hello, Aelia."

My chest lightened at the sight of this reaper—Hadron, my old acquaintance.

Many fear death when he comes for them, but not me.

I had died before.

I smiled back at him.

"Aelia."

Hadron's calming voice soothed my aching soul.

I stared at his expressionless face. No pupils graced his eyes, only white nothingness.

"I'm ready," I said, swallowing hard. My voice little more than a whisper.

He chuckled, shoulders bouncing as he shook his head. "It is not your time. The Trinity has other plans for you."

"Please," I begged, but Hadron did not oblige.

Taking a glowing ball of life from his shabby twill satchel, he placed it in my chest. Electricity radiated throughout every limb of my body. My lungs constricted.

"Breathe, Aelia."

Surrounded by a white light, the magic worked its way through my blood, healing the torn flesh. A feverish heat brought sweat to my brow.

I shut my eyes.

Caiden's voice pulled me back from the other side. "Breathe, Aelia. Fucking breathe. Trinity, help us."

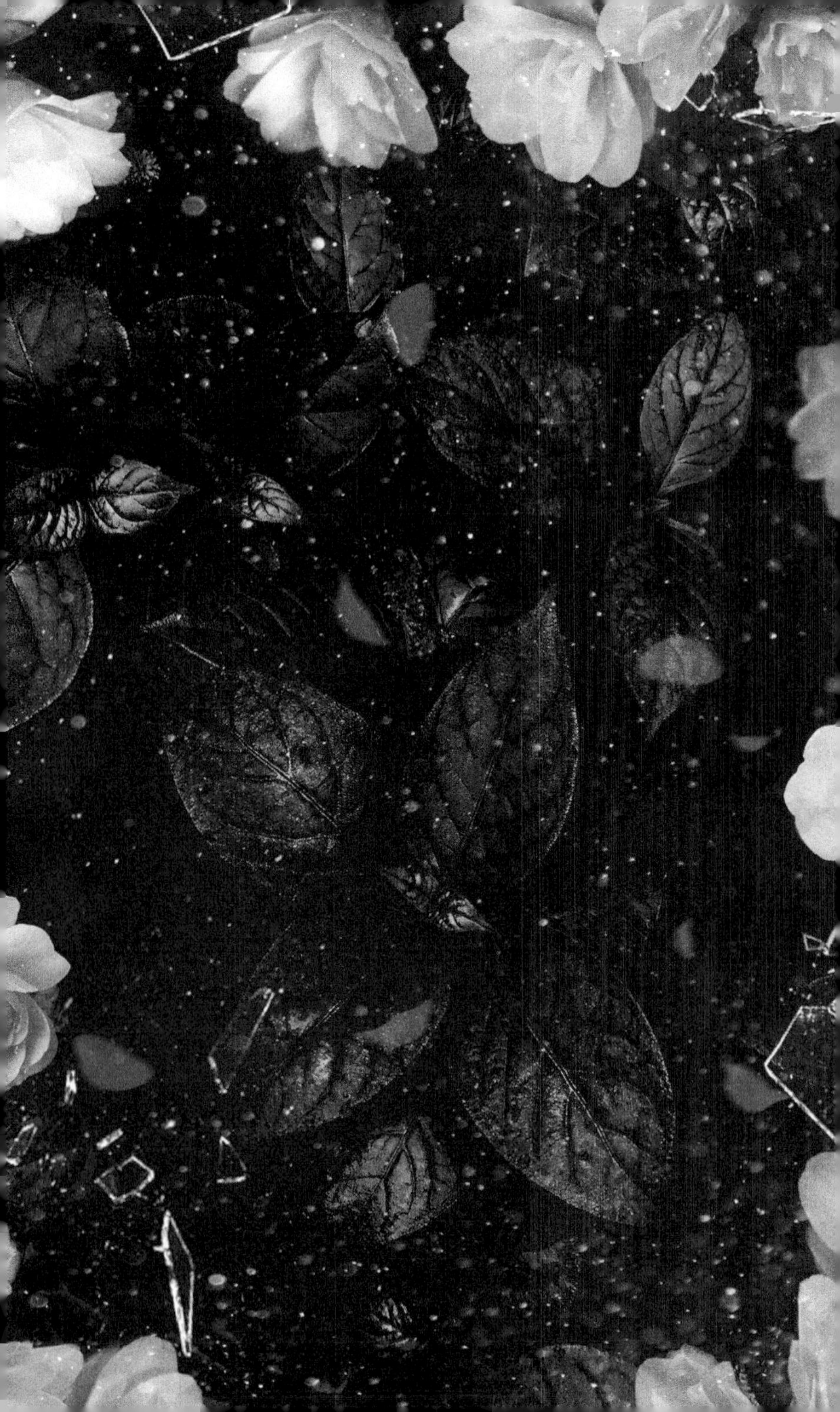

8 AELIA

I opened my eyes to find Caiden crouching over me, his muscled arms pressing on my chest. "Focus on me, Aelia."

Despite my hazy vision, I tried to keep my eyes on Caiden—tried to focus on every piece of stubble on his olive skin, but the darkness crept in.

"Turn her over," Amolie commanded.

Frigid air kissed the wound as they ripped the shirt from my back, sending a shiver down my spine.

Rubbing healing salve into the wound, Amolie clicked her tongue with worry. "That should hold her until we can get her to a proper healer."

My eyes flickered open.

"Aelia, chew this."

Something hard and chalky filled my mouth.

"It's charcoal. It will help to clear the iron and ash from your blood."

I nodded as best as I could.

"She can ride with me," Caiden said, mounting his gray mare. Lucius and Roderick lifted my broken body onto the horse. Pain ripped through my every muscle as I lay against Caiden's warm chest.

The charcoal worked its way through my system. I craned my neck to see the dismembered bodies of the Blood Riders and their mounts.

We rode into the Court of Sorrows territory, setting up camp along the river Nyrinx. Caiden and Roderick gently helped me off the horse.

"When did Gideon gain the Blood Riders?" I said, propping myself up against a rock.

Caiden did not look up from where he built a fire. "Lord Greaves gave them to him in exchange for a stewardship over Elyria."

"I should've known." I rested my hand on my chest. Elyria had been my home. The crown jewel of the Midlands. The breadbasket of Moriana. Gideon needed it to feed his growing army.

As for the new steward of Elyria, Lord Greaves had once been an advisor to my father, the owner of the largest private army in Moriana, including the Blood Riders—half men, half monsters bred from an elite line of sylph warriors and human mothers.

"What else has happened since I've been away?"

"Nothing good." He sighed. "The Sylph Council is divided. It's every lord for himself. Some have partnered with the elves, others with humans. Gideon is considered the unifier."

I raised an eyebrow. "Things must really be bad if the sylphs are willing to partner with their former masters."

Caiden took a seat in front of the fire. "The sylph and elven war ended five hundred years ago. Despite our long lives, sylphs have short memories."

"I hope they remember the Treaty of the Three Faces," I said, wrapping my arms around my knees, trying to hold on to any warmth. Humans partnered with the sylph during their rebellion, and, in return, the sylph pledged to protect the human kingdoms from invasion.

Caiden gave me a coy smile. "Oh, you don't want to go back to old ways when sylph prayed on weak humans for fun?"

"I prefer things the way they are."

Caiden poked the fire with his stick, bringing the flames to life gilding his chiseled features. "Well, if the Wild Courts have their way, you'll be back to glamoured slaves in no time."

I laughed. "Trinity be, I hope not. What about the Fates? Are they still scheming, too?"

"They are always scheming," he said, flicking an unruly piece of hair out of his eyes.

"I'm sure Erissa has her hand in that as well." I held my hands up to the warm flames.

"I suspect she's had a hand in everything since the reign of Crom Cruach. There's no telling how old she is." Caiden tossed another log on the fire. "Elven mages are revered for their magical abilities. I've never heard of another being banished from their order before."

I bit the inside of my cheek. "Dealing in blood magic is a dangerous thing. I imagine there is more to her story than we know."

"I hate talking about her." Caiden grimaced. He had his own history with Erissa, and it tore at both our hearts. Another scab to be picked at.

"You don't think her name turns to ash in my mouth?" I asked.

"That was a long time ago, Aelia. Let it go. I told you what happened. I'm sorry." He grimaced at the memory festering in his mind.

"It doesn't make it hurt any less," I hissed at him.

An elongated lifespan didn't make it any easier to let things go. It amplified the pain. When you have an eternity to think about something, you turn it over and over in your mind until you know every facet, nook, and cranny of the memory.

"You were married to someone else!" A heat grew between us. Old wounds ripped open. Anger and frustration boiled to the surface.

I pushed on it.

Holding my hand to my heart, I smothered the tears welling behind my eyes. "You were supposed to love me. You were supposed to protect me."

I never loved you. You are nothing to me. I never want to see you again.

"I wanted to save you!" His cheeks flushed. Chest heaving, lightning flashed in his eyes. "You know what? Let's make the deal, Aelia. Once we rescue Baylis, you will erase every memory of us from my mind."

"Gladly," I said, holding out my hand, knowing the laws of the land would bind us to our words. We could not come back from this.

He grabbed my hand. Magic burned hot as it sealed the promise. I would have to erase Caiden's memories of us—a solution to the hurt that rotted our hearts.

Once, we belonged to each other, heart and soul.

A memory floated to the surface of my mind.

The day we met—Caiden nursed a terrible hangover. I had been running late to a meeting with him. My hair tousled from riding, and with no opportunity to change, I arrived in a white riding tunic paired with leather riding pants.

Normally, emissaries were old men, ready to be put out to pasture. Not Caiden. My heart skipped a beat when I saw him.

The chair scraped across the stone floor as he stood to greet me, stumbling over his words. "Hi, um, er, you're her… and I'm him."

"Princess Aelia Springborn." I curtsied. "But you can call me Aelia."

Dimples cut into his cheeks as his face brightened with a smile. "Caiden."

What started as a lustful wanting turned into something deeper as we got to know each other. My father's illness made it impossible for him to travel, so my mother made me the royal emissary. Meaning Caiden and I saw a lot of each other. Often the youngest at state dinners, our friendship was born of proximity. We created a signal system for when one of us needed rescuing from a winded dignitary: Four taps on the right side of our nose with our ring finger.

He got me through the tough times when my father's illness consumed everything in our lives. I counted down the days until I could see him again—the smile on his face—the whistle as he walked down the halls.

For five years, we kept our true feelings hidden from one another. It wouldn't be prudent for a human to marry a sylph. Although the sylph and the humans had a treaty, both still preferred to keep their bloodlines pure. Deep down, we knew our fates would never intertwine. Ostara offered us a chance to indulge in our desires. The one night a year when all carnal acts were permitted among humans. A night to honor the goddess Ammena and her fertility. It was a fleeting moment of freedom when we could glimpse a future that would never be ours.

Our love burned and died like a candle being lit and blown out —a life forever out of our reach. We savored the night. Our fates were sealed before our lips ever touched.

"What are you two doing?" Amolie's face turned to a grimace as we made a promise bound by magic older than the world itself.

Caiden pulled me in closer, gripping my hand. "One more thing."

My eyes widened.

"You will get off the dust."

"It's medicinal," I spat back.

"Aelia, please…" His eyes were as hard as stone.

I swallowed hard. For five years, it had been my crutch, a way to erase the pain and guilt tearing me apart inside.

Caiden saw the hesitance in my eyes. "I will help you, Aelia, if you care to remember. I, too, was addicted to drowning my sorrows."

"It's not the same," I said. But our hands were locked. The magic bound me to the promise.

"I'll help, too," Amolie said, putting a reassuring hand on my shoulder—a knot twisted in my chest. I didn't want to let go, but I had no choice.

"Fine, but with one caveat. Once I am erased from your memory, I will no longer be bound to the bargain."

"Deal. I won't be around to watch you kill yourself."

The taste of copper filled my mouth as magic swirled around us, binding our words. We were playing a dangerous game. Magic demanded balance, and it took its payment one way or another.

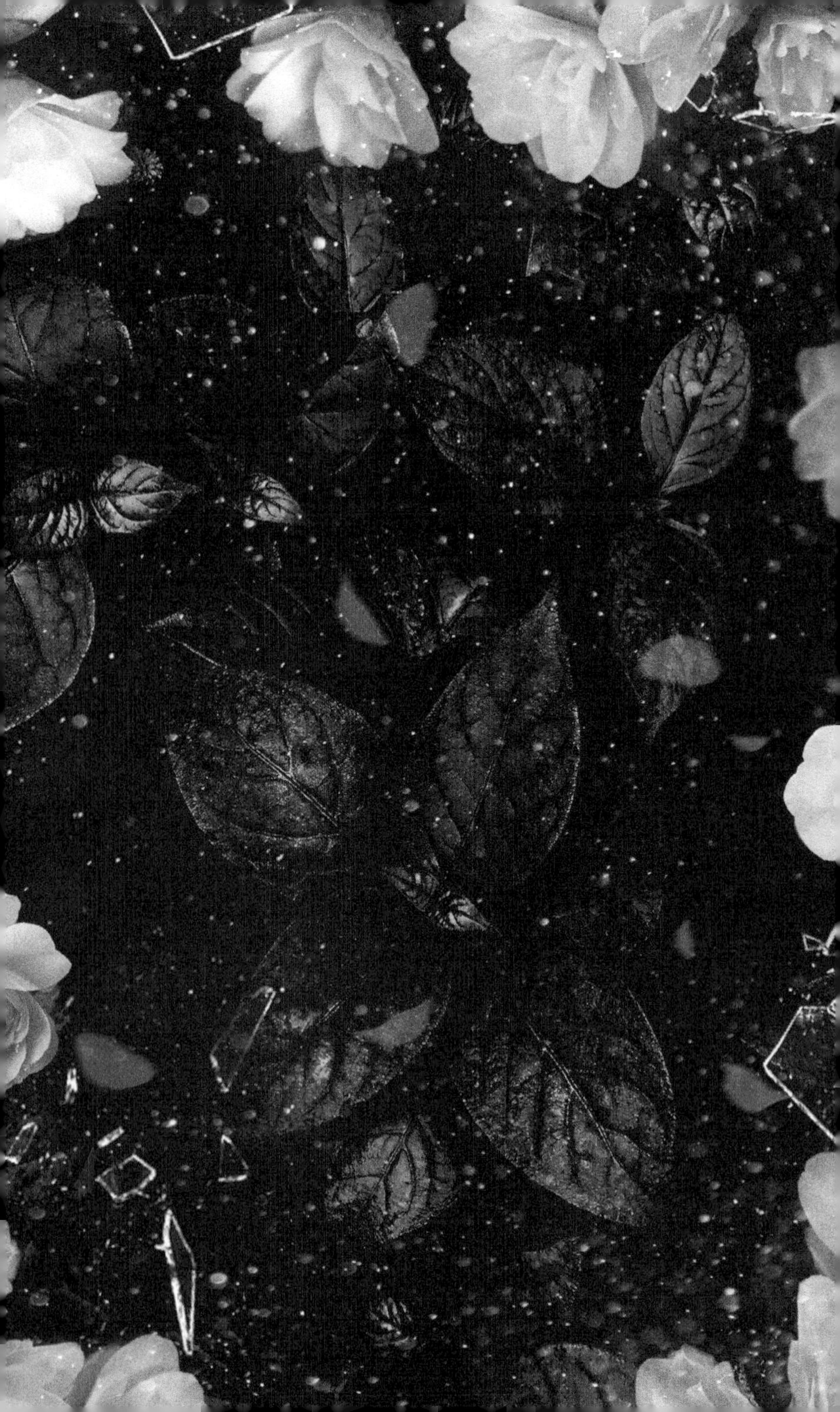

9 AELIA

Lucius and Roderick went fishing in the river while Amolie spread salt around our encampment—enough to deter any kelpie or nixie lurking in the river nearby.

"We'll have to go to Ruska to get clothes for our dinner with Queen Nysemia," Caiden said, throwing a log on the fire. "Even Wild Courts have a high level of decorum."

"Do you think Gideon will follow us there?" I asked. My head throbbed both from the poison of the ash arrow and my body's need for dust. A rough night awaited me. Already, a clammy sweat dampened my brow. Despite the advanced healing the sylph blood coursing through my veins offered, withdrawal from dust would take days.

Caiden scoffed. "Queen Nysemia hates humans. She would not make a treaty with one. Especially one who gained his powers from drinking the blood of the sylph."

"Then I'm sure she's going to *love* me." I pressed my hand to my heart.

"We'll discuss it when we get to Ruska." He looked around the darkened wood. "You never know who or what is listening out here. Nysemia could have spies in the trees."

Roderick and Lucius returned with a rack of fish for our dinners.

"And what if we get caught?" I swallowed the dread blooming in my stomach.

"Not an option," Caiden said, skewering the fish so they could be cooked over the fire.

"Wonderful." I tightened my cloak around me. Night closed in on us.

"You two will need dresses for the Alder King's ball. Multiple. You know how the sylph love pomp and circumstance."

I rolled my eyes. I had been to enough diplomatic dinners to know how much the sylph loved a show. Their balls were elaborate, their food enchanted with spells to make you giddy for days. Before the Treaty of Kings, the sylph had considered humans a necessary nuisance. We were good enough to grow the food they ate but not for much else.

Roderick handed me a cooked fish. Its flakey flesh melted in my mouth. My hands shook from the withdrawal as I picked the bones clean. I hoped to keep it down long enough to nourish my healing body.

"Have you discovered who the emissary will be at the ball, Lucius?" He probably hadn't, but I needed a distraction.

"I sent a raven when we reached Oakton. I am hopeful to hear something back soon."

Heads hung low. Tired bodies picked at the meager dinner. No one said a word. The events of the day took a toll on us all.

After dinner, we lay by the dying light of the fire. I curled my knees into my chest, hoping to keep the dinner down. Winter nights could be brutal in the northern kingdoms, and my healing body wasn't doing me any favors. Although being part of sylph had its advantages. My withdrawal would be shorter than most humans.

Through heavy-lidded eyes, I surveyed the camp. Lucius slept as he always did—standing up—a trait I chalked up to his wraith curse. Amolie and Roderick huddled together. His large body cradled hers under his cloak.

The shakes made it impossible for me to sleep. Sweat coated every inch of my body, making me both hot and freezing at the same time. I tried not to wake the others but knew they could hear my misery.

Fleeing to the shore, I hurled my dinner into the river. My stomach tightened. I spit acidic bile into the water. Heat radiated off my clammy skin. Cupping the icy water in my hands, I splashed my face. The sting provided a moment's respite.

I gazed at my reflection. Hollow eyes stared back at me. What had become of my life?

I wanted to go back to the days before I married Gideon. When Caiden and I were young and in love. Seeing him now stirred something inside me I thought had died long ago.

As if summoned, Caiden appeared next to me. His warm hands rubbed my back. "You'll be okay, Springborn."

For the first time since we set out on our journey, I detected sympathy in Caiden's voice. Although, I winced at the name. Only Roderick and Lucius had ever called me that.

"Does this remind you of the ball in the Court of Tears? When someone slipped me faerie wine?" I asked through chattering teeth.

Caiden let out a laugh—a true lighthearted laugh, like the ones we used to share so long ago. "You were such a mess. You thought you could dance in a sylph circle."

"I can't believe you still wanted to kiss me after that." I splashed more water onto my face. The cold distracted me from the agony.

Caiden continued to rub circles on my back. "I've wanted to kiss you every day since the first time I laid eyes on you."

My breath hitched in my throat against feelings I had buried rising to the surface. "I'm sure your wife would *love* to hear that." *Don't catch feelings, Aelia, he's married, and you're a mess.*

"She knew we both had pasts. That's part of what made me fall in love with her." Sadness filled his voice.

Daggers twisted into my heart. Why did I think Caiden wouldn't have moved on? I had my fair share of lovers since I last saw him. They were just distractions, though. A way for me to feel something other than pain and to ease the sting of loneliness. I didn't trust anyone enough to let them get close to me. The rug had been pulled out from underneath me twice before. My heart could not bear it a third time. So, I built a wall around it, so high and so thick no one could ever hurt me again.

Caiden filled the awkward silence between us. "You know, you're not old, Springborn."

I laughed. "To you, I must seem like an infant."

Although not immortal, like the elves, Sylph lived for hundreds, sometimes thousands of years. At thirty, I must have seemed like a child to him.

"Even for a human, you are young." He continued to rub circles on my back, reminding me of how my mother would do the same when I was a child.

I studied him through lowered lashes. Though we looked the same, I calculated his age at nearly seventy.

Dipping my hand into the black water, I let the river cool my fever. "I feel old. Like I have lived a thousand lives since I left Elyria."

"A long life is hard. It makes the sylph petty and violent. Life is less precious when it extends hundreds of years."

"You'd think it would make them less dramatic," I said, only to hurl more of my dinner into the river.

"What's life without a little *drama*?" Caiden patted my back.

I wiped my mouth on my sleeve. "I think I've had enough drama for multiple lifetimes."

Caiden laughed before looping his arms under mine and helping me to my feet. "Let's get you back to camp. There's no telling what lurks in the waters of the Court of Sorrows." He wrapped his powerful arms around me, pulling me closer. I couldn't help but catch the scent of bergamot on him. Some things never change.

Caiden wrapped me in his cloak. "Do you want me to lay next to you? To keep you warm."

Words escaped me. I blinked stupidly at him. It was the first time Caiden had touched me in years.

A chasm of silence formed between us.

"I'll just lay here…" He pointed to a spot near me. "If you need anything… wake me up." He sat down, motioning for me to do the same.

I laid down and pulled the cloak over my mouth so that only my eyes showed, inhaling his intoxicating scent.

"Goodnight, Aelia," Caiden said as we lay back-to-back.

"Goodnight, Caiden," I replied.

The embers in the fire still glowed as I tried to find sleep.

"Aelia?" Caiden said, his voice heavy with sleep.

"Yes?" I answered.

"I don't hate you."

I swallowed the lump in my throat. "I hate myself enough for the both of us."

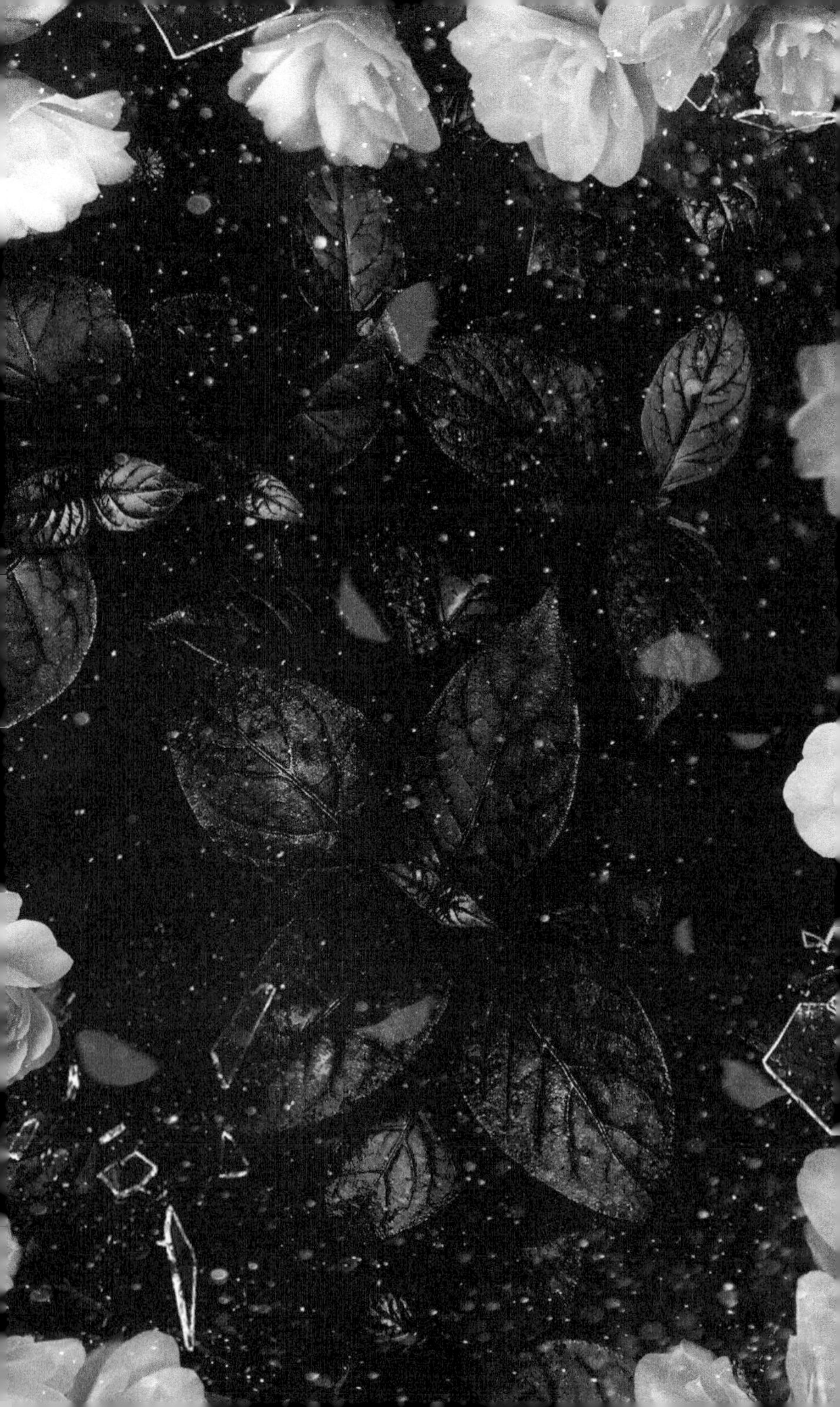

10 AELIA

The ride to Ruska would take weeks.

I heaved myself onto Arion's back. My body still recovering from being thrown off a building.

"You okay back there, Springborn?" Roderick said, giving me a radiant white smile.

Amolie handed me some more charcoal to settle my stomach.

"Never better." My heartbeat pounded in my ears.

"We will follow the river for most of the trip. Be alert. Sirens have taken refuge in the Court of Sorrows," Caiden announced as we moved out.

With my head and body feeling the way it did, it would be merciful for a siren to take me below the waves.

Ruska, a port on the banks of the Atruskan River, lay across from a solitary island, the Tower of Fate. Home to Clotho, Decuma, and Morta, the Three Fates. The Trinity's divine presence in the world.

I shivered at the thought of being so close to them.

When we stopped for the night, I offered to catch fish for our dinner. I needed something to quiet my mind as it begged for the high I'd been feeding it for five years. Lucius accompanied me.

"You know, you should take it easy on him," he said, not bothering to look at me while we weaved a trap from reeds as we sat on the river's shore. "He's been through a lot."

"Yeah, well, he got to keep his home and marry the woman he loved, so forgive me if I'm not sympathetic." I tossed a trap into the water.

"It is more complicated. The fight you two had before you disappeared… it broke him."

I never loved you. You are nothing to me. I never want to see you again.

I stared across the river. I knew I hurt Caiden. Hurt him in a way only a lover can. Deep and personal. I made sure it hit all the sensitive spots—the places where the hurt would fester.

"I wanted someone to hurt the way I did. I couldn't let him come after me." I rubbed my arm awkwardly as if I could wipe the shame.

"I always appreciated that." Lucius tugged on the trap, hoping to attract fish. "You never led him on afterward."

I ran a nervous hand through my hair.

"I was a mess, Lucius. Every emotion was like touching an open nerve. I couldn't stand to exist."

"I know. But you must understand, he has suffered too." He pulled a trap filled with fish from the river. "Look, it's not my place to tell the personal details of his life. I just think you should cut him some slack. He is here now, Aelia."

I bit my lip, wrapping my hands around my lean body. My anger was an integral part of me. I no longer knew myself without it.

I lit a cigarette.

As we carried our catch back to camp, my mind drifted to Baylis. Guilt thickened my throat at the thought of my innocent sister, who lived a pious life, served the goddess Ammena faithfully, and loved her family. She must be so afraid. I should have protected her.

Back at camp, Amolie and I cleaned the fish while Roderick took a small harmonica out of his pocket and struck a tune. Caiden and Lucius joined in.

The sylph loved their tragedies almost as much as they loved to sing and dance about them. I tapped my foot to the beat as we roasted the fish.

They were risking everything to save Baylis. Just as they had done so for me five years prior, I owed it to them to try my best to get clean. More than Baylis's life hung in the balance. I swallowed hard at the thought.

Caiden approached me when the song was through, tugging at his ear nervously. "Take a walk with me?"

"Now?" I looked around. The others were engaged in a heated conversation over the merits of each of the goddesses of the Trinity.

"Yes, it's important." He cleared his throat. "The others won't notice or care."

I sighed. "Fine."

Caiden offered me a gloved hand before I could protest any further.

We tramped through the snowy woods to a small clearing near a pond covered by ice. "Why are we out here, Caiden?"

Caiden rubbed the back of his neck. "I'm hesitant to tell you…"

I took out my cigarettes, tapping them on the palm of my hand. "That bad?" I said, lighting one with a match and taking a long drag.

Caiden swallowed hard, gazing out over the frozen water.

I blew a smoke ring. "Just tell me. You've seen the worst of me. It can't be worse than anything I've done."

Caiden kicked the snow. Moonlight streamed across his face,

illuminating his rugged features. He scratched at the stubble on his chin.

"My wife is dead."

My breath hitched, nearly choking on the smoke from my cigarette.

"I… Uh… I'm sorry." Those two words echoed throughout my life. They were the last words my father had said to me before he took his own life. It's what Gideon would say after he hurt me. Two paltry words you said when you didn't know what else to say.

Caiden hurt as much as I did.

"I don't need your pity. I need your help." Caiden stood with his back to me, the moonlight casting shadows on his muscular build.

"What do you mean?" I asked, pulling my cloak tighter around myself—the winter air cut at my sleek figure.

"Gideon killed my wife. I cannot prove it, but I know he did. We found a piece of iron ore on her pillow."

The Highlands were known for their deposits of iron ore. Almost every piece of steel in Morina came from iron in their mines, making the country prosperous and the men cruel.

I winced. "He did it to punish you for helping me. Didn't he?"

He did not have to answer. Gideon had always been jealous of Caiden.

Caiden stared straight ahead, biting on the inside of his cheek.

I wanted to comfort him, but a chasm of hurt lay between us. Slowly, I slid my hand over the top of his. A single tear trickled down his cheek.

We sat in silence for a moment. Each of us unsure of what to say.

Finally, when my teeth started to chatter, I asked, "So, is there more to this plan than just saving Baylis?"

Caiden clicked his tongue. "It's not politically wise of me to kill Gideon in the Court of the Alder King. But… if you could cause him some pain with your mind…"

I raised my hand, cutting him short. "I hoped to never see Gideon again, but I owe you a debt for saving my life in Ryft's Edge."

Caiden shook his head. "I did it out of love. You owe me nothing."

A lump rose in my throat, but I pushed it away. I hadn't felt this much in a long time. Every part of me was raw. A clammy sweat still dampened my brow. I knew this day would come—the day I would have to give up my crutch. I didn't think it would come this soon.

"Everything will be forgotten after we free Baylis." He squeezed my hand.

I shut my eyes. Our debts would be erased along with his memory.

"Then why are you telling me this?"

Caiden turned, meeting my gaze. His blue eyes were full of warmth and my body relaxed.

"Because I understand you now, Aelia. I understand why you were so angry. Why you shut out the world. I don't hate you, but I am ready to be rid of the memories haunting me."

I understood what he meant. I had never encountered another telepath like me, but I would've asked them to wipe my mind if I had—would've paid any sum they asked.

Caiden and I walked in silence back to camp. No words to bridge the gap between us.

"Caiden?" I stopped outside of the salt circle. He turned to look back at me. His eyes red from tears. "I'm sorry for what I did."

"I know," he said, turning to lay by the embers of the fire, leaving me alone in the cold.

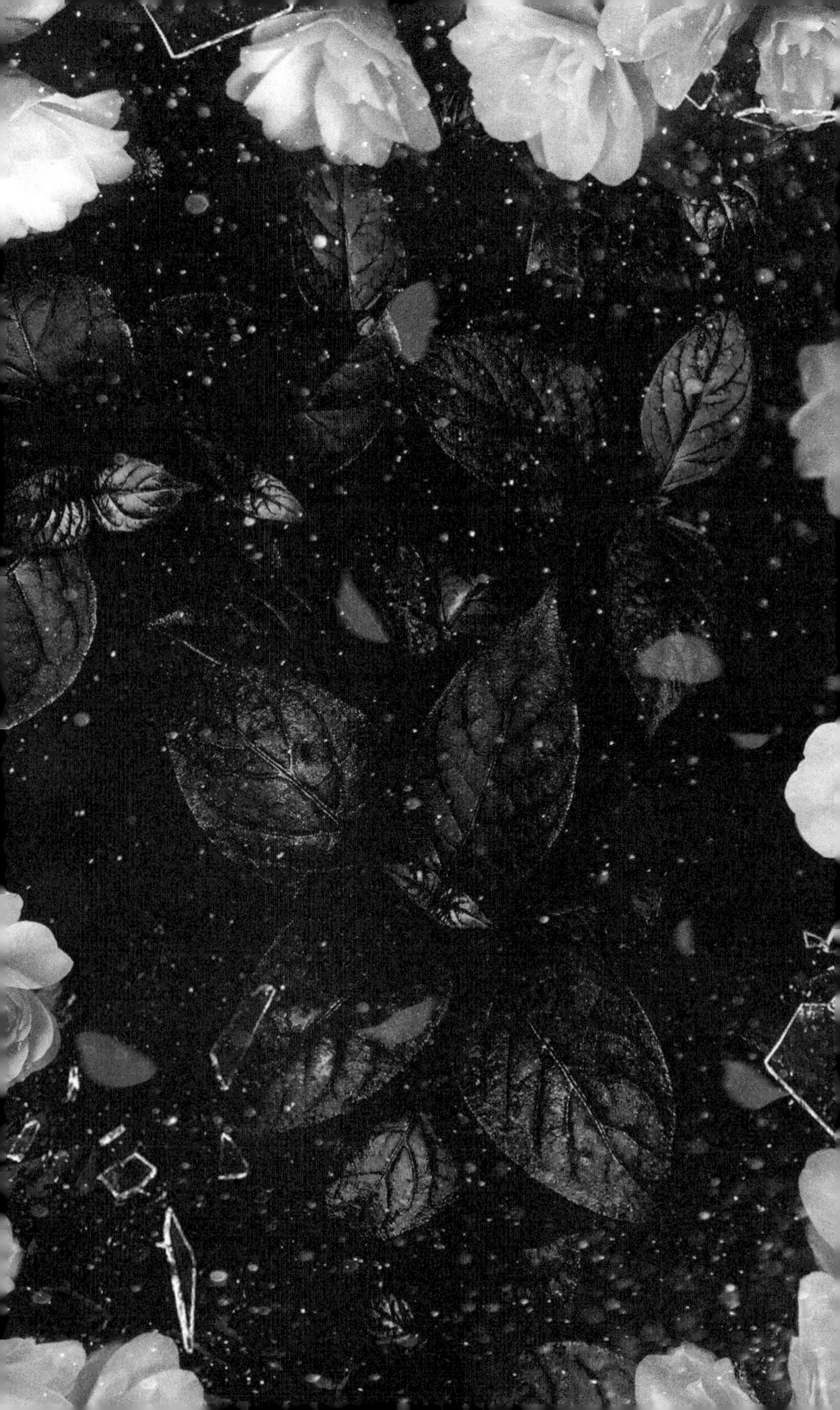

11 AELIA

BY THE TIME WE REACHED RUSKA, A HEALTHY GLOW HAD returned to my face.

Home to humans and magus alike, the city overflowed with culture and character. Made rich by the Fates, at the height of their power, kings would send barges of gold to the city to curry their favor. Though few believers remained, the city still bustled with life.

Our horses' hooves clicked on the cobblestones as we made our way into the heart of the city, passing through its many layers. Stone houses on the outskirts dated back thousands of years, while the affluent part of the city boasted huge granite and marble palaces.

"The Court of Storms has an embassy here for state visits," Caiden said as we pulled our horses into the stable. "It's around the corner."

Large stalls filled with straw adorned with intricately carved wooden doors and chandeliers hung overhead. A lavish stable for the affluent of the city.

"How many days for the 'orses?" the elderly stable master asked as he looked over his spreadsheet.

"At least three," Caiden replied.

"One gold coin per day, per horse…" He tallied up our total, his fingers shaking with age.

Caiden plopped a sack of gold coins on the desk.

The man's eyes widened. "Anything you need, sir, please let me know." Humans were always kinder to others when they knew they had coin.

We left the stables and headed for the safe house, located down a long alley. Had it not been for two lanterns embellished with the crest of the Stormlands—a lightning bolt striking a single tree—I would have passed the place by.

Caiden ran a jeweled finger over the stone wall.

A door of solid, cold-pressed iron appeared. He tapped on the surrounding bricks, and the door swung open, revealing a plush townhome draped in linens of dark blue and silver. The colors of the Stormlands. After sleeping on the ground for several nights, I fought the urge to run to the nearest bed.

A small hobgoblin no bigger than a toddler with the face of a mouse appeared.

"Eek! Prince Caiden." His whiskers twitched as he straightened his satin suit. Hobgoblins or "hobs" were household sprites known as much for their cleaning as their tricks.

"It's alright, Ernie. We won't be here long. Please have rooms made up for each of us."

"Prince Caiden. A message came for you." He handed Caiden a small roll of parchment.

Caiden examined it before handing it over to Lucius. "For you."

Lucius's eyes widened at the sight of the script. "Excellent."

"Thank you, Ernie," Caiden said.

The hob bowed and returned to his duties. His long ears dragged on the floor behind him.

We filed into the large dining room, where Caiden laid out a map of the palace at the Court of Sorrows on a dark mahogany table. Glass lamps painted the room in a warm golden glow. Their flickering light danced off the ornate wallpaper decorated with flowers. This house must have cost a fortune.

"Your target will be Tharan Greenblade. The infamous bastard son of the Alder King," Lucious said.

My skin tingled. "Sounds exciting."

"Don't get any ideas, Springborn." He tapped a painting of an empty chair on the wall. "Show us Tharan Greenblade."

An image appeared in the chair. Tall, handsome, with cutting features. Lord Tharan Greenblade stared back at me. A jagged scar split his face in two. One eye clouded white, the other a piercing green. High cheekbones shadowed hollow cheeks, and a curved nose added to the elegance of his look. Sloped ears peeked from underneath a blanket of burgundy waves.

Terrifying and beautiful at the same time, my heart fluttered at the sight of him.

"Close your mouth, Aelia. You look like a fish," Caiden snapped at me.

Amolie whistled at the sight of him. "Where has he been hiding?"

"He rarely leaves the Woodland Realm, but once he was known throughout the land as a fearsome warrior before fading into obscurity. Now, I hear he's a lush playboy, amusing himself with pleasures of the flesh," Lucius said, a warning in his tone.

"I can work with that." I tapped my index finger on my lips, staring at the painting. "Do you think he has training against telepaths?"

Lucius shrugged. "If he did, it's probably long since lapsed. Everyone thought telepaths had been erased after the war. I'm surprised Erissa found one."

"Think you're charming enough to catch a prince, Springborn?" Caiden picked at his nails lazily.

"I caught you, didn't I? I'm sure I can hook another one." Years of trial and error taught me you catch more flies with honey than vinegar.

Caiden rolled his eyes.

Tension filled the space between us.

"I'll need to get him alone. You will have to provide cover for me. Planting an idea is like threading a needle. You don't always get it on the first try."

"Of course," Lucius turned to the map on the table. "This is the Nightmare Palace."

I stared at the map—a maze of corridors and doors leading to nowhere. "This is... complex."

"It's chaos." Lucius sighed. "But we can use that to our advantage. It's the perfect place for getting lost with someone."

I lit a cigarette, took a long drag, and leaned back in my chair. "Easy. I've done this job a million times."

"Are you sure you can do this, Aelia? There will be a lot of temptation there." Caiden gave me a condescending look.

"I've been clean for weeks." I held out a steady hand. "I think I can handle one night."

"I guess this will be a test."

Ernie entered the room, wearing a black suit with silver trim. "Dinner is served, Your Highness." He wrinkled his furry nose at me, and I abruptly took my boot off the table.

From the kitchen came a line of other mouse-faced hobs, each garnishing a silver platter. We all took our places at the table as, one by one, the platters revealed a myriad of foods. Roasted lamb, a cooked goose, fruits, and vegetables graced the heavy oak table. My stomach grumbled at the smell of herbs and spices wafting through the air.

Ernie poured each of us a glass of wine before returning to the kitchen.

I tore into a lamb chop, savoring each bite. Famished from five years of living on cigarettes and hate.

"Easy there, Springborn, save some for the rest of us," Roderick said, tearing into a goose leg. As sylph, they consumed much more food than a human. Wielding magic made their metabolism fast.

As the night wore on, our companions headed to their respective chambers, until only Caiden and I remained.

"Not tired?" I took a sip of hot cocoa.

Caiden shook his head, slouching into a plush chair with a glass of brandy. "I rarely sleep these days."

"I haven't slept in a decade. Dealing with my father's illness and then Gideon—I feel like a sponge that's been squeezed out too many times—ragged and useless."

"That would make anyone frazzled." Caiden took a drink. "You're going to have to turn on the charm when we go to the Court of Sorrows."

"I am charming."

Caiden barked out a laugh. "Sure, ten years ago."

Little did Caiden know I had charmed royalty all over Moriana.

Breaking into someone's mind required trust. You couldn't just dive into it. The subconscious protected itself at all costs. You had to entice them to let you in.

Many nights, I laid on the laps of dignitaries, pouring honeyed words into their ears until they became putty in my hands. Then I went in. Sometimes, I did it right in front of entire courts. No one knew. They assumed I was whispering sweet nothings, when really, I was hard at work, rewriting their memories or erasing them entirely. I have yet to find a drug to match the high of crushing a king's mind while his court looked on, oblivious. Simply delicious. Just thinking about it made my pulse quicken.

"You don't think I know how to be charming anymore?" I gave Caiden an incredulous look.

"You've been out in the wild for years. Your emissary days are far behind you."

I leaned into him. The smell of sweet liquor permeated his lips. "How do you think I made a living all these years?" I slid my thumb down his jaw.

His muscles tensed under my touch.

"I can see into the hearts of men. Their desires, their wants, their needs." Closer now, my breath on his neck. Goosebumps speckled his skin.

"Your tricks won't work on me, Aelia." He swallowed hard before pushing me away.

Flicking my hair behind my back, I said, "That's what you think."

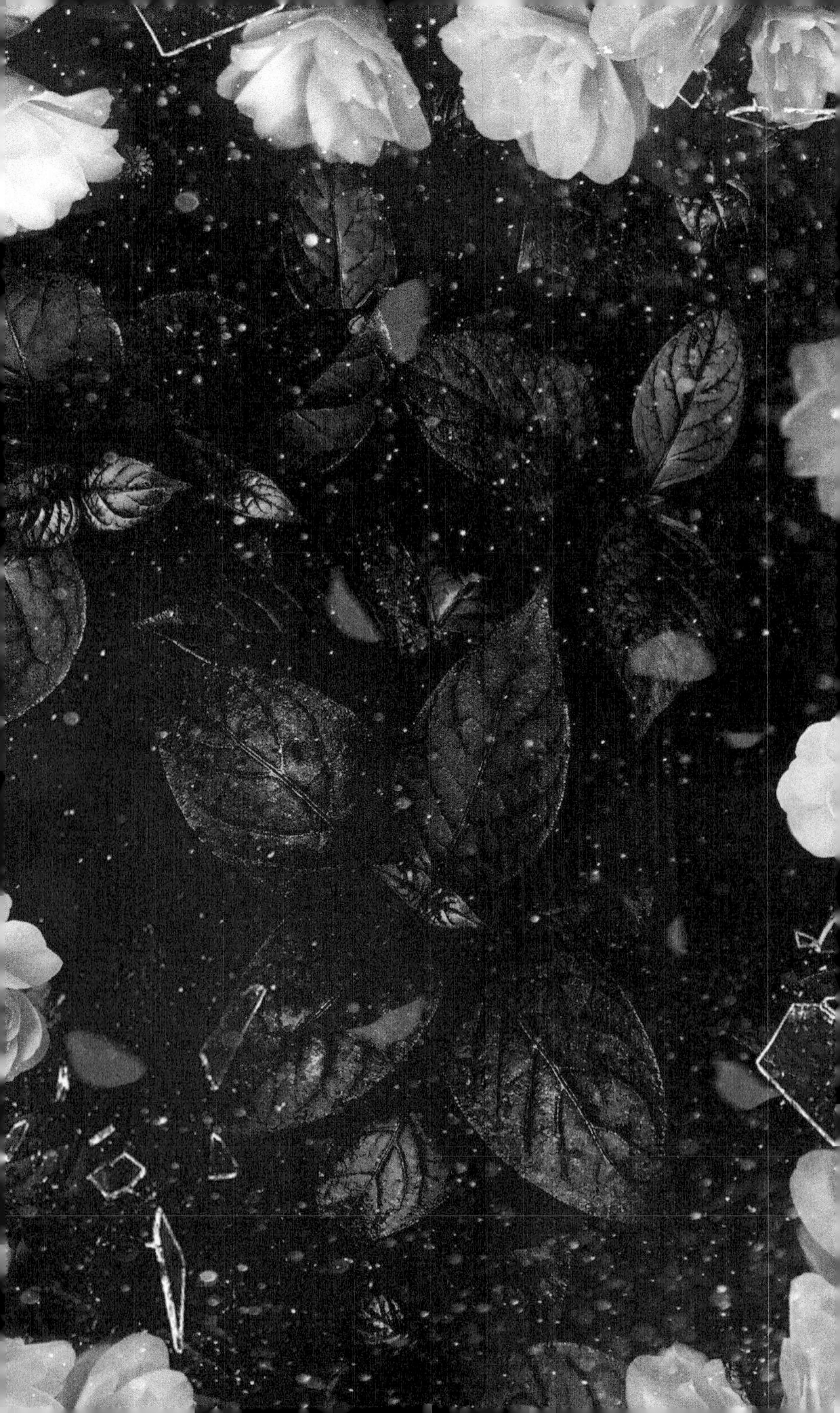

12 AELIA

Caiden didn't look at me the next morning as we sat in the parlor for breakfast. A light winter sun streamed through the large, shuttered windows.

I flashed him a shit-eating grin as I munched on a piece of toast with butter.

"Either of you want to tell me what's going on?" Amolie said, reading the tension between us.

"Caiden thought I had lost my charm. I proved him wrong." I took a sip of my tea.

Amolie's eyes darted between Caiden and me.

"You two didn't…"

"No!" we both shouted. Caiden took a long drink of his coffee.

Roderick nudged Amolie, whispering something in her ear, turning her face red.

I stood, fixing my soft wool dress. "We better get going, Amolie. The shops fill up fast."

Amolie nodded and downed her own cup. Ernie brought us both fur-lined cloaks before opening the iron door.

"Have a good day," he said as a winter wind poured through the house.

"You too!" Amolie and I shouted as we headed into the cobblestone streets.

Dressmakers decorated their windows with the finest garments they could produce in the bustling textile market. Free cities, like Ruska, were said to have the finest dressmakers in all of Moriana. Even the elves in their lofty towers made a pilgrimage to Ruska for formal wear.

The sylph rules of decorum demanded we dress elaborately. Only Itra's designs would do.

"Hello, your majesty," Itra said in a low voice, bowing her head in respect as we entered. We were old acquaintances from my days as an emissary.

"It's just Aelia now. I haven't been royalty in quite some time."

"As you wish, Aelia." She held her hand to her heart. "How can I help you today?"

Reams of colored fabric hung on the wall. I ran a yard of plum velvet through my fingers. "This is for tea with the king."

Itra remembered the code for when I needed a dress discreetly. She locked the doors and drew the shades—moving with a grace that only came from centuries of living. Her white hair, tied in a long ponytail with black pearls placed throughout. Wrinkles near her eyes marked Itra as one of the elder sylphs.

She led us over to a sketching table where pencils and paper were waiting. "So, what's the occasion?"

"We will each need a few dresses. They will need to have hidden compartments for weapons and potions."

Itra's eyes widened in surprise. "You will want a protection spell woven into the fabric, then?" She started to sketch frantically.

"We'll be attending a banquet in the Court of Sorrows and the Alder King's Yule Revelry."

Itra paused, her brow knitted in concern. "Have you ever been to one of the Alder King's Revelries?"

We both shook our heads.

"It is the most extravagant party you will ever attend." She clapped her hands together in excitement. "Others put in their orders months ago."

She didn't have to say it. The dresses were expensive.

I dropped a sack of gold onto her desk. "A down payment. I'll have the rest when we return to pick up the dresses."

Itra's eyes widened. "Of course. I'll get right to work on these. The Court of Sorrows' dresses should be ready by the day after tomorrow. I'll just need your measurements."

She pointed to a large stool.

I stood with my arms out. Itra took a golden tape measure out of her pocket and encircled it around my feet, letting it slog its way up my body, taking down my measurements for her. Once finished, it recoiled upon itself and returned to Itra's hand.

After she finished measuring Amolie, we said our goodbyes and headed to the butcher's shop.

A fresh blanket of snow coated the lamp-lined streets. Peaked roofs of timber-framed houses bore heavy caps of white.

"Do you want to tell me what happened this morning?" Amolie asked as we stopped at the butcher to grab some meat and cheese for dinner.

I gave her an innocent look. "I don't know what you're talking about."

A smile curled at the corner of her mouth. "Sure."

"I don't kiss and tell, Amolie." I gave her a coy smile.

"I knew it!" she exclaimed, interrupting the business of the shop.

"Shhh." I widened my eyes and held up a calming hand. "Did it ever occur to you to tell me that not only did Caiden have a wife but that she died?"

Amolie's eyes fell to her feet. "I didn't think you could handle it."

I clicked my tongue at her. "I'm not *that* fragile."

Amolie looked up at me, her brunette curls surrounding her face like a halo. "You were *that* fragile for a long time. I didn't want you to spiral."

Amolie's words struck me right in the heart. I knew I had been hard to be around for years. What else people were keeping from me?

"Did you meet her?" I pointed to some aged gouda behind the counter and signaled to the butcher I wanted the whole round.

"No, but Roderick mentioned she and Caiden were happy together."

I flinched.

"Sorry."

"It's fine. I'm glad he found happiness for a time." I collected myself, pushing a stray hair back into place, before taking the cheese from the monger and sliding it into my satchel.

Amolie squeezed my hand.

"Are you going to tell me what has been going on with you and Roderick?"

Pink flushed her cheeks, and a beaming smile crossed her face. "Well, you know we've been close for a long time..."

"I do..."

"And well, recently, we decided to be together." She dug her toe into the wood floor of the shop.

My mouth fell open in surprise. "You're a couple?"

"You could put it that way," Amolie said as she surveyed the contents of her satchel.

"Be careful. You know how he is. I remember Caiden having to pull him out of some precarious situations." Roderick's gift of honey tongue had led many lovers to his bed.

"He's changed," Amolie said, taking a salami wrapped in wax paper from the butcher.

I rolled my eyes. In my experience, people didn't change. "You can let him know; if he hurts you, he'll have me to deal with."

Amolie laughed. "All right. I'll let him know."

A lump grew in my throat. "I am happy for you, Amolie."

"Thank you, Aelia. It means a lot to me."

"Of course…" I wrapped my arm around her shoulders. "We've been through the wringer together. It's time one of us found happiness."

Amolie's shoulders sank. "I will be sad to see you erase Caiden's memories."

"Me too," I said, swallowing the lump in my throat.

Winter's chill bit at us as we headed down the cobblestone street lined with townhomes toward the potions shop.

Pinky's Potions gained fame for its extensive selection of rare herbs, crystals, and tonics. Pinky herself, a tall and slender witch with dark skin, a button nose, and her signature pink hair—the result of a tinting potion gone wrong—greeted us as we entered.

"Aelia, I see you've survived another contract," she said, rearranging a shelf of brightly colored vials. A regular at Pinky's, we knew each other well.

"Sorry to disappoint," I said, heading for the medical section.

"Nonsense. It's great advertising for the shop."

The smell of cardamom and orange peels wafted through the air—a staple of the Yule season.

"Pinky, this is Amolie of the Ravenwood Coven." I pointed to Amolie who beamed back at Pinky with her gummy smile.

Pinky placed her hands on her hips. "Ooh, a Raven girl. We don't get many of you around here."

"We're a small coven, but it's not the size that counts, as they say," Amolie replied, grabbing some dragon's breath from the herb section.

"The Ravenwood are skilled in the art of potions, I hear."

Amolie nodded, turning over an eye of newt in her hand.

"Well, what can I do for you girls for today?" Pinky returned to binding herbs.

"I need the usual," I said, handing her my list. My usual included one jar of healing ointment, one contraceptive tonic, and one dye tonic for my hair. A natural brunette, I now kept it jet black as part of my cover.

Pinky nodded and went to fetch my things.

While she arranged my order, I glanced over at her wide assortment of tinctures, everything from love potions to a death kiss. One in particular caught my eye—a glowing vial containing a bright yellow liquid.

"Pinky, what's this one do?" I said, holding up the vial.

Pinky's eyes brightened. "It's new. They call it The Last Wish. Deadly and undetectable once it's in a liquid. Elvish made."

"I'll take one," I said, setting the vial next to the other items on the counter. "And anything Amolie wants as well."

Amolie piled herbs high on the counter. "You never know what we'll need." She gave me an innocent look, shrugging.

"What kind of adventure are you off to now?" Pinky asked.

"We're headed to a party," I replied, not wanting to give too much away, never knowing where Gideon's spies lurked.

"I'm not sure I want to go to whatever party needs this kind of supplies," she said, surveying our purchases.

Gold coins clinked on the counter. "See you later, Pinky. Always a pleasure."

"Be safe out there," she called after us.

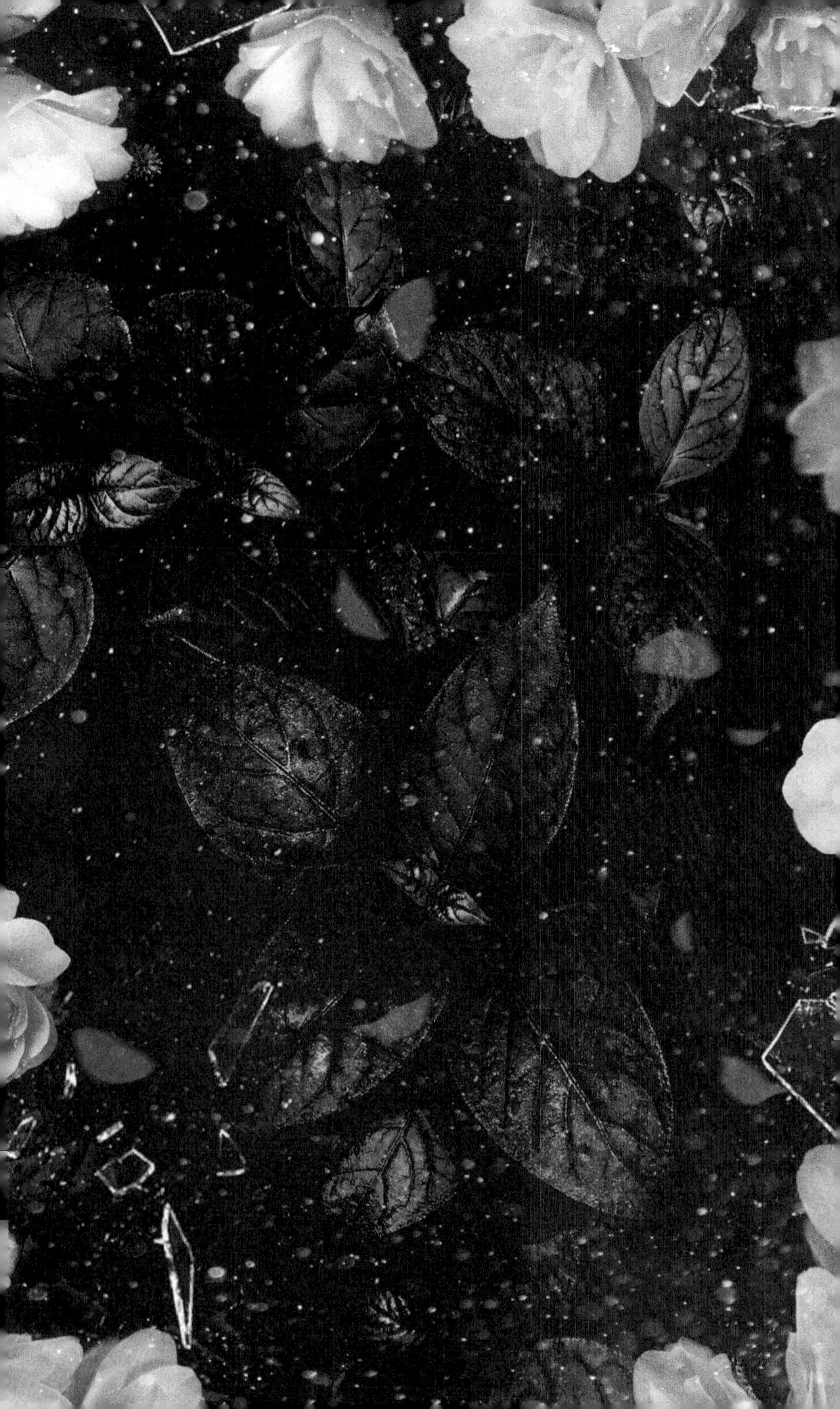

13 CAIDEN

"Are you going to tell us what happened last night, or are we going to force it out of you?" Roderick put Caiden in a headlock before he could react.

"Fine, fine, I'll tell you." Roderick released him from his iron grip, and Caiden stumbled backward, almost knocking a vase over.

From the doorway, Ernie frowned at the men. "You are not children anymore, master. Please be careful."

"Sorry, Ernie," Roderick said, his green eyes falling to the floor.

Huffing in annoyance, Ernie left the room.

As soon as the hob disappeared around the corner, Roderick's face brightened once more. "Anyway... Did something happen between you and Aelia last night?"

Caiden ran his hands along the edge of the velvet couch, contemplating whether he should divulge his secret. "She kissed me, and I did not turn away," he said sheepishly.

"Don't get attached," Lucius said while studying a map of the Court of Sorrows.

Roderick waved Lucius off, flopping onto one of the plush

couches. "I know what you're thinking, Caiden. You shouldn't feel guilty. You two were madly in love once. It makes sense the flame reignited once you were together again."

Caiden sighed, brushing his thick hair out of his eyes. "It wasn't real. She was just using me to make a point. Whatever love Aelia felt for me died long ago. Besides, it would be foolish of us to start anything when we have made a deal."

"You and I both know there are ways to get out of bargains." Roderick leaned his elbows on his knees.

"Yes, ones involve immense pain and potential death," Lucius said from the other room. "If you ask me—"

"We didn't," Roderick cut him off.

Lucius glowered. "*If you ask me*, you should be glad to be rid of Aelia. She has caused you nothing but trouble."

Lucius had never been a fan of Aelia. He saw the heartache Caiden endured when they freed her, and she fled into the wild. Lucius was there every time she broke his heart anew.

Caiden knew he should have been angry with Aelia—hold her accountable for Cassandra's death, but she could not have saved her. He had been the one to risk everything to save Aelia, and he knew there would be consequences. But love blinds even the most careful planners. Caiden couldn't have known events he set into motion years ago. Gideon had killed the spirit of the woman he loved, and his heart ached to save her.

"*Better to mourn her and move on,*" Lucius said to him when Aelia had fled the Highlands.

"You're so bitter for someone who has never been in love," Roderick told Lucius, pulling Caiden back into reality.

"How do you know I have never been in love?" Lucius asked, donning a pair of round-reading spectacles.

Roderick and Caiden sat stunned on the couch. In all the years they had known Lucius, he had never spoken of any lovers. Not even the kind you take after a battle when your blood runs hot. Caiden assumed he took them in secret or not at all.

"Well, have you?" Roderick asked, his eyes wide with excitement.

Silence filled the air.

Caiden held his breath in anticipation.

Lucius shrugged. "Love is not in the cards for me."

"Bullshit," Roderick said, sitting up straight. "If I can fall in love and settle down, anyone can."

Lucius bit his lip. "Well, we can't all find partners like Amolie now, can we?"

Roderick slapped Lucius on the back, sending the thin man hurtling forward. "There's someone out there for you, Lucius. I know it."

"Anyway... we'll need supplies for the Court of Sorrows. Amolie and Aelia are picking up potion materials, but we'll need weapons we can easily hide. I've made an appointment with Tiernan, the blacksmith, to get us equipment." Lucius pushed away from the table where he sat. Ernie brought out the cloaks.

The three men headed into the cold winter streets of Ruska. The smell of burning wood stoves filled the crisp winter air.

"Let's make this quick," Roderick said as they crossed the busy avenue where carriages crowded the street. "I hate the cold." He rubbed his hands together for warmth.

"How are we getting to the Court of Sorrows?" Lucius asked.

"There is a portal in their embassy we can use. It will drop us outside the gates," Caiden said as they entered the blacksmith's shop. Tiernan greeted them, holding up a sword still hot from the fire. A towering man with a bright orange beard—part giant, Tiernan made Roderick look childish.

"Ah, trouble's here," he said, finishing his last bit of hammering on a piece.

The smell of fire and sweat filled the air. Caiden tugged at his collar, trying to ease the sweltering heat of the shop where intricately designed weapons lined the walls. Tiernan was known for his enchanted weapons... and rare artifacts... although few knew of the latter.

"What can I do for you?" He sat on a stool so small Caiden thought it would crumple under his weight.

"We need some discreet weapons," Caiden said, motioning to some of his smaller daggers.

"How discrete are we talking?" Tiernan twisted his braided beard in his blackened fingers.

"Hidden in plain sight."

Tiernan nodded. "I've got some things you may be interested in. Follow me." He went to a door in the back of his smithy, so small that Caiden thought he wouldn't fit. Turning sideways, the hulking man easily slid through the doorway.

The three men followed.

He pulled an earring from a glass case. "First, we have this." It appeared to be a typical stud with a thin gold chain attached.

Roderick's brow knitted in confusion. "An earring?"

"Not just any earring. When swung at the correct angle, the chain enlarges and becomes a whip."

"I'll take it." Roderick's face brightened with glee as he placed three gold coins on the counter.

"And for you, my prince. This ring." He held up a solid gold ring with a line running down the center. "It will detect poison in your drink."

Caiden turned the heavy ring over between his hands before slipping it on. The ring sized itself to fit his fingers.

"And for the spy?" Tiernan asked Lucius, who leaned against a wall in the back of the room, staring out the window. The light washed out his already pale complexion.

"I have all I need." He didn't bother looking at Tiernan.

Tiernan shrugged. "Suit yourself."

The men paid Tiernan and headed back to the townhome. As they reminisced about their academy days, Caiden caught the distinct red of a Highland soldier's uniform from the corner of his eye. He stopped dead in his tracks, signaling the men to remain vigilant. They paused, their bodies tensing as adrenaline lit up their systems.

"Let me check." Lucius transformed into a wraith, becoming nothing more than a wisp of a ghost with translucent skin and hollow eyes.

Were they here for them? The neutrality of this city meant nothing to Gideon. Sweat dampened Caiden's brow as his thoughts drifted to Aelia and Amolie.

Lucius returned a moment later, appearing through a brick wall.

"It's them."

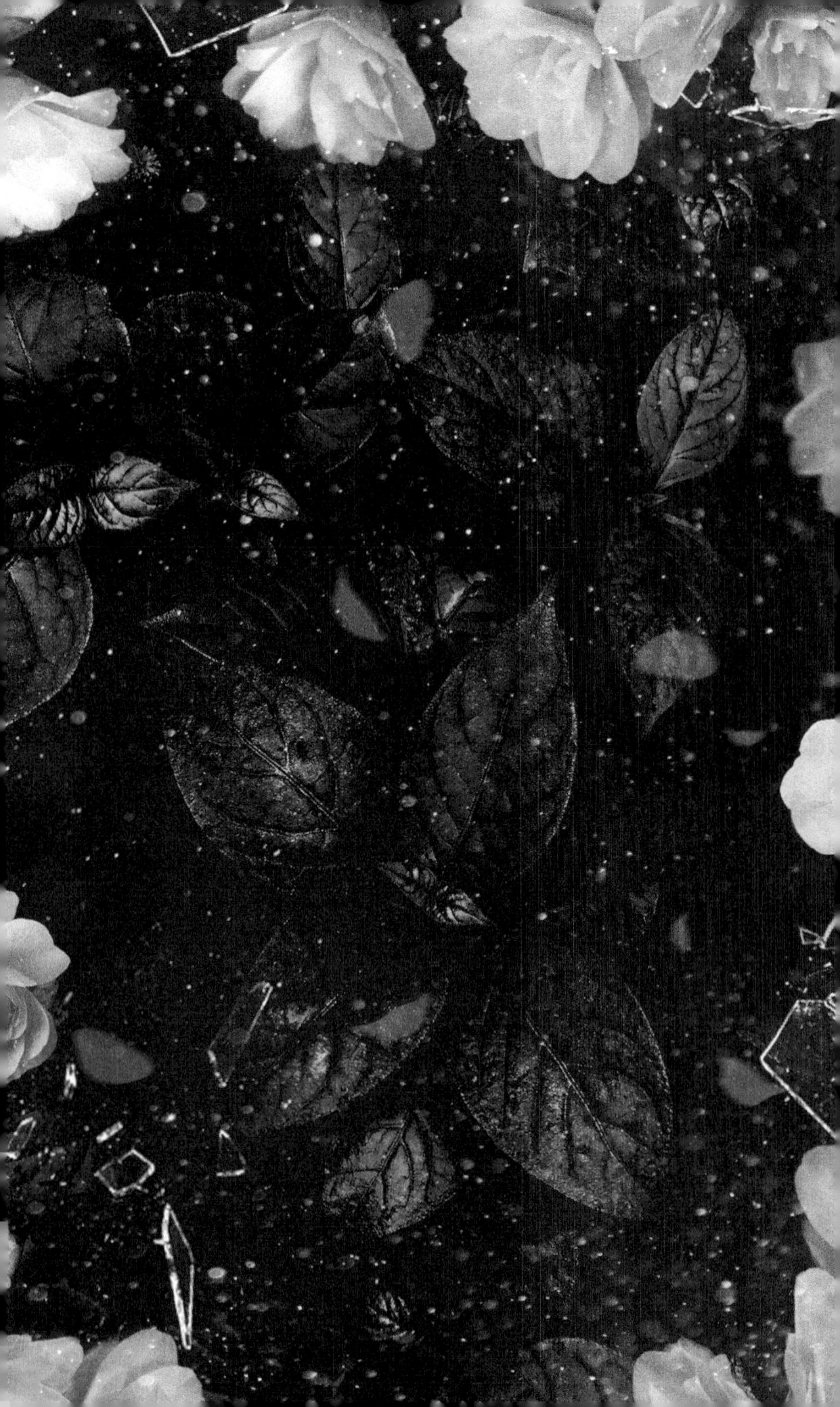

14 AELIA

THE CITY SPARKLED AS THOUGH COVERED IN A LAYER OF SUGAR as Amolie and I made our way back to the townhome. My mouth salivated at the thought of Ernie's rich hot cocoa waiting for us.

Patrons hurried through the streets, eager to get home to a warm meal. We took our time, enjoying the light snow. I noticed an unmistakable mark chiseled into one of the granite walls—a pixie sprinkling dust. Thoughts of the euphoric substance running through my veins made my fingers twitch.

I fought the urge to mark where the sign had been. It would be so much easier to face my fears sedated. I swallowed hard and pushed the temptation away. *You're stronger than this.*

Shame washed over me at the thought of my sister seeing what I had become. She wouldn't recognize me. I rubbed my hands on my cloak as if I could wipe the embarrassment away.

When we reached the house, Caiden, Roderick, and Lucius waited in the living room. Their faces filled with gloom and apprehension.

"What's going on?" I asked, handing my cloak to Ernie.

Caiden stepped forward, putting his hand on my shoulder. "Gideon is here."

A pit opened in my stomach.

Amolie grabbed my hand, steadying me.

Reading the panic on my face, Roderick chimed in, "At least, his men are. We didn't *actually* see him."

I paced around the room, lighting a cigarette to calm my nerves. "He can't know I'm here." My whole body shook in fear.

Ernie frowned at me from the stairwell.

"You can enchant the smell away later." Caiden waved him away. "You're safe here, Aelia. His magic can't penetrate the wards around this house."

I took a drag of my cigarette, letting the smoke burn in my lungs. "It's not him I'm worried about. He's too lazy to learn how to use his magic properly. Erissa could if she wanted to."

Caiden turned to Amolie. "Then we best not give her a reason to snoop around. Amolie, can you put a salt barrier around the inside of the house?"

Amolie nodded and headed upstairs.

"Aelia, I think it's best if you don't leave the townhome until we depart for the Court of Sorrows. Itra can bring your clothes here." Caiden wrote a message down on a piece of parchment. "Have this delivered to Itra Davenport in the textile district." He handed the paper to Ernie.

"Right away, sir." Ernie took the parchment, the wax seal of the Court of Storms visible.

"And make sure it is kept discrete," Caiden warned.

Ernie nodded.

After dinner, we gathered on the terrace of the townhome. The lights of the city twinkled below us. Roderick held Amolie close while Caiden, Lucius, and I gathered around a small fire.

I lit another cigarette, without dust to lean on, every emotion hit me like a tidal wave.

"I'm going to scout for Highland soldiers tonight. Maybe I can figure out why they are here," Lucius said.

"Be careful. We don't need to alert them to our presence." Caiden took a sip of brandy.

Lucius gave Caiden a look that made my stomach turn. "I am your Master of Shadows. Please give me some credit."

"You're right." Caiden held up his glass to salute his friend.

Pulling a dark cloak over his head, Lucius disappeared into the darkness of the night.

I bit my fingernails as memories bubbled to the surface like a boiling kettle, slow at first, then faster until I wanted to scream.

"You know, you can talk to me," Caiden said.

I shut my eyes. "I've already burdened you enough."

"You're going to erase my memories, anyway."

I pondered for a moment. Perhaps it couldn't hurt to let Caiden in.

Amolie and Roderick were lost in their own world, holding each other tightly, whispering sweet nothings.

With a heavy sigh, I let some of the tension out. "It's more than just the memories of abuse. It's the shame that eats away at me every day. I let him in. Let him manipulate me." Bile rose in my throat at the admission.

Caiden's glance softened. "Your father had just died, and you had been ripped from your home. It's not your fault he preyed on your sorrow. A leech doesn't feed off a sick host, Aelia." He pulled me in closer to him.

I rested my head on his shoulder—chest tight from the emotions building within.

"I know, but I hurt so many people." A pressure built behind my eyes. "Including you."

Caiden rocked me as I hyperventilated. "You can't go back and change the past, but you can move forward with your life."

Caiden had been my lifeline for so long.

A memory bubbled to the surface.

It was the day after my Promise Ceremony. Baylis had woken me early in the morning. Before the first light of dawn. "Mother needs us at the castle." The fear in her eyes made my heart leap into my throat.

We ducked through alleys and back passageways to remain as hidden as possible.

When we arrived, my mother was waiting in our father's study with a glass of whiskey. A glaze covered her emerald eyes. Her long black hair draped over her shoulders.

"He's dead," she said to no one in particular. "Your father is dead."

A sense of relief flooded me at the sound of those words. For ten years, we had walked on eggshells around my father. One wrong move sent him into a downward spiral we could not pull him out of.

We were free.

The reality of the situation did not register until she led Caiden and me into my father's chambers, where he hung from a rope. His eyes were glassy, like a doll's.

I left my body: his snapped neck, his rigid limbs. The guards hacked to bits on the floor beneath him. It was all too much. I retreated inside myself.

Caiden held my hand the entire time—a tether to this world—the last intimate touch we would share for years. The next day, I was shipped off to the Highlands. Where a fate worse than death awaited me.

Baylis's last words echoed in my mind.

Do not let them break you, Aelia.

My sadness so consumed me that I hadn't noticed that sentence's nuance. *Them.* Did she have the sight then? Was she trying to warn me of what was coming? Why had I been so thickheaded? *Stupid idiot.*

My chest lightened after telling Caiden the simple truth. Gideon had made a fool of me—a brilliant plan. "A broken girl makes for a willing victim," I said, wiping my nose on my cloak.

Caiden lifted my chin so that our eyes met. "You were never broken to me." Lightning flashed in his blue eyes as if he were seeing me for the first time.

Both suffering when we met, we poured ourselves into one another, half empty, looking for something to make us whole again.

"I am hollow inside. Gideon sucked the life from my veins." Tears muffled my words. Truthfully, I accepted love from any source. I allowed Gideon to abuse and manipulate me because of desperation to be accepted… to be loved.

Taking my hand in his, a serious look crossed his face. "Let me help you, Aelia."

"You can't." I breathed deeply. "You won't know I exist when this is all over."

Firelight danced across his chiseled face as his mouth tightened into a thin line.

I focused on our intertwined hands. "I cannot let myself get attached to you again. I have to protect my heart."

"We didn't specify a timeline in the bargain. We could hold off on it." Caiden ran a loving hand across my shoulders.

"You and I both know the longer we wait, the harder it will be. The more the magic will demand the bargain be fulfilled."

The laws of the land demanded balance. Once we saved Baylis, the scales of the universe would be off. Magic liked equilibrium. It would pull us together, demanding we finish what we started.

Caiden's stubble pricked my fingers as I stroked his jaw, examining the man I had loved and hated for all these years. "We were never meant to be, Caiden."

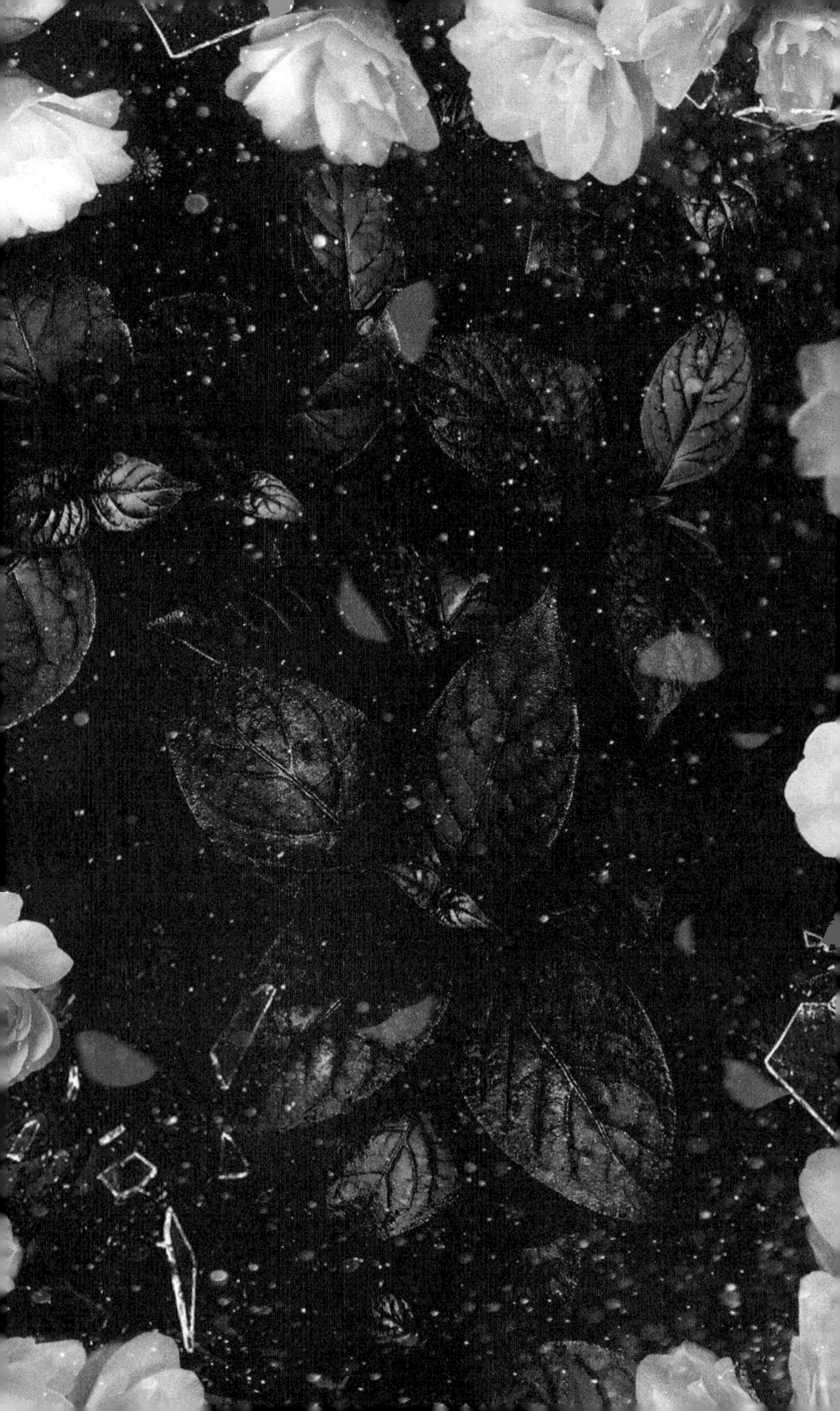

15 AELIA

Lucius sat on the bench in front of one of the large kitchen windows with one leg dangling in the air. Shadows ringed his eyes as he stared out the window.

"Did you sleep at all?" Caiden asked, sitting at the table laden with fine pastries. The smell of fresh berries filled the air. The sylph loved sugar. They put it in everything from pies to eggs. Wars had been fought over sugar.

"I followed the soldiers we saw earlier to a house on the outskirts of town and waited." Ernie poured him a hot cup of coffee, and Lucius took a long swig before continuing—being part wraith, he ate very little, if at all. "Erissa and Gideon are here, but I did not discover if they knew of our presence."

"What did they discuss?" I held my breath.

"Mostly domestic political matters. From what I could gather, they are here preparing for the Yule Revelry."

"You should have killed him," Amolie chimed in from across the room.

"Easy." Lucius held up a hand. "That's not how diplomacy works." He sipped his coffee. The morning light illuminated his pale skin.

A fire burned in my belly, rising into my throat. "If anyone is going to kill either of them, it's going to be me," I said, squeezing Caiden's hand under the table.

"Her goons are here, too," Lucius said, his eyes peeking out from beneath a curtain of white hair.

I shuddered at the thought of Ramus and Remus, Erissa's bodyguards and the architects of my worst nightmares. Twins born to a giant mother and sylph father, with the strength of a hundred men. They towered over every creature.

My hands shook, and my chest tightened at the memory of their abuse. I could leave my body while they did what they pleased with it. But the names they'd call me were forever burned into my skin. Tattoos only I could see. At least I could take solace in having made them earn every ounce of flesh they took from me.

The metallic taste of blood filled my mouth as I bit the side of my cheek. Caiden squeezed my hand, bringing me back to reality. "Everyone needs to keep a low profile until we leave for the Court of Sorrows."

"Did you see my sister, Lucius?"

Lucius shook his head. "I'm sorry, Aelia. No."

I bit my lip, imagining the various forms of torture Gideon could put my sister through.

Ernie cleared his throat. "Lady Itra is here."

Amolie and I headed into the plush parlor decorated in silver and blue with accents of gold. Itra sat in a leather armchair drinking tea. Her jovial face brightened when she saw us.

"Hello, my beauties." She set down her cup. "I have outdone myself with your dresses."

From a leather case sprung seven dresses, each more ornate than the next. The dresses twirled in the air as if ghosts adorned them.

"You each need to try on one. Aelia, we'll start with your

Court of Sorrows dress." She kicked the leather case with her foot, and a small wooden stool and full-length mirror popped out of the bag. "Some privacy?" Itra glowered at Ernie, who clapped his hands, closing all the doors in the room.

I undressed and, with Itra's help, donned the elegant gown. Its skirt consisted of black satin with a slit running up one side. At the same time, the top sported a design reminiscent of velvet cobwebs that crawled from my waist to my chin, leaving the skin exposed yet retaining an element of intrigue. An image of a queen stared back at me from the mirror. The memory of my reign made my stomachache. I ran my hands down my hips. Where once luscious curves could be felt, now there was nothing more than jagged bone.

Itra straightened the skirt of the dress.

"Protection enchantments are woven into the fabric. No curses should be able to penetrate it."

"Thank you, Itra. It is beautiful." I ran my hands over the delicate lace.

"No need to thank me. You have always been one of my favorite customers. The others and a set of wings will be delivered in a few days. In the Alder King's court, they are required. Women go to great lengths to have the most ornate wings."

Some said before the sylph were taken as slaves, many had wings, but the elves bred it out of them. No sylph had been born with wings for centuries.

As I returned to my everyday tunic and leathers, Itra helped Amolie into her dresses. "Since you are a witch, my dear, I went with the theme of the forests for your dresses."

The dress hugged Amolie's curves in all the right places. A tight bodice descended into a flowing train like the wing of a giant monarch butterfly. Amolie's amber eyes glistened with pride at her appearance. Her long hair fell in tight curls over her bare shoulders. Itra adorned her head with a crown of enchanted butterflies, each one's wings flapping as if they were just landing.

"You look radiant," I said as Amolie twirled in the dress.

Her eyes brightened, and she splayed her hands in a curtsey. "I feel like it."

"I can't wait for Roderick to see you." I gave her a wink. Pink flushed her cheeks. "Thanks, Itra." I handed her a sack of gold coins. She felt the weight of the bag and nodded in gratitude.

"You are too kind to me, Lady Aelia. Anytime you need something made, whether it be a gown or a coat of armor, I hope you come to me first," she said, finishing her tea.

"Of course."

"If there is nothing more, I will take my leave. Good luck." She floated out of the room with an ancient grace.

Caiden and I played cards after dinner. While Amolie worked on her potions, Roderick sharpened his sword, and Lucius studied the maps of the Court of Sorrows.

My fingers drummed the table as Caiden took his turn.

"Nervous about something?" he asked, scrutinizing his cards.

"Gideon is too close for my liking. I can feel his hands around my neck. If his power has grown, he could—"

Caiden cut me off before I could finish. "You are protected here. Three of the finest warriors to walk Moriana sit beside you."

"I know, but I still worry." My legs fidgeted under the table. Even protection spells could not calm my nerves. I tried to focus on the game.

"You know, you will have to see him at the Alder King's Revelry." Caiden played his hand.

I lit a cigarette. "I don't know how I'm going to sleep tonight."

Caiden set down his cards. "Amolie, do you have a sleeping potion?"

Amolie tossed a vial filled with purple liquid to Caiden. "It's valerian root. You only need a little."

Caiden handed me the vial. I tipped it so one drop hung on the cork top before leaning my head back and dropping it onto my tongue. An oaky taste filled my mouth. Instantly, my eyes felt heavy.

Caiden and Roderick helped me up the stairs to my bedroom and into bed.

Gideon haunted my dreams. In one, he climbed through my window and dragged me out by my hair. In another, I awoke to find him suffocating me. Squirming underneath his firm grip, my heart raced. The sedative kept me locked in my nightmares. Screams scraped at my throat.

A voice called from beyond the veil. "Aelia, wake up, Aelia. It's just a dream."

I opened my eyes to find a shirtless Caiden shaking me awake. Sweat drenched every inch of my body.

"It's a dream, Aelia." Caiden pulled me in close.

Burying my face in his chest, I sobbed. "I can never escape him."

"I'm here now. He can't hurt you here."

My body trembled, and a hot cry bubbled in my throat. "You can't protect my mind."

Caiden held me tighter. "I'm staying with you the rest of the night."

I didn't have the energy to fight with him. "Fine." My body relaxed.

He gave me a warm smile. "Let's get you out of those wet clothes."

Without thinking, I let him peel the clothes from my slick body.

When he returned with the pajamas, he gasped. "Your back."

I shut my eyes tight, blocking out the memory.

Caiden swallowed hard at the sight of my mangled flesh.

"Whips infused with iron and nightshade." The words caught in my throat. I tore the silk pajamas from Caiden's hands, covering my shame.

"Do they still hurt?" A crease formed between his blue eyes.

I pulled the satin shirt over my head as I pushed back tears, fighting a scream that lingered under the surface of my skin. "Only in my mind."

"I'm sorry," he said, lowering his eyes.

"You didn't cause them. They are a part of me now." I fiddled with the gold stud in my left ear. The simple piece of jewelry hid my deepest cut.

His eyes asked the questions his lips did not dare.

"The twins did this to me. Gideon didn't get his hands dirty with such things."

Caiden fell to his knees before me, grabbing my waist. "I failed you. I should have protected you."

I ran my hands through his thick hair. "There was nothing you could do. My fate was sealed before I ever set foot in the Highlands."

It had taken me a long time to accept that.

"Still." He buried his face into my abdomen.

I cupped my hands around his face, forcing him to meet my gaze. "You saved me in so many ways, Caiden. You were my escape. My refuge in a storm I couldn't see a way out of. Every night, I replayed the memories of us over and over in my mind. You were a light when I was surrounded by darkness."

"Aelia... I... I don't know what to say." His eyes softened. I had cracked some invisible barrier guarding him.

For hours, we lay in bed, holding one another. I tried to imagine my life if we had run away and been married in secret, despite knowing it did not do me any good to dwell on what could've been. Still, it hurt my heart to think about leaving him.

Caiden and I were like a rock cracked in two. Over time, the elements had worn away at each of us so that we could never go back together again.

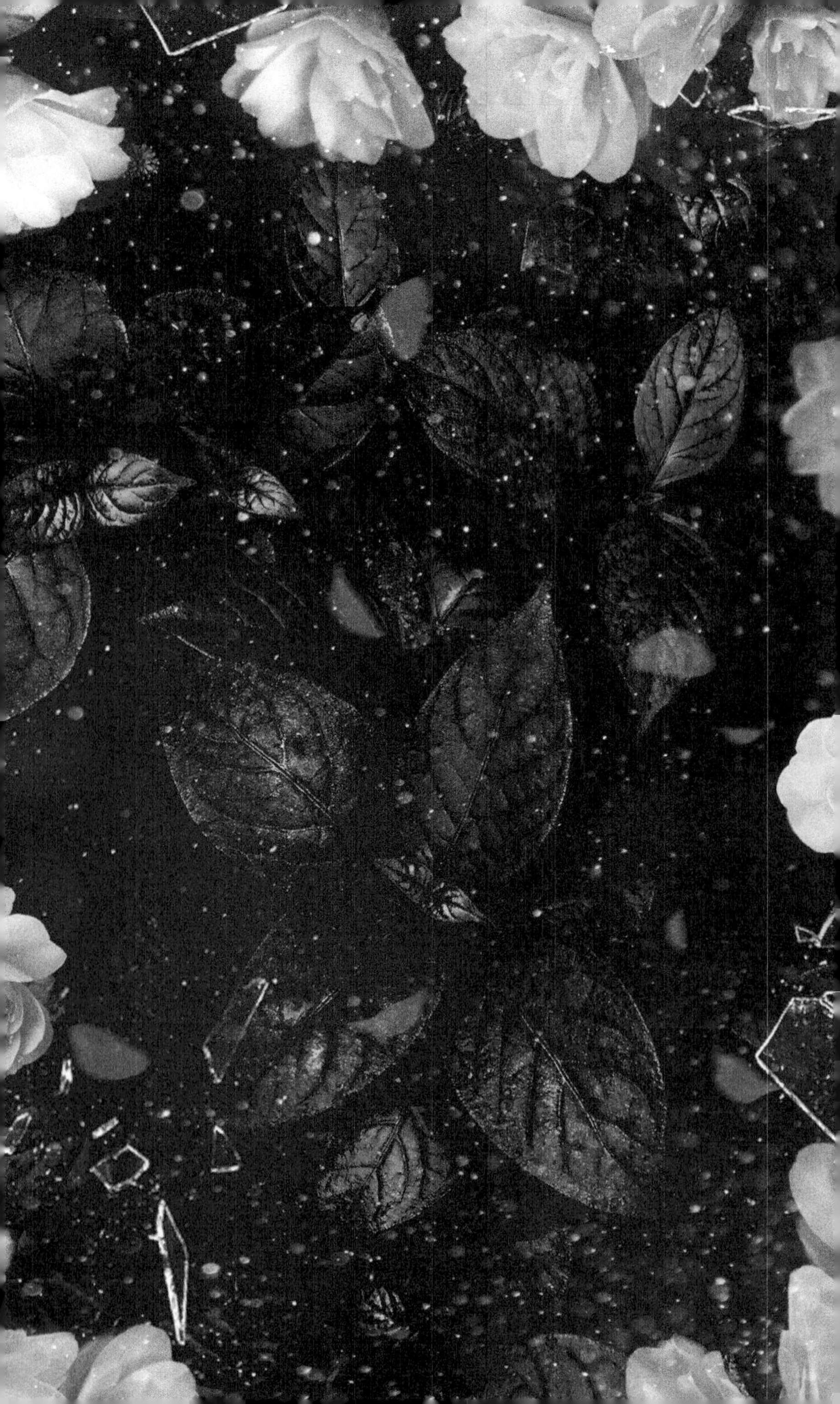

16 AELIA

"Are you nervous?" Amolie asked as she braided my hair, intertwining the strands with a diadem.

I blew out a long breath. "No, this is just another job."

She fastened the braid with a pin, holding the others between her teeth while she wove the hair. "Well, that's one way to look at it."

I bit my lip.

"What?" Amolie asked.

"Baylis used to braid my hair before royal events." I pushed down a sob.

A memory rose to the surface of my mind. *Elyria—Baylis sat before me in our dressing room, which smelled like fresh flowers. Her round face smiled back at me from the mirror as I braided cherry blossoms into her hair. Her two black shepherd dogs lay at her feet.*

"My first ball. I'm so excited." Her sun-kissed cheeks seemed to radiate joy.

"No one will be able to take their eyes off you," I said, placing a bloom.

"There's only one boy's eyes I want to catch."

"Oh? Whose?"

"Peter Avilard." Her eyes fluttered. *"He's so handsome; his father is the Master of Coin."*

"Peter Avilard is a good match for you."

"Do you think so?" She turned to face me. Her gray eyes full of hope.

"I do. He's from a respectable family. He seems to have a good head on his shoulders."

"Could you plant a seed with our mother and father?"

"Of course," I said as I put the final blossom into place.

"Aelia?" Amolie said, waving a hand in front of my face.

"Sorry, what were you saying?" I shook the bitter sting of regret off. I hadn't mentioned Peter to my parents. I knew what the answer would be.

"Oh, nothing. You need to be careful tonight—you know how Wild Courts are. There will be a lot of temptation for you to use."

"I know. I'll be fine. But thank you for worrying about me, Amolie. If you didn't, no one else would."

She clicked her tongue. "You're not as hard to love as you think, Aelia."

I applied a thick layer of kohl to my eyes and reddened my lips. The sylph loved to dress up.

"We need to go, ladies," Lucius called from the parlor.

Amolie strapped my dagger to the outside of my leg so its carved stallion hilt did not dig into my thigh. I slipped into the spiderweb gown, letting the mesh and velvet hide the scars on my back, then helped Amolie into hers.

"Beautiful and deadly," Amolie said as she stepped back, allowing me to glimpse myself in the mirror. I did not recognize the woman who stared back at me. A queen of darkness replaced the mercenary.

The three men stared at us, mouths agape, as we descended

the elegant marble stairs. Even Lucius looked taken aback by my appearance.

Caiden wore a dark blue velvet vest embroidered with lightning, Roderick wore traditional Court of Storms armor, and Lucius dressed in all black.

"You all look nice as well, except for Lucius. You look like you are attending a human funeral."

The others laughed while Lucius pulled his hood over his head. His face disappeared into nothing.

Caiden extended a hand to me. "Shall we?"

"Let me cleanse us before you leave." Amolie lit a bundle of dried sage. "To get rid of any negative energy on you." She waved the smoldering herb over us, filling the room with the sweet, earthy aroma.

I hugged her tight before heading into the snowy night, where a black carriage waited outside to take us to the Court of Sorrows' embassy.

Caiden kept a reassuring gloved hand on mine as we traveled through the white city. It scared me how easily I accepted his support. I should not become accustomed to something that would not last.

The black stone embassy of the Court of Storms stood out like a sore thumb among the white-marbled houses of the city. Two wraiths stood guard outside, holding obsidian spears. Their long black robes hovered above the ground. Hoods covered their gaunt, hollow faces.

Wraiths were shadows of men who had been cursed. Their bodies died long ago, but the essence of their spirits lived on. They served the owner of the curse until the owner's death. Notoriously hard to kill, the wealthier of the Wild Courts collected them as a symbol of their strength. How Lucius came to be part wraith, I did not know, but I had my suspicions.

Caiden flashed an invitation embellished with the Court of

Sorrows sigil of a spider battling a serpent. The wraith motioned for us to enter, waving their hands to open a giant stone door featuring the sigil.

A lump grew in my throat at the sight of the spider. Every strand of fur visible as though a live creature had been cast into the door.

"When the doors open, they won't open to this house but to the Court of Sorrows," Caiden said, reassuringly touching my small back. "It will be as though no time has passed, but we will have traveled hundreds of miles."

The doors opened, and a damp fog crept from the mouth of a cave, covering our feet. Caiden grabbed my hand, escorting me into the darkness. Roderick and Amolie followed. The sound of his armor echoed through the empty cavern. I looked for Lucius but couldn't find him.

I struggled to see in the pitch-black as we stood, unsure of our next move. The cave smelled of damp soil, and only the trickling of water could be heard.

A light flickered at the end of the tunnel, followed shortly by a sylph with pale white skin and hair as dark as ink. Vampires—a sylph who lived solely on blood. The pupils of his eyes turned red from a millennium of drinking the life force of others.

"Welcome, Lord of Lightning." He bowed to Caiden then turned to escort us to the palace. "Please follow me."

Damp air seeped into my bones. Shivering, I pulled my cloak tighter around me.

We reached a set of opulent stairs carved into the mountain. "My queen is waiting for you," the vampire said, motioning for us to climb. Torches illuminated our way, making monsters out of our shadows as we ascended. Caiden did not let go of my hand.

Queen Nysemia waited with a myriad of other servants and courtiers at the top of the stairs in a rotunda of stone and stained glass. The little light trickling through cast a rainbow of colors across their macabre faces.

"Welcome, guests," she said in a voice as rich as dark chocolate.

Nysemia's captivating beauty held me spellbound. Her skin was a deep purple, her hair the hue of fresh snow. Amber eyes entranced me, refusing to release their grip. A sheer dress adorned with diamonds gripped her curves, leaving little to the imagination. Around her neck coiled a golden snake, not a mere necklace but a living serpent, its tongue tasting the air. A crown of jagged bone rested on her pale hair.

"It has been too long since the Court of Storms visited us." She flashed a smile. Her sylph fangs sparkled in the firelight. "I thought you didn't like me."

Caiden kneeled, kissing Nysemia's outstretched hand. "It is time our courts reconciled."

Nysemia smiled, running her jeweled hand down Caiden's jaw. "Rise and join the festivities. We have much to catch up on."

Nysemia clapped her hands. Two large doors heaved open, revealing an enormous ballroom filled with sylphs and faeries from across Moriana. In the center of the room, a chandelier filled with thousands of candles hung from thick chains. Fire sprites danced between them, ensuring their continuous burning.

The queen's carved throne of adamant sat on a dais in the center of the room. Behind it, a wall of live insects hummed with life. The smell of incense and wine filled the air, and creatures danced lasciviously to the music of a string band. Two massive fireplaces heated the stone ballroom, bathing everything in a warm glow.

I scanned the room for Tharan, but what my eyes befell made my blood run cold. Lounging in the center of the room sat Gideon, dressed in his signature red vest and black cloak with gold buttons. Ever the handsome king, his dark hair was neatly styled, framing his face and giving him an air of sophistication. Brown eyes stared intensely at the woman he was flirting with. A straight, well-proportioned nose with a slight curve at the bridge added to his distinguished appearance.

I squeezed Caiden's hand as the world darkened around me. My throat thickened. I couldn't get enough air in.

"Be strong, Aelia. I'm here," Caiden whispered to me.

I didn't feel strong. I felt like cracked glass waiting to shatter.

The ladies surrounding Gideon laughed flirtatiously, their faces blushing at whatever joke he told.

I remembered those feelings. The charm, the way he made you feel like you were the most important person in the world to him. A bitter taste filled my mouth. "I need a drink."

"What's he doing here?" Lucius said, loud enough for the room to hear.

"Keep your voice down." I slapped his shoulder. "I don't need his eyes on me."

But it was too late. Gideon's head jerked toward us.

Fuck.

A devious smile crossed his handsome face. He excused himself from the conversation and headed straight for us.

"Well, well, if it isn't my wife. I thought I sensed you coming in." He downed a goblet of wine. "Come to ask me to take you back?"

"I'd rather die," I said through gritted teeth. Caiden gripped my hand tightly.

Nysemia floated up to us, stroking the snake around her neck. "Oh, you two know each other? How sweet."

Gideon launched into my mind. *Play nice, and I won't have to hurt your sister.*

Clenching my jaw, I plastered a smile onto my face. "You could say that."

Very nice, Gideon purred in my mind.

Nysemia hooked a finger under Gideon's cleft chin. "Isn't he delicious?"

Words stuck in my throat. I knew what she saw in him. I saw it too, once. He was hard to resist. Charming, handsome, rich, and a fierce soldier, who wouldn't fall head over heels for him?

"Absolutely." The words pained me to say.

"He's come all this way to attend my party. Isn't that sweet of him?" Their eyes were locked.

"He's the sweetest," Caiden said, trying his best to hide the sarcasm in his voice.

"Come, my dear, let us go someplace more private." She grabbed Gideon's hand, leading him away from the crowd.

I let out a sigh of relief.

Lucius jerked Caiden to the side, whispering something in his ear. Caiden's gaze shot to Nysemia and then to me.

"Change of plans." Caiden ushered us to a secluded study. He tapped his temples, and I opened the door to his mind.

What is it?

'*Gideon is up to something.*'

No shit.

'*Something big, Aelia. All that mattered was the invite.*'

I huffed in annoyance. *So, what's the plan?*

Caiden looked around for prying eyes. "We need to split up. Aelia—go find Tharan. Amolie and Roderick will stay at the party and watch out for Nysemia and Gideon, while Lucius and I try to find the scepter before Gideon does."

"Do you know where it is?" I asked.

"Likely in her study or her bed chambers," Lucius said definitively.

"And what if she's in either one with Gideon?"

"I'm part wraith, stealth is my specialty." He snapped his fingers and transformed into a ghostly figure.

I bit my lip. "Fine."

We each headed in a different direction.

I grabbed a goblet of wine and headed toward the balcony, hoping to calm my nerves with a cigarette.

The moon shown over the acrid bog, the stench of sulfur wafted up on a chilly breeze. I lit a cigarette, letting the smoke burn away the tension in my chest.

Palms flat against the cold stone railing, I craned my neck, hoping to glimpse a famed creature of the swamp.

"Don't jump," a voice as smooth as velvet said.

I whirled around to see a tall man with hair the color of mulled wine standing behind me, lighting a cigarette. Tharan Greenblade had come to me.

"Do you mind if I join you? These revelries can be painfully dull." He took a drag.

"Be my guest." I motioned to a place next to me on the balcony.

"I haven't seen you at one of these before. Who are you here with?" He leaned his body against the railing, looking up at the stars. He wore a fine green satin vest with golden embroidery, a white tunic underneath, and leather pants. His side bore a curved sword.

"I'm here with Lord Stormweaver," I said, examining the stranger.

Smoke billowed into the night air, forming a haze around us.

"Oh, since when does a Council Court deign to dine with the likes of the Wild Courts?"

I tapped the ash of my cigarette on the railing. "I guess times are changing."

"Perhaps." He took another drag. "But you still didn't tell me who you are."

My mind fizzled and popped. His presence unnerved me in a way I hadn't felt in a long time. I wanted to touch him—to feel his lips on mine. "Aelia," I blurted out.

A smile tugged at the corners of his lush lips, revealing two sharp fangs. "Pleasure to meet you, Aelia. I'm Tharan."

My cheeks flushed, and attraction tingled in my chest.

"It's nice to meet you." I extended my hand as was customary.

Tharan leaned down, laying his lips gently upon my soft skin. My breath hitched in my throat at his touch. "The pleasure is all mine."

We stared awkwardly at each other for a moment. My eyes followed the jagged scar across his face. I envied his confidence.

"So, are you with Lord Stormweaver?"

"With him as in his lover?" I asked, arching a brow.

Tharan nodded.

Biting the inside of my cheek, I hesitated. "Oh, um, not like that. We're old childhood friends."

Tharan's face brightened. "Then I guess he won't mind if I dance with you tonight."

"I thought you said these parties were dull?"

Tharan tongued his sharp incisor. "Well, now that I have someone to dance with, the night just got much more interesting."

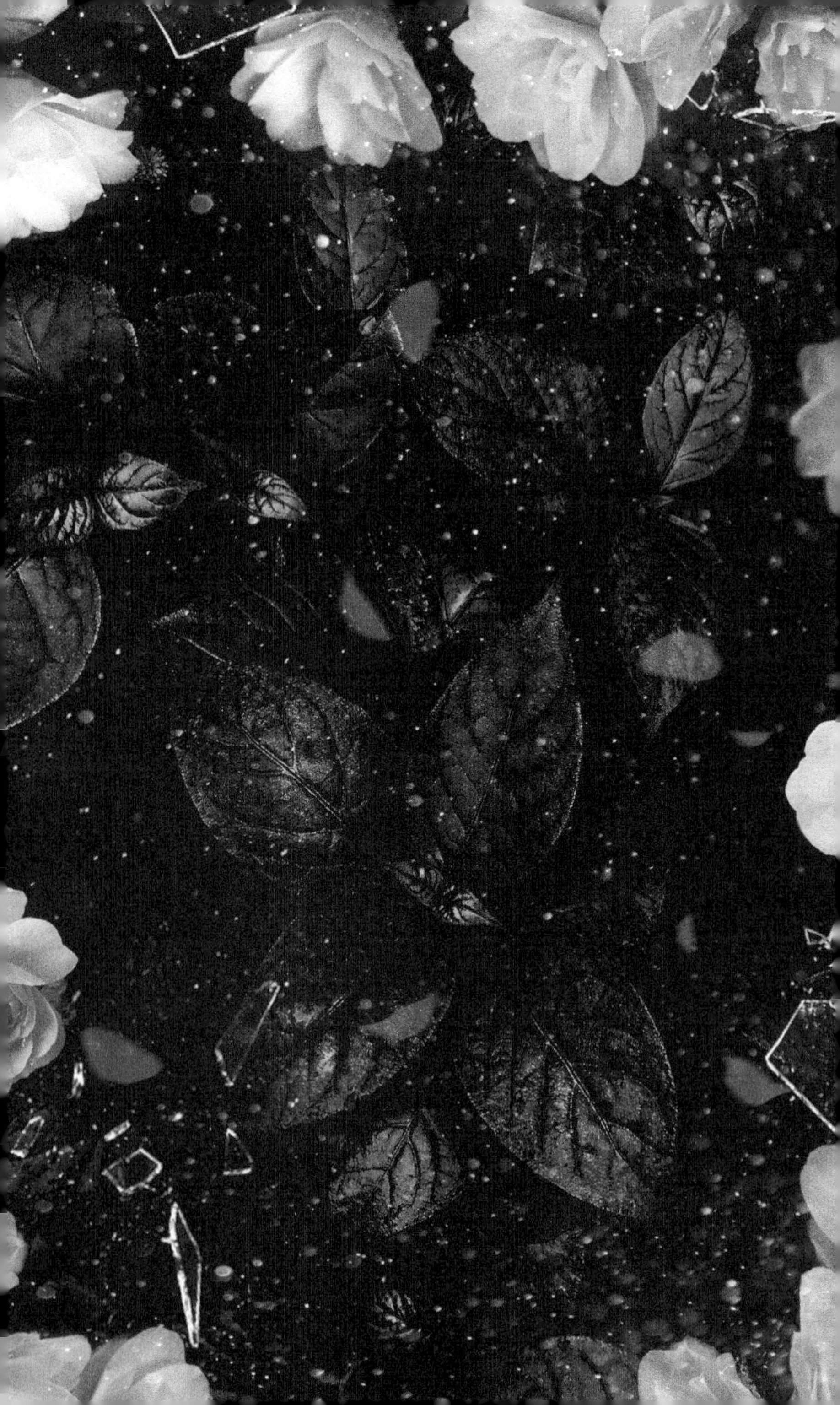

17 CAIDEN

Caiden downed a glass of enchanted wine and then promptly spilled another down the front of his vest before mussing up his hair.

Music echoed through the stone hallways of the palace as creatures indulged in carnal delights. Trails of spilled liquor stained the floors. Wraiths kept watch at the end of every corridor—though much was permitted, some areas were off-limits to guests.

Leaning against Lucius, Caiden feigned intoxication. No one batted an eye as they passed through the circuitous hallways Lucius had memorized before they left. They tried room after room, each filled with sylph and other creatures delighting in the pleasures of the flesh until they found somewhere secluded.

Shutting the door, Caiden sprung to life. "Okay, tell me what I need to do."

"You need to stay here and pretend to be sick. If people come looking for us. Just make yourself sick in some chamber pot."

Caiden blinked at the wisp of a man. "That's it?"

"That's it. Leave the rest to me." Closing his eyes, Lucius

transformed into a being of smoke. His eyes merely two black holes on an indistinguishable face.

"Fine." Caiden plopped onto the plush bed with a huff. "Be careful."

Floating in midair, Lucius passed through the wall and into the corridor above. With most of the staff tasked to work the party, the royal wing sat silent, waiting for its queen to return. Lucius snuck into the nearest room. Shelves of books and scrolls lined the walls. A portrait of Nysemia holding a skull hung above a dormant fireplace. In the center of the room sat a large stone desk adorned with candles perched on spines. Correspondence littered its top.

Behind the desk sat a glass case, a scepter of engraved bone with a crow's skull perched on a satin pillow inside—arrogant queen. For centuries, no one dared challenge Nysemia, making her lazy and conceited.

Lucius clicked his tongue as he approached the glass case, looking for a protection spell. He wouldn't set off any physical alarm in his wraith form, but that didn't mean there weren't other means of ensnaring him.

Examining the case, Lucius noticed something odd: the script on the bone blurred in places it shouldn't have—an illusion spell.

Shit.

He needed a spell breaker. He needed Amolie, but there was no way to get her here unseen.

Taking a moment to collect his thoughts, Lucius scanned the room for other hiding places. If this was a decoy, the real one might be hiding in plain sight.

He ran a hand over the skulls embedded in the stone desk. Each one stuck in place.

"Damn."

Lucius stared up at the painting of Nysemia, his brows knitted. "If I were you, where would I—" His shoulders slumped.

"No... it can't be. She wouldn't be so arrogant as to hide it behind a picture of herself."

Lucius floated up to the portrait and delicately pulled it down, revealing a cutout with a safe inside. "Oh, Nysemia, you foolish woman."

He reached for the safe. Cold iron seared into his skin. Shit. He needed to get the key.

Lucius floated back down to where Caiden waited.

"About time," he said, popping up from the bed. "Did you find it?"

"I think it's in a safe in Nysemia's office." Lucius returned to his normal opacity, smoothing his white hair behind his ears.

"How are we supposed to get in there?"

Lucius tapped his boot on the floor. "We need a key. I can't penetrate the iron."

Caiden sighed. "And where is that?"

"I assume Nysemia keeps it on her. I would."

"Shit." Caiden paced back and forth across the bearskin rug. "What are we going to do?"

Lucius chewed his nail, lost in thought. "We need a distraction." He looked at Caiden's stained shirt. "You can get close to Nysemia. Closer than any one of us."

Caiden arched a brow.

"She's infatuated with Gideon, and she's probably drunk. All you need to do is accidentally bump into her and steal the key."

"That's not a very good plan, but it's all we've got." Caiden rubbed his temples. "Let's get this over with."

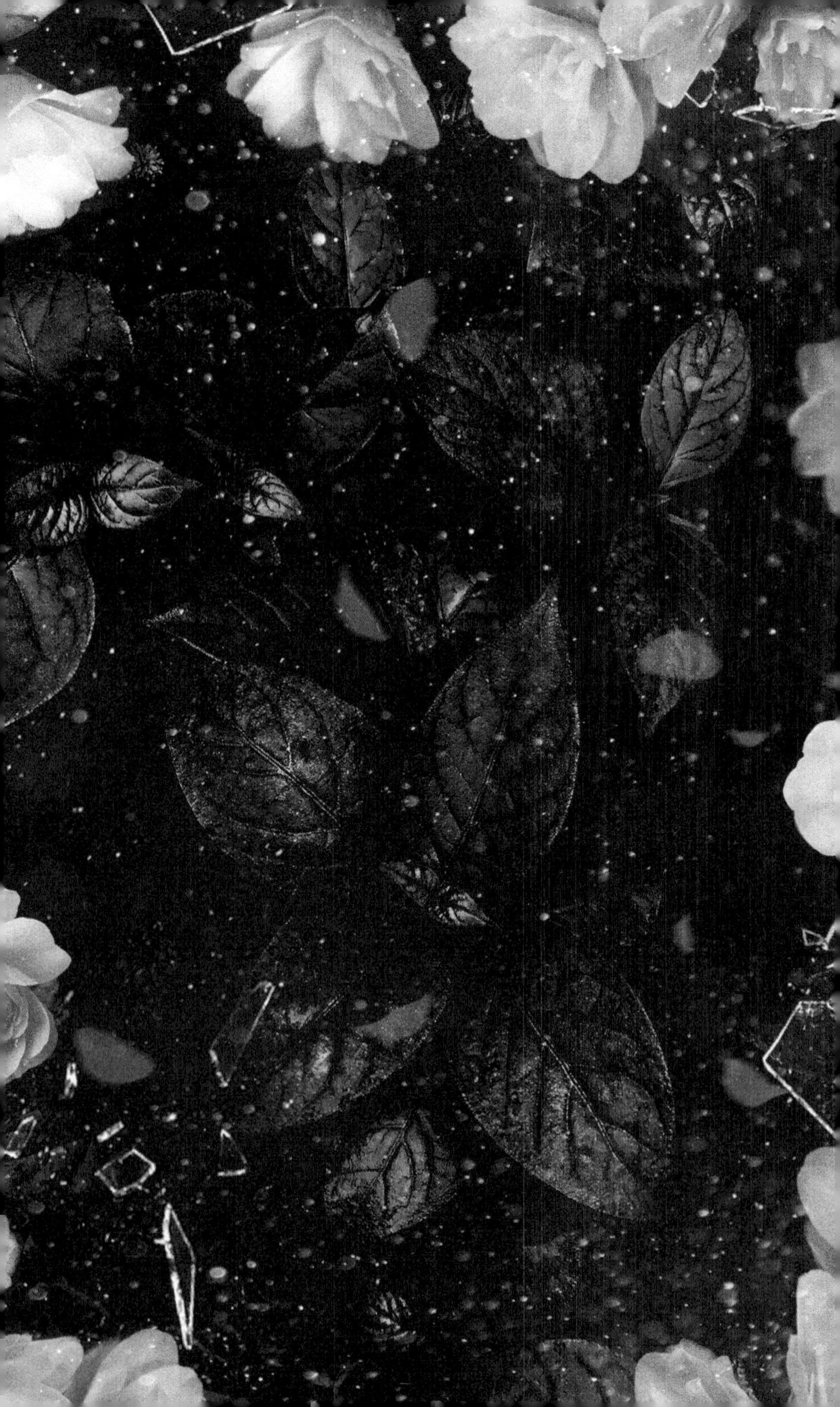

18 AELIA

THARAN CARESSED MY THIGH AS I POURED ENCHANTED WINE INTO his mouth. We lay on a plush chase lounge in one of the smaller parlors. A lutist played in the background, gently strumming his instrument in a calming melody.

"Why haven't I seen you at one of these before?" Tharan asked. "I'm familiar with the Wild Courts, and I've never seen you before."

"I don't get out much." I took a drink of wine. I needed to have him sedated if I wanted to enter into his mind, but it would look off if I didn't drink, too.

"Well then, I'll have to give you a night to remember, mystery woman." He downed the last bit of wine with a hiccup. His cheeks flushed red.

I had to act fast.

I launched into his mind. A tangled web of vines and trees guarded his precious psyche.

Let me in, Tharan. I'm not here to hurt you.

The vines tightened their grip.

Focusing, I made my mind relax, trying to blend into the surroundings. When entering a mind, you have to be careful not to trip the traps the unconscious mind sets. I ran a finger over the vines. A pink flower with white edges bloomed at my touch. But, instead of a pestle at the center, a large thorn hissed at me.

I took a step back. His mind was trained. Fuck. I was going to have to fight my way in.

Pulling my sword from my sheath, I hacked at the vines. The flowers spit poisonous spikes at me. I ducked, narrowly avoiding them.

The flowers shriveled and died. The vines untangled, opening to a forest of toadstools and tall pines.

I stood in the clearing, contemplating my next move. The mind was my playground. I cracked my knuckles, rubbed my hands together, and created an invite.

The forest creaked around me. The subconscious recognized a foreign presence. I quickly laid the invite on a red and white mushroom before bolting out of his mind.

Tharan blinked at me. "Where did you go? You looked so far away for a moment."

I smiled. "Oh, I'm just thinking about something I shouldn't be."

He curled a strand of my dark hair around his finger playfully. "I hope it was about me."

A devilish grin made my heart skip a beat.

"Maybe it was, and maybe it wasn't. Kiss me and find out."

Tharan bit his lip. "If that's what you want."

I leaned in, planting my lips on his. A heat grew between us.

His tongue teased mine while his hands gripped my waist, holding me close.

My breaths came faster. Arousal bloomed in my chest. I wanted more. He tasted like wine and clove cigarettes. The combination made me ravenous with need.

'Having fun, Little bird?'

I pulled away from Tharan.

Get out of my head, Gideon. This doesn't involve you.

'*Everything you do involves me. You are mine. And I won't have my wife whoring herself out to a dirty sylph.*'

Tharan cupped my face tenderly. "Hey, what's wrong?"

Tears trickled down my cheeks.

GET OUT! I pushed Gideon out of my mind, cursing myself for being so weak.

"Nothing," I said, rubbing my knuckles over Tharan's jaw. "I just had a little too much wine."

He hopped to his feet. "Well then, let's get you something to eat."

Shaken, I followed Tharan into the ballroom. The lights burned low, casting everyone in shadow.

I eyed Gideon and Nysemia flirting in a corner. My stomach churned. How could everyone love him? Didn't they see the monster he was? Maybe it was just me. Maybe I was unlovable.

Amolie and Roderick nodded at me as I followed Tharan to the buffet of cooked meats and fruits splayed out across two massive tables. I didn't have the heart to tell him—my stomach was in knots.

But before we could eat, a massive wind blew open the doors to the ballroom, snuffing all the candles, blanketing the room in darkness.

Tharan pulled me closer.

I gripped him tight.

A flame flickered through the open door.

The crowd held their breath. All eyes fixed on the dancing flame.

The fire twisted and turned, taking the form of a hooded figure.

From the opposite end of the room, Nysemia stood, a torch in her hand. "What is the meaning of this?"

The figure snapped their fingers.

Screams rang out from beyond the doors. The sound of scales slithering on stone made my blood run cold.

A basilisk slithered into the ballroom. Its iridescent skin shined in the light of a single flame. Its tongue tasted the air.

For a second, the room froze. Everyone collectively held their breaths, wondering if this was a part of tonight's entertainment.

The hooded figure spoke in a raspy voice, "Go, my child, devour what is yours."

Screams rang out, and the hall echoed them back. Chaos erupted. Creatures tried to flee, but the exits were barred. Panic hung thick in the air as they scratched desperately at the door.

The snake snapped at people, swallowing some whole. Their fists banged against the reptile's soft flesh as they descended into its gut.

"Wraiths arise! Protect my people!"

Through the floor, dozens of cloaked ghouls appeared. Faces empty under tattered hoods. Each carried a sword and a mace, swinging them menacingly as they approached the king and his mage.

Tharan drew his sword.

I searched the room for Amolie and Roderick but couldn't see anything through the haze of darkness and panicking bodies.

"We need to go. Out the back." Tharan pulled me toward the throne.

"But my friends—" I tugged at his arm.

"You are no use to them dead, Aelia. This place is about to be a blood bath."

The hooded figure swirled their arm around their head, creating a vortex of wind around themself and the basilisk.

The wraiths closed in, but they were no match for the hooded figure, whose wind shredded them as though they were made of nothing.

Through the doors, an army of goblins marched. Pale-skinned, with eyes as red as blood and pointed floppy ears. Their leader let out a guttural cry, before sticking his sword through the gut of the nearest man.

Nysemia released her wall of insects, sending them flooding into the crowd, devouring everything in their path.

Tharan and I dodged bodies being consumed by ravenous insects. The protection spell woven into my dress repelled their advances.

Darkness hindered our escape.

My thoughts went to Gideon. He hadn't tried to get back into my head.

Through the haze of the crowd, I watched as he took on the basilisk.

The creature snapped at him with giant fangs.

A master of swordplay, he sidestepped each attack with a flourish, slicing the snake's hard skin.

The creature reared up before striking, nipping his leg.

I smiled to myself. *Good.*

Gideon narrowed his eyes at the creature. No one made him look foolish and lived.

Pulling his sword back, he charged the creature, thrusting the blade through its open jaw. The basilisk screeched in pain, its body flailing, trying to hold on to any ounce of life.

Gideon jumped onto the back of the snake.

Holding on for dear life, he crawled to the head of the beast.

Pulling a long dagger from his bandolier, he drove it into the creature's skull.

The snake collapsed onto the marble floor.

Gideon dismounted, straightening his vest, proud of the work he'd done.

Meanwhile, Roderick sparred with the hooded stranger.

I bit my lip, unsure where I could help. Where was Amolie?

The sound of swords clashing muffled the screams of the

dying. Tharan fought off attacks on all sides: giant insects, goblins, even the sylph were attacking one another.

My heartbeat drummed in my ears.

A goblin reached for me with clawed fingers, but I buried my dagger in his skull before his callous hands could reach my flesh.

"Through this door," Tharan said, leading us into a deserted hallway.

Blood trailed through the hallway, smeared by the train of a dress. Had Nysemia come through here?

Tharan barred the door.

We rounded the corner to find Caiden crouched over the dead queen. Blood covered his hands.

"I couldn't save her."

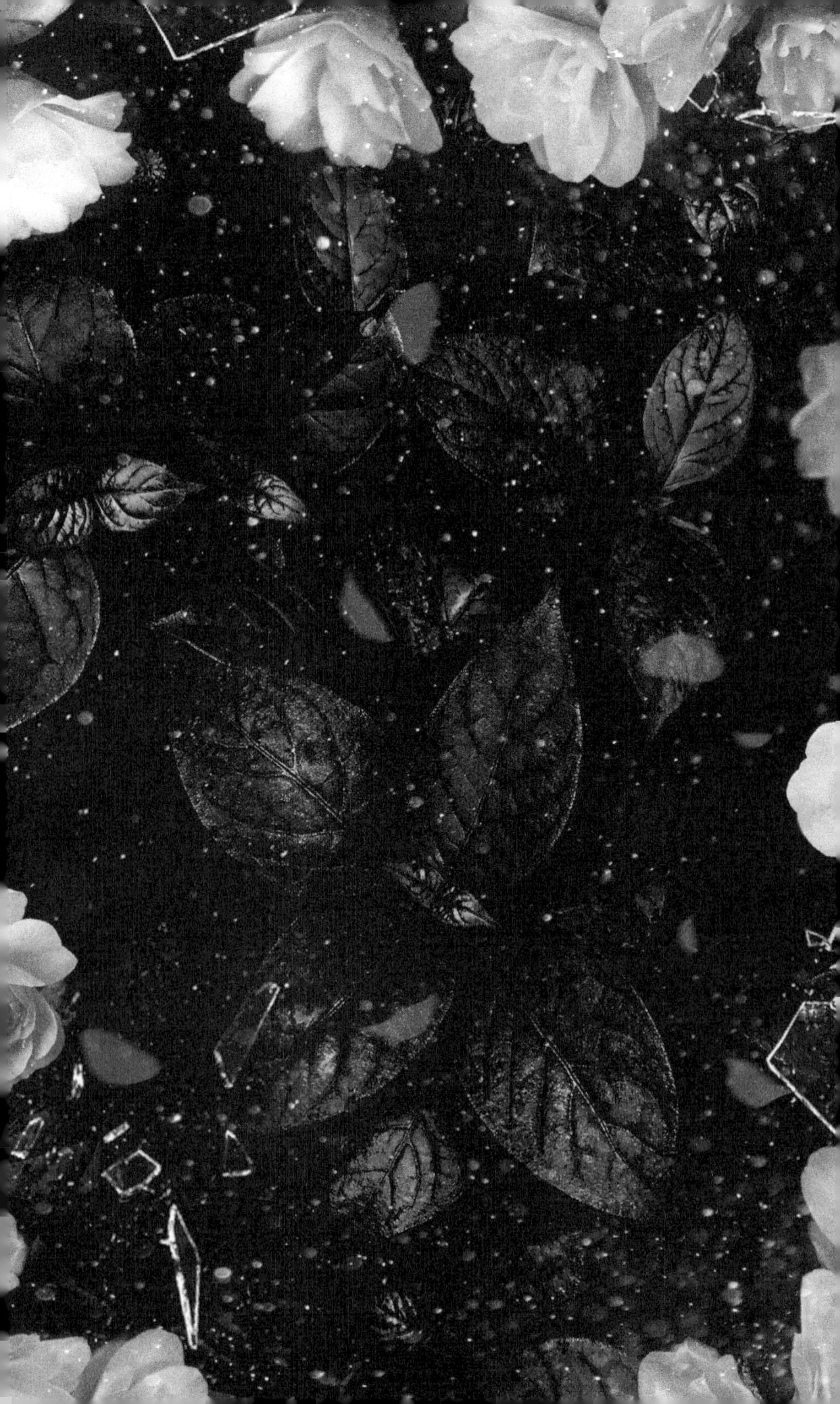

19 AELIA

"What did you do?" Tharan yelled.

"I didn't do anything. I found her like this." Caiden waved his bloody hands in the air.

"Sure, a Council Court comes to a Wild Court after decades, and it just so happens that an attack occurs?" Tharan held his blade to Caiden's neck. "Were you planning this?"

Nysemia stirred, reaching a bloody hand "My army... take it before he does..."

The golden snake uncoiled itself from around her neck and slithered up her palm where it transformed into a golden key.

Caiden's eyes flitted between Nysemia and Tharan. "See, I told you."

"She's talking about Gideon," I said, snatching the key from her hand. "What is this about?"

Tharan lowered his weapon. The men exchanged knowing glances.

Goblins beat against the door. "Tell me what this is about right now!"

Caiden reached for the key, but I yanked it away.

"Tell me or I'll take it..."

Caiden's mouth twisted into a straight line. "Nysemia controls an army of ten thousand undead soldiers."

My jaw fell open. "You didn't think this might be something I'd want to know?"

"You didn't need to know, Aelia."

Hurt tugged at my heart. I thought Caiden trusted me more. Perhaps I was as foolish as they all said.

"Give me the key, Aelia." Caiden held out his hand.

I gently placed it in his palm.

"Let's go."

"You think I'm going to let you take control of the world's most powerful army?" Tharan twisted his blade in his hand.

"We can debate who has control of the army later, but right now we need to make sure it stays out of Gideon's hands."

Tharan lowered his weapon. "Fine."

We hurried up the empty corridors to the royal wing leading to Nysemia's study. Where a painting of the queen holding a skull hung over an ornate fireplace, her vibrant white hair and purple skin radiated with life. A vision of her crumpled body flashed before my eyes.

"Is this it?" Caiden stood in front of a glass case containing a scepter made of bone and the skull of a crow, resting on a satin pillow.

"No." Lucius caught Caiden's hand before he could touch the glass. "That's a decoy." He pointed to the painting. "The real one is behind her."

Tharan stood with his arms crossed, staring intently at the queen.

Caiden inserted the golden key into the steel safe.

Click. The door swung open, revealing the real Scepter of the Dead.

Handing it to Lucius, the men examined the artifact. Runes in an ancient language covered the hilt.

"Tharan, can you read this?" Caiden asked.

Tharan ran a finger over the bone, then quickly yanked it away. "It shocked me."

"Don't touch it, just read it," Lucius said.

Sinking to his knees, Tharan examined the bone again. "I think... I think it requires some kind of sacrifice. Only the blood of the chosen will rule the dead." He bit his lower lip, trying to make out the dead language. "I can't read the rest."

"Great," Lucius said. "All this, and Gideon couldn't even use the thing."

"Maybe not. But I'm sure Erissa could figure out a way to activate it." Caiden said, wrapping the scepter in a satin handkerchief. A sullen look crossed his face. "Where are Amolie and Roderick?"

My heart sank. "Last I saw of Roderick, he was taking on the hooded figure."

Caiden and Lucius both shook their heads in disbelief.

"He never could resist a fight," Lucius said. "I hope they're alright."

Caiden put a hand on his friend's shoulder. "They both know how to handle themselves and how to get back to the townhouse safely. Roderick is the best warrior I've ever seen. I'm sure they will be fine. We need to worry about getting out of here, fast."

"What about the scepter? It belongs to the Wild Courts." Tharan placed a hand on his sword.

No one moved.

Tension pulled like a taught knot in the air.

The sound of goblins approaching echoed through the hall.

We didn't have time for a dick-measuring contest.

I launched into Theran's mind. Grit filled my mouth.

Frantically, I searched through memories of the night. My heart skipped a beat as he laid eyes on me. His affection had been genuine.

Pushing my guilt aside, I moved to when the serpent attacked. Tharan thought only of me, of my well-being. An overwhelming urge to protect me consumed him. Pain tickled the back of my throat. This was wrong. Tharan cared about me.

I had to focus on the specific memory.

Carefully, I erased our time in the hallway behind the throne, taking any memories of the key or the scepter—replacing them with nothingness. Normally, I would concoct an elaborate alternative history, but time was not on my side. Black spots would have to do.

Caiden handed the scepter to Lucius, who disappeared into a cloud of smoke.

Tharan blinked at me blankly. "What happened?"

"You blacked out," I said, hoping my lie stuck. "There's no time to explain. We need to get out of here."

Caiden mouthed a silent "thank you" to me.

We fled down a back passage to the entrance from which we came, but the portal we entered through had closed.

"Shit, what are we going to do now?" Caiden whispered, running a hand through his blond locks.

Goblins stalked the corridor above us. It would only be a matter of time before they came looking this way.

"The caves…" Caiden headed toward a crack in the wall. "This way."

With no other option, I reluctantly followed him.

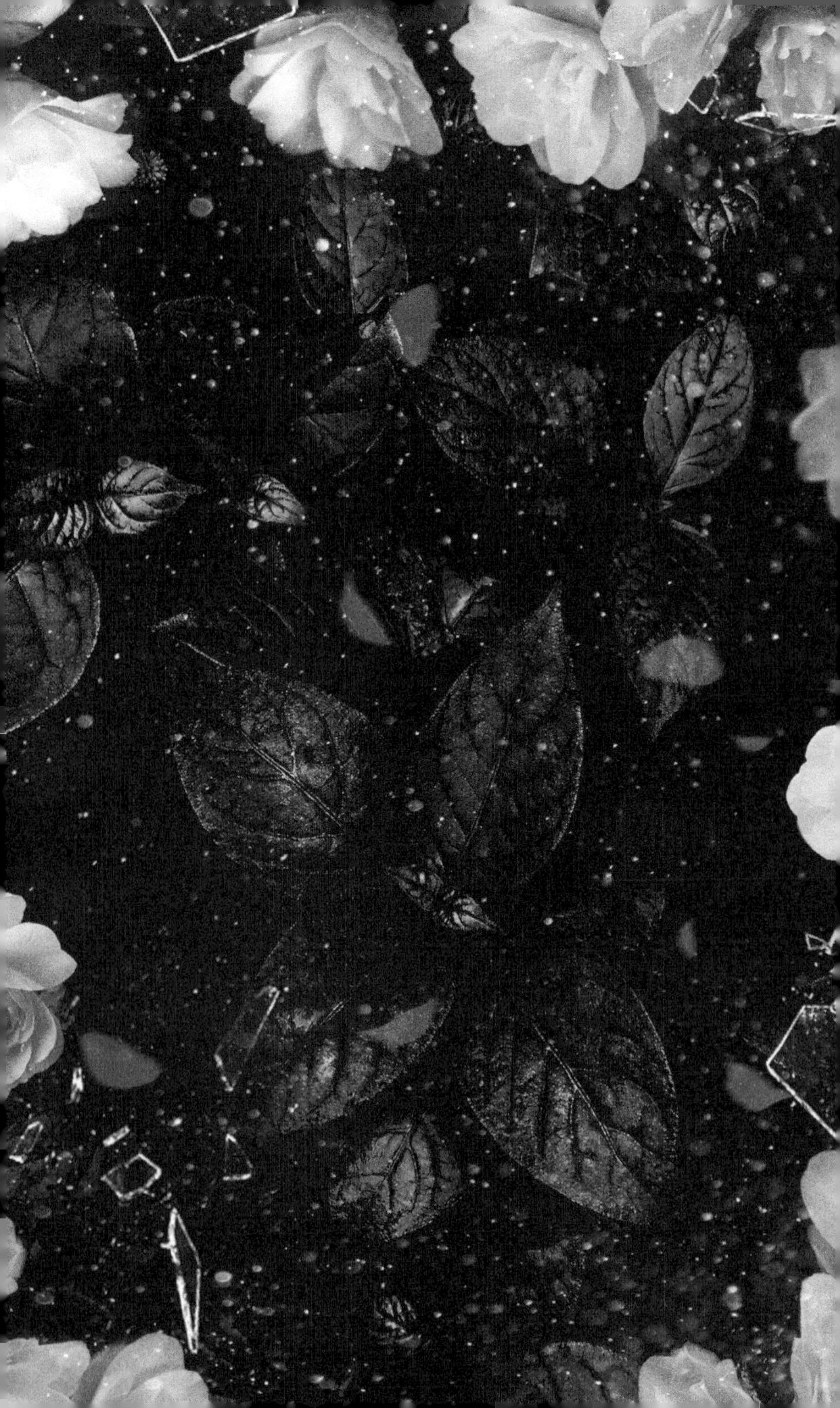

20 AELIA

Tharan made a torch out of his undershirt and the matches he carried. The light barely fought back the ever-encroaching darkness.

The tunnels in the cave twisted and turned, playing tricks on our minds. Dampness seeped into my bones, making my teeth chatter with cold.

"We're never getting out of here," I moaned. My body begged for sleep, but my mind ran wild with questions. Who was the cloaked sorcerer? Where were Amolie, Roderick, and Lucius? My chest tightened with concern over things I had no control over.

"These tunnels can't go on forever," Tharan said. "We'll find a way out."

Caiden rubbed his arms as we headed through the treacherous passages.

We entered a cavern where a pool of black water lay still as glass below a narrow bridge. Putting his finger to his lips, Tharan pointed to the water, wiggling his fingers. I got the hint: a monster lurked in the underground lake.

I held my breath as we crossed the narrow pathway over the water, the torch's light reflecting off the still surface below.

With every step I took, my pulse raced faster. Tharan moved gracefully as if he had done this a thousand times. The sound of our padding feet on the bridge undulated through the massive cavern.

My heartbeat blasted in my ears: *thump, thump, thump.* I prayed we were almost across.

A wave rippled across the placid lake beneath us. I swallowed hard. We needed to move quickly. Whatever lurked in the water knew we were here.

The bridge dipped down. We were near the end. My heart soared, but something felt off. The water was too still.

The hairs on the back of my neck stood on end.

"Aelia!" Caiden called from behind me.

A slimy tentacle wrapped itself around my waist, pulling me into the abyss. My head went foggy as the creature slammed me into the water.

I screamed, but the water filling my lungs stifled my voice.

Nothing but murky blackness surrounded me as pain ripped through my chest.

Stabbing at the tentacle, I fought to get free.

The kraken released me, howling in pain, and I clawed my way to the surface.

I burst through the surface, gasping for air. "Caiden, your electricity. Use it!" My voice cracked as I swam aimlessly in the water.

"It'll kill you too, Aelia."

"Just do it!" I screamed before another tentacle hooked itself around my leg, dragging me back under. This time, my eyesight adjusted in time to see a set of vertical teeth, the size of a grown man, chomping at me.

Lightning cracked, and a flash of white light filled the cavern. Heat like a thousand fires blazed through my body. The water muted my screams.

The creature released me.

I floated to the surface. My muscles spasmed uncontrollably. Barely able to move, I tried my best to stay afloat.

"Aelia, grab the vine," a voice called from above.

My hand shook as I reached for the smooth bark of the vine. Wrapping itself around my wrist, the three men heaved me out of the water, where I dangled.

The beast stirred back to life beneath me.

"Hurry!" I cried, just as a force pulled me down—down closer to the abyss.

"We're trying," Tharan said through a clenched jaw.

The slap of a tentacle sounded below, spraying me with water. The creature failing to retake me. I didn't dare look down, but I could feel the monster rising to the surface. The sound of water running off something significant echoed through the cavern.

I focused on the flickering torch, trying to regain my breath.

Above, Caiden created a ball of lightning between his hands.

"Shut your eyes, Aelia," he said, expanding the size of the orb.

I did as he commanded, but not before taking one last look at the monster hunting me. The light grew larger and larger in the creature's black eyes until the two collided, sending a wave of energy throughout the chamber.

The kraken howled and thrashed in the water until taking one final death roll. Silence surrounded us once more. Its massive body floated lifelessly.

The men pulled me onto the narrow land bridge. Water dripped from my heavy skirt. I dug my fingers into the dirt, gasping for breath, while saying a silent prayer of thanks to Ammena for saving my life.

"Are you okay?" Caiden said, kneeling, patting my back, attempting to get the water out of my lungs.

"Just... give... me... a... minute." I focused on the dirt

between my fingers as the reality of what had occurred came crashing down upon me. I wanted to cry, but no tears came as a knot I couldn't untangle twisted in my chest.

"We have to go," Tharan said in a voice as hard as adamant. The torch flickered in his green eyes. His gaze focused on something behind us. "They're coming."

Through the darkness, the light of a single torch came into view.

"Gideon's men?" I asked.

"Worse." Tharan pulled his sword from its sheath. "Cave trolls. Can you run?"

I nodded, feeling returning to my limbs. "I think so."

My heart raced as Tharan cut my heavy skirt off. The fabric fell into the black water below. With it went any protection I had.

"Caiden will lead us. Aelia will go next, and I will follow."

Everyone nodded in agreement.

Tharan dropped his torch into the water.

Massive white trolls appeared at the other end of the narrow land bridge.

The creatures sniffed the air, tasting our scent. Fucking cave trolls—smelly beasts without eyes who lived off the organisms in the rocks but had a taste for blood should the opportunity present itself. Notoriously hard to kill because of their armor-like outer shells. Leading the army of blind beasts was a goblin with batwing ears and beady black eyes.

My breath hitched in my throat at the sight.

"Run," Tharan said.

We took off across the land bridge into complete darkness. I could barely make out Caiden's silhouette as we made our way through the circuitous tunnels of the cave. An army of trolls marching behind us. Their heavy footsteps shook the earth beneath our feet.

Caiden swore under his breath.

"What is it?" I asked, trying my best to keep my voice steady.

"It's narrow up here. I think we'll have to go one at a time. When you get through, sprint to the mouth of the cave. The trolls won't dare cross into the forest."

A jagged crevasse cut like a scar against the smooth rock. Inhaling deeply, I maneuvered my body into the gap. Rough stone scraped my face as I made my way through.

Rays of sun shone through, beckoning me forward, while the sound of clashing swords reminded me of the danger lurking behind us.

"Keep going," Tharan yelled loud enough for me to hear.

I squeezed through, falling to my knees on the other side.

Come on, come on, make it through. I bit my nails, waiting for the men on the other side.

Another flash of light streamed through the crevasse—the last of Caiden's power. The gifts of the sylph were not infinite. Caiden would be exhausted. *If* he made it.

I held my breath as another figure made his way through the fissure. Tharan joined me, gasping for air.

Caiden came through after. His movements slowed by the weight of exhaustion. I bit my lip but did not look away until I saw the gold ring on his left hand slide out of the crack.

He collapsed onto the hard ground.

"Caiden," I gasped, running to his side and pulling him into my lap.

"I'm so tired," he said as his eyes fought to stay open.

"He needs to eat something." Tharan went to the mouth of the cave, digging his hand into the damp morning soil. Holding it up to the sun, he whispered something in a language I did not recognize. To my amazement, two mushrooms sprouted from the dirt.

"Here, give these to him. They should help."

I took the two yellow mushrooms from his palm. "How do I know these aren't poisonous?" I arched a questioning brow.

"The ring. The band will glow if there is poison near."

I held the mushrooms near the ring. It did not change colors. A weight lifted off my chest. I smashed the fungi into a paste and placed it on Caiden's tongue.

"I need you to chew," I commanded.

Caiden mashed the yellow mush lazily. A grimace crossed his face, but alertness returned to his eyes.

"Energy mushrooms," Tharan said, wiping his hands on his pants.

"Thank you, Tharan." I rubbed Caiden's chin with my knuckles.

Caiden got to his feet, brushing the dirt off his white pants, stained with blood. "Thank you. Both of you." Caiden nodded to Tharan before giving me a dimpled smile.

"We should go while the sun is still high in the sky. It will take us hours to reach the border of the elven lands." As Tharan headed toward the forest, a trail of blood leaked from his leg.

"You're hurt," I said, pointing to the gash.

"It'll be fine," he said, keeping pressure on the wound. The winter wind bit my exposed legs as we trudged toward what we hoped was safety.

The Forest of Needles was aptly named—skeletal trees reached for the ashen sky like twisted, bony fingers. Leafless branches, barren of life, clawed at the air as if frozen in a perpetual state of agony. A thick, suffocating stillness permeated every living thing, broken only by the occasional creaking and groaning of the lifeless limbs in the wind. The air itself seemed to carry a whisper of melancholy, as if the very essence of life had been drained from the surroundings. Gnarled trunks cast long, foreboding shadows playing tricks on my mind.

With every step, the snow burned my bare skin. Caiden offered me his coat. I took it gratefully, burying my nose in the fabric smelling of bergamot and leather.

The sound of Tharan's teeth chattering drowned out my own. Shivering worse than me, his wine-red hair whipped in the icy wind—a slight limp in his gait from the fight.

"We need to stop and light a fire. Tharan and I will not make it much further," I said, wrapping my arms tighter around myself.

"We must cross the border before nightfall. There's no telling what hunts in these woods once the sun is gone," Caiden said, not bothering to look back at me.

I gave Tharan my best *I'm sorry* eyes.

He mustered the best smile he could.

An eerie sense of calm inhabited the forest.

"We're just passing through," Tharan whispered under his breath. "We will be gone soon."

A stick cracked in the distance. The men's heads snapped to the left. Caiden held up his hand, stopping us dead in our tracks. Tharan muttered something under his breath while we held ours. Perhaps the cold had made him go insane.

"Something is watching us," Caiden said, scanning the ridge above for predators.

"Let's keep going. We are almost at the border," Tharan replied.

"Do you know what hunts us, *Prince*?" Caiden asked, snark dripping from every word.

"If we keep moving, it will leave us alone. This forest is old and likes the taste of blood. It's best not to linger for too long." Tharan kept limping along.

Hooking my arm around Tharan's waist, I let him lean on me. He gave me an appreciative smile, showcasing his long sylph fangs.

"There is a town close to the edge of the forest. They are not kind to outsiders, but they will tolerate you if you're with me. We can get a hot meal and a place to lay down," Tharan said.

Darkness chased our footsteps, awakening the forest with it. I didn't dare look back. Tharan's wound attracted the eyes of the forest.

From the edge of the forest, the roofs of a small town came into view. Sheep dug in the snow for grass on rolling hills. Elven lands were foreign to me. They did not take kindly to outsiders.

Opulence dripped from every nook and cranny of the elven town. Streets paved with iridescent cobblestones wound through meticulously manicured gardens where vibrant flowers and enchanted flora bloomed even in the dead of winter. Sculpted homes mirrored the surrounding forest—a testament to the elves' craftsmanship.

Tharan stopped before a large marble building with two statues of Eris, the elven goddess of the Trinity, standing guard.

"This is the governor's residence. I will ask for a safe harbor for the night." He took a deep breath before climbing the marble stairs and disappearing behind two gold-plated doors. Caiden and I sat on the hard steps and waited for him to return.

"Thank you for what you did back there," Caiden said, fiddling with his rings. "Did you plant the seed?"

"I did, and you're welcome." I wrapped Caiden's cloak tighter around me. "Everyone will think Gideon is a hero now." A bitter taste filled my mouth at the thought of Gideon being hailed a champion.

"He's cunning, I'll give him that," Caiden said, gazing around the immaculate marbled town.

"What are we going to do now? He'll be more emboldened than ever."

Caiden rubbed eyes. "We're going to continue with the plan as is. His arrogance will be his downfall."

"Let's hope it works," I said, rising as Tharan bounded down the stairs.

"They said we could stay for the night. The portal to Ruska opens in the morning." Tharan led us down the pristine street to a small inn where he presented the innkeeper with a permit for outsiders to stay.

Dark wooden staircases and gold accents greeted us when we entered the inn. An elderly elf with long, bony fingers and soft creases around her eyes greeted us.

"Hello, Prince Tharan. The governor sent word ahead and said you would be arriving with…" She eyed Caiden and me with distaste. "Guests soon."

Tharan laid a pouch of gold on the mahogany counter. "Yes, they are to be treated with the utmost respect."

"As you wish," she said with a hint of disdain, grabbing keys to three rooms.

Her hands slipped on the polished railing as she escorted us upstairs. Despite their immortality, time still took its toll on the elves.

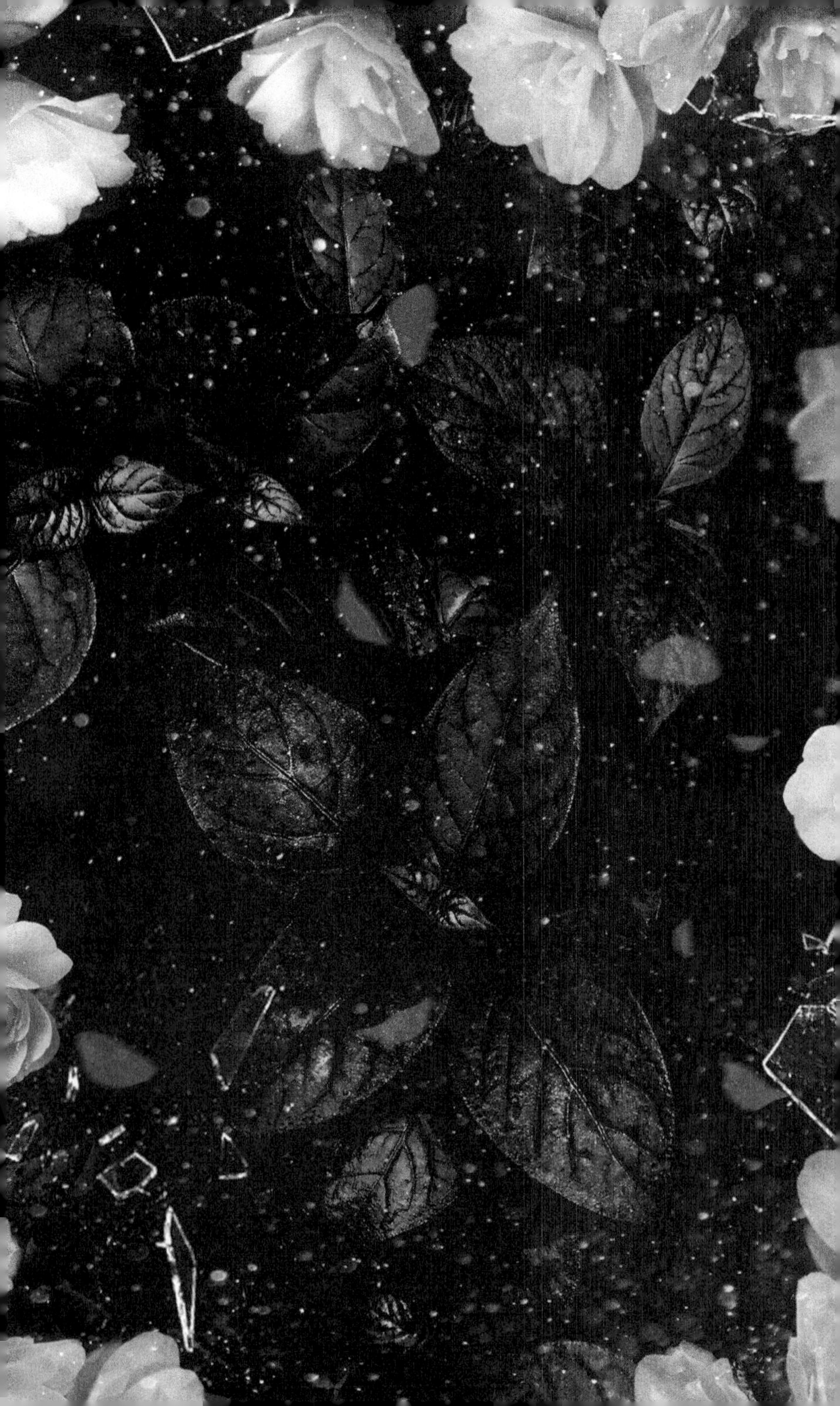

21 AELIA

I DREAMED OF MY SISTER.

Baylis woke me in the middle of the night.

"What's going on?" I asked, bolting upright.

A smile crossed her round face.

"Shh... follow me." She held up a small lantern.

I pulled on my cloak, and we headed into the night. The Ostara festival had begun, and our parents were out dancing the night away. We made our way down the back stairwell, where Baylis grabbed a picnic basket.

"What's that for?" I asked, sleep still clung to my eyes.

"You'll see."

The moist grass stuck to our feet as we scrambled to evade the guards. Our little hearts pounding in our chests as we hustled to the old lookout. Music from the Ostara festival floated on the crisp spring air.

We took the stairs two at a time until we reached the old lookout. Two blankets waited for us.

"Did you plan this?" I asked, shocked my little sister had so much foresight.

"Happy Ostara, Aelia!" she said, bringing out a bottle of

sparkling wine she had nicked from the cellar. We shared sips, letting the bubbles go to our heads.

"There's one more thing." She pointed upward as fireworks burst overhead, illuminating the sky with bright lights.

"I hope you like it," she said, sipping the bubbly wine.

"I love it, Baylis." I pulled her in close for a hug.

We stayed until the fireworks ended and then snuck back into our beds, giggling to ourselves. Drunk on the idea we had gotten away with something.

The sound of our parents' footsteps echoed down the hall. We shut our eyes, pretending to be asleep.

The door creaked open. Baylis and I did our best to pretend to be asleep.

"They're so precious," our mother said.

"They really are beautiful," our father replied before shutting the door.

Baylis and I let out the laughs we had been holding in. Little did we know by the next Ostara, our lives would be completely different.

Suddenly, I was underwater, trying desperately to swim to the surface, but something dragged me down. My screams were muffled by the water filling my lungs.

I awoke covered in sweat, yearning for dust to calm my nerves. I reached for my cigarettes only to find they had been ruined.

Exhausted, dirty, and needing a bath, I rang the bell in my room. A young-looking elf with rosy cheeks appeared at my door within minutes.

"How can I help you?" he asked in a cheerful tone.

"I'd like to take a bath, and I'll need a change of clothes." I motioned to my torn gown.

Clicking his heels together, he tipped his hat at me. "Would you also like a wool cloak? Elves spin the finest wool in

Moriana."

"Yes." I had no gold on me and, therefore, no way of paying for any of this. "Is it possible to send an invoice to my bank?"

The attendant looked up from drawing me a bath. "Lord Greenblade has covered all your expenses. He also asked me to give you these." He handed me a leather pouch filled with clove cigarettes. A note lay inside.

I figured you would need these.
- Tharan

A mixture of excitement and guilt swirled in my heart. I should not feel this way. Caiden and I did not belong to one another, and soon, he would not know I existed. I needed to move on with my life and leave the past in the past.

An assortment of dresses lined my bed, each crafted in the elven style, favoring function over fashion. I chose a high-necked olive green one with golden leaves for buttons. In human lands, this dress would cost a month's wages, and here I had four of them and a black cloak lined with fox fur.

My stomach grumbled with hunger. Caiden wouldn't be up for hours. Perhaps Tharan would be awake.

Hesitantly, I knocked at his door.

Tharan answered, dressed in only his pants—his bare chest exposed. I tried not to stare at his toned body as he rubbed the sleep from his eyes.

"Well, if it isn't the mystery woman," he said, giving me a coy smile. My stupid knees weakened as he leaned a forearm on the doorframe.

"Thank you," I said, giving him a wink. *Who was I? I was a woman who gave winks, apparently.* "Would you like to get something to eat?" I wiped my sweaty palms on the expensive dress.

Tharan yawned, stretching so I could see the muscles in his abdomen tighten. "Sure, come in. I'll get dressed." He left the door ajar and went to change. I hesitated before stepping in. Gideon's words from the night before echoed in my head. *Whore.*

Squeezing my eyes tight, I tried to shake off the shame.

Tharan threw on a thick wool sweater, the color of stained oak, buttoning it to his chin.

We headed out onto the promenade, where elves gave us dirty looks. If it bothered Tharan, he did not show it. I envied the lightness of his steps.

We entered a large dining hall with long wood tables where elves sat chatting with one another, drinking wine, and eating roasted lamb. The smell of roasted meats and vegetables wafted through the air, making my stomach rumble.

Taking a seat at one of the less crowded tables, Tharan hailed a servant, ordering us ale and two plates of lamb stew. "Hope you're hungry," he said, handing me the tin plate.

"Starving," I said, popping a roasted carrot into my mouth. The potent flavor exploded on my tongue. I devoured the rest without so much as a whisper to Tharan, who I noticed reached for seconds when a server came past.

We ate until our bellies groaned.

"Thank you for everything," I said, sipping the mulled wine—savoring the taste of spices. Pulling the leatherbound cigarettes from my pocket, I placed them on the table between us.

Tharan's face brightened. "You got my note."

I had to admire anyone who could be cheerful after almost being killed several times in one night.

"I did." Arching my eyebrows at him, a cigarette between my lips, I tried to be as seductive as possible. "Thank you."

I exhaled the smoke into the hall.

Tharan took another drink of his mulled wine before reaching across the table and taking the cigarette from my hand.

Electricity roiled in my veins. Tharan exuded sensuality in a way I had never experienced before. Yes, Caiden possessed handsomeness, but Tharan was an entity unto his own. His scars displayed for the world to see instead of hidden beneath a glamour like mine.

"So, are you going to tell me who you are?" He took a drag from my cigarette, letting the smoke billow into the air. "Judging by your incisors, you're not fully human."

Taking back my cigarette, I brought it to my lips, letting the smoke burn in my lungs. "You are correct. I am a half-breed, as they say."

"Interesting." He leaned in closer. The candle's light cast devious shadows across his scarred face. "Which sylph lord bed your mother?"

"None." I bit my bottom lip, afraid to tell the truth. "Blood magic turned me."

His expression darkened. "That's punishable by death. I thought everyone knew that."

My eyes flitted around the room. I couldn't look at him—couldn't tell him the truth. "It wasn't my idea." Tears welled behind my eyes. "I was turned against my will."

Tharan reached for my hand. "Who?"

My words stuck in my throat. "King Gideon of the Highlands. He and I were… are… married."

"Interesting." Tharan leaned back, crossing his arms over his chest.

I took a long drag of my cigarette while I waited for his response.

"You probably think I'm a—"

"I don't think anything about you, Aelia Springborn."

My shoulders dropped with relief, but still, I could not look at him.

Tharan leaned forward, hooking a finger under my chin,

forcing our eyes to meet. "I have been around long enough to know—life sometimes places us in impossible situations."

I sucked in a stifled breath. A heat grew between us. I wanted him to touch me, but I dared not move closer.

"I'm sure Caiden's told you all about me."

I let out a half-hearted laugh. "He told me you were not to be trusted."

"He was right. You shouldn't trust me." Mischief gleamed in his emerald eye.

My breath hitched in my throat. "Why?"

"Because I am the Lord of Nothing. A bastard son who drinks too much wine and pours honey into the hearts of princesses, only to shatter them later."

"Lucky for you, there is nothing left of my heart to break."

A smile tugged at the corner of Tharan's lips. "That makes two of us."

We clinked our mugs together in acknowledgment of one another.

Tharan and I walked back to the inn in comfortable silence. I didn't have to be anyone around him. The people who knew me before expected me to act like the old Aelia—the one they knew in Elyria before I married Gideon. That Aelia died a long time ago, and I couldn't resurrect her.

Lanterns hung from every tree, giving the promenade a warm glow. Tharan walked with purposeful grace, keeping his hands behind his back. The lush I met in the Court of Sorrows replaced by a dignitary.

I did not know Tharan's story, but if it mirrored my own, the scar on his heart proved worse than on his face.

"How about a smoke before we turn in?" Tharan motioned to the golden railing encircling the roof of the inn.

"Maybe one more," I said, pulling the cigarettes from my cloak pocket. Excitement bubbled in my chest.

A quiet swept over the city as townsfolk turned in for the night. From where we stood, the lights of the town twinkled like stars on rolling hills laid out as far as the eye could see.

I lit a cigarette. "Have you been here before?"

Tharan tucked an unruly piece of hair behind his ear. "I was born here," he said, taking out his own leather pouch of cigarettes and tapping the pack on the palm of his hand.

"So, your mother is from here?"

"No," he chuckled. "My birth was a cursed one. She fled here to escape her father's wrath."

"Ah, it was a forbidden romance?" I arched an eyebrow.

Smoke plumed around Tharan. "Like you, I am a half-breed. You know the laws of this land. No elves and sylph may mate. Even if they are in love."

"I guess I thought the law only applied to commoners," I said, staring at the town blanketed in snow.

Tharan sighed. "My mother's father is the elven king, Aerendir. It was a disgrace on the crown."

I touched his arm tenderly. "What happened to her?"

"She was discovered here and taken back to the elven capital of Elohim and killed. I was sent to my father's doorstep in a basket of thorns." He took a long drag of his cigarette. "He hadn't known my mother was pregnant."

"You never knew your mother?" My heart broke for him. I couldn't imagine never knowing my mother.

"No." He lifted his head toward the heavens, silken hair shining in the moonlight. "Sometimes I like to imagine she looks down on me from wherever she is."

It would be easy to fall in love with Tharan. Few were this candid with a person they'd just met. He made you feel like every word he shared was a secret, known only to the two of you. I yearned to kiss him again, to alleviate whatever pain resided in his soul.

My tendency to fall in love too easily had always been my downfall. I would not step into a trap again. Tharan was an asset to exploit. For all I knew, he could be using me. I needed to give him something in exchange for the story about his mother—a wound for a wound.

"My father fell ill when I was young. He descended into madness before taking his own life on my twenty-fifth birthday."

Tharan did not look upon me with pity as most others did. In his eyes, I saw a reflection of myself. "We are both children of sorrow," he said, taking my gloved hand.

We stood together in the silence of the night. Here, we could be vulnerable with one another. Here, we were two people enjoying each other's company. No titles branded us—a traitorous queen and a bastard prince.

When the winter wind became too much to bear, we reluctantly headed inside.

"I've enjoyed this time with you, Aelia. Even if you are still a mystery to me."

A fuzzy feeling grew in my chest. "I as well, Lord of Nothing. I hope we can be friends in the future."

He leaned in and kissed me on the cheek. "I'd like that," he whispered in my ear.

Goosebumps pricked my skin, and my heart fluttered. I wanted to reach out and touch him, bring him closer to me.

But I was not that person anymore.

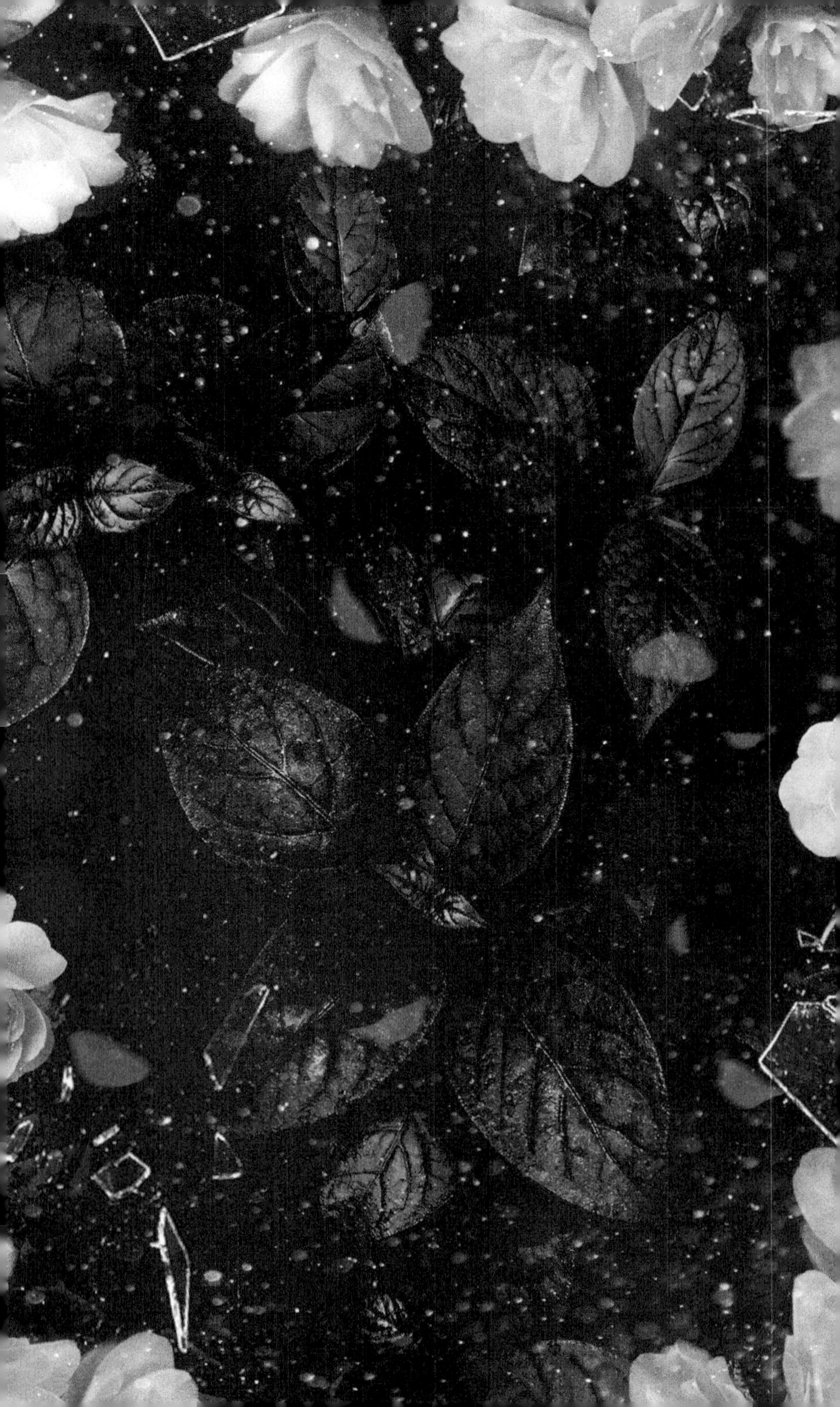

22 AELIA

I LAY IN MY BED, CONTEMPLATING MY FEELINGS TOWARD CAIDEN and Tharan. I did not need to be getting involved with someone new.

The weight of everything pressed down onto my chest. These two men were a distraction from my real problem—Gideon possessing my sister. I hadn't seen Baylis in five years. Part of me wondered if we would recognize one another. He showed his power in the Court of Sorrows. The hooded figure who attacked was likely Gideon's elven mage, Erissa, but I'd be lying to myself if I didn't suspect Baylis. Gideon and Erissa created monsters.

We needed to come prepared with a plan for the Woodland Realm if we wanted to get Baylis back.

The clock on the wall read 3:00 a.m. The portal to Ruska opened in six hours—more than enough time to set my plans in motion.

I flung off the blanket, throwing on a fur shawl.

Padding down the hall on silent feet, I made my way to Tharan's room, ensuring to avoid Caiden's. I paused, pressing my ear to the door. Nothing stirred on the other side.

I knocked lightly.

Nothing.

I knocked again.

Nothing.

Out of frustration, I tried the knob.

The door opened.

Only the light of the moon illuminated the room. Tharan's bed lay empty, but I could sense his presence.

The cold tile sent a chill through me as I crept into the suite. Tharan lay curled in the copper tub, covered by a thick pelt of furs. I recognized the pose. After I escaped Gideon's clutches, it took me months to regain the ability to sleep in a bed. The mattress seemed too big, too open. More often than not, I slept in the bathtub.

Kneeling, I rubbed his arm. "Tharan," I whispered. "I need to tell you something."

He stirred in his sleep.

Cracking open one green eye, he said, "Yes, mystery woman. What do you want?"

"I need your help to kill a king."

His eyes sprang open. "And here I thought you wanted to take me to bed. This sounds much more interesting. I'll call an attendant to bring us some spiced cider." Hopping out of the tub, his full chiseled physique was on display.

Mouth agape, I averted my eyes as he wrapped a robe around himself.

The attendant arrived shortly with two steaming cups smelling of cinnamon and apple. Tharan handed me one, motioning for me to sit on his bed.

Inhaling the comforting scent of nutmeg, I clung to the mug for warmth.

"So, what king are you killing?" He sipped his mug from a leather armchair by the fire. The picture of royalty.

"Gideon of the Highlands."

"Ah, I should've guessed." He took another drink. "He will be hailed as a hero for his display in the Court of Sorrows. Only the three of us know what Nysemia implied with her dying breath."

I gathered my thoughts. I had so much to explain. "Once upon a time, Gideon was my husband." I tapped my fingers on the copper mug, contemplating if I should reveal my secret to Tharan. "I am who they call the Traitorous Queen."

His eyes widened. "I knew you were interesting." He took another sip, leaning back in his chair. "Are the stories true? Did you destroy your own kingdom?"

My eyes fell to the floor in shame. "Women do stupid things for love."

"Everyone does stupid things for love." A knowing acceptance reflected back at me. "That's how I got this scar." He traced the path of pink flesh across his face.

I smothered a lump growing in my throat.

"I, too, fell in love with someone I should not have, and I paid the price." He twisted a piece of his long hair around his index finger.

"What happened?" I asked, unsure if I wanted to know.

Tharan hesitated.

"Sorry if that's too forward of me." I bore a hole into my cider with my gaze.

"No, it is fine. The more I talk about it, the easier it becomes." He sighed. "During the sylph and elven war, I fell in love with an elven woman, Lyra. She defected from the elves and joined the rebels. I was a junior captain and still unfamiliar with my own powers." He stared off into the distance as if reliving the moment. "One night, I awoke to find Lyra gone. I tracked her deep into the forest. Where I found her leaking information to an elven scout. When I confronted her about it, she denied everything, insisting she was getting information from him. I believed her because I loved her."

I shut my eyes. I knew how this story ended.

Tharan took a long drink. "Turns out I was a fool, just like you. She had used me to gain information. It almost cost us the war. When my father learned of her treachery, he had me kill her as punishment. Little did I know she was wearing a protective amulet." He paused, trying to find the correct words. "I wanted it to be quick. To be painless for her. So, I convinced my father to let me take her life with magic. But when I cast the curse, it bounced off the amulet and hit me." He tapped his scar. "I was humiliated in front of my father's entire court. Once the amulet was removed, I placed it in the hilt of my sword, amplifying its power." He did not look at me, choosing to stare into the fire as if he were watching the incident in the flames. "I split her in two, Aelia. I poured every ounce of hatred and embarrassment into that final blow."

I swallowed hard.

"From then on, I vowed never to be tricked again. So, I keep everyone at a distance. Let them believe I'm cursed." He looked at his hands. "Spell or not, I am cursed. Cursed to live knowing it is because of me thousands of my people are dead. Cursed to remember the look on my lover's face as I split her skull in two."

I grimaced, knowing what a poison self-loathing could be. "I'm sorry." Those two miserable words were all I could conjure.

"I paid for my sins, Aelia. Two hundred years in the mines of the Stone Kingdom. I lived off gruel and suffered through the beatings. Reduced from a famed war hero to a prisoner, all because I chose the wrong woman to love."

My heart ached. I knew all too well the pain he felt. To be betrayed by the one you love. Nothing in this world can prepare you for it. The shame, the guilt, the embarrassment, it eats away at you until there is nothing left but bone and regret.

"Did you feel better once you had killed her?" I asked, fixing my eyes on his. I fantasized about killing Gideon a million different ways.

"For a moment," Tharan said, rubbing his fingers up the side of the mug. "Emptiness and regret filled the hole she left. I became the creature you see before you. Heartbreaker extraordinaire."

I bit my lip, running my hand over the fur pelt lining the bed, trying to fight the pressure building behind my eyes. Tharan sat next to me—pulling me in closer. Tears spilled down my cheeks. "I'm so angry, and I don't know who I'm angrier at, myself or Gideon."

Tharan said nothing, letting his acceptance fill the space between us. I buried my face in his chest, releasing years of pent-up emotion to a man I had just met.

"Gideon has my sister," I said, finding my voice again. "He's going to offer her to your father at the Yule Revelry for use of the Wild Hunt."

Tharan laughed. "What would my father want with a mortal girl? He has consorts of every species and gender. She would need to be a literal god for him to lend his prized Wild Hunt."

I knew what I had to do. The piece of the puzzle that would make everything fit into place. "Our mother is the human Fate, Morta."

He pulled me from his chest. His eyes searched mine for a hint of a lie. "What? I had heard she went missing, but I never imagined..."

"She never showed her power to us. Until five years ago, we knew her as Queen Isadora of Elyria."

Tharan's mouth straightened into a thin line. "That's how you survived the shock..."

I gave him a puzzled look.

He paced the room as he fiddled with his hair, tying it back in a low bun.

"In the cave with the kraken. Caiden sent enough electricity into the water to stun an animal the size of this city block, but you didn't flinch. Do you possess other powers as well?"

"Nothing akin to our mother's," a half lie.

Tharan continued pacing and muttering to himself, holding his pointer finger to his lips. "If she could see the future, she would know the outcome of battles. Fix failure before it happens. My father *would* be intrigued by that."

A pit opened in my stomach. "Help me stop it. She is no seer. She is a regular girl who wound up in the wrong hands because of my mistakes."

"It has been five hundred years since the war, and my father and I still have our differences. I don't know what I can do, but if I can help, I will."

The weight lifted itself from my chest. "Bind us to the words." I held out my hand, and we shook on it, letting the magic tie us to the bargain.

As I went to leave, Tharan grabbed my arm. "You are brave to make a deal with the Lord of Nothing."

To which I replied, "Perhaps it is you who is brave to make a deal with a known traitor?"

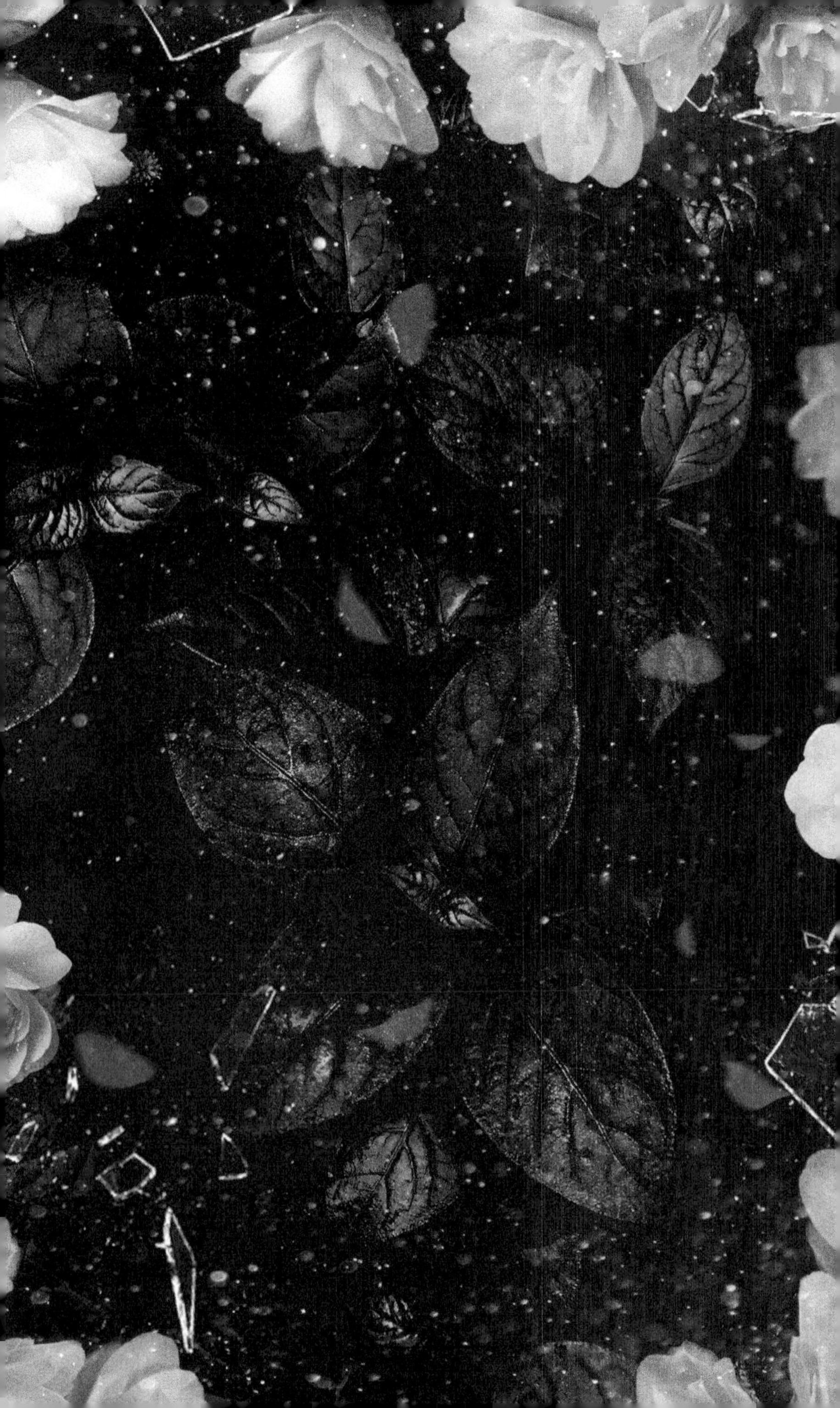

23 CAIDEN

Caiden breathed deeply, happy to be back on neutral ground. "Ah, Ruska, never thought I'd be quite so happy to return to this city again. But after the past few days, it's never looked better to me."

Aelia twiddled her thumbs nervously as they walked toward Caiden's townhome. "I hope Amolie and Roderick made it out alive."

"Roderick is the finest warrior in all of Moriana. Maybe the world, but he knows when to cut and run. He wouldn't let Amolie be harmed."

"I know, but I hate being in the dark." Aelia pulled her cloak tighter around her. "I just want to know if they're okay."

Caiden rubbed her back. "They are. I know it."

They walked in silence the rest of the way. Both braced for the worst.

The door swung open, and Ernie greeted them. "Prince Caiden." His whiskers twitched as he bowed. "The others have already arrived."

Aelia pushed past the hob. "Amolie! Roderick! Lucius?"

Amolie bounded through the parlor, hugging her friend. "You're okay. I was so worried."

"Me? I was worried about you. I saw Roderick take on the hooded figure, but I couldn't see you."

Amolie glowered at Roderick. "This one would have stayed and slayed every goblin there if I had let him."

Roderick blushed. "We're fine. I wasn't worried for a minute."

Amolie rolled her eyes.

Aelia collapsed onto the couch. "I'm exhausted. I need to sleep before we discuss the mess that was the Court of Sorrows."

"Come with me, and I'll heal you properly." Amolie pulled her friend into the kitchen, leaving the three men alone in the parlor.

Lucius waited until after the women had left to show himself. "We need to talk about the scepter."

"We should take the scepter to the Sylph Council. They will know what to do with it," Caiden said, staring at the bone with the bird skull lying on the table.

"They will use it for war," Lucius said. "We should hide it until this business with Nysemia is resolved."

"The Court of Storms should keep it," Roderick chimed in.

Lucius and Caiden turned to look at him, their mouths agape.

"With the Army of the Dead on our side, we would be invincible." Chaos flickered in his pale green eyes.

Caiden rubbed the back of his neck as he considered his options. Why should the council get the scepter? The Stormlands had a formidable military, but they could rule the continent with the scepter. He could descend upon the Highlands to seek retribution for his wife, and no one could stop him. His mind jumping to laying siege to the kingdoms scared him. "There is no suitable solution here."

No one knew they possessed the Scepter of the Dead. Nysemia had no heir, meaning her court and her army were free for the taking. "Does Gideon hold the Court of Sorrows?"

Lucius clicked his tongue. "My spies say armies from all over Moriana are marching to lay claim. Although who holds the palace is up for debate."

Caiden nodded, nervously rubbing his chin with his palm. "Where are our troops located?"

Roderick tapped the table, and a map of Moriana appeared. "They were moved to protect the border, sir."

"Call them back. I don't want the elves to get the wrong idea and think we are invading in this time of chaos."

Roderick chewed his cheek, moving the invisible chess pieces in his mind. "I would like to return to the Stormlands, my lord. My men will need to see their leader,"

"That is wise," Caiden said.

Roderick nodded and went to collect his things.

Lucius's expression darkened. "There is something else you should know."

Caiden put his hands on his hips. "Out with it."

"My spies told me Baylis Springborn is not a captive of Gideon's. She travels with him unguarded and unchained."

Caiden's eyes widened at Lucius's declaration. "Lies. Baylis would nev—"

Lucius cut him off before he could finish his thought. "I think she was the hooded figure in the Court of Sorrows, not Erissa."

"Bullshit."

"Perhaps her power lay dormant or bound by an ancient spell. The Fates are goddesses of the old world. Morta is powerful enough to conceal their magic." He tapped his long finger on his pale lips. "Look at what Erissa did to Aelia. There is no telling what she could have done to Baylis."

Caiden bit the inside of his cheek, filling his mouth with metallic blood.

Lucius continued. "We should be prepared when we go to the Court of the Alder King. Roderick will bring a legion to the Woodland Realm. It is not uncommon for a lord of your stature to travel with one."

Pinching the bridge of his nose, Caiden tried to relieve the pressure building in his head. "Let's hope Aelia got that right."

Lucius gave him a knowing look. "I saw the way Lord Tharan looked at her in the throne room. The way he defended her while she trembled in fear. Perhaps she planted more than just an invitation in his mind."

Caiden's stomach hardened at the thought of Aelia with Tharan, but he couldn't intervene. They would never be together. A lump grew in his throat at the thought of everything they had shared. Who would he be without those memories? He smothered the jealousy gurgling in his gut.

"This will break Aelia." Caiden's voice cracked.

Lucius clicked his tongue as he poured himself a cup of tea. "We will not tell Aelia any of this. At least not until we're *sure* Baylis is working with Gideon."

"You're right. There's no need to worry her for no reason." He could hear the words leaving my mouth, but deep down, he knew what Lucius said was true. There was a reason they hadn't been able to find Baylis for five years. She did not want to be found.

Lucius sipped his tea, then setting his cup down, leaned over the table. "I know what you are thinking."

"You do?" Caiden's blue eyes went wide.

"You're thinking you may need to kill Baylis."

Lucius's statement knocked the wind out of Caiden. "I wasn't, but now that you bring it up…"

"I will do it for you if it comes to that. Let Aelia hate me," he said nonchalantly.

Caiden placed a reassuring hand on his shoulder. "You're a good friend, Lucius, but let's not rush into killing princesses."

Lucius shrugged. "It's my job to plan for the worst."

Caiden let out a sigh. The last three days took a toll on him. He never expected to fight Gideon, steal the Scepter of the Dead, and fight a horde of trolls.

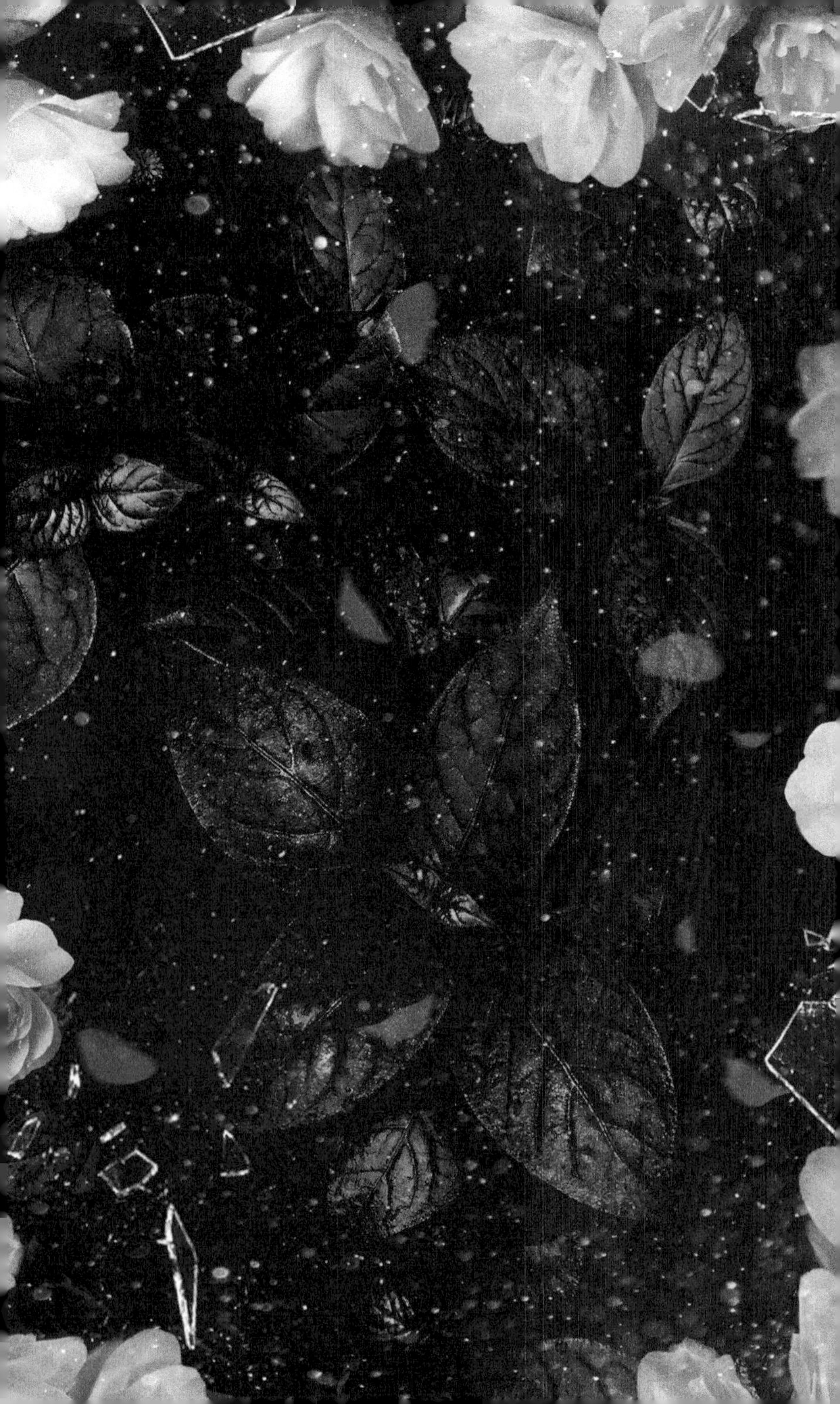

24 AELIA

G*IDEON HELD ME BY THE NECK OVER THE BLACK POOL WHERE THE kraken's razor-sharp teeth snapped at my feet.*

"Do you see the things you make me do, Aelia?" His black eyes were full of ire. "You drive me crazy."

He tightened his grip on my neck as I squirmed. "Please, Gideon. Please don't do this." Tears streamed down my face.

"You make me hurt you."

"I will be good, I promise. Please, Gideon." My voice cracked with fear.

Gideon's eyes gleamed with delight as he pressed me closer to the kraken's champing jaws. I held my breath, preparing for the creature's fangs to rip through my flesh.

Pulling myself from the dream, I shot up in my bed.

A hot scream formed inside my lungs, scraping at my insides, begging to be released. Grabbing the nearest pillow, I yelled until my lungs gave out. For years, I dulled my pain with dust, and now, I found myself exposed—forced to face my fears sober. My brain burned with the need for a high.

Caiden burst through my door.

"Shh—it's okay," he said, running his hands through my sweat-slicked hair as I heaved ragged breaths into his chest.

I gripped his back tight, anchoring me to reality.

Fear coiled in my gut. How would I face him again?

Baylis had always been the stronger of the two of us. While I busied myself with royal dinners and sylph princes, she managed the domestic policy work at home. Every day, she visited my father in his chambers. He didn't recognize her most days, but that never diminished her hope.

A memory floated to the surface of my mind.

"How was he today?" I asked as we walked down the cobblestone streets to the River House.

Her gray eyes darted to the ground. "For a moment, I thought he was himself again."

"Really? What did he say?" Our father rarely recognized any of us anymore. The potions Ragana brewed kept him in a near catatonic state. It was safer that way for all of us.

Baylis sighed. "He said he knew who I was."

I arched an eyebrow, smothering any flicker of hope. "And?"

Baylis shook her head. Strands of blonde hair escaped its meticulous bun. "It was odd. I swear to the Trinity, he recognized me. It was only for a moment, but his eyes told me he knew who I was."

I shrugged. "Well, that's more than I got the last time I visited him."

She squinted, focusing on the memory. "He said something before he slipped back into his fugue."

"I'm sure it was riveting and not dribble at all."

Baylis ignored my vitriol. "He said something about two little birds. One high on a mountain. The other, lost in shadow. He said both would be broken. I wonder what that could mean." She bit her lip, pondering the ravings of a madman.

"I don't know how you do it, Baylis."

"Do what?" she asked, as if awakening from a trance.

"Visit him every day."

Baylis pondered my question for a moment. "I don't want him to be alone. It must be scary wherever he is. I want him to know we still love him. At least, that's what I'd want my family to do for me. I guess a part of me still thinks if I love him enough, he'll find his way back to us."

A sob rose in my throat at the memory of my sister.

I took the opposite approach, opting to act as though my father and his demons did not exist. His lucid days were the worst. For a moment in time, we glimpsed the father we knew, only to watch him fade into nothingness.

I wanted to reach out and grasp him. To keep him here, in the present, with us, but there was nothing to grab, like a light dimming through the night until you were left in utter blackness.

For years, I prayed to Ammena to heal him. I bargained, smashed things, and finally accepted he was gone. He was forty-five when they lowered his body into the unforgiving earth, but he had been dead long before that. The maggots could ravage his corpse for all I cared. I would not shed another tear for him.

Melancholy wrapped itself around me like a warm blanket. With my emotions depleted, I had nothing left to give anyone. I slept for weeks, only rising so the sheets could be changed.

A succubus in human form, Gideon fed off my pain, absorbing it like soil absorbs the rain.

A willing victim, I confided all my deepest fears in him. Little did I realize he would manipulate those fears to his advantage, unraveling my emotions until I was held together by threads. He cut the remaining strings one by one until I became the puppet he desired.

I died in Ryft's Edge. Only my corpse continues, fueled by hate and the lust for revenge.

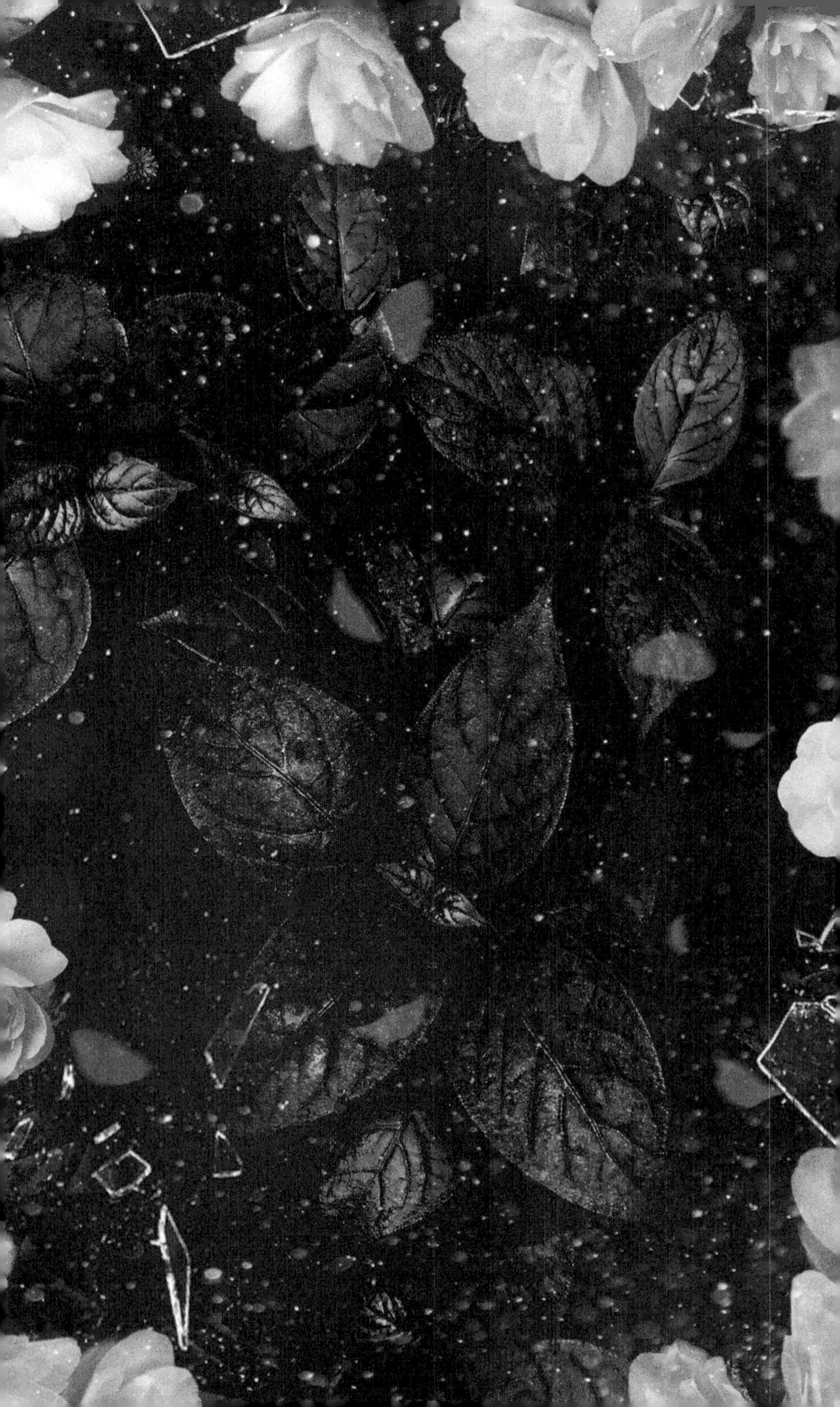

25 AELIA

ERNIE'S DEEP VOICE ECHOED THROUGH THE QUIET TOWNHOME, "She is in the parlor. I will escort you."

My heart jumped at the thought of Tharan standing in the doorway. I quickly fixed my hair, straightened my simple smock dress, and neatly placed my tea next to the book I was reading.

Ernie approached, bowing his head. "Lady Aelia, there are some messengers here for you."

I cleared my throat. "Let them in."

Three Woodland Realm soldiers entered the parlor. Their armor of golden leaves laid atop one another to form a chain mail. Their helmets crowned with cascading ferns resembled a living crown camouflaging them amidst the lush foliage. Thin vines adorned with tiny blossoms crisscrossed their armor, providing additional protection and a touch of natural elegance. The soldiers moved with quiet grace, their leafy attire rustling softly, a symphony harmonizing with the whispers of the wind through ancient trees. Elegant, long swords fell at their sides.

My mouth fell open as the middle soldier kneeled before me, extending a velvet pillow on which an invitation sat.

I picked up the letter, breaking the green wax seal of the

Alder King with my nail. My eyes flitted to the doorway, where Caiden, Lucius, and Amolie stood, jaws gaping at the three soldiers.

The letter read:

> To the Traitorous Queen Aelia,
> You are cordially invited to the Alder King's Yule Revelry, which begins on the night of Winter Solstice and lasts through the new year. Your companions are welcome to attend as well.
> Your Friend,
> The Lord of Nothing.

"Thank you," I said, trying to steady my voice.

The soldiers bowed and then left.

Lucius, Caiden, and Amolie came rushing into the room. I held up the invitation for Caiden to inspect.

His eyes darted back and forth across the parchment. "Excellent."

"Good work, Springborn," Lucius said.

"And you all thought I couldn't be charming." A satisfied smile crossed my lips.

"Well, given your past, you could see how we would have reservations..." Caiden said.

I needed fresh air and some time to think. Arion had been cooped up in the stable for too long and would also want a run.

"Amolie, do you want to go for a ride with me?" I asked as I buttoned my wool cloak.

"You don't have to ask me twice," she said, grabbing her cloak.

The streets of Ruska bustled with people gathering supplies for their own Yule celebrations. As one of the few holidays celebrated throughout Moriana, the merchants usually made a killing.

Arion bobbed his head up and down in excitement when he saw me.

"Hello, boy, I've missed you." I ran a gloved hand down his muscular neck, taking in his distinct smell.

He mouthed my hands, looking for treats.

"Okay, here you go." I flattened my palm, placing a carrot on it.

Arion lovingly nibbled it.

The stiff leather saddle sent a chill through my bones, but I needed to escape.

The Tower of Fate loomed behind us as we made our way to the open fields.

"I can't believe your mother is in there," Amolie said, staring at the twisted stone tower rising into the heavens.

"It's her prison." I didn't look back—I couldn't.

"Don't you wonder about her at all, Aelia?" Amolie rode beside me.

I bit my nail. "I wonder why she allowed me to be sent to my own personal hell."

"At least she's alive, Aelia."

My chest tightened. Amolie's mother had been burned alive by Gideon's father during the witch hunts twenty years ago.

"I'm sorry."

Those stupid words again.

Amolie waved me off. "Those things can't hurt me anymore. I couldn't have saved my mother."

"Still. I should not have been so thoughtless with my words."

"It's fine."

The horses plodded along happily through the snow.

"I'm afraid to see Gideon again," I said. My words were shaky like my nerves.

"I would be too. He's so charming. I wonder how long he'd been courting her."

"It doesn't take long to fall for him. He's great at love-dumping." I fought the memories of our sweet beginning rising to the surface. He swept me off my feet like no one had before, showering me with affection, making me believe he was my soul's mate.

"He's going to put on a show for the Alder King, of that we can be sure." Amolie's normally cheerful demeanor darkened. "And likely, Erissa will be with him."

I rolled my eyes.

"Let's talk about something more exciting like... the forest boy."

I straightened in my saddle. "Yes?"

A coy smile tugged at her mouth. "He seems nice."

"We're just friends." My heart skipped a beat at the memory of our night together.

"I didn't imply you were anything more. I think it's interesting he would send you such an intimate invitation. You must have charmed him... or you planted something in his mind."

I scoffed. "Why does everyone believe I can't be charming? I am charming, for Trinity's sake."

Amolie laughed. "You can be prickly."

I thrust my hands up into the air, startling the horses. "Prickly? I was a queen and an emissary."

"That was a long time ago, Aelia."

"For Trinities sake—it wasn't *that* long ago."

"Fine, fine, you're still charming."

"Thank you." I held my head high like the queen I was.

Amolie sighed as our horses plodded along. "I miss Roderick." Sadness filled her voice. "I know he's doing his duty, but my bed feels so cold without him."

"You can always sleep with me, Amolie."

She smiled at me.

I patted Arion's neck. "Care to tell me how you and Roderick…"

"Became a couple?" She finished my sentence for me.

"Yes. I didn't think there was anything between you."

"There wasn't at first. We were just friends. Lucius would sometimes send him to rendezvous with me. One day he caught me reading a poetry book and he let it slip that he too loved poetry…" She stroked her pony's silken mane, her cheeks flushing at the memory. "And we bonded over it. He'd leave me little poems in my tack box or have a bouquet of roses sent from the royal florist."

My eyes widened at the thought of Roderick, hero of the sylph, writing poetry and buying flowers. "Are we talking about the same Roderick who used to wear the ears of his kills around his neck?"

Amolie nodded, her curls bouncing like springs. "The very same one."

"Huh… I guess people *can* change."

"We are not our labels, Aelia. You should know that by now. Sometimes it is easier to live in the armor we build for ourselves than let the world see who we really are."

I sucked in a breath, ashamed of my ignorance. "You're right, Amolie. I'm happy for you."

"That means the world to me, Aelia." She reached out and squeezed my hand.

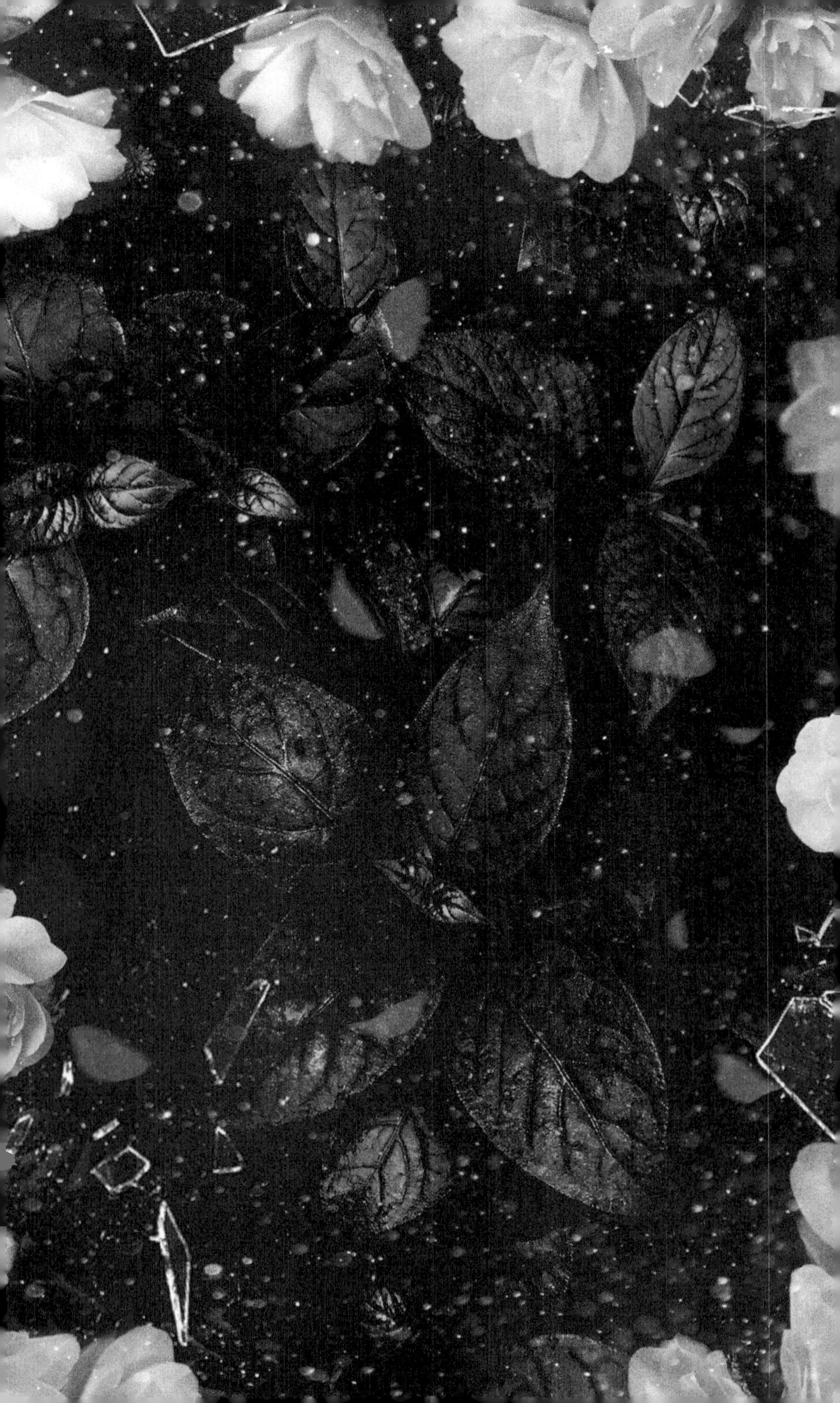

26 AELIA

Caiden arranged for a sleigh and an entourage to transport us to the Woodland Realm, where a legion had already set up a camp. Lords liked to bring along armies as a demonstration of their strength.

"The sylph are so dramatic," I said, covering myself with the fox-lined cloak Tharan had given me. We all clambered into the covered sleigh pulled by six dapple gray workhorses with bells braided into their manes.

"Life is a show, Aelia," Caiden said, sliding into the seat next to me. Lucius and Amolie took the seats across from us.

"The horses are fed an enchanted grain. They will not tire for days. I am having one of my men take Arion to the camp." He wrapped his hand around mine. I didn't know how we had fallen back into touching each other so easily again, but it felt nice.

"Thank you." I gave him a reassuring smile.

He pushed in closer to me. "Do you know where I got the enchanted grain?"

"You are a magus. I assume you can enchant anything."

He shook his head, chuckling to himself. "I got it from Baylis."

I perked my head up. "What?"

"You didn't know your sister was a scientist?" he asked, cocking his head to one side.

"I knew she met with the farmers of the kingdom. She must have worked with them to develop such a hearty crop." Maybe I didn't know as much about my sister as I thought.

Caiden let out a sigh. "She was quite something."

"She still is," I said before laying my head on Caiden's shoulder.

Shadows ringed my eyes. The steady motion of the sleigh lulled me into a dreamless sleep. As I drifted off, Caiden kissed the top of my head, and I burrowed myself farther into his warm embrace. My heart chafed at the feeling of the kiss. Torn between my need to be loved and the inevitable heartbreak that would follow.

The trip seemed endless. We passed the time by playing cards, telling old stories, and singing. On the third night, we stopped at an inn in the human province of Leighton. I stretched, arching my back, relieved to be free of the sleigh for a moment.

The inn had two suites available. Amolie and I split a room while Lucius and Caiden shared the other.

"How are you feeling about the revelry?" Amolie asked as we lay in bed, listening to the wind rattle the windows.

"Hesitant, excited, sad, a million different things and nothing simultaneously."

"Do you want to use?"

"I want to use every hour of every day." I picked at my fingernails.

"For what it's worth. I'm proud of you. I know this isn't easy."

I squeezed her tight, inhaling the sweet scent of sage seemingly baked into her hair. "I knew this day would come. I wish I had gotten sober sooner."

"You weren't ready, Aelia." She stroked my back. "I feel bad for enabling you for so long, but I didn't know how to help you."

"You couldn't have helped me, Amolie. I was determined to kill myself slowly. I had to come to that realization on my own."

"You deserve happiness too, Aelia. Don't forget that. Don't let your past control your future."

A sigh escaped my lips. "I wish I could."

The beauty of the Woodland Realm took my breath away. Towering, ancient trees with twisted branches and luminescent foliage formed a canopy filtering sunlight into a kaleidoscope of dappled hues. Their leaves glowed an otherworldly radiance, casting a gentle, ambient light bathing the forest floor in a surreal glow. The fragrance of unseen blossoms floated in the air, carrying hints of sweet nectar and the untold mysteries of the arcane. Birds sang to one another. Magic flowed like water here. I could feel its presence in every living thing.

The forest held an ancient history, one that extended beyond recorded accounts. Legend said the forest birthed the Alder King to serve as its protector.

Our camp lay in the middle of the forest, near the river. Other courts arrived and could be seen setting up their tiny tent villages as well. A market set in the center of the camps provided goods and services for weary travelers.

In the distance, a giant sycamore tree rose from the earth like a castle on a hill.

"The Alder King's palace," Caiden said, noticing me staring at the mighty structure.

"I've never seen something so grand."

"Wait until you see inside." He led me over to the tents. Our new home until the end of the Yule season. They contained all the comforts of a home, including a roaring fire, a plush bed piled with furs, two leather chairs, a desk, and even an ornate rug for the floor. Two soldiers dressed in Stormland armor stood guard outside the entrance to Caiden's tent.

"Why all the protection?" I asked as I plopped down onto his bed.

"So that women like you don't take advantage of hopeless romantics like me," he said, lying next to me, stroking my hair.

"Cute, but what's the real reason?"

"You know what we carry."

I shot up, having almost completely forgotten about the scepter. "Why would you bring that here? Do you think you're going to call on an ancient army to destroy Gideon?"

"I could if I wanted to."

"We don't even know how the scepter works and you brought it here, close to our mortal enemy?"

"Well, I wasn't going to leave it behind." Our faces nearly touched.

Knots tied themselves in my stomach.

Something like love flickered in Caiden's eyes. Any feeling of guilt I had faded away as his lips touched mine.

I sucked in a breath as heat grew between my legs.

All the feelings of love and longing I pushed aside for years came rushing back the moment our lips touched. I wanted him in a primal way—wanted to show him the girl he fell for all those years ago still lived inside me—full of lust and passion. No reason to play coy. Only I would remember this.

I slipped my tongue between his lips. He groaned with pleasure, laying me down on the blanket of furs.

He pulled away from me. "Are you sure you want this?" he asked as he undid his wool jacket.

"Yes," I replied through ragged breaths, fumbling with my buttons.

My pulse quickened at the sensation of his hands gripping my hips, making my mind go blank.

He knew my body better than I did. Caiden loved me. Loved me when I was human. Loved me when I was broken. Loved me when I did not love myself.

Tears poured down my cheeks.

"What's wrong?" He cupped my face in his hands.

"I'm sorry for everything." My voice caught in my throat. "I don't deserve you."

"Let me be the judge of what I deserve." He pressed his lips against mine once more.

Parting mine, I let his tongue explore my mouth before he moved down to my chest. For a moment, I hesitated. The last time Caiden and I lay together, my breasts were plump and round. Years of self-loathing and starvation had left them flat and deflated. He did not bat an eye at my new body.

A fire grew in my core as he took one of my nipples into his mouth, teasing me with his tongue. I let out a long moan.

"That's right, princess. I remember how you liked it." His voice was rough and cracked.

"Do you remember what I taste like?" I said, spreading my legs wide so that he could see my slick core.

His face brightened as he lowered his head between my legs. Delicate fingers grazed over my body, making the tiny hairs on my neck stand on end.

"I've dreamed of the day I would get to taste you again." His tongue circled my throbbing sex before diving deep into my core.

I came undone, letting out a moan the entire camp could hear. He continued to thrust his tongue in and out of me. Fingers teasing me at the same time.

Pleasure surged through my body, leaving me whimpering with each flick of his tongue.

Digging my fingers into his hair only increased his pace. My body trembled with exhilaration.

A back-arching, toe-curling orgasm ripped through me like a bolt of lightning. I let out a primal cry of ecstasy.

"Good girl," he said, giving me a sly smile as heaved himself up, revealing his erect cock.

I pulled him on top of me, allowing him to lower his throbbing erection into my slick cunt. He thrust in and out, stoking the flame of my desire.

"Don't stop," I said, burying my fangs into his shoulder.

He let out a cry of pleasure, hastening the pace of his thrusts.

Another orgasm grew in my core, demanding to be released, but Caiden wouldn't let me, pinning my hands over my head.

"Oh, Trinity," he exclaimed, his body going limp on top of me. "I'm sorry. I…"

I lay stunned at the man on top of me.

"It's okay," I said, kissing him on the forehead.

Blush colored his cheeks. "It's just… I haven't been with anyone since my wife. So, I'm a little out of practice. Let me finish you."

I winced at the word "wife."

"That's okay." I sat up, awkwardly pulling the blankets around me, regretting letting it go this far. We shouldn't have let our feelings get the better of us.

"Aelia, I…" He fiddled with his thumbs. "I don't know what to say."

Running a soft hand down his square jaw, I gave him a loving glance. "You don't have to say anything at all. The blame is on me."

Caiden nervously mussed his hair. "I don't know what came over me."

I nuzzled my nose into the crook of his neck. "Lay down with me. We can try again in the morning."

Something tugged at me from my sleep, but when I opened my eyes, only darkness surrounded me. The dying embers of the fire throwing their last bits of light. I tried to return to my slumber, but the tugging continued. *Tug, tug, tug.*

I pulled myself from Caiden's warm embrace, wrapped myself in his coat, and went to investigate the source of my discomfort. It pulled me toward Caiden's desk.

'*Aelia,*' a ghoulish voice whispered in my ear. '*Aelia, my queen. I am here, waiting for you.*'

"Who are you?" I whispered into the darkness.

'*I hover in between worlds, not fully alive, but not fully dead either. Only one who has been beyond the veil is worthy of commanding the dead.*'

"What are you talking about?"

A drawer of Caiden's desk popped open, revealing a leather box.

'*Open it,*' the ancient voice commanded.

Shaking hands unclasped the golden latches, exposing the scepter made of a long bone with symbols I did not recognize engraved on its hilt.

'*Take it,*' the voice commanded. '*You are the only one who can command the dead.*' The ruby eyes of the bird glowed.

"I don't want it." I tried to steady my voice.

'*You are my chosen one, Aelia Springborn. Prick your finger and bind us together until death do us part.*'

Everything inside me told me to run, but part of me yearned for power. My whole life, I had been powerless. Unable to save my father, my sister, and myself. As commander of the Army of the Dead, I would be unstoppable.

"What's the catch?" I asked the voice.

'*Don't you want to be the Queen of the Dead?*'

"Queen of the cursed is what you mean." I ran my fingers over the inscriptions carved into the hilt. Pure power radiated from the scepter. A lesser woman would jump at the chance, but I wouldn't tie myself to the damned for an eternity.

The voice hissed at me. '*Hard as you may try, Aelia Springborn, you will command the dead.*'

A gust of wind blew through the tent, extinguishing the last embers of the fire, slamming the box shut.

A long breath escaped my lips. I rubbed the sleep from my eyes. Was I delirious? Had my drug-addled brain dreamed this up? Hopefully, a good night's rest would solve my burning mind.

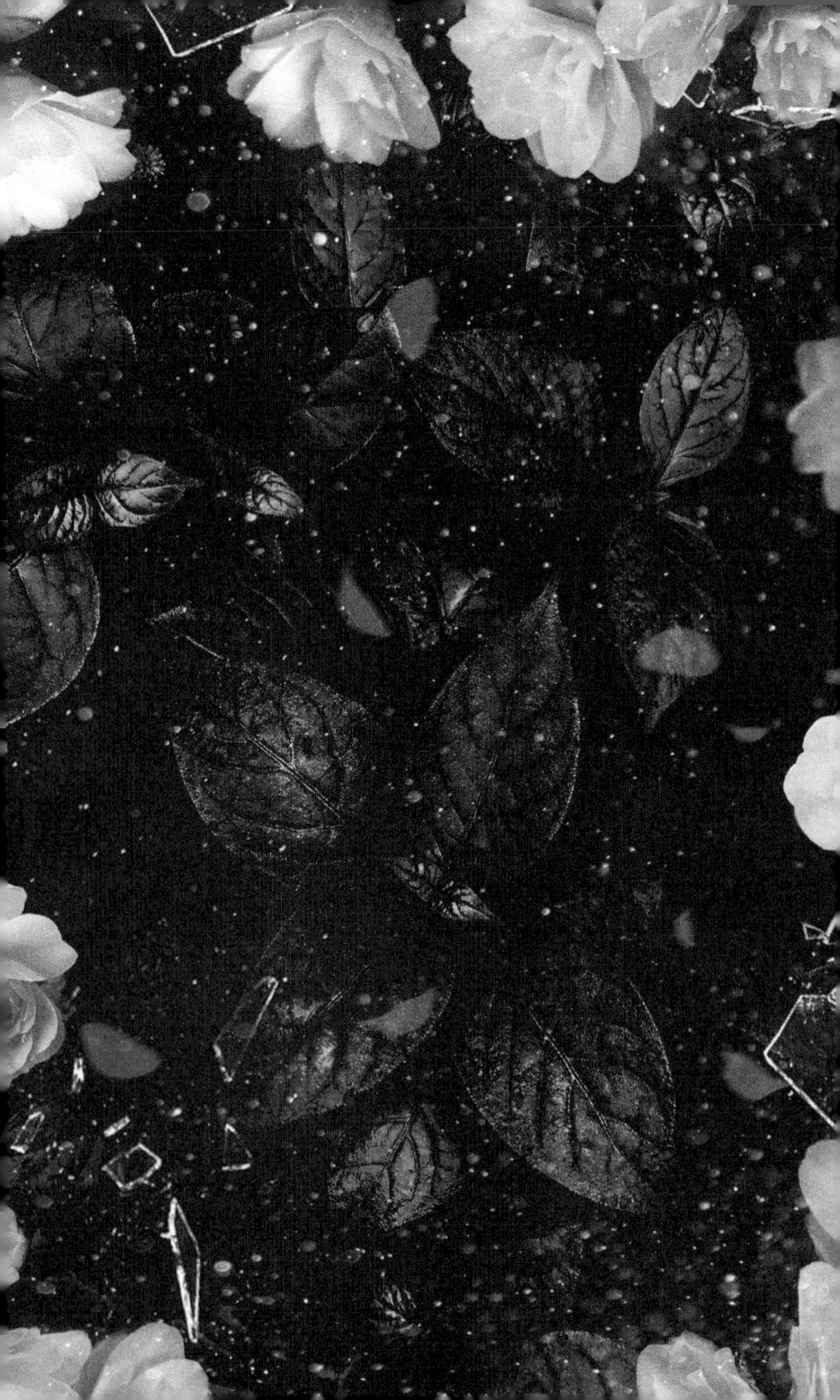

27 CAIDEN

Lucius tossed his thick braid over his shoulder. "Gideon left the Court of Sorrows after we did, leaving the scraps for other lesser courts to pick at."

"Meaning they *were* there for the scepter." Caiden bit at his cuticles, carving off tiny pieces of himself.

Lucius gave a curt nod. "I believe so."

Roderick entered the tent, whistling a cheery tune. "The legion is prepared." He picked up the scepter, twirling it in the air.

"What are you doing?" Lucius shouted, grabbing the scepter from Roderick's powerful hands.

"Just testing it out. You said it won't work without a sacrifice, anyway. It's useless to us as is." Roderick plopped onto Caiden's bed. The mattress strained against his giant figure.

"I said it *might* require a blood sacrifice. I'm still deciphering the runes." Lucius held the carved bone close to a lantern by the bed. The ancient script glowed eerily in the light.

Roderick leaned over. "Amolie could look at it. She researches ancient texts for her spells."

Lucius wrinkled his nose. "Absolutely not. The last thing we need is Aelia finding out how the scepter works and doing something rash."

Caiden's blood boiled. "That's enough." He slammed his fist on the desk. "I will not have you speak of Aelia as if she were some impulsive girl. She nearly killed Gideon in the Court of Sorrows and hasn't touched dust since we got to Ruska. Give her some credit."

Lucius threw up his hands. "If you want to put your faith in an addicted, traitorous queen, then so be it." He pointed a slender finger at Caiden. "But I will not be a part of the downfall of our kingdom." He stormed out of the tent.

Roderick plucked an apple from a nearby tray, biting into it. "Dramatic."

"He lets his hatred for Aelia cloud his judgment." Caiden sank into a leather chair, letting his exhausted body finally relax.

"And your love for her clouds yours," Roderick said, taking a bite of his apple.

Caiden buried his face in my hands. "You're right."

Roderick sat up on the bed. "You have a decade-long history with Aelia. It's natural these feelings would resurface after Cassandra's death."

Caiden let out a long sigh as he fiddled with the gold ring around his fourth finger. "I feel guilty every time I think of Aelia…"

"Cassandra would want you to move on with your life."

Caiden shrugged. "I suppose you're right."

"It looks like there is a decent showing of courts here," Roderick said, changing the subject. "Court of Rabbits, Court of Flies, even a few human kingdoms."

"The Alder King likes an audience," Caiden said, running his fingers over the bone scepter.

Roderick moved beside him. "With the Army of the Dead, you could be more powerful than the Alder King."

Caiden's mouth straightened into a thin line. A look of determination crossed his face. "Fetch Amolie to decipher these inscriptions. Make sure she can keep a secret."

"Right away." Roderick left to get Amolie.

While Amolie studied the scepter, Caiden walked along the camp, chatting with the men, looking for Aelia. They spent the morning wrapped around one another. He could still smell her scent of jasmine on his skin. In ten years, her scent had not changed.

The camp spread between the wood's giant pine and oak trees, creating a much-needed cover from the harsh winter winds. While a river snaked its way through the forest, providing water for the attending kingdoms.

As Caiden rounded a corner, three riders on horseback caught his eye. He ducked behind a tree. Hairs pricked on the back of his neck. Gideon led the group, riding his black stallion. Erissa followed, dressed in her usual silk robes, her unmistakable red hair shining like a beacon against the desolate winter landscape. Caiden couldn't make out the face of the third, whose baby blue hood hid their face.

He followed them.

Carefully, he crept between the massive pines of the wood, trying his best not to arouse suspicion.

Their camp lay situated at the base of the river traversing the Woodland Realm. Gideon brought his strongest legion as a show of strength to the other kingdoms.

Caiden sunk into the snow at the foot of mighty pine. A bitter wind wiped at his face as he tried to ascertain the third person's identity.

The stranger stood next to Erissa. From where Caiden hid, he could only make out a dainty hand as they reached for an apple.

Caiden's throat grew thick.

Baylis had fair skin and hair.

He needed to get a closer look.

Slowly, he crept around the other side of the camp, hoping to catch a glance at the mysterious figure's face. A crate of onions provided the necessary cover. The overwhelming scent stung his eyes.

C'mon, turn and face me.

As if answering his silent plea, the person turned, removing her hood.

Caiden gasped as Baylis locked eyes with him from across the camp, blinking once before turning to kiss Gideon.

Caiden's heart leapt into his throat. She was not a captive. She was in love with Gideon.

He needed to get out of the camp.

Sprinting through the forest, still in shock, he replayed the event in his mind. Baylis did not appear to be under duress. Not a mark blemished her pale skin. She was under Gideon's spell now, and that was a hard enchantment to break.

This would break Aelia's heart. He had to tell her before the revelry. She would never forgive him if she learned he had kept this from her.

He always ate with his men on the road. It kept the morale high to know their lord and commander respected their sacrifice and ate with them.

Caiden fiddled with his food, nauseous. Aelia looked so happy singing and dancing with the soldiers.

His heart fluttered when she smiled at him. How could this creature he had spent years hating to be so enchanting?

He returned her smile, and she motioned for him to join her.

"Where have you been all day?" She pulled him into a warm embrace.

Caiden swallowed hard, trying to find the courage for what he needed to do. "There's something I need to tell you."

Her expression darkened as she released him. "About what?"

"Let's go back to my tent." He signaled for Roderick, Lucius, and Amolie to follow, and took her hand, leading her through the snowy trees. Each step brought him closer to the point of no return. The fate of this mission rested in Aelia's hands.

"Please, sit." He motioned to the leather chair in front of his carved oak desk.

"What's this about?" She looked at Amolie, who shrugged.

"It's about Baylis." Caiden crouched down, taking Aelia's hand in his. Her hazel eyes frantically searching for an explanation.

"Is…" Trembling hands twisted with apprehension. "Is she dead?"

Caiden's mouth tightened into a straight line. He nervously ran his hand through his thick hair. "No, she is alive, and she is healthy."

Her shoulders relaxed. "Oh, thank the Trinity." Aelia held her hand over her heart.

"It's just…" Words escaped him.

Lucious said what Caiden could not. "It's just she's working with Gideon. She may be in love with him."

Aelia blinked at the men. "That is not true. She wouldn't."

"I saw it myself, Aelia." A lump formed in Caiden's throat. "She is not their prisoner."

Aelia covered her face in her hands, taking in the moment.

They sat in silence as she mulled over the information.

When enough time had passed, Caiden touched her shoulder.

Lifting her head from her hands, her nostrils flared, a defiant look reflecting in her gold-flecked eyes. "Show me."

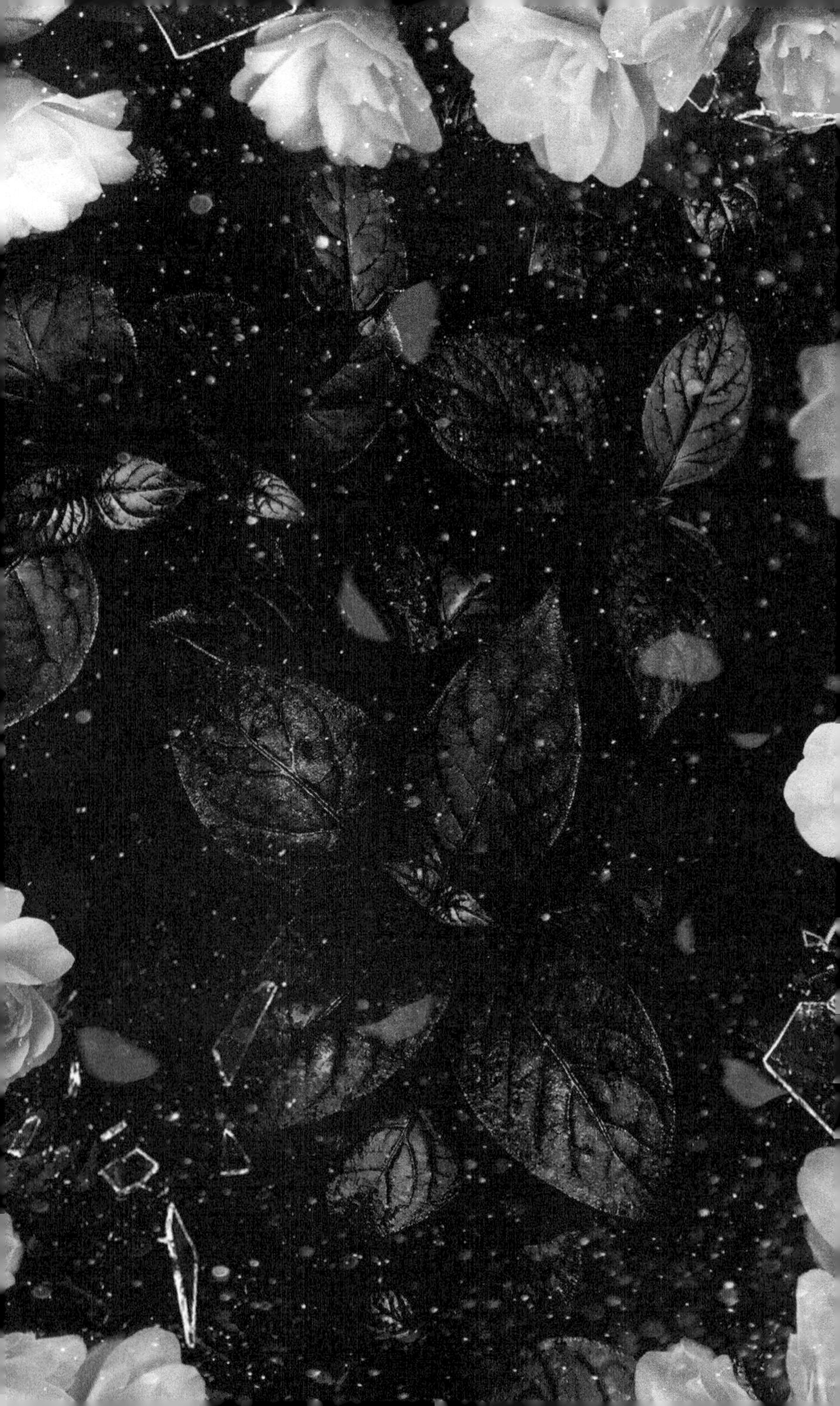

28 AELIA

I didn't want to believe Caiden.

Baylis had never been foolish. She always led with her head over her heart. There had to be a reason for her to work with Gideon.

Caiden led our party through the pristine woods down to the river, where Gideon and his men were camped.

Night blanketed the forest. Fires and dim lamps lit the basic tents. Smoke billowed from fires where men sat huddled next to one another, trying to escape the cold.

We found a covered spot on a hill overlooking the camp, laying our bodies in the cold snow to evade detection.

"She's down there," Lucius said, pointing to the ornate tent Gideon and Erissa occupied.

Amolie handed me a pair of binoculars, and I crouched under a log to get a better look.

Erissa's bodyguards, Remus and Ramus, stood outside the tent, their muscles taut against their shirts. Their faces red, not from the cold but from the sheer number of bulls' testicles they consumed. I looked around for Baylis, hoping to see her silhouette through the tent. There were three figures, but nothing identified her.

"I need to go down there," I said, pushing myself out of the snow.

"No," Caiden said firmly.

"I'll wait until everyone is asleep."

"No," he whisper-yelled at me.

"You know you can't stop me, Caiden. You know I will do this, with or without your permission." Fire roiled in my veins.

A look of resignation crossed Caiden's chiseled face. "At least let us provide cover. We have a good view from up here. Use your telepathy to talk to me."

I mulled over his proposition for a moment. "Fine."

We huddled together for warmth until the camp quieted and the men returned to their tents.

On silent feet, I snuck down the hill to the camp, wedging myself between two supply carts for cover. The smell of mud and livestock brought an acrid taste to my mouth. Gideon's tent stood directly before me.

I opened a line between Caiden and me. *Do you see anything?*

'*The twins are out front of the tent, but if you go to the back of the tent, you should be fine.*'

On tipped toes, I slipped between the tents, holding my breath each time I sprinted. Most of the men were drunk or busying themselves with the prostitutes Gideon's army traveled with.

In the time since I left the Highlands, his army had grown in both size and brutality. Through the tents, I could see men in a makeshift boxing ring, beating each other bloody while others drunkenly cheered them on.

My stomach turned at the thought of what I might find within the tent.

'*Aelia, be careful. Guards are patrolling nearby two tents away.*'

I edged along the side of Gideon's tent, listening for Baylis's voice, trying to silence the sound of my heart beating wildly in my chest. The sound of the canvas flapping in the wind muted everything else.

"Tell me what you see," Gideon said, pacing back and forth, the pallet floor squeaking beneath him.

I smothered the fear blooming in my chest, whipping my sweaty palms on my pants.

"I see a blood moon, my king." The sound of Baylis's voice brought a tear to my eye. My precious sister. What had Gideon done to her?

"Good, my darling." Gideon's voice crept like a rot into my brain. I wanted to scratch it out. "Do you see a victory?"

She could look into the future. They had unlocked our mother's gift. Bile gurgled in my throat. I did not know this woman—this was a stranger.

'*Do you see Baylis?*'

Tears rolled down my cheeks. '*Yes, she's here. She's working with Gideon.*' This had to be a spell. I needed to get her out. Maybe Amolie could cure her.

There must be a way to get her out of here.

'*We can't do it now. It's too risky. Come back, and we'll decide at camp.*'

I didn't want to leave Baylis, but Caiden had a point.

"All will bow to you," her voice floated on the breeze, far away.

'*Aelia, you need to get out of there.*'

I could not tear myself away. The world spun around me as I came to accept the lies I believed for so long.

'*Aelia! Now!*'

I looked up in time to see Ramus clasp a massive hand on my shoulder.

"Well, well, well, if it isn't the l'ttl bird," he said, a wicked grin cutting his face in two, displaying a host of rotten teeth.

"I'm not your little bird anymore," I said through gritted teeth. Slamming the blade of my dagger into his wrist, I made a run for it.

He cried out in pain. Blood gushed down his arm. "Remus. She's here!" he yelled to his brother.

I picked up my pace.

The twins' heavy steps clambered behind me. Their screams alerted the camp.

I prayed to Ammena that I could make out.

'Aelia, they're coming. Dozens of them. Duck left.'

I did as he said, running through the rows of farm animals.

Piss and shit coated my boots, but I did not stop. Men appeared at the other end of the row, coiling ropes in their filthy hands.

Determination buzzed in my chest like a thousand angry bees —I would not be tied like a hog.

'Aelia, through the pig pen. Then, over the chicken coop. You can make it.'

The men drew nearer. The delight of the hunt sparkled in their eyes.

"Come here, little kitty," one said, making kissing sounds at me. "We just want to have some fun."

I cut left over the waist-high fence surrounding the pig pen. The smell of feces made my eyes water. Deep slop slowed my stride.

I could feel the men behind me. Their heavy bodies struggled to wade through the mud and shit. Pigs squealed in horror as they trounced through their home.

Climbing over the shoddy wooden fence, I leapt toward the chicken coop. As my hands touched the roof, someone grabbed my leg, slamming my face into barbed wire. A sharp pain seared into my skin—stars blurred my vision. I looked back to see Remus's bulbous nose and rotten smile.

"Thought you could get away, did you? My mistress will be upset if I let you go."

"Fuck you." I kicked as hard as I could straight at his face. The sound of shattering bone rang in my ears.

"You bitch." He stumbled backward, releasing my leg.

I scrambled up the coop's roof and dropped to the other side, landing in a stack of crates and twisting my ankle. I screamed in pain, but I could not stop. Not now.

'*Run, Aelia,*' Caiden's voice urged me forward. '*Get up and run.*'

I heaved myself up, stumbling through the deep snow. My ankle throbbed in pain. My hot breath turned to vapor in the cold air. I looked back to see the twins, followed by a dozen men, gaining on me.

My muscles burned. When the agony of my ankle became too much, I got on all fours and crawled to the top of the hill. Gideon's men were mere feet behind me.

'*Aelia, if you can make it to me, Amolie thinks she can create a barrier.*'

I summoned the strength to push myself to the top. My limbs shaking with fear and exhaustion. The fallen tree lay so close. I could almost touch it.

A blast of wind knocked me to the ground, banging my head against the rough wood.

I looked up to see Gideon in his long black coat and gold-accented tunic. His leather riding boots crunched in the snow as he slowly approached me. My eyes struggled to focus on him.

He let out a devious laugh, making my blood run cold. "Your sister said you would come, but I didn't think you'd be foolish enough to pluck her from under my nose."

I braced myself against the log. Blood snaked its way down my face. "What do you want with my sister?"

A wry smile crossed his handsome face. "You think I'm holding her against her will?" He crouched in front of me, wiping the blood from my face. "That's so cute."

I recoiled at his touch.

"She is everything you could never be, Aelia." His voice scratched at my brain like nails scraping glass.

"Just let her go," I said, my vision blurring.

Throwing his head back, he scoffed, his quaffed hair fell over his dark eyes. "She sees my vision. Unlike you, who broke like a twig under pressure." His eyes raked over my body. "Look at yourself, an addict and a fool. You disgust me. I can't believe I—"

I spat in his face before he could finish his sentence.

His eyes flared with hatred.

"Now, now, Aelia, that's not nice." He wrapped his gloved hand around my neck. "And haven't I always been nice to you?" He squeezed tighter.

I gasped for air, panic rising like a wave in my chest. Every memory of my time in Ryft's Edge flashed through my mind. We had been here before—replayed this scene a thousand times. I was not the weak woman I was before.

I fumbled in the snow for my dagger while I tried to reach into Gideon's mind, but he built a wall, blocking me.

"Looking for this?" He held up the dagger so its iridescent blade shone in the moonlight. "Perhaps you like a scar to match the one you're hiding with a glamour."

I choked on the taste of sand. What other experiments had he been doing on himself to give him this kind of ability?

The sounds of swords clattered behind me as Caiden, Roderick, and Lucius sparred with Gideon's men.

Gideon jerked his head in an unnatural motion. "Ah, your lover. Always the valiant knight."

Delight gleamed in his black eyes. He loved making me squirm. My breaths were shallow now, my vision going in and out. I barely noticed when he scraped the dagger over my cheek.

"Get it over with," I said, clenching my jaw.

He kissed my cheek before whispering in my ear, "There is no fun in killing you. I want you to worship me like you do that filthy sylph prince."

A primal fear built in my chest, but I pushed it aside. "You'll never be him."

A horn sounded in the distance. The men stopped fighting, and Gideon released my neck as three riders on wolves the size of horses approached.

I hit the snow, gasping for air.

"In the name of the Alder King, we command you to cease," a deep feminine voice said.

The riders dressed in the same black and gold armor as the ones who delivered the invitation. Rows of teeth woven together in intricate designs hung around their necks while their fists coiled around tungsten spears.

These were no ordinary soldiers of the Woodland Realm. These were three riders of the Wild Hunt. Their mere presence made my breath hitch in my throat.

"I was just having a simple conversation with my wife." Gideon dropped my dagger into the snow.

"This woman is a guest of Lord Tharan Greenblade, Prince of the Woodlands. She is not to be harmed." The wolves pawed at the snow. One of them snarled at Gideon. "Touch her again, and we will banish you from this court." The female soldier's voice radiated confidence. Gideon did not scare her.

Nostrils flared, Gideon burned with hatred. No one told him what to do. He fiddled nervously with his belt as the wheels turned in his head. He had no power here, and he knew it. "Fine, she's free to go." He threw up his hands.

The warrior extended an armored hand to me, pulling me onto the back of the dire wolf.

"We will escort you and your comrades back to your camp. Do not let us catch you fighting again."

I nodded, clasping my hands around the female's waist. The others climbed onto the backs of the other wolves.

We rode, swift as shadows, through the forest until we reached our tent.

"If you need medical attention, Lord Tharan has a healer we can send for," the soldier said as I slid off the back of her wolf.

"It's okay." I motioned to Amolie, who stared enamored at the giant wolves.

"Very well. Goodnight." The trio turned and disappeared into the night.

We all stood silent for a moment, trying to make sense of everything.

"I need a drink," Roderick said, heading toward Caiden's tent. "Anyone else?"

A screeching noise brought me to my knees before I could enter the tent.

'You may think you are safe with your prince and your protectors, but I will always be able to reach you here.' Gideon's voice bore into my head like a hot knife.

Get out of my head!

I pulled myself into the tent.

The voice silenced.

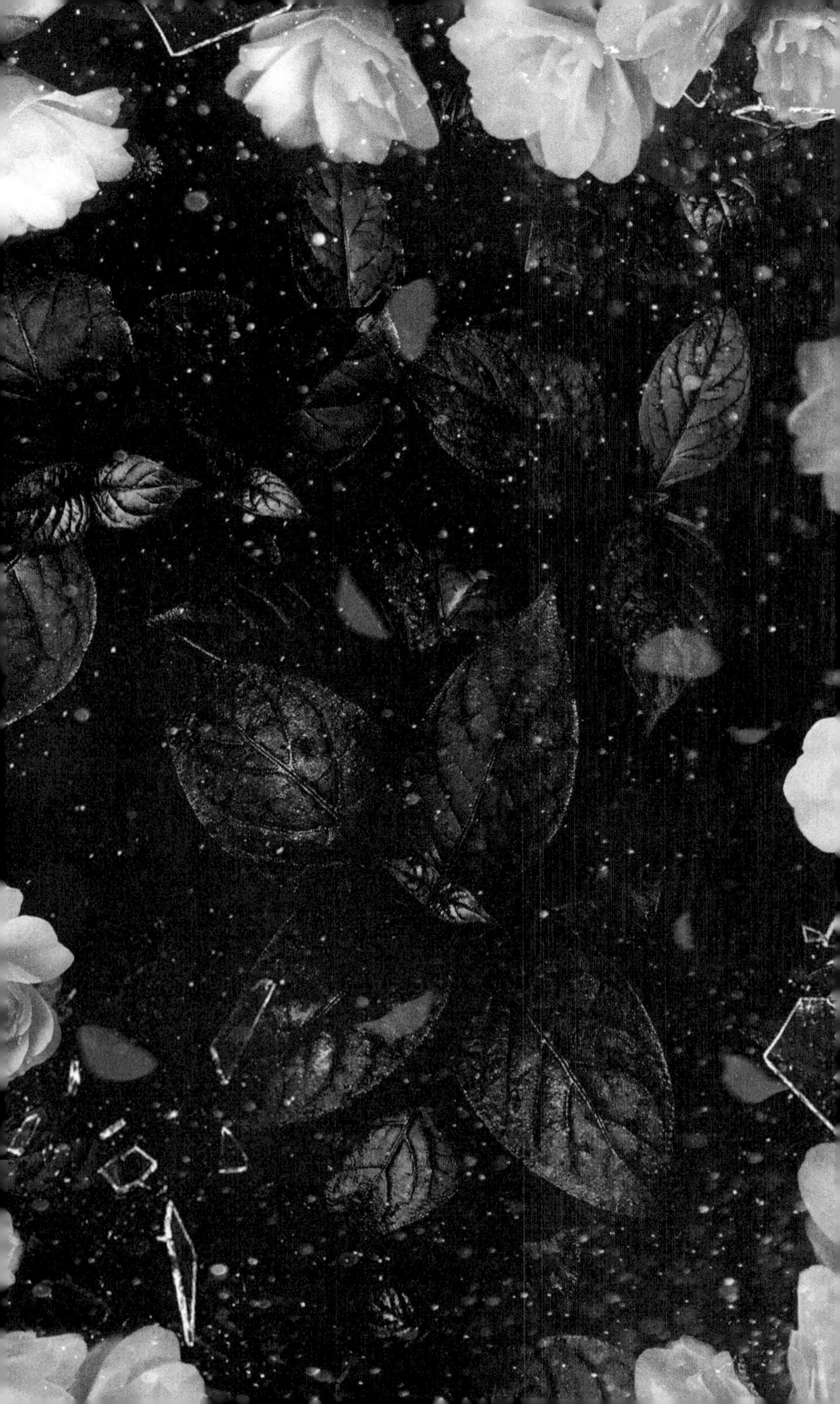

29 AELIA

"Aelia?" Caiden and Roderick rushed to where I lay crumpled on the floor, heaving me onto the bed. Emotions whirled inside me like a cyclone. This could not be the world I lived in. A world where Baylis allied with my tormentor. A world where I erased the mind of the only person who had truly loved me.

"I need a minute," I said, curling myself into a ball. My ankle throbbed with pain. I wanted a mountain of dust. I didn't want to feel anything ever again. My breaths came faster as the world closed in on me. My vision tunneled, growing smaller by the minute.

"I can't breathe." The air in my lungs diminished.

"Aelia, breathe. You must breathe."

I could hear Caiden's voice, but it sounded far away. With each shallow breath, I drifted farther away from my body.

Caiden lay next to me, wrapping his warm body around mine. "Do not let this break you, Aelia."

Tears cascaded down my face. What did I have to live for anymore? Everyone I loved was gone. I wanted to rip my soul into a million pieces and scatter it into the wind.

I buried my face in his neck. This world had beaten me.

Caiden pulled me in closer. "Aelia, look at me." He held my face in his hands. "This will not break you."

"I've been broken for a long time," I said through tears, gasping for air. "There is no fixing me."

"You are not broken, Aelia Springborn. You are strong. I remember the girl I met ten years ago. The girl who has faced death. She is in there somewhere. I know it." His eyes searched mine, for the woman he loved.

I did not know if I had the strength to resurrect her.

"Okay." I sank into Caiden's embrace, matching my heartbeat to his.

Amolie brought a healing tonic. The green viscous liquid tasted like sap and pinecones.

"When this is through, you better serve Gideon's head on a platter." She eyed the two sylph men in the tent.

"Oh, we're planning on it," Roderick said, cracking his knuckles.

"Good... because if you don't. I will." Her voice dripped with vitriol. I wasn't accustomed to seeing this aspect of Amolie.

"Oh, I know you will, my love." Roderick put an arm around the witch.

"His father killed my mother, and he nearly killed my best friend. I will carve his heart from his chest."

I tried not to choke on the tonic as I stifled a laugh. "Thanks, Am. Thank all of you." A calm washed over me.

Everyone nodded.

"I think Aelia needs her rest," Caiden said, hurrying everyone out of the tent. He stoked the fire. The light danced on his face. I wanted to live in this tent with him forever.

Caiden brought me a plate of roasted chicken and vegetables, filling the tent with the mouth-watering aroma of thyme and rosemary.

As I ate, I glanced at Caiden's desk, where the bone scepter slept, waiting for me to return.

"What are you looking at?" Caiden asked.

"The scepter... it calls to me. Talks to me in my head."

He set his plate to the side, a seriousness overtaking his features. "What does it say?"

"It wants my blood. It wants to bind itself to me. I have been beyond the veil, and it knows." Leaning back on the bed, I let out an exasperated sigh.

Caiden shook his head in disbelief. "Lucius was right. It requires a blood sacrifice."

"I don't think it needs an entire sacrifice. Just a prick. You sylphs are so dramatic." I rolled my eyes.

"We need to tell Lucius."

"I don't need a lecture from him."

"He needs to know. Will any blood work? Or just yours?"

I shrugged. "Would you like me to ask it?"

"Yes, of course." Caiden bounded out of bed.

I regretted asking. Of course, they wanted me to communicate with a talking scepter who controlled the Army of the Dead.

"Tomorrow. I am too tired tonight to argue with an ancient artifact."

"Yes, my apologies, you need your rest." He pulled back the pelts from the bed and slid in next to me, pulling me close and running his calloused fingers down my back.

We lay there, holding one another until late into the night.

"Remember when we were looking for the crack in the wall surrounding the bog?" I ran my hands over Caiden's broad chest.

"Of course. It was the first time I got to see your swordplay. You took down an Arachnai on your own."

"And you told me beer tasted better after a battle," I chuckled.

"I was a charmer," he said, stroking my hair.

"You were, and I ate up every bit."

We both laughed.

Caiden's face darkened. "I should have taken you away. Run as far away as we could get. We could've had a family."

I pressed my fingers to his lips. "It does no one any good to dwell on what could've been."

Grasping my hand, he pulled me in closer. "I want you to know. I thought about it. About stealing you away."

"Stop." Hot tears burned behind my eyes.

"Your Promised Day almost killed me." His voice cracked like sharp glass. "I watched you on your pedestal, dressed in white. All those eyes on you. It was unbearable."

A sob caught in my throat. "Caiden, please…"

"And then when your father announced your betrothal to Gideon Ironheart of Highlands. It took everything in me not to slit his throat right there and run away with you."

"I wish you had." A smile crept through my tears.

"Me too, Aelia. Things would have been different. Maybe they would have been worse, but at least we could have been together."

"We have each other now," I said, pulling him in close. "We need to treasure the time we have together."

Caiden squeezed me tight. We could have ruled over the Stormlands together. I wouldn't be this terrible crossbred creature. Shaking my head, I pushed the thoughts from my mind. I couldn't let delusions of grandeur get the better of me now.

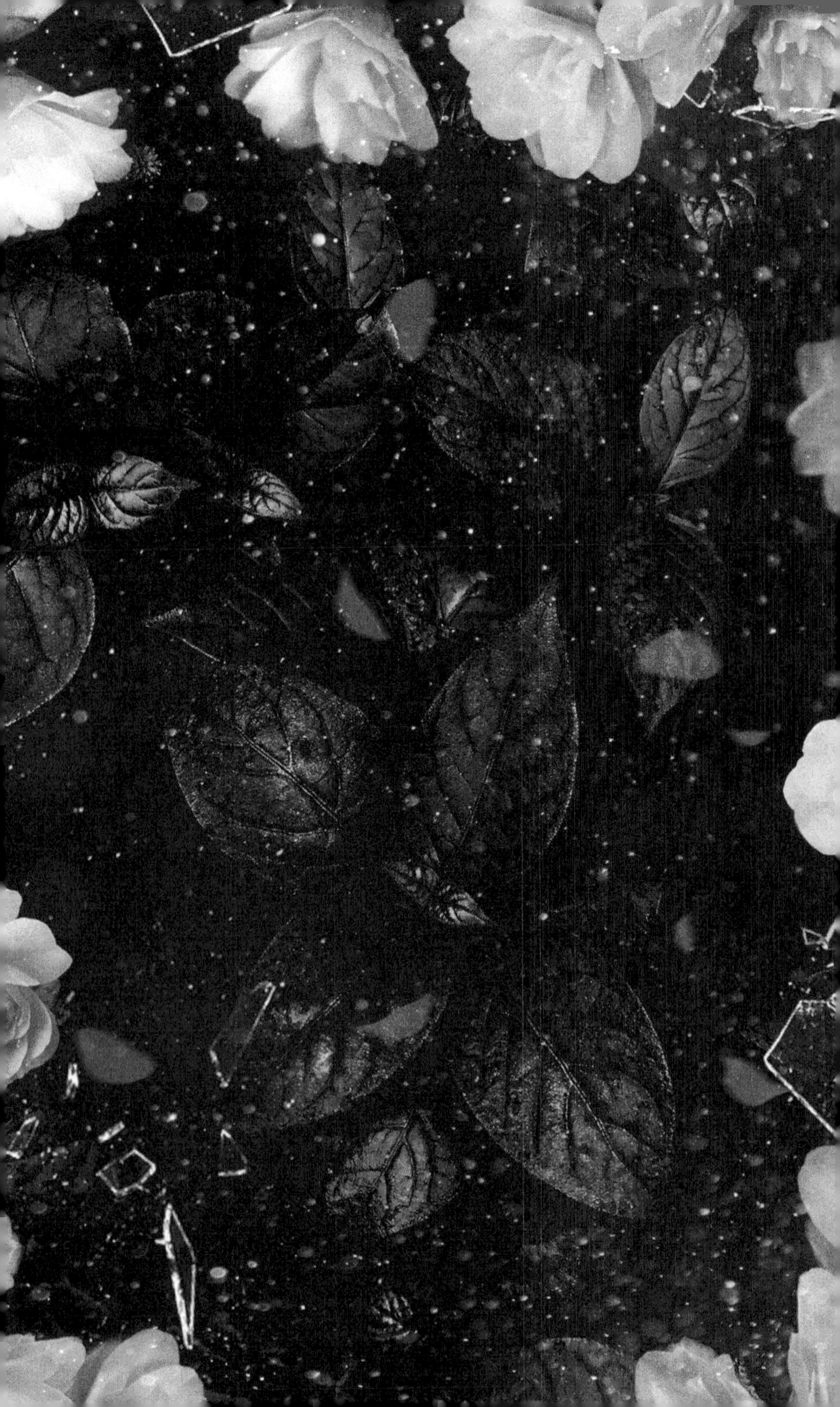

30 AELIA

'*I knew you would be back,*' the voice in the scepter hissed in my ear.

I rolled my eyes. "Who else can control the army?"

'*One who binds their blood to my bones. But you are my chosen one, Aelia.*'

I relayed the message to the group, who stared at me in amazement as I held a conversation with a piece of bone.

"And who are *you* exactly?" I stared at the roof of the tent, expecting something to materialize.

'*Long ago, before the Trinity, before the reign of Crom Cruach, they called me the Morrigan. Goddess of death and victory. All who sought success in war prayed to me. In the War of Three Faces, I tried to turn the tides, but he caught my deceit, scorching my body, binding my soul to these bones.*'

"So, you control the Army of the Dead?"

'*When I died, my legion died. Cruach cursed them to serve him forever.*'

"How did Queen Nysemia come to control you?"

'*Nysemia found me in the deepest part of the Mountains of Lenore, where I had rested for thousands of years. I saw a way back into the world through her. She treated us fairly. But now she is dead, and I require another master.'*

"And you want me to control your army?"

'Only one who has straddled both worlds can control me.'

"What about Lucius? He's half wraith."

I did not want this responsibility.

'He is of the dead, yet he has not stepped beyond the veil.'

"And what if I don't want to be your master?"

'Then bury me in the earth and leave my bones to rot. My army will not fight for the powers of darkness conspiring in secret.'

A bitter chill bit at my heart. "Do you know who is conspiring?"

'I can only speak of those on this side of the veil. But there are souls here who seek to reclaim what they lost long ago in the War of Three Faces. And some have waited longer... Since the Trinity first tamed this land.'

I rubbed my temples. All I wanted was to get my sister, go home to Seaside, and disappear from the world. I needed time to think—time to sort through my feelings.

Caiden, Lucius, Roderick, and Amolie waited for my answer with bated breaths.

"I will think about it," I said, putting the scepter back into its box.

'Be quick, Traitorous Queen, before another finds me.'

The Morrigan quieted.

"With this power. You could rule Moriana," Roderick said, touching the leather box.

"Nysemia had this power, and it got her killed." I turned and threw myself on the bed, covering my face with my hands.

"But you are not Nysemia," Caiden said, taking my hand and kneeling before me. "Become the queen you were always meant to be, Aelia. Rid this land of Gideon and the evil he carries with him before it's too late."

My breath hitched. "I'm not strong enough. I came here to save Baylis, which I intend to do. The dead can wait."

"And what if she doesn't want to be saved?" Lucius asked.

"There is no other choice, Lucius. That person I saw in the camp is not Baylis. Now, let's make a plan."

"Can I interject?" Amolie asked.

"What is it?" I said, my blood running hot.

"If Baylis has the power of sight, could she see us coming?"

"That's not how sight works," I said, tightening my braid. "It takes a great deal of magic to conjure a vision, and she needs to be looking into the future for something specific. Gideon knows we're here. He won't waste her powers on us. He'll want her to be able to perform in front of the Alder King."

Lucius and Roderick spread out a large map depicting a cross-section of the Alder Palace.

"All the courts and kingdoms who attend the revelry will present to the Alder King." Lucius pointed to the throne room on the map. "This is where Baylis will be presented. We will grab her here as she walks off."

I gave Lucius a puzzled look.

"It is the one time she will not be heavily guarded."

"And you're okay with this?" I shot Caiden a look. They risked damaging their fragile relationship with the Alder King.

Caiden shrugged. "What he doesn't know won't hurt him."

Lucius cleared his throat. "May I continue?"

I waved him on.

"Amolie will brew smoke bombs for us. We will position them around the throne room." He pointed to four areas—two at the throne's base and two on a balcony above. "When Baylis comes forward, Amolie will unleash the smoke. Roderick will grab Baylis and make a run for it. There's a side exit here. Where one of my men will wait with a horse."

"Everyone knows their duties. I think we should all get some rest before the ball. We're presenting to the Alder King." Caiden ushered everyone out of the tent.

Amolie lingered, biting her lip.

"What is it?" I asked.

"I think we should talk in private." She motioned for me to follow her.

We walked through the snowy forest to her tent. Once inside, Amolie handed me a hot mug of licorice root tea.

"What did you want to tell me?" I asked, blowing on the hot mug.

Amolie paced back and forth in front of the small stove. "I examined the scepter. The speech is ancient, but I could decipher some of it."

"And?"

"If you bind yourself to the scepter, it will eventually kill you."

I arched my brow as I sipped. Magic demanded a price.

Amolie shook her head. "From what I can tell, it uses your life force to control the dead. Eventually, there will be no more life to take."

"Nysemia had the scepter for hundreds, maybe thousands of years. She looked healthy before her death."

"Nysemia never used the army. It has to be called upon to drain the user."

"So, I'll have an entire army at my disposal but won't be able to use it?"

Amolie shrugged. "If you want to continue living." She twisted her curls around her index finger. "I could do some research on how to break the curse. I once read of magical springs the Trinity placed around Moriana. The text said they were pools of pure magic the Trinity hid away to keep them from falling into the wrong hands. They are said to be able to reverse any curse."

I set down my drink. "Let's focus on tomorrow, and then we can decide if I should bind myself to a talking bone."

Amolie nodded, her hands on her hips.

"Do you think Baylis is under a spell?" I asked.

"Did he put you under a spell when..." She grimaced.

Gideon excelled in manipulation. Even before our minds became entwined, he understood my thoughts—discerning my emotions from my body language and anticipating them before I felt them.

Endearing at first, I quickly learned how dark love could get. The manipulation started subtly, placing doubt in my mind over minor things, planting false memories, and using my father's illness to make me question my sanity.

Seeds of doubt sprouted in my mind. Over time, he picked away at me, piece by piece, as if I were a painting he wanted to change.

I transformed into a specter of my past self, overly willing to fulfill his desires. He became the focal point of my existence, encompassing my entire world. Every breath I drew was dedicated to him. Consequently, I complied without hesitation when he requested me to betray my kingdom. I would have sacrificed my life for him had he commanded it.

"No," I said, taking Amolie's hand. "But that doesn't mean she won't need help."

Amolie gave me a reassuring smile. "I can brew a clarity potion."

Rubbing my thumbs in circles on her silken hands, I gave her a reassuring smile. "You are the smartest person I know. I wish I had some way of thanking you."

"Promise me you won't lose yourself in the darkness again,"

she said, squeezing my hand. "I don't know if I could bear to watch you slowly kill yourself again."

I let out a long breath. "I'm sorry, Amolie. I shouldn't have asked you to aid in my self-destruction."

"I did it willingly. Better to have you half alive than dead."

I gave her a smirk. "Still. I will not ask it of you again."

"I am worried, Aelia. Worried about you and Caiden. Worried when the time comes for you to erase his mind, you will disintegrate along with the memories."

I feared that too—feared I could not do what the bargain demanded of me. Feared I would float away with every memory I erased.

"I'll be fine." Clearing my throat. "Keep the whole scepter soul-sucking thing to yourself for now, will you, Am? I don't want Caiden to worry."

"If that's what you want." She raised her mug to me as I left.

Caiden brought two attendants from his court to help us prepare for the ball.

I winced as the attendant pulled my hair into an intricate braid, entwining fresh flowers into the strands. The sheer dress I wore left little to the imagination. In a Sylph Court, such attire would hardly draw attention; beings adorned solely in wings and sparkles were the norm. Unlike them, I lacked a fondness for exhibitionism, choosing instead to complement my outfit with a shawl crafted from the fur of a white rabbit.

The wings Itra fashioned for us hung heavy on our backs.

Placing a diadem on my head, I peered at myself in the mirror, baring my fangs. A creature of the blood stared back at me.

"You look stunning." Caiden's reassuring voice wrapped around me like a warm blanket.

"Thank you. I have never worn something so…"

"So, sylph?"

He wore a velvet doublet with streaks of lightning intricately embroidered into the fabric. A lengthy navy cape lined with wolf fur flowed down his back. Impeccably styled hair and a crown of silver lightning adorned his head.

"No wings?" I gave him a chiding smile. Wings were reserved for the women of the sylph courts.

"Not tonight." He kissed my gloved hand.

It felt peculiar to have a layer of silk separating me from the world. Nevertheless, his lips touching my hand sent a rush of excitement through my veins.

"We better get going. We don't want to be late for the Alder King."

"Just a moment." I pulled him in for a kiss. His body tensed and then relaxed under my grip.

His mouth agape, he blinked furiously at me. "What was that for?"

"I don't know how many more times I'll be able to do it."

A smile pierced his lips, although his eyes told me the inevitability of our bargain scratched at his heart.

"Get a room," Roderick said, standing in the doorway, dressed in his finest Stormlands armor, holding Amolie's hand.

"We have one, and you're in it," Caiden said, giving Roderick the finger.

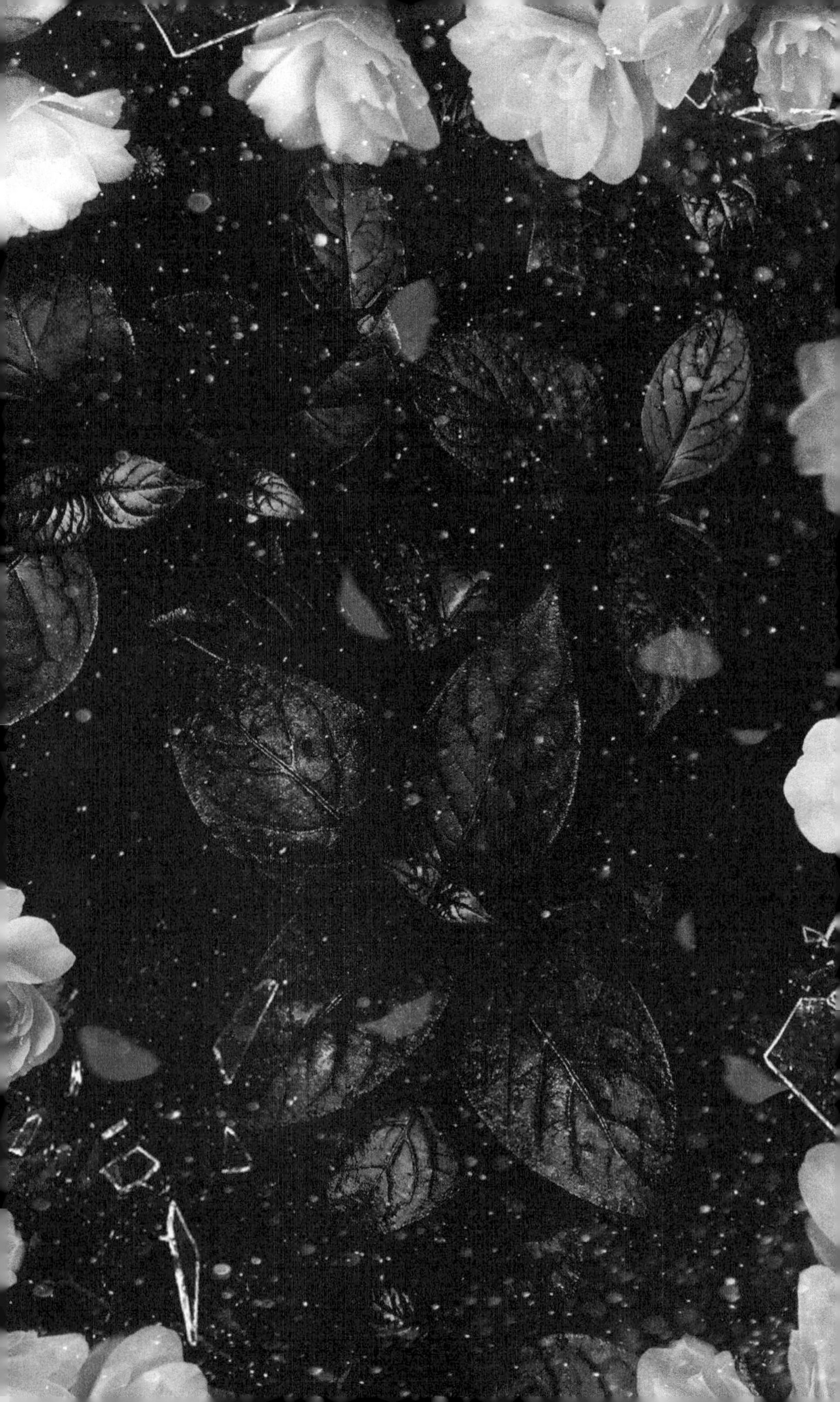

31 AELIA

THE ALDER PALACE PROVED OVERWHELMING UP CLOSE. DESPITE being winter, flowered vines wrapped their way up the trunk of the massive tree. The fragrance of blooming flowers wafted through the air, enveloping the palace in an intoxicating blend of sweet, natural perfume. Birds called to one another from extended limbs. A waterfall cascaded gracefully down the side of the ancient tree, sparkling like jewels in the winter sun. Degloving my hand, I let the cool water calm my racing heart.

Creatures of every race and creed waited to be ushered into the great hall for an audience with the Alder King.

Amolie elbowed me in the ribs. "Centaurs, look, actual centaurs." She bit her nails, trying to contain her excitement.

A herd of centaurs waited to be announced, swishing their tails back and forth. Their human halves adorned with intricately designed leather armor. A blanket of woven snowflakes covered their horse halves. Legendary warriors, they kept to their own.

Behind the centaurs waited the halflings—short creatures, no taller than a child, with pointed ears and round faces. The southern halflings were known for their ability to mine the most precious jewels, and the northern halflings were considered the finest brewers of ale in Moriana.

I searched the crowd for Gideon and Baylis but could not find them. My heart pulsed with anticipation. *Breathe, Aelia, just breathe. Everything will be fine.*

A courtier called our name. "Lord Caiden Stormweaver of the Court of Storms."

We entered the great hall. Garlands of flowers hung from the wooden rafters. The smell of fresh-cut wood cloaked everything. Sylph, fairies, and other creatures crowded the throne room. Some watched the procession and whispered to one another, while others dined on elk hearts and cake. At the far corner of the room, men held their mouths open while naked women drowned them in enchanted wine. The red liquid spilled out of their mouths and over their chests, but still, they begged for more. In the distance, a lute played.

Caiden and I led the way, followed by Amolie and Roderick. Eyes watched us as we descended the petal-covered aisle toward the dais, where the Alder King perched above his court.

"Don't look at him until he addresses us," Caiden had warned us on the ride over.

I stared at my feet, watching my glass shoes smash the fresh petals, releasing their sweet aromas.

Reaching the dais, we fell to our knees, honoring the Alder King.

"Rise," a voice older than time proclaimed from high above.

Alder King: an ancient creature whose existence predated the sylphs. Skin like weathered leather stretched over a refined bone. Atop his silver mane rested a crown crafted of golden antlers. His serene white eyes locked onto mine, captivating me with his merciless stare as he lazily tapped his throne with long, clawed fingers.

Next to him, Tharan sat wearing a kelly green velvet vest

embroidered with golden trees. His wine-red hair brushed to a lustrous sheen. A bored expression splashed upon his elegant face.

His sister, Briar, sat poised opposite her brother. Her dark hair cascaded onto the dais: a pale woman, half of her face replaced by decaying wood. A faint light flickered where an eye should have been. She did not acknowledge my presence.

"Your court has not visited for an age." The king stared at Caiden.

Caiden cleared his throat. "My king, I know our kingdoms have a rocky history, but let us come together to celebrate the solstice and the dawning of a new year."

The ancient kind nodded approvingly. "Allies are always a good thing."

"They are indeed. Let me present to you a token of our friendship." Caiden mustered lightning between his hands, pulling and manipulating it into a long wand. The Hunt aimed their spears at Caiden but lowered them at the king's behest. Twisting and turning, Caiden shaped the lightning into a staff. With one final flick of his finger, the lightning hardened.

"For you, Lord of the Forest, a staff of pure lightning."

The king's stoic demeanor lightened to one of joy. "I've always envied the Stormweaver line. Illya favored your line."

"You are more powerful than any Stormweaver could ever hope to be, my lord," Caiden said, presenting the staff to the Alder King.

"Thank you," he said, twirling the staff.

A courtier motioned for us to leave.

We hurried to an alcove, scanning the room for any signs of Gideon.

I released the breath I had been holding in. "He's intimidating."

Caiden slid a reassuring arm around my shoulders. "Would you expect anything less from an ancient god?"

"I guess you're right."

He twirled his index finger in a circle. "Alright, everyone, spread out. You know what you must do."

We dispersed, each carrying a tiny smoke bomb in our pockets. A familiar silhouette appeared as I climbed the wooden stairs to the balcony. Ursula. I'd recognize the curve of her body anywhere. Her fish-like face lit up at the sight of me.

"Glad to see you made it out of that shithole town in one piece." She kissed me on the cheek.

"You're looking lovely, as usual." I meant it. With blue hair pinned back in waves and a dress of woven scales, I couldn't help but put my hands on her waist.

"Care for some bubbles?" She handed me a flute of sparkling wine.

"Thank you," I said, taking the flute from her and downing it in one gulp.

"Someone's thirsty," she said, giving me a wink.

My eyes darted around the room, looking for any sign of Gideon, Erissa, or Baylis, but found nothing.

I leaned over the polished balcony. The false wings were heavy on my back, straining my core. I watched Tharan presiding over the line of kingdoms, who had yet to pay homage to the king. His playful demeanor replaced by a regal one.

"Care to tell me what you're doing here, Springborn? Council Courts don't attend Wild Court revelries." She slid her arm around my waist. "This dress looks beautiful on you," she whispered into my ear, her breath on my skin, pricking the hair on the back of my neck.

"Thank you." My cheeks flushed. From across the balcony, Caiden gave me a warning look.

I rolled my eyes at him, removing Ursula's arm.

Ursula frowned. "This is a job, isn't it?"

I studied my nails. "Everything is a job, Ursula."

She ran her pearlescent hand down the side of my face. "Even on a holiday?"

"Mercenaries don't take holidays."

She leaned closer, the smell of wine heavy on her breath. "What about a break?"

"I think that could be arranged."

She pulled me in for a kiss.

I leaned into her, savoring the briny taste of her lips.

Remember why you're here, Aelia. Reluctantly, I pushed her away.

"You're no fun." She pouted. "Come and find me when you're ready to party." She kissed my cheek before disappearing into the revelry.

I shed the pair of heavy wings, stashing them in a closet, then returned to the balcony, where Caiden waited for me. "Everything alright?"

"Just old friends catching up." I pulled him in close, kissing his ear, dropping the smoke bomb in a nearby plant.

"Clever." His hands gripped my waist, igniting a fire in my chest.

I clicked my tongue. "Don't get distracted, Lord."

We waltzed around the great hall, keeping our eyes peeled for any sign of Gideon. A string band played. Creatures, already drunk on honey wine, danced seductively. A small satyr offered a tray of cubed elk hearts on gold toothpicks.

"No, thank you," I said, waving him off.

The dancers moved into a more formal line, preparing for the traditional sylph waltz.

"Would you like to dance?" Caiden extended his hand, leading me toward the dance floor.

"Just like old times," I said with a smile.

We took our places in the line, bowing to one another, before joining hands, bringing me back to when we danced together at the Ostara Ball in Elyria. A lifetime ago.

Caiden and I had stirred up quite a commotion. It was customary for a princess of the Midlands to dance with potential suitors during Ostara. However, in my eyes, no other person existed in the world but Caiden. We danced until our feet throbbed with exhaustion. I wore a bloodred satin dress, my head crowned with a wreath of roses. Caiden sported an outfit of white and gold, highlighting his golden locks.

My heart ached at the memory. The world seemed so simple then.

I gave my body to Caiden that night, letting him teach me the ways of love. Our bodies entwined, sweat dripping from every pore as rain pelted the glass-roofed cottage.

The world disappeared around us as memories of lustful youth danced in my head.

The music changed, and we switched partners. To my surprise, Tharan waited with an outstretched hand.

"Hello, Lord of Nothing." I gave him a coy smile.

"Hello, Traitorous Queen." His hand around my waist made me weak in the knees. "That's quite the dress you have on."

"I'm surprised a sylph would bat an eye at such a thing."

He twirled me. My dress sparkled in the firelight like the sun glinting off a thousand diamonds.

"I can still admire you," he said, bringing me in so close I could smell the pine on his skin.

I blushed. "Thank you for saving me the other day."

"It was nothing. No guest of the Alder King will be harmed while in his domain." His hand on the small of my back hitched the breath in my lungs.

I stared into his eyes. I could not help but be drawn to him. He looked at me in a way few had.

I swallowed the lust blooming in my chest. "Do you know if Gideon is here?"

Tharan shook his head. "No, but not all courts will come on the first night. There are smaller balls taking place throughout the kingdom. Many people attend multiple gatherings in one night. This one is very formal. The others are… more debaucherous."

I nodded as if I understood.

Tharan leaned in close, making the hairs on the back of my neck perk up. "I am glad to see you, Aelia of the Midlands." His sultry voice made my mouth dry.

The music changed once again, and we parted ways.

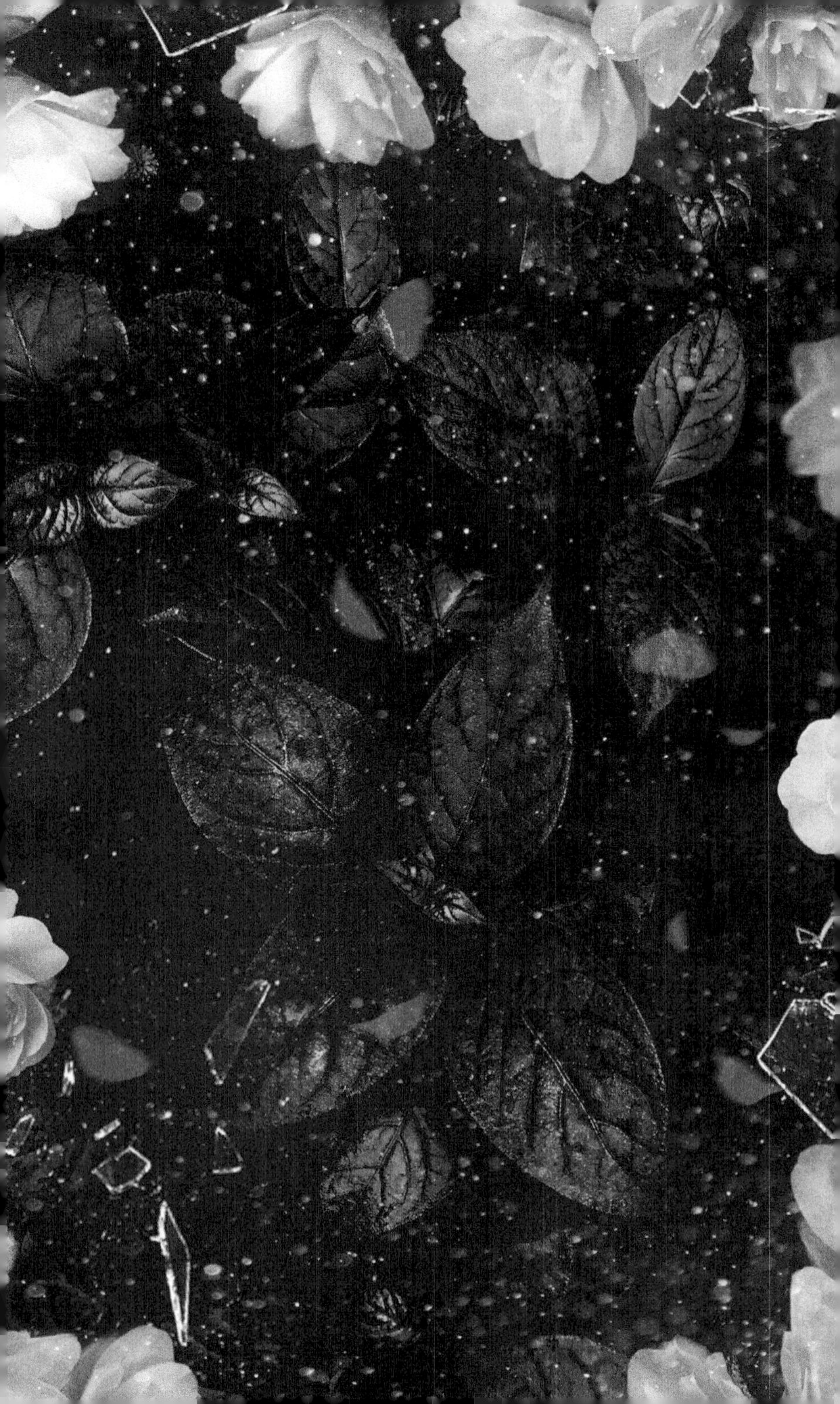

32 AELIA

I headed to the bar, where Caiden stood chatting with Amolie and Roderick. My skin still tingled from Tharan's touch.

"I've never seen so many creatures," Amolie said, sipping wine.

"The Alder King is of the old world. Many creatures pay homage to him," Caiden said as he surveyed the crowd. "Did you have fun with the Prince of the Forest?"

"He's my friend," I said, staring at Tharan, who flirted with a pack of fauns. The females twisted their hair around their fingers, laughing at whatever joke he made.

The night grew late, and Gideon still hadn't made an appearance. "This is pointless. Baylis isn't coming." I slugged back another glass of bubbly, letting the liquor loosen my limbs.

Caiden sighed. "I'm sorry, Aelia, maybe the Hunt spooked them."

Shrugging, I downed another glass of champagne. "She's not my sister anymore."

Caiden gave me a knowing glance. "We can regroup in the morning. Let's not waste tonight."

We danced until sweat dripped down our bodies, and my dress

stuck to my skin. I had not been this free in a long time. I pulled Caiden in close for a kiss. He tasted like spring rain. His greedy mouth enveloped mine as if I were a delicious desert he could not get enough of.

A hand tapped me on the shoulder. I turned around to see Ursula; her sea-glass eyes glowed in the dim light of the dance floor.

"Save some for me," she said, pressing her lips against mine. This time, I did not hold myself back, pressing my body into hers, letting my hands wander.

Caiden joined us in our lustful embrace, snaking his tongue up my neck while his hands went to Ursula's hips.

The room spun as Caiden and Ursula pulled me off the dance floor toward a more secluded hideaway where we could fully explore one another.

Before we could make our escape, the door to the throne room swung open, and a male guard stumbled in, holding his neck, blood stained the pale wood floor beneath. The music stopped, and the crowd parted as the young man fell to his knees before Tharan.

"Goblins," he said before collapsing into Tharan's arms.

The crowd erupted into chaos. Creatures fled. Lords called for their armies. The Alder King stood, directing his Wild Hunt to defend the palace.

"We need to go," Caiden said, dropping my hand and signaling for Roderick to follow him. Roderick pulled the earring from his earlobe, the chain transforming into a whip of pure light.

I tried to shake off the liquor coursing through my veins. *Focus, Aelia, focus.* I stumbled over my feet, falling into the door, knocking my head on the brass knob.

My head throbbed.

Tharan's voice thundered in my ears, "Aelia, look at me."

His face came into view.

"What happened?" I felt the sore spot on my head.

"You hit your head. We need to get you out of here." Amolie held a piece of Tharan's shirt to the bloodied bump.

"It'll heal shortly. Let's go," I said, kicking off my glass slippers.

We returned to the throne room, where the Alder King consulted with two of his warriors. A woman, the height of a giant with deep umber skin and black hair, stood beside a slender male with amber eyes and skin the color of pea soup.

Tharan sat me down on the steps to the dais. "Just wait here a moment."

"Aelia, I'm scared," Amolie said, taking my hand in hers.

I patted her hand reassuringly. "It's nothing Roderick can't handle."

A blinding pain blasted through my head, while a hot scream burned in my chest. Had I not already been sitting I would have been brought to my knees.

"Apologies for our tardiness," Gideon's voice echoed through the now-empty hall.

I forced my eyes to open.

Gideon, Erissa, and Baylis stood at the far end of the throne room, dressed in the red battle armor of the Highlands. A hawk etched into their breastplates.

"What is the meaning of this?" The Alder King's thunderous voice rattled in my aching head.

"I'll make you an offer," Gideon said as he approached the king, his black cape swaying behind him. Picking up an apple drenched in sugar, he ran a callous finger along the desert before tasting it and grimacing. "Disgusting."

Amolie and I exchanged glances. The smoke bombs were still

set. Amolie could use her magic to explode them, but we had to time it correctly.

The Alder King stood like a statue, unmovable and unyielding. "An offer for what?"

The warriors at his side drew their swords.

An evil grin cut Gideon's face in two. "Give me your Wild Hunt, and in exchange, I will let you live."

A wave of horror swept over me as I glared at my sister standing next to Gideon, her long blonde hair braided behind her ears. The flickering of the torches played with her features, casting shadows across her delicate face. No longer a sacrificial lamb but a hardened member of Gideon's inner circle.

Aiming her crossbow at the Alder King, determination flared in Baylis's gray eyes.

The Alder King laughed. "The Hunt has served me for ten thousand years. They are bound to my blood. They will never serve you."

"Then I guess I'll have to take that from you, too." He nodded to Erissa. The mage stretched out her arms, pooling her magic into the green bloodstone resting on top of her wooden staff.

The two warriors leapt off the dais, but before they could reach Gideon, a wall of smoke blocked their way. The soldiers coughed as the gas filled their lungs.

The Alder King's eyes rolled white, bringing the thorns of the throne to life; wrapping themselves around their master, they created an armor for the king.

Growing into a massive being, light exploded from his fists. "This is my court, and it will remain my court until the day I walk into the abyss." Gripping the staff Caiden had given him earlier, he sent a bolt of lightning toward Gideon, which he deflected.

My eyes frantically searched for Tharan.

Conjuring her magic, Erissa sent a flash of a green bolt hurtling at the Alder King. Holding up his staff, he tried to block her attack, but it was useless. Erissa's magic disintegrated the lightning rod, turning it to ash in the Alder King's hands.

He staggered backward in shock. "What is this?"

A wind blew into the throne room as Erissa called upon an ancient power. "I possess the power of Crom Cruach, who demands retribution for his exile beyond the veil." Her voice echoed through the chamber.

The Alder King's eyes widened at Erissa's show of force. Her power rivaled his own.

From the ceiling, a storm of thorns as thick as my arm rained down on Gideon.

Reaching a hand into the air, Erissa turned the thorns into petals. They floated daintily, coating the room in a colorful blanket.

Amolie and I stowed ourselves in an alcove out of the way. My chest heaved as I tried to piece together how my sister had become entangled in all this. Did she know what she was doing? Was she under his control? The dreaded thought crept into my mind, freezing the blood in my veins. Was I going to have to kill Baylis?

The warriors cut through the smoke, their steel blades shining in the flame light, feet crushing the fresh petals. Baylis fired her crossbow at the weak points in their armor, catching the female in the shoulder. The bolt didn't stop her.

Holding her sword high, she pounced on Gideon. Blood Riders emerged from the darkness, their long fangs on display, wedging themselves between Gideon and the Hunt. Sparks flew as their weapons clashed.

"Do you know what destroys a forest?" Erissa said, a ball of fire in her hands.

"You think your puny fire can harm me?" A thicket of thorns grew from the floor, building a wall between Erissa and the king.

Hammering the wall with fire, Erissa set the palace ablaze.

Fear coiled like a snake in my gut. I reached for Amolie. We had to get out of here.

Behind the trio, Tharan crouched, fingers to his lips. A serpent-like vine sprang from his palms, slithering silently across the floor.

"We have to do something," I told Amolie, whose fingertips sparked with magic.

"I'll cover you," she said, forming a shield with her magic.

Calling Little Death to my hand, I hurled the dagger toward the mage.

It hit her wrist. She cried out in pain, sending a fireball flying into the rafters.

Tharan's vines struck at Gideon, grabbing him by the neck and pulling him to the ground. Baylis screamed as Gideon struggled against the vines.

The Blood Riders and Wild Hunt continued to battle one another. Blood soaked the floor, but neither side backed down.

Erissa turned her gaze upon me. "You bitch. Stay out of this." She fired a bolt of dark magic my way.

Amolie threw up her shield, blocking the attack.

"Run!" I yelled.

"Where? They've locked us in," Amolie said frantically.

Erissa moved towards us gracefully. "There is no place for you to go."

Behind her, Tharan and Gideon engaged in heated swordplay.

A flash of light blue caught my eye. "The king," I said to Amolie. "Baylis is going for the king." A gaping hole smoldered in the wall of thorns. I called my dagger, but it would not return to my hand.

Erissa cackled. "You and that fucking dagger. You thought you could beat me once again. But I know where to put my strikes now." She held up a hand, sending a blast of energy, knocking the

Alder King to his knees. He grasped at his neck as though an invisible rope choked him.

In an instant, she stood before him, pinning the king against his throne.

"Amolie. Now!"

Amolie triggered the smoke bombs, filling the room with a thick, acrid fog. She pushed a piece of damp fabric into my hands—valerian root.

The smoke burned my eyes as I ran toward the throne. "Baylis, don't!"

I reached the king in time to see Baylis plunge my dagger into his heart. Hate and joy flashed in her gray eyes. The Alder King cried out in pain.

A hot scream formed in my throat, dragging its claws against soft tissue. I unleashed it into the ether.

I dove on top of Baylis, knocking us both off the dais. The ground rocked underneath us. The king and the land were connected, and the land called out to its master—feeling his pain.

"Don't fight me, Baylis. I'm trying to save you!" She squirmed underneath my grip.

"I don't need to be saved," she said in an alien voice.

I held the cloth over her mouth, and she quieted, her body going limp.

"This is all just a bad dream," I said, pulling her sleeping body to the side.

Through the smoke, the Wild Hunt arrived on the backs of their dire wolves, pouncing on the Blood Riders and tearing them to shreds. The sounds of screams echoed through the massive hall.

Once the Blood Riders were desecrated, the wolves directed their attention toward Erissa. Sparks flew from her fingertips as she frantically struggled to open a portal.

The clash of weapons distracted me from Erissa. Gideon's sword pressed down upon Tharan's, pinning him to the floor.

I had to help him.

'*Gideon.*' I tried to make my voice as alluring as possible. '*Gideon, I know you can hear me.*' I cracked an eye open to check if he reacted, but he remained focused on Tharan.

This called for drastic measures. I conjured the magic inside me, hurling it like a lasso around Gideon's mind, pulling it tight.

Gideon let out a cry of pain, stumbling backward, releasing Tharan.

I pulled tighter.

What are you doing? He held his hands to his head, wincing in pain.

'*Something I should have done a long time ago.*' I pulled the lasso tighter.

Gideon cried out in pain, dropping his sword.

Stop. Please! The desperation in his voice filled me with glee.

I tightened the lasso one last time. I wanted him to beg.

Seeing an opportunity, Tharan ran his blade through Gideon's gut.

He grasped his abdomen, trying desperately to stop the blood, a look of shock plastered across his devilishly handsome face.

Erissa let out a shrill scream, knocking the room to their knees. She scrambled to where Gideon lay, pounding her staff into the floor.

A glowing portal opened.

"You will all pay for this," she said before pulling Gideon's lifeless body in and closing it.

Tharan rushed to his father. "No, no, please, no." His hands fumbled to stop the bleeding.

The king held his son's face in his hands. "I know we've had our differences, Son." His voice grew fainter with each word. "But I want you to know… you are my greatest achievement."

Tears welled in Tharan's verdant eyes as he gripped his father's wrists. "Father, please. A healer! We need a healer!"

Amolie ran to where the king lay, pulling the dagger from his heart. She plucked a small piece of bark from her skirt, placed it in her mouth, and chewed it vigorously before mashing it into the gaping wound in the king's chest.

We all held our breaths as she worked. "The wound is deep. The dagger was made to kill gods."

The king's breath shallowed as he reached for his son. "It is your time to rule." With his remaining strength, he placed the crown of antlers on Tharan's head. "You are the Alder King now."

"No," Tharan whispered, holding his father in his arms. "I'm not ready."

But the king could not hear his pleas.

Hadron, the reaper, appeared. He gave me a knowing smile before lifting the soul from the Alder King's body, taking it to the land beyond the veil.

No one moved.

An original was dead, and my sister had killed him. If Tharan wanted to kill Baylis, I wouldn't blame him, but I would die defending her.

Tharan kissed his father's forehead.

Amolie was beside me then, grabbing my hand. "We need to get Baylis out of here."

Tharan stood, surveying the bloodied throne room, shaking his head, unable to comprehend his father's death.

The remaining members of the Hunt fell to their knees before him. No longer was Tharan the Lord of Nothing, but the Alder King.

Tharan's eyes searched the room for a familiar face, for guidance, but he found none. Swallowing hard, he turned his gaze to his blood-soaked hands as if they held the answers he sought.

A slow clap rang out from the back of the room.

Princess Briar stood with her blue eyes locked on Tharan. "Well done, Brother. I wondered how you were planning to take the throne from me."

"I do not want this," Tharan said, his voice little more than a whisper.

"Once the crown is placed, there is no going back. This kingdom is yours."

She kicked the doors to the great hall open, revealing a forest set ablaze.

"Good luck." She leaned her head back, cackling like a lunatic, before fading into the shadows.

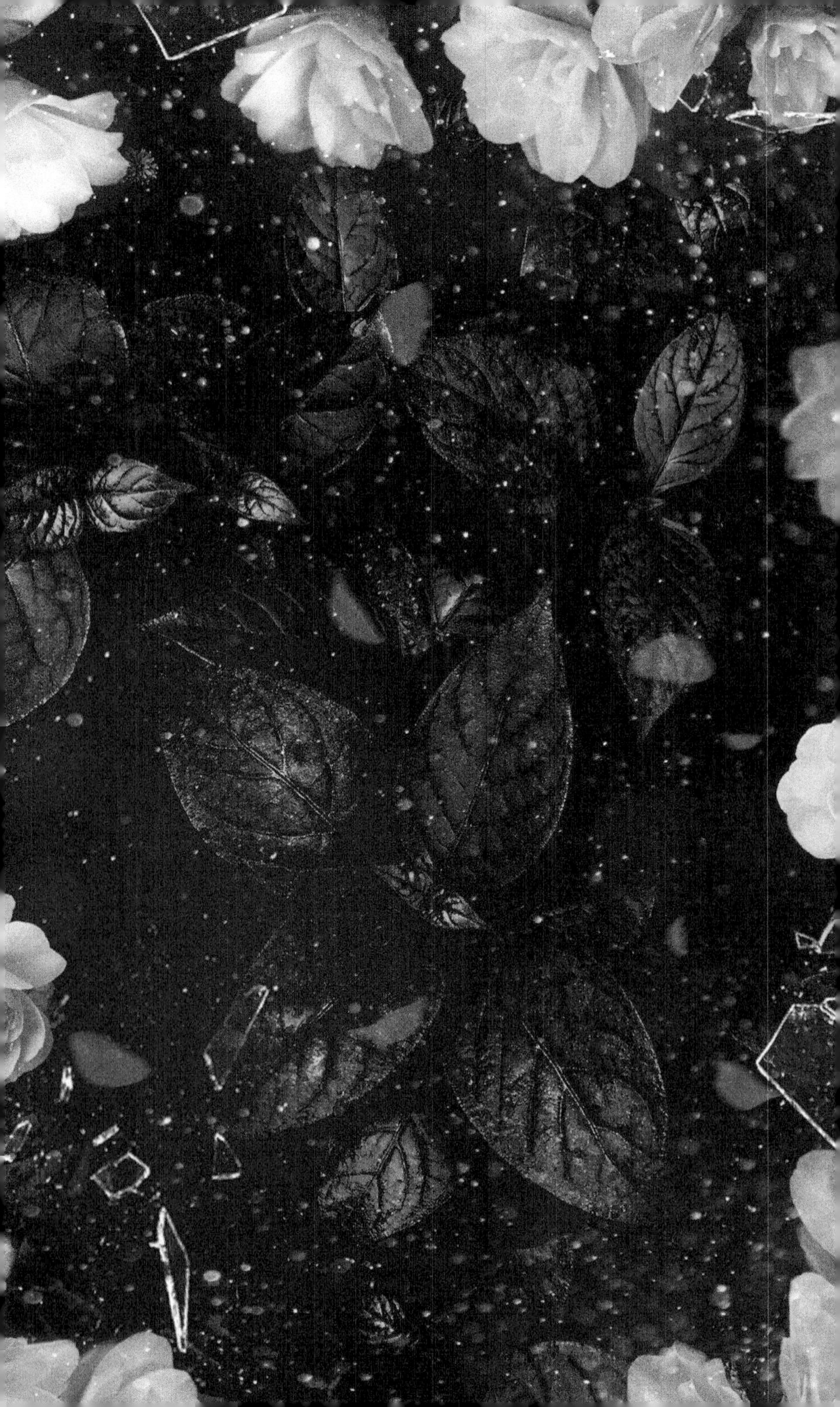

33 CAIDEN

Fires enveloped the entire forest. While the courts and kingdoms had been distracted by drinking and fornicating the night away, Gideon had been busy. How long had he been allied with the goblins? What had he promised them in return for their help?

Lucius waited with two horses. "Quickly," he said as the fires consumed everything in sight. The smell of ash and burnt bodies hung heavy in the air. "I saved some of our items. The goblins came out of nowhere."

Caiden choked on the heavy smoke as their horses' hooves thundered on the charred earth, the fires ravaging the once-lush forest, burning through the freshly fallen snow.

"Where's Aelia and Amolie?" Lucius asked.

"They're in the palace. Tharan is protecting them. It's safer there until we have this under control." The heat seared the men's skin as they rode. "And what of the scepter?" Caiden yelled over the sound of battle, coughing with each breath.

"I hid it," Lucius said firmly as they approached the camp. The Stormlands army fought back the goblins, using their gifts of rain to help put out the fires where they could.

As they neared the battle, Caiden leapt from his horse, pulling his sword from its sheath, bringing it down on a goblin's head. Green blood oozed from the gash.

Known for their brutality, mountain goblins were no ordinary foes. Tall with thick, leathery skin and heat-seeking red eyes, their ears could sense their opponent a mile away. Luckily, the sound of the forest burning drowned out their ability to sense any incoming attacks.

Roderick used a battle ax and his whip to cut through throngs of goblins while sylphs from the Court of Wings flew on Pegasus, impaling Gideon's men on golden spears.

A declaration of war. Gideon wanted to make a statement. He wanted them all to suffer.

The ground trembled as a wave of energy erupted from the Alder Palace.

"Hold on," Roderick called as they braced for impact.

Caiden created a dome of electricity around them, letting the wave crash over it.

A groan came from the earth itself.

"What's happening?" Lucius yelled from across the camp.

Caiden pulled his sword from the gut of a goblin, wiping the sweat from his brow. "I don't know. The forest is… angry."

Roots sprung from the ground, wrapping themselves around the fallen goblins. The creatures screamed, digging their nails into the earth. Their eyes pleaded for help, but there was none to be had, for they had angered the ancient forest, and now it would take its revenge. Dragging the creatures beneath their gnarled trunks, the trees silenced the screeching creatures.

Caiden fought to catch his breath. They needed more men.

Gideon's army moved in on the camps, using the goblins as lambs to slaughter before they came to finish who remained.

Not one kingdom had been foolish enough to bring their entire army, but they had all brought their best soldiers as a sign of strength. Gideon wanted this—he wanted to wipe out the strongest.

A pack of centaurs appeared at the edge of our camp. Their mighty spears glowed with the Light of Illya, a sacred stone for concentrating magic.

"Join us," the head centaur said, his face carved by the winds of time. "If we band together, we can beat them."

"Form a line," Roderick shouted, raising his battle ax high in the air. The remaining soldiers joined with the centaurs and other courts.

Gideon's men wore their traditional red armor with the black hawk crest. Winged helmets adorned their heads. The size of Gideon's army seemed to have tripled, no doubt hidden with a cloaking spell until they were needed.

The men stood stoically in perfect formation, banging their fists against their iron armor. A human army had not taken on a sylph hoard in the history of Moriana. The crows would feast on their corpses in the morning.

"They're glamoured," a centaur said.

Oblivious to their impending deaths, the men stared fearlessly into the oncoming armies.

"Ready!" the centaur called. The flapping of wings overhead filled the air as the forest burned around them, gilding the battlefield in a golden hue. Caiden took a deep breath, steadying his racing heart. *Illya guides my sword.*

Gideon's men did not move, did not flinch at the threat of imminent death.

Brutus Strong, Gideon's chief commander, rode a gray stallion through the rows of men, his face cracked from years of harsh terrain on countless battlefields. Behind him, two thick draft horses pulled a siege crossbow on a wagon. Four men sat atop the structure, loading a bolt into the bow.

Arrows rained down from the trees where the halflings had taken up residence, killing the men closest to the trees but missing the crossbow.

"Forward!" the centaur commanded. The armies of the sylph moved together in formation. Still, the Highland army stood firm.

The Court of Wings blasted the siege crossbow with their spears, killing one soldier, but that could not stop the inevitable.

The crossbow fired a heavy bolt of solid adamant into the air, skewering a Pegasus. The creature cried out in a deafening scream, falling from the sky. Its body slammed into the earth, killing two sylphs.

Gideon came prepared for war.

Lightning flickered at Caiden's fingertips.

"Forward!" Brutus called to the men. Gideon's army marched on. Their rhythmic footsteps shook the ground beneath their feet.

Caiden's heart beat wildly in his chest.

The soldiers outnumbered them ten to one. He had to think fast.

Scanning the sylph forces, he spotted a centaur carrying a shield polished to a mirrored shine.

"Hold up your shield," Caiden yelled over the sound of marching feet. The centaur nodded in understanding, tilting the shield toward the oncoming legion. Caiden sent a blast of lightning that ricocheted off the mirrored surface, splaying out like an electric scythe, taking off the heads of an entire row of soldiers.

Unfazed, Gideon's men marched forward.

The clash of weapons echoed across the burning forest as creatures fought to maintain control of the Woodland Realm. Without the aid of the Wild Hunt, they would soon be slaughtered.

Cries of pain rang out as the fighting continued. Death hung in the air. Caiden had been to battle before, but this was a slaughter.

There would be no honorable cease here. Gideon wanted them on their knees. And they would not go without a fight.

The three men fought side by side, revealing the blood coating their skin. Each kill, a notch on their belt.

"Hell of a solstice party? Am I right?" Caiden said through ragged breaths, as he stuck his sword through a Highland soldier. The boy's youthful face stared up at him with empty eyes. Caiden swallowed the guilt in his chest. Gideon had sent his greenest men to be fodder.

"I always like it when they keep it interesting," Lucius said, taking down a fat goblin with an arrow through the head. The creature toppled over like a sack of potatoes.

Roderick snapped his whip of light at two Highland soldiers, ripping them from head to pelvis. Three goblins jumped him from behind, but they were no match for the mammoth man. Pulling them off, one by one, he buried his ax in their thick skulls.

"Follow me! This is what we were born for," he yelled to his men. Chaos danced in his eyes. His men would follow him anywhere, even into the bowels of hell if he asked.

Caiden did not know how long they could hold them. As if Illya had heard his prayers, a blinding light shot out from the Alder Palace, reaching into the heavens. The fighting ceased as soldiers from both sides stared, mouths agape, at the blinding light.

"The Alder King is dead," said a voice from the crowd.

At the heart of the battlefield grew a twisted tree. Ripping through its gnarled bark, Tharan appeared, the crown of antlers resting on his head.

Caiden's heart leapt into his throat at the sight of him. A fearsome king replaced the playboy prince. His green eyes shone with rage, and his scar glowed silver.

Tharan towered over the soldiers. Where once he had nails, now thick claws emerged from his fingers. He tilted his head back and howled a deep guttural sound, sending a shiver down Caiden's spine. A call to the Wild Hunt.

"Enough," he said in a deep and ancient voice. "This is my kingdom. My domain. You will not tread where you are not welcome."

No one moved, for no one had seen an original's power in a millennium. A growling sound came from the trees. The Hunt emerged with their golden bows knocked, waiting for Tharan's signal. The hackles on their wolves' backs raised.

Gideon's men did not move.

"Hold steady," Brutus yelled from atop his horse. "The Lady Erissa protects us!"

Tharan turned his head to face Brutus, eyes rolled white, his red hair gleamed in the firelight. "Your mage has fled, and so should you."

His words shook Caiden to his core.

Power radiated from him.

"We will die before we bow to you, sylph scum," Brutus said in his graveled voice.

"Have it your way." Tharan signaled to the Hunt.

Arrows flew, striking their targets. Gideon's men fell in waves. The Hunt moved in, killing any Highlander in their path. The screams burst Caiden's eardrums.

Tharan sent a wave of energy blasting through the legions, knocking men to the ground, their bodies enveloped by feral roots.

"Retreat!" Brutus said, pulling his remaining men back.

Tharan fell to his knees. His eyes fluttered, no longer lit from within.

"Help him," Caiden commanded.

Lucius and Roderick ran to his aid.

The Wild Hunt chased after Gideon's men, tearing apart any they could catch.

The forest continued to burn, and Caiden dispatched any of his men who still possessed the power of rain to help put out the fires.

Roderick and Lucius pulled Tharan into one of their remaining tents. He clung to life, his breaths faint.

"His powers are new. They require a lot of life." Lucius searched the tent for any healing potions.

"Watch over him. I need to find Aelia," Caiden said, donning a thick wool cloak.

"I'm coming with you. Amolie is out there, too," Roderick said, grabbing his whip.

As if sent by the Trinity, Arion waited for them outside the tent.

Fires still smoldered, but many had died down by the time they reached the great hall.

"Aelia! Amolie! We're here!" The men ran through hallways and corridors, searching for any signs that the women were still alive. The once magnificent palace, now a tomb. Dead sylphs lay scattered about. Gideon's Blood Riders stalked the hallways, looking for anyone still alive.

"Fuck," Caiden muttered under his breath. "Let them still be alive."

Keeping to the shadows, they desperately searched for any signs of life. A small scream came from behind. Caiden turned around to see Roderick with his dagger in a Blood Rider's neck.

"Sleep now," he said, laying the man on the polished floor as blood pooled around their feet.

"Thanks," Caiden said, nodding to Roderick.

In the study, another Blood Rider lay dead on the floor. From his body, a trail of petite bloody footprints led to a grate under a bookcase. "Look at this." Roderick pulled the grate from the wall, revealing a hidden passageway. "This is how they escaped."

Caiden let out a sigh of relief. "Can you fit?"

They both knew Roderick couldn't.

"Go back to camp. Help Lucius and Tharan. I will find them and bring them back."

Roderick nodded, replacing the grate after Caiden crawled into the dark tunnel.

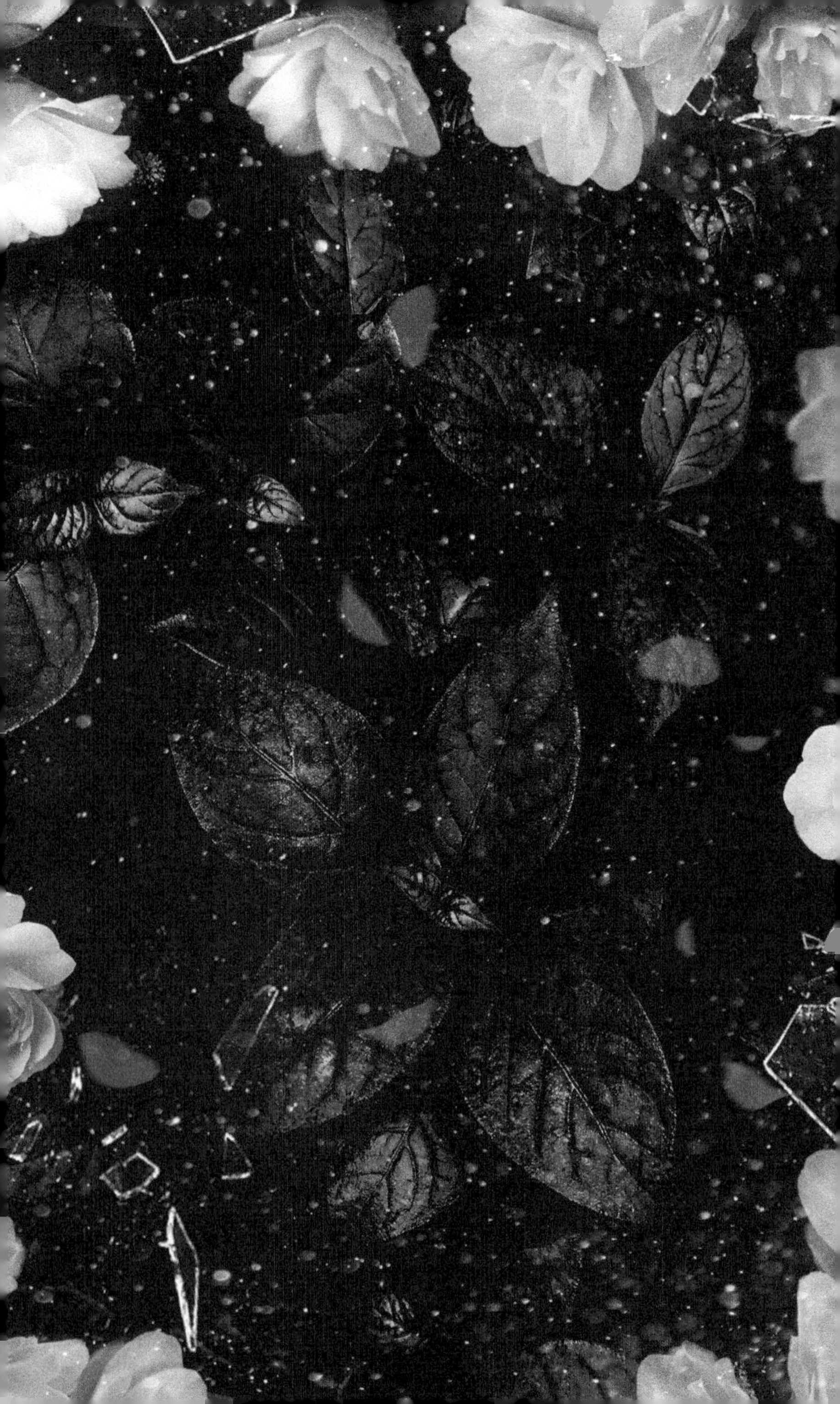

34 AELIA

The jewels on my dress scraped against the hardwood of the tunnel as we crawled toward freedom, dragging Baylis's sleeping body as we went.

"When did she get so heavy?" Amolie said through panting breaths.

Gritting my teeth, I heaved her body forward. "I just hope she doesn't wake up while we're in this tunnel."

Crawling relentlessly, the end nowhere in sight, panic overtook us as our strength dwindled.

"Listen," Amolie said, pressing her hand to the roof of the passage. "It's water. We must be near the river."

The knot in my chest untied at the sound of rushing water. "If we can get out, we can build a simple raft for Baylis and, hopefully, get her to camp."

"What's left of it," Amolie said half-heartedly.

We'd both seen the forest ablaze. The heat had radiated throughout the great hall as the Hunt battled the Blood Riders.

A new Alder King had been crowned. Half-sylph and half-elf, his power would be limitless if he could control it.

Once the great hall had emptied, Tharan invoked his

newfound power. A formidable vine emerged from the wooden floor, coiling around him before descending back into the earth, carrying the newly crowned king with it. The Wild Hunt echoed with their eerie howls, faithfully trailing their leader into the tumultuous blaze. Amolie and I narrowly evaded the vengeance of the remaining Blood Riders.

"Can you see an exit, Aelia?"

I squinted, trying to find my way through the endless darkness.

A tinge of light became visible. "The end of the tunnel is near. Just a little further."

Exhausted and dirty, Amolie and I pooled our strength and pushed Baylis with all our might until the river came into view.

Mud squished between our bare toes as we sank to our knees. The ground sent shivers through my body.

I lay on my back, gazing up at the canopy emitting smoldering embers. The scent of burnt wood and fresh blood drifted on the wintry breeze. The illumination I initially confused for the early dawn unveiled itself as the voracious inferno engulfing the Woodland Realm.

I pressed my ear to Baylis's chest, confirming her continued breathing.

As children, Baylis and I often shared a bed. Even at the River House, the beds always seemed too large for us, and we invariably gravitated to Baylis's bed on the second floor, overlooking the river through its window. I would read stories to her many nights until she drifted off to sleep. Cherished tales of ancient knights who vanquished dragons and defeated monsters, secretly yearning for a knight to rescue us. Her room transformed into our own little sanctuary. When our father fell ill, we grew up quickly, but Baylis's room remained the one place where we could still hold onto the innocence of our childhood.

"I hope the men are alright," Amolie said. Cries of pain echoed over the river in answer.

"If we can get down the river, we may still help them," I said.

Amolie ripped strips from her dress, using them as ties to make a raft for Baylis, while I frantically cut reeds for Amolie to fasten together. Despite the fire, a cool wind swept through the valley, sending a chill up my spine, reminding me of the sheerness of my dress.

We loaded Baylis onto the raft, lowering our bodies into the icy water.

Amolie's teeth chattered.

I shook uncontrollably as the cold snaked its way straight to my bones.

The river wound through several camps where courts tended to their wounded and wrapped their dead.

"Is the battle over?" I asked a sylph woman with silver hair and the eyes of a serpent, trying her best to heal a wound on a large sylph man.

"The battle is over. King Tharan and the Hunt triumphed. But we suffered many losses."

"Do you know about the Court of Storms? Are they still standing?" Fear frayed my already frazzled nerves.

"Lord Caiden was at the front of the last line of defense. I do not know his fate."

A skeletal hand tugged at my heart. "Thank you." I shot Amolie a look of urgency. "We have to get back to the camp."

Amolie nodded, and we picked up our pace, wading through the water until we reached a turnoff for the camp where the Court of Storms had been. Our muscles burned as we fought against the current.

"I'll stay with Baylis. Run up and see if anything is left of the camp," I said. We pulled the makeshift raft onto the shore.

Freezing water dripped from Amolie's dress as she scrambled up the embankment.

The smell of death and blood lingered in the air. Many had fallen. I silently prayed to Ammena, Illya, and to any god listening. *Please let Caiden be safe. Please let him be unharmed.*

Heavy rain fell from the sky, extinguishing the remaining fires. Desperate, I searched for his mind in a sea of agony. But he did not return my call. Sinking into the muddy bank of the river, heart heavy, I buried my face in my hands. Tears welled in my eyes. I shouldn't have gone into Gideon's camp the other night. We'd brought this nightmare upon everyone.

"I hope you're not crying over me," a familiar voice said.

My heart leapt at the sight of Caiden coming up the riverbank. The light of the dying fires flickering on his golden hair. Blood stained his armor. A picture of the fierce warrior I had fallen in love with. "I thought you were dead."

"It takes more than some mountain goblins to kill me." He pulled me into his arms, wrapping his cloak around us both. I reveled in his warmth. The smell of blood and steel lingered on his skin. "I'm glad you're safe, Springborn."

I buried my face in his chest, not wanting to let him go. "Help me get Baylis into camp."

"Amolie's potion was strong," Caiden said, waving his hand in front of Baylis's face.

We heaved her up over the small hill to where a few tattered tents remained.

"Roderick, Lucius?" I gave Caiden a panicked look.

"They are fine. Tharan is here, too. He's resting in a tent. Roderick and Lucius are looking after him. They've got Amolie working on a potion."

I gazed at the men bandaging their wounds. "We need more healers."

"Most of my men will heal themselves. Illya's gift protects

us." He pulled open the tent where Tharan lay on a table in the center of the room. Amolie stood over a bubbling cauldron.

"Put her over there," she said, pointing at a cot near Tharan.

"Make sure you tie her to it," Lucius said, pulling a pair of manacles from his pocket. "If she is brainwashed by Gideon, she may try to attack us."

"No, I won't have her tied," I said, pushing Lucius away.

"It's for her own good and our safety," Lucius said, holding the manacles up.

Caiden lay a reassuring hand on my shoulder. "It'll be alright, Aelia. If she wakes, she might try to run or attack us."

I bit my lip in contemplation. "Fine, but make sure they aren't too tight."

Laying Baylis on the bed, we secured her hands and feet. I stroked her hair lovingly.

The large female member of the Hunt I had seen in the palace entered, her helmet tucked under her arm. She looked at Tharan, smoothing his hair over his sloped ears.

"We've been friends since childhood." Tears welled in her eyes. "He defended me when no one else would."

"He'll be alright," Amolie said, touching the female's ironclad hand. "What is your name?"

"Sumac," the sylph woman said.

I recognized her voice.

"You saved me. The other day, it was you." I bowed my head. "Thank you for your kindness."

"It was him." She motioned to Tharan. "He could... sense you were in trouble."

Tharan's chest moved up and down with his breath.

"He always knows when those he cares about are in trouble," Sumac said, more to herself than to anyone in particular.

A flush warmed my cheeks. I looked away, avoiding Caiden's gaze.

"Hold him steady," Amolie said.

Roderick and Lucius each braced one of Tharan's arms as Amolie poured a mixture of dandelion and enchanted honey into Tharan's mouth.

Tharan coughed, jerking his body violently.

"Easy," Roderick said, helping him upright.

Black soot and the dandelion potion dripped from Tharan's lips. His eyes caught mine, and a smile brightened his face. "Glad to see you made it."

"I could say the same about you." A flush reddened my cheeks.

"Without you, I'd be dead." He brought my trembling hand to his lips. A bolt of lightning shot through my body. The room watched silently as the Alder King bowed to the Traitor Queen.

The sound of Baylis waking brought everyone back to the present. Her eyes blinked in disbelief before she thrashed violently against the ties.

"Let me go! Let me go! Dirty fucking sylph lover. Dirty fucking witch!" Her voice was harsh and foreign.

I rushed to her side. "Hold her down," I commanded.

Roderick and Caiden moved to help, but Tharan held up his hand; a force pinned Baylis to the cot.

Frozen with fear, I could only blink awkwardly at my sister. "Do you see a glamour, Amolie?"

Hate flashed in Baylis's gray eyes. Our father's eyes.

"She's not glamoured," Amolie said, examining Baylis.

"Can you go into her mind, Aelia?" Caiden asked.

I bit my lip. "I can try."

Closing my eyes, I reached out a tentacle of my power, searching for Baylis. The door to her psyche hung open. The same simple door that led to the temple of Ammena in Elyria—basic wood with a small apple carved in the center. *Darkness surrounded me. I focused my energy, feeling for any sign of life.*

Stars flickered around me as if I were standing in the middle of the night sky.

"*Baylis? Are you here?*" *The great expanse echoed my voice back to me. I swallowed hard. What was going on here? Where was my sister?*

A cackle came from all corners of Baylis's mind, making my blood go cold.

Erissa's laugh.

The mage's slender figure materialized out of smoke. "*Hello, little lamb.*" *Her pearlescent robe fell in waves around her curves.*

I clenched my fists, digging my nails into my palms. "*What are you doing here? Where is my sister?*"

Erissa circled me, taking long, graceful steps. "*Oh, she's still here. I've just locked her away. For safekeeping, of course. I needed to access her full abilities.*" *An evil smile cut Erissa's ethereal face in two.* "*It's a shame you wouldn't let me do the same to you. I have a feeling there's a well of power not yet tapped within you.*"

"*You will never have me again,*" *I said through gritted teeth.*

On the outside, I possessed no supreme power, but I could bend the mind to my will here. I sent a blast of energy toward Erissa, knocking her to the ground.

"*Aelia! Help me. Please,*" *Baylis called, her voice everywhere and nowhere at the same time.*

"*Where are you?*" *I searched frantically for my sister.*

"*Here, I'm still here.*" *Baylis's voice flickered in and out.* "*There's little time, so listen. Erissa took my soul from my body. She's controlling my mind, using the parts she wants. The amulet around her neck. Break it and set me free.*"

Erissa pounced on me, knocking me to my knees. Kicking her as hard as I could, I ran for the exit.

"*I've got your sister right here,*" *Erissa called after me, holding up a bloodred amulet.*

I opened my eyes.

Everyone stared at me.

Baylis lay asleep.

"She's trapped," I said, through heavy breaths. "Erissa is controlling her mind." I collapsed into a chair. It took all of my power to get out of Baylis's mind.

An inky stain crept through my veins, inching up my arm. The bargain with Caiden—Baylis's rescue completed it. Magic sought balance, and though the pain remained bearable for now, delaying the erasure of Caiden's memories would only exacerbate it. Hastily, I wrapped Caiden's cloak around myself, praying that no one else saw the telltale mark.

"There is a library in the Alder Palace. If it's intact, perhaps it might shine a light on the spell. We can have rooms made up for all of you." Tharan nodded to Sumac, who left to fulfill his wishes.

"I'll mix up a potion and put Baylis in a deep sleep until we can figure out a plan," Amolie said.

"We should keep her in a secure room, away from the rest of us," Lucius said, towering over Baylis. His once-white hair now stained red with blood. "We don't know if she can be used as a conduit."

"You mean lock her in a cell?" I growled.

Lucius glowered at me. "We do not know what she is capable of. It's what is best."

The thought of keeping Baylis locked up like some kind of lunatic turned my stomach, but Lucius was right. If Erissa could control her mind, there was no telling what she could do.

Tharan stood. "We will honor the dead and burn the bodies on pyres in the sylph tradition. Then we will discuss what to do next about King Gideon."

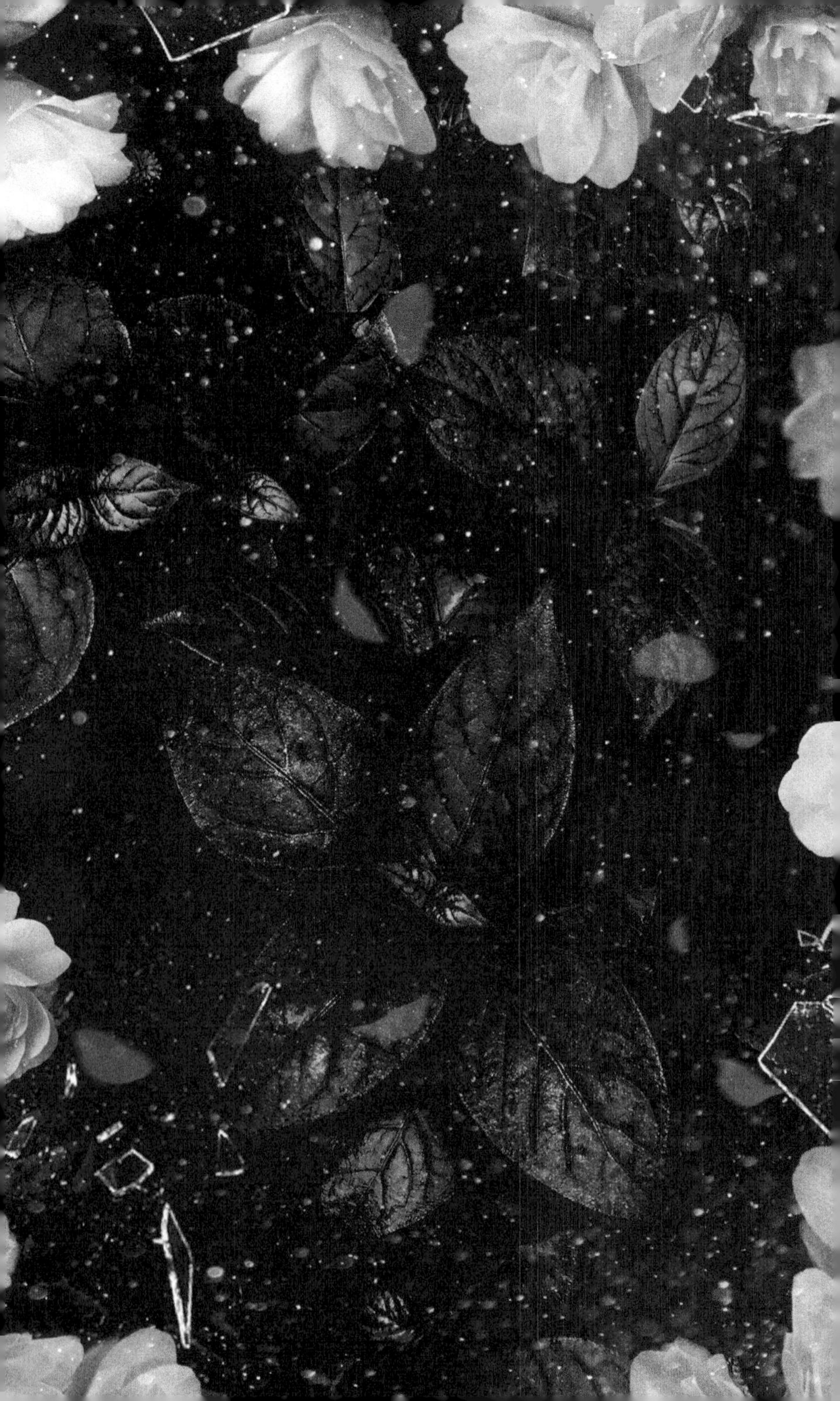

35 AELIA

Pyres burned for three days.

None brighter than the former Alder King's.

Dressed in a black satin dress and matching veil, I stood beside Caiden as the Stormlands honored their dead.

Priestesses from Ammena and Illya temples presided over the funeral ceremonies. Normally, humans are buried in the earth to return to the soil what they took from it in life. To honor their sacrifice, the few human kingdoms who had attended the revelry burned their dead along with the sylphs. Hoping Moriana would see the smoke and feel their grief.

Ursula fled to the sea, not bothering to return for the funeral—typical mermaid.

On the third day of the burning, Tharan assembled the heads of the courts to discuss their response to the attacks. Caiden and I sat with Roderick and Lucius.

The pain from the rot claiming my body for not upholding the deal with Caiden was still dull, but I knew the longer I waited, the worse it would get. Amolie cast a glamour to hide the dark mark. I looked for signs of the bargain taking its toll on Caiden but saw nothing out of the ordinary.

"We should retaliate now! Hit the Highlands while they think we are licking our wounds." The Lord of Rabbits slammed his fist on the long wooden table. An elder with long, gray hair and a salt-and-pepper beard, his face showed a fierceness in sharp contrast with his court's name.

"It is unwise to attack the Highlands. They are allied with the Elven High King, Aerendir. We do not want to start another war." Tharan took to the part of the Alder King well. He sat in the center of the center of the room, flanked by Sumac and the green sylph, Hopper. The crown of antlers gleamed in the firelight. Butterflies flitted in my stomach at the sight of him.

"War is at your door, young king," a centaur with a jagged cut across his face chimed in. "There is no going back now. We must show strength."

Caiden squeezed my hand under the table. I opened a line of communication between our minds.

'*It is never wise to go to war,*' Caiden's voice filled my mind. '*Millions will die. There will be bloodshed for thousands of years.*'

I nodded. War represented the final recourse, yet the sylph hungered for conflict, their essence imbued by the goddess Illya.

Caiden stood, wearing the Court of Storms battle leathers, endowed with boning to conduct his lightning. "As the only court here, who answers to the Sylph Council, I will need to take this to the chairman. The sylph courts need to appear united. If the elven king hears we are divided, he will not hesitate to exploit our weaknesses."

A grumbling rippled through the crowd. Tharan cleared his throat. "I am the leader of the Wild Courts. My word is the law. I will send my emissary to parlay with the Sylph Council. Until they return, no one is to attack the Highlands unless otherwise provoked."

The lords returned to mumbling, but no one challenged Tharan's word.

The meeting adjourned, and the courts returned to their homelands.

Caiden and the Court of Storms would return to the capital city of Vantris with Tharan's emissary in the morning. Amolie and I would stay in the Woodland Realm and search for a cure for Baylis.

Caiden and I lay in bed together.

"I'm going to miss you," I said. Caiden laid his head on my chest. "I didn't think I'd ever say those words again, but I am."

"I was stupid to make the bargain with you." He hugged me tighter.

Pressure built behind my eyes. "We both said things we didn't mean."

"I wish I could take it back."

A lump grew in my throat as I stroked his soft, blond hair. "I know."

I pulled my sleeve back, wiping away the glamour Amolie had covered my arm with.

Caiden's eyes widened at the sight of the mark. He pulled back his sleeve, revealing one of his own. "I wanted to keep loving you until I couldn't take the pain anymore. I too covered it with glamour." He sat on his knees, pulling me in close. "I'm sorry, Aelia. I'm sorry I did this to us."

Our time was at an end. No more sweet kisses or stolen glances. No reminiscing about our youth. Only I would carry our memories. Cursed to remain while Caiden moved on.

"We did this to each other." My words stuck in my throat as tears poured down my face.

The bargain needed to be completed before he left for Vantris tomorrow.

I struggled for air, the futility of our struggle cementing within me. There would be no reversing it. Tomorrow, I would gradually vanish from Caiden's memory, like sand carried away by the wind.

"I love you," I said, looking into Caiden's blue eyes. "I know you won't remember, but I hope your heart keeps the memory your mind won't."

Taking my face in his hands, he thumbed my cheek. "I will find a way back to you." He kissed me passionately. "I love you, Aelia. I loved you even when I hated you, and I will keep a space in my heart for you until the end of time." A promise he couldn't keep.

Laying me down on the bed, tears wetting both our eyes, we indulged in one last night of passion.

Tomorrow, I would be a stranger to him.

We made love until the sun rose; neither wanted to waste our last precious moments together sleeping, hoping our bodies could convey what our words could not. Caiden held me until the morning bells chimed. I committed everything I could about him to memory. His smell, the dimples on his cheeks, the way one piece of his unruly hair fell over his eye. These memories were for me.

A knock woke us from our dream.

We quickly dressed.

"Come in."

The door creaked open, and a sleepy-eyed Amolie strolled in carrying a comprehensive book and a mug of coffee.

"Sorry to disturb you, but I found something." She laid the massive tome on the desk.

Pulling my hands through my disheveled hair, I hoped the smell of sex wasn't too pungent.

"What is it?" Caiden asked.

Amolie motioned to the tome. "This is a book of ancient spells. From a time before the Trinity."

The book was full of old pages, yet the colors on the paper were still vivid even after thousands of years. I delighted in the smell of old parchment. "You can read this, Amolie?"

"The scholars in the library helped me to translate it." She pointed to the text. "This is a spell to bind a soul to an object. I'm guessing Erissa used it to bind Baylis's soul to her amulet."

I ran my fingers over the words. "Can the spell be broken?"

Amolie sighed. "It says here to free the soul, the blood of the bound must be spilled upon the object."

"So, we need to take Baylis's blood?" I asked.

"Yes." Amolie put her hands on her hips. "Only the blood of the soul can free it."

I took a deep breath, raising my head to the heavens. "I have to go back to the Highlands, don't I?"

Amolie sipped her coffee. "It looks that way."

I needed time to think. I hoped never to return to the place of my torture, but to save Baylis's soul, I would endure the fires of hell itself.

A long breath escaped my lips. "Okay."

"There might be another way. I'll have to do more research, but—"

I cut her off before she could finish. "This is the only way. We will get Baylis's blood, find the amulet, and free her soul. I know the castle at Ryft's Edge like the back of my hand. I can sneak in without being seen."

"Are you sure?" Amolie gave me a questioning look.

"Yes."

Caiden's hand entwined with mine.

Amolie shut the book and made her way toward the door. I grabbed her arm. "There's one more thing we need to do. Gather the others."

"What?"

I laid my arm bare. Black rot crept through my veins like ink in water. "It's time, Amolie. We need to complete the bargain before it takes our magic, and our lives."

Amolie's mouth tightened into a straight line. "I'll get them."

The door silently shut behind her. Caiden slipped an arm around my waist before burying his face in my neck. "I wish I could go with you."

"You will be with me," I said, placing his hand over my heart. "You'll be right here."

We held each other until the others came.

Caiden and I stood hand in hand as we addressed our friends. Their sullen faces made my voice crack. "I am going to finish my part of the bargain today. Baylis is safe. The rot on our forearms will hinder our magic. It makes sense to do it before Caiden leaves."

"Isn't there another way?" Amolie said, biting her nails.

"No," Caiden said, squeezing my hand. "We made a bargain, and now we must fulfill it as the laws of this land command. Eventually, the rot will kill us if we do not."

Hot tears welled in my eyes. "Are you ready?"

Caiden nodded, taking a seat on the bed.

Pushing my feelings aside, I knelt before him, focusing my mind. A sandy grit filled my mouth.

"Wait." He ran his hand through my hair and down my jaw one last time. "I want you to know I love you."

"I love you too." I kissed him one last time, savoring every moment. "Now close your eyes and show me your first memory of us."

I connected our minds.

We stood in the library of Caiden's mind. Each book represented a memory.

"This one first," Caiden pulled a leatherbound book from the shelf and handed it to me. I swallowed hard before opening it.

The first day we met.

My hair was a brown mess of curls tied together in a bun on the top of my head. I had just finished riding. Through Caiden's eyes, I looked like a goddess. His pulse quickened, and my chest felt light. He smiled at me. I erased the memory.

My heart shattered. I couldn't do this. This history belonged to both of us—but I had to.

Releasing a breath, I pressed on, erasing our adventures together as emissaries and the holidays at the River House. Every memory rewritten took a piece of my heart with it: all the kisses, the hugs, the stolen glances—all gone.

Our memories intertwined. It killed me to wipe them away.

I stumbled upon the memory of my wedding day. As an emissary, he was obligated to attend. He arrived late, entering through the rear of the throne room, likely hoping to avoid me. However, we collided as I waited to be escorted down the aisle. It was an odd feeling to revisit a memory shared with someone else, seeing and feeling it from their perspective.

Dressed in a high-necked ball gown, a white veil covered my face. Caiden's heart went cold when he saw me. Tears poured down my face. I had never felt more alone than on that day. None of my family could come to the wedding as my father had just died, and they feared leaving the Midlands unattended.

Reaching out, he grabbed my hand. We shared one last moment.

"You'll always be my princess," he whispered before the guards escorted him away.

Those simple words carried me through the darkest days of my life. I should have thanked him for that. He'll never know how he helped me.

With tears in my eyes, I wiped the memory away.

Taking another breath, we entered the darkest part of our past.

The hard memories were easy to erase.

"*I never loved you. You are nothing to me. I never want to see you again.*"

I wish I could erase who I was then. So full of hate and vitriol—a rabid dog who attacked anyone who got near me. I wish I could take those memories from my mind, but they were a part of me—a lesson I needed to learn.

We reached the most recent memories. I took them all—the Court of Sorrows, the cave trolls, the nights we spent entwined in each other's arms.

Back in the library of his mind, Caiden gave me a half-hearted smile. "This is it. The last memory."

He handed me a few pages containing our memories from the morning.

Tears welled in my eyes. This was all that remained of us. Just a few pages. Already Caiden's mind closed in on me, no longer recognizing me as a friend, but as an intruder.

"I'm sorry," I said, lighting the papers on a nearby candle.

"You'll always be my princess," he said as the look on his face transformed from sadness to neutrality.

I blew out the candle, cloaking myself in darkness. He wouldn't know me from a stranger on the street.

When I opened my eyes, they'd already blindfolded Caiden. I snuck out of the room on padded feet before taking refuge in an intricately carved alcove, letting out the hot cry boiling in my chest.

From a balcony high in the Alder Palace, I watched Lucius and Roderick load Caiden into a carriage. The process made us both weak, and it took all my energy to climb up the massive circular staircase. I kept my gaze fixed on Caiden until the carriage disappeared, yearning for one final glimpse of him before he vanished forever.

Lowering myself to the wooden floor, the weight of grief pressed down on my very being. Tears flowed freely. I cursed the Trinity, the Fates, and every force that seemed to conspire against Caiden and me. My breath seared in my lungs.

I screamed until my lungs crackled like the embers of a fire.

Closing my eyes, I allowed the flood of emotions to engulf me —a teaching from the Trinity, a trial of my resilience. Caiden had departed, taking my vow of sobriety with him. The temptation to surrender to a blissful numbness and never resurface overpowered me, but I couldn't yield to it. I had Baylis to consider and refused to be a victim any longer.

A hand decorated with golden rings extended toward me. I looked up to see Tharan standing in front of me.

"You look like you could use a drink." He gripped my wrist, pulling me to my feet.

I wiped my nose on my tunic. "Maybe two."

Giving me a reassuring smile, his aura radiated soothing energy, lifting the sadness from my bones.

"How are you doing this?"

"A gift from my mother's side of the family," he said, leading me down the winding stairs of the Alder Palace. The midday winter sun cast an ethereal light throughout the branches as craftsmen busied themselves, mending the ancient tree. "We are more alike than you know, mystery woman."

I didn't want him to see me like this, but somehow, I knew he would understand.

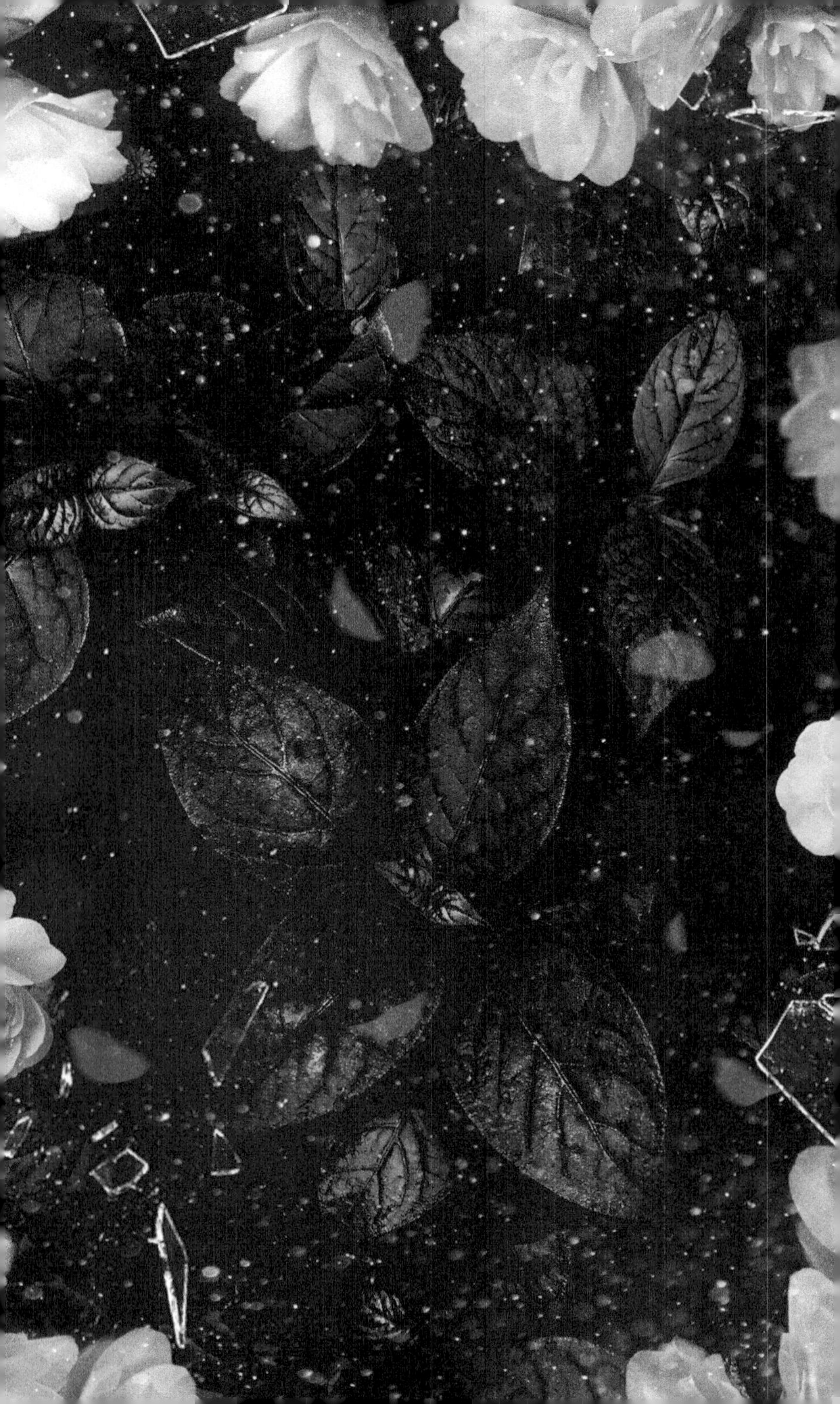

36 AELIA

"You don't have to tell me why you were screaming your lungs out, but if you want to, I am here to listen." Tharan handed me a hot mug of spiced cider.

I took a sip; warmth filled my chest. "It's a long story."

"I am nearly immortal. I have nothing but time." He leaned back in his brown leather chair. Seated in one of the palace's immaculate studies, books and scrolls lined the walls. A fire roared in the hearth. Yule garlands adorned every eve, filling the place with the scent of spruce and berries.

"By now, I'm sure you've discovered the power I possess." My voice trembled.

Tharan nodded. "You are a telepath."

"Yes." I fidgeted in my chair, guilt built in my heart. "Caiden and I were…" A lump grew in my throat.

"In love." Tharan finished my sentence for me.

"Yes. It's a long story," I repeated lamely.

Tharan laid a pack of cigarettes on the table between us. "We've got time."

I lit one, taking a long drag before diving deep into the intricacies of my relationship with Caiden. The words flowed like a river being released from a dam. I laughed and cried and talked until my voice went hoarse, all while Tharan nodded along, placing a supportive hand over mine.

I told him everything: the love Caiden and I shared, the way he helped me through my father's illness, my Promised Day, and my father's untimely death. I told him about the darker parts of my history when I was a much different person. Caiden had seen every iteration of who I was, and now he was gone.

By the time I finished my tale, fuchsia painted the dusk sky. Sleep tugged at my eyelids.

"Now you know everything." I took a drag of my cigarette. "I am not a good person. Everything they say about me is true. I am an addict, a mercenary, a traitor who burned her kingdom to the ground."

Tharan leaned in close to me. "I don't think you're a bad person, Aelia Springborn." He sucked in a drag from his cigarette. "This life forces us into situations we never thought we'd be in. We can only move forward."

A smile tugged at the corners of my mouth.

Tharan lifted my chin, our eyes met. "Your past is just a story, Aelia. Anytime you wish, you can start a new chapter."

My breath caught in my throat. I saw myself reflected in Tharan's vernal eyes. Words escaped me. Half of me wanted to melt away into nothing, and the other half wanted to kiss Tharan and never stop.

A knock at the door broke our gaze. Awkwardly, I rubbed my sweating hands on my pants.

A satyr with brown fur and ram's horns entered the room. "Dinner is served in the dining hall, my king."

"Thank you, Albie." Tharan nodded. "Shall we?" Extending his hand to me once more.

"We shall," I said, taking it.

Amolie and Sumac were waiting for us when we entered the

dining room. Roasted elk, wild mushrooms, and carrots adorned the expansive oak table—an ancient text propped open in front of Amolie.

"Nice of you to join us," Amolie said, taking a bite of meat. Tharan took his seat at the head of the table. I took one across from Amolie. Dozens of candles cast dancing shadows across the walls as we ate.

"Did you find anything in the library to break the spell on Baylis?" Tharan asked.

Amolie nodded. "I did, but it will require blood and espionage."

"You've piqued my interest. Tell me more." Tharan took a sip of his wine.

As Amolie explained the intricacies of the amulet, my thoughts drifted to Caiden riding away in the black carriage, oblivious to my existence. In some memories, I merely removed myself, while others, I wiped entirely. To him, I existed as Baylis's sister, a sibling he had never encountered.

Tharan massaged his chin, pondering the whole thing. "I want to go with you."

The clanging of silverware interrupted the conversation. "Over my dead body," Sumac said, food flew from her mouth.

"The Highlands attacked my kingdom. I need to do reconnaissance."

"Send me." Sumac rubbed her shoulder where Baylis's crossbow had hit.

"I need someone to stay here and defend the Woodlands. You and Hopper can run things until I return."

"But—"

Tharan placed a reassuring hand on top of Sumac's. "I know you want to protect me, but I am the Alder King now. I will be fine."

Sumac nodded, returning to playing with her food.

"Is there a chance Gideon could be dead? I skewered him through the gut."

"I think I would know... or have a feeling if he was dead," I said.

"Knowing Erissa, she could probably bring him back. Elves with their breaths and all," Amolie said, not looking up from her book. "It's a tricky thing, bringing someone back from the dead. No one truly returns. Sure, their body is alive, but you can see the differences over time. Little things, like their sense of humor changes or goes away."

"How do you know about all of this?" I asked.

"There used to be a coven of witches known for their necromancy. Whoever casts the spell must give some of their own life to bring the person back." She returned to studying her book.

After dinner, Tharan and I shared a smoke outside. Leaning against the railing, I stared at the stars, blowing smoke rings at them.

"Tell me about your sister," Tharan said, gazing over his massive kingdom. The forest embarked on its own healing process. Glimpses of green emerged amidst the charred branches of trees.

I sighed. "I know you must hate her for what she did to your father. I'm sorry I couldn't stop her."

Tharan turned to me. His verdant eyes accepting. "I know it wasn't really her. My father's blood is on Gideon's hands." He took another drag of his cigarette. "He was as old as the world. Born from the very trees in this forest—a king to lead them. He ruled for nearly ten thousand years, fought countless wars, helped the Trinity cull the land, and united the Wild Courts. His people loved him, and I hope I can be like him. We had our differences, but I knew he loved me." He took a deep breath as if the crown weighed heavily on him.

"Thank you," I whispered, lowering my head. "She's not that person."

He placed his hand over mine, making the hairs on my arm stand on end. "I know the love siblings share."

"Is Briar your only sibling?" I stomped on my cigarette butt.

"Originals differ from you and me, Aelia. The Trinity chooses when they will sire offspring."

I leaned in closer. Moonlight shone off his silken hair. "What of your sister? Will you look for her?"

Tharan dug a finger into the wood railing. "Briar has always walked her own path. The root rot she contracted as a child transformed her. Some think the rot seeped into her brain."

"Is that what you think?" I arched my brow.

A sigh escaped his lips, turning his breath to mist in the night air. "I think Illya gives us all special gifts. Sometimes, our gifts may be hidden from others, or it may take time to find them, but they are still there. Briar will do whatever Illya wishes her to do. Should she return, I would welcome her with open arms."

I rubbed the spot on my arm where the inky mark had been just hours before. "Were you close?"

"We were once. She is the daughter of my father's only wife, Maple. My father favored her above all others until the rot took her magic. She and I used to play for hours. We were best friends." He paused. "After the rot, she changed. She secluded herself away from the outside world. Ashamed of what the illness did to her. I tried to help her, but she did not want to be helped. So, we grew apart."

I placed my hand on his. "Sometimes it is easier to sink into the roles already given to us than to fight for a new one."

"I didn't want to be king, Aelia. But now that I am, I want to do right by my people. To be their strength." Tharan ran his hand anxiously through his silken hair. "And that starts with seeking justice for what the Highlands did to my beautiful forest."

"I understand. Baylis is a better person than I'll ever be." I said, tracing the grains in the wood with my fingers.

Tharan raised an eyebrow at me.

"She cared about others. I only cared about myself."

"Did you ever consider she poured herself into others to distract herself from your father's illness? The way you poured yourself into Caiden?"

"Perhaps. She exuded perpetual confidence, effortlessly excelling in everything she pursued. As a child, she dreamed of becoming an archer. Our father arranged for her to have a teacher. In just a few years, she ascended to become the kingdom's finest archer, capable of dispatching a rabbit without it ever suspecting a thing. Our father often had her showcase these talents at gatherings, yet Baylis never boasted.

"She held the title of the best archer in the Midlands and perhaps in all of Moriana, but she remained unwavering in her loyalty to Ammena and the Trinity, praying at the temple daily. Even when she knew our father wouldn't recognize her, she visited him every single day." Guilt gnawed at my heart. "I wish I possessed her level of devotion."

"Everyone copes in their own way, Aelia." Tharan squeezed my hand.

A lump grew in my throat. I had not thought about my father in a long time. I shook my head, trying to empty the guilt lingering there.

"So, what are you going to do when all this is over?" Tharan asked, lighting another cigarette.

I plucked out another as well, lighting it to collect myself.

"I'm going to kill Gideon. But first, I'm going to humiliate him the way he did to me. A quick death is too easy for him." Smoke billowed into the night air.

"From traitor to king killer." Tharan held the cigarette to his pursed lips.

I hung my head. "Do you think I'm crazy for wanting revenge?"

"No." He smiled into the night. "I think your need for vindication is justified.. We have a common enemy. However, you can't kill him yet. He needs to be held accountable for what he did during the Yule Revelry."

I huffed. "And why not? I would be doing you a favor."

Tharan blew smoke into the cool night air. "Sylph laws demand a trial. Even if the verdict will certainly be guilty."

I knitted my brow, grabbing Tharan's hands in desperation. "Allow me to carry out justice as I see fit."

A smile tugged at the corners of his lips. "I will make the case to the Sylph Court."

"Thank you…" I twiddled my fingers. "For everything. For being my friend." I surveyed the forest kingdom below us. Snow-capped trees of all kinds spread out for as far as the eye could see. The magic of the ancient forest seeped into my skin, making it tingle.

Tharan leaned on the railing like he did the first night we met at the Court of Sorrows. His angular features illuminated by the moonlight reminded me of the god he was. "Your past means nothing to me, Aelia. You have shown me kindness and bravery. I am proud to call you my friend."

I resisted hugging him. "Perhaps when this is all over, I could come back here. To be in your service."

An arched eyebrow. "I do need advisors I can trust."

My chest lightened at the thought of being near Tharan, protected in this forest oasis.

"But before we can get you a title, we must first bring Gideon and Erissa to justice."

I tried not to blush. "When do we leave?"

"A few days." He offered me his arm.

Escorting me to my room, we said our goodbyes. He kissed

me on the cheek before heading off to his own chambers. "Goodnight, mystery woman."

I couldn't hide the smile lighting my face. This is how so many women had fallen for him.

The room I occupied with Caiden for weeks seemed hollow when I stepped inside. Our intimate moments were erased along with Caiden's memories. The long leather box containing the Scepter of the Dead lay on the mahogany desk. I did not have the energy to quarrel with the Morrigan's ghost, so I put the box into a drawer.

'You will not get rid of me that easily, my queen,' her ancient voice hissed at me.

I rolled my eyes. "I don't have time for you right now, Morrigan."

'I know what happened at the revelry. Bind me to you, and my army will be yours.'

"And you'll suck the life from my bones. No thanks. I'll pass."

'There are ways of getting around that.'

"Oh, another quest? I'm booked solid on quests at the moment. Try again later."

'You will need me, Traitorous Queen. Our fates are intertwined.'

"Great. Goodnight." I rolled over in my bed, feeling the cold emptiness where Caiden once lay. My heart ached at the thought of never seeing him again, never feeling his touch. Burying my face in my pillow, I screamed my lungs ragged.

The door creaked open. Amolie peeked her head in. "Thought you might want some company."

"You know me so well, Am." She crawled into bed, and I laid my head in her lap. "I miss him already."

"I know; I miss Roderick too," she said, running her hands through my hair. She always knew how to comfort me. "It's going to hurt for a while, but you will learn to live with the pain. Some days, you won't feel it at all."

I didn't want to let the pain go. I wanted to tattoo it onto my skin, forcing the world to look upon my sorrow to know my truth: someone loved me once.

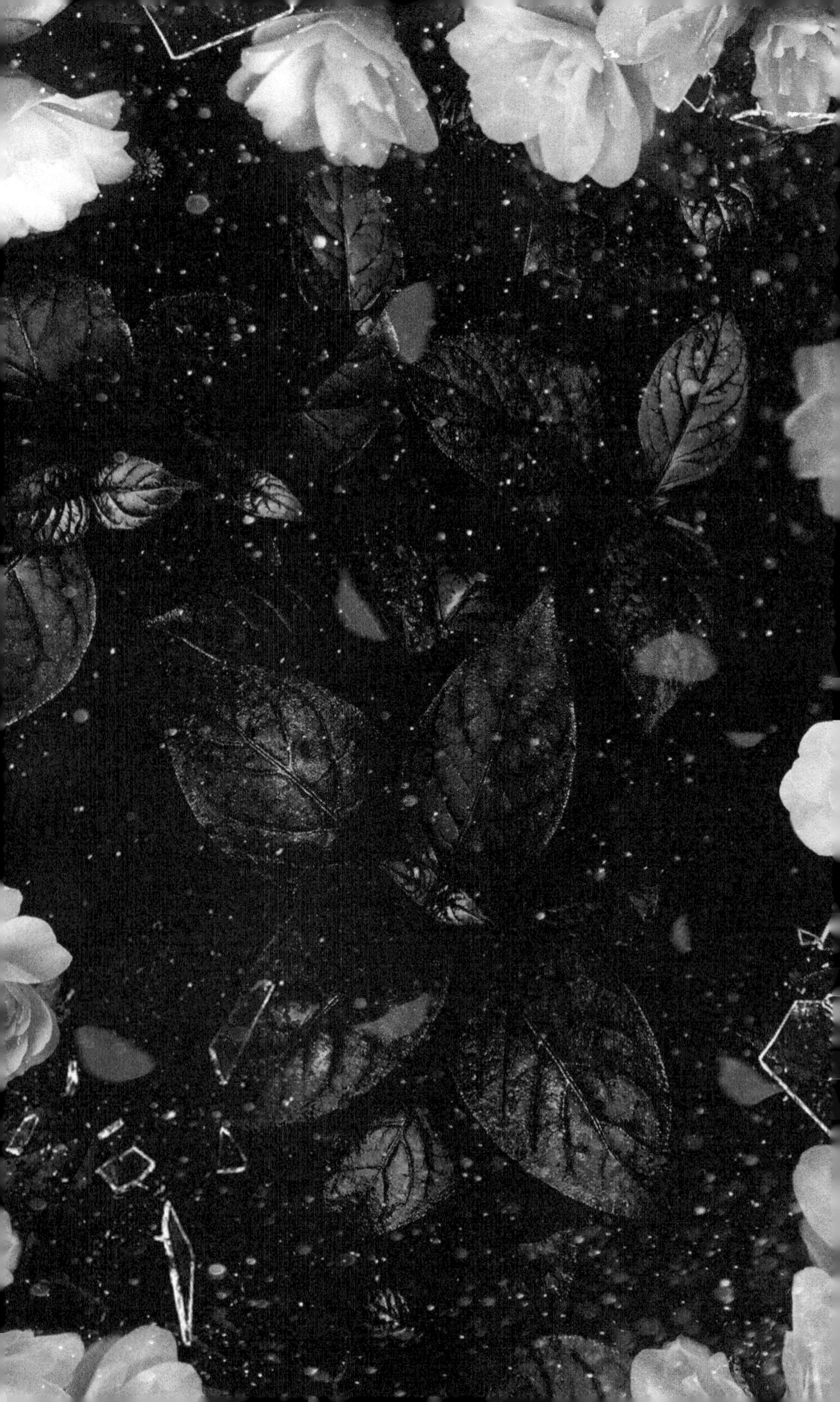

37 AELIA

I LAY IN BED, TRYING NOT TO LET MY GRIEF CONSUME ME, wrestling with the fact I could not save the people I loved. In two days, I lost Caiden and found my sister, only to lose her again.

I allowed myself this day to wallow in sadness. But there was no room for self-pity on the journey ahead.

I visited Baylis. We heeded Lucius's warning and kept her secured in a secluded part of the palace. Amolie mixed a powerful sedative to keep her peacefully asleep until we could free her soul from the amulet.

Sitting next to her, I rubbed my thumb over the delicate skin of her hand. This was the sister I remembered, the wise, generous, and kind girl who held onto me during nights when our father's demons overtook him—the one who eased my nerves on my Promised Day. There was so much I wanted to tell her, but there would be time for all of that after we saved her. I squeezed her hand one last time before I left. I wanted her to know I cared and would rescue her every day for a thousand years if that's what it took.

I lit a candle beside her bed and prayed to Ammena to keep her safe. Sometimes, I wondered why I still prayed to a goddess who never answered me. I think it was more the act of praying than the answer. I envisioned the words floating into the heavens, reaching the Trinity, wherever they were. Truth be told, I did not know how to stop praying despite having stopped believing a long time ago.

Leaving Baylis's room, I ascended the long, winding staircase to Tharan's study. The ancient tree whirled with magic and a renewed sense of hope I had not felt before, as if waking when Tharan became the Alder King. All around me, new growth sprouted from the walls, healing the fire damage.

Dark wood paneling covered the walls of the study, and candles scattered the massive bookshelves, creating a cozy atmosphere. While outside fat snowflakes fell lazily.

With his burgundy hair tied back in a low bun, Tharan hunched over the schematics of Ryft's Edge, a cigarette between his lips, and two wolves sleeping at his feet.

"Some added protection?" I said, glancing at the dogs.

Tharan gave me his signature smile, eyes sparkling with delight. "They are dire wolf pups. I had always wanted a pair of my own, but my father never wanted to spare any." He scratched one wolf behind the ear. "Winter and Frost. The white one is Winter, and the one with the blue tint is Frost."

Winter nudged me for pets. I obliged, sitting cross-legged on the floor, rubbing her belly.

"They're so sweet. Amolie would love them. You should show them to her. She's great with animals." A genuine smile crossed my face for the first time since the revelry.

"You're going to make them soft if you keep coddling them," Tharan said, tossing hunks of meat to each wolf.

"No, I'm not." I laughed as Frost licked my face. "My sister had two shepherds. But they were as black as night. Luna and Melvin."

Tharan arched his brow. "What kind of name is Melvin for a dog?"

I shrugged. "She was twelve when she got them. I guess Melvin sounded like a good name to her."

"I have not been a child in nearly a millennium; I guess that makes sense." He shrugged. "Why don't you come here and tell me about the Highlands?" He pulled me to my feet.

I stared at the map. "The Highlands are flanked by mountains on the northern edge of the territory and the sea on its eastern shore. They were prosperous even before they allied with the elves. The alliance, however, made them wealthier than any other human kingdom in Moriana."

Tharan ran his hand over the mountain range on the map. "They mine the other side of the Chayne Mountains."

I nodded. "Yes, they mine the ore that makes iron and steel. Every blade in Moriana originated in the Highlands. It's dirty and dangerous, but the payoff is worth every lost life."

"Charming," Tharan said, examining his blade. Sylphs used obsidian in place of steel or iron in their weaponry. "And what of the people?"

"The classes of the Highlands are divided, with a few ruling houses pulling rank over the rest of the kingdom. Gideon rules with an iron fist over all of them. Though, you'd never know it from the outside. His brutality is unmatched. Many residents live in squalor on the outskirts of the city. The lowest ranking class, the servants, have their tongues mutilated at birth, so they cannot sell the secrets of the palace."

Tharan shut his eyes in disgust. "Barbarians."

"The Highlands are both beautiful and brutal. Some say the beauty of the land makes the men cruel."

"What do you think?" Tharan set his cigarette into an ashtray.

I picked at my nails nervously. "I think thousands of years of brutality breeds a certain type of man."

He nodded decisively. "I agree. Now tell me what your plan is."

In front of us lay a large schematic of the castle at Ryft's Edge. A shiver ran down my spine at the sight of it.

I pointed to the Chayne Mountains. "There is one path through the mountains. They call it the Ryft. Half guarded by the Stone Kingdom armies; the other half guarded by the Highland armies. The center of the land trades between the three human kingdoms. Without it, everything must be shipped in via the sea or through the Bog of Eternal Suffering, and no one dares to venture there."

"How are we going to get in?" he asked.

"We can either cross the mountains on foot, come in through the sea, or…"

Tharan groaned. "The bog?"

"The bog."

I ran my fingers over the Ryft on the map. "I think we can avoid it. We'll need to be glamoured to make it through the Ryft, but I think we can make it."

"I'll call for the spell weaver." He rang a bell, and a satyr entered the room. "Send for Elrida."

"Right away, your majesty." The satyr bowed and left.

I continued telling Tharan about the Highlands' customs until we heard a knock at the door.

"Enter," Tharan said in his royal voice.

Hunching as she walked, her weight supported by a thick hickory cane, the elderly sylph bowed as best she could. "You called for me, your majesty."

"Take a seat, Elrida."

The ancient woman slowly lowered herself into a plush chair. "How can I be of service?"

"We'll need two glamours. Human ones. A married couple. Have the scribe draw up marriage documents as well. You know how humans love their bureaucracy."

"Of course, my king. I will get to work on weaving something right away." Elrida hobbled to the door. "Don't fall in love with each other now."

Tharan gave her a knowing look. "We're just friends, Elrida. I appreciate the concern, though."

Elrida winked at me before slipping back through the carved doors.

"Now, where were we?" Tharan said, scanning the maps and rubbing his palms on his green vest.

"We'll go in through the sewers." I pointed to the entrance points around the city. "Best to do it at night when no one is watching. Then, we'll work our way to this passage under the castle. It's used by servants to transport goods without being seen by royalty. The royals hate seeing servants, so they keep them hidden as much as possible. We can take one of these doors into the main castle. Erissa's room is here." I pointed to Erissa's chambers on the map.

Tharan nodded. "Easy enough."

"We'll also need servants' clothes to blend in while we're in the tunnels."

Tharan bit his lip, lost in thought. "Can you draw something up for the palace tailor?"

"That won't be a problem. The servants also use hand signals to speak. I know the language, so let me do the talking."

Tharan signed. "Like this?"

I smiled, blinking rapidly. "Of course, you know sign language."

"I'm seven hundred years old. You don't think I've been bored enough to learn sign language?"

"I'm thirty, and I will never live to be the age you are now. I don't know what immortality is like."

Tharan shrugged. "Well, I know sign language."

"Great, then we should be fine. Just some humans scouring the sewers, looking for an amulet with a soul inside. What could go wrong?" A flicker of my old self sprung to life.

"You'll be with the Alder King. I'll keep you safe." The heat from his arm around my shoulder lit a fire underneath my skin. I breathed in deeply, trying to keep my arousal concealed. "The stable master will bring up a cart for Arion to pull. We'll look like farmers selling our goods.

"Are you excited about this?" I asked, my hands on my hips, the same way my mother would stand after I did something stupid. Tharan had never been a normal citizen before. He had always been a prince and now a king. Being normal might be fun for him.

"Kind of." He shrugged, giving me a mischievous smirk. "I have spent little time in the mortal lands. When you're as old as I am, things like this excite you."

"Don't set your expectations too high." I patted Winter before heading out.

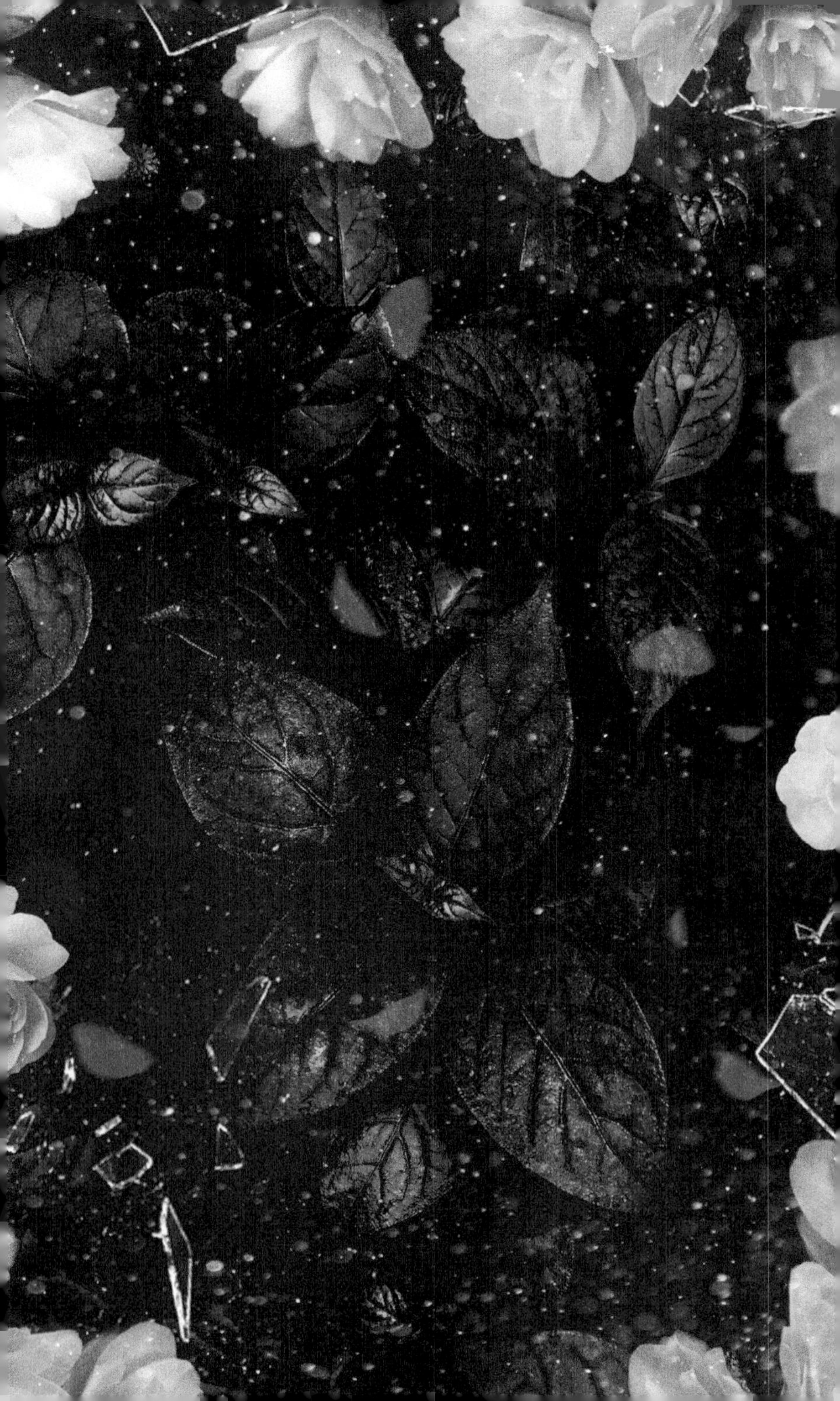

38 CAIDEN

"What was a Council Court doing at one of the Alder King's revelries?" Daynaris, lord of the Court of Light and head of the High Sylph Council slammed his palm on the podium. The council sat around an elevated dais. The ten representatives whispered to each other as Caiden stood before them, feeling foolish, squinting as blinding sunlight streamed through the floor-to-ceiling windows.

"We were invited. After the attack on the Court of Sorrows, I saved the Alder King's heir, Tharan, from a cave kraken. He invited the Court of Storms as a sign of gratitude."

Lord Daynaris stroked his dark beard with his thick, ringed fingers, contemplating Caiden's words. "Did you sanction this trip, Tonin?" He turned to Caiden's father.

"Caiden does not need to seek my approval. I trust his judgment." He nodded to his son.

Lord Daynaris let out a hearty laugh. "You always loved your children too much to see their foolish actions, Tonin."

Caiden interrupted. "Now is not the time for parenting advice. The Highlands allied with the mountain goblins and attacked the Woodlands during a holy festival. That cannot go unpunished. I have brought an emissary from the Court of the Alder King with me to attest to what I am saying."

A slim purple-haired sylph female stepped forward, wearing the crest of the Alder King. "It is true, my lord. The Highlands attacked without cause. We only survived because all the courts banded together."

Members of the council grumbled to one another. Caiden had been in this situation before. When Baylis's father, King Philip, died, he pleaded with the council to send aid to the Midlands. They refused, and the Midlands fell to Gideon. He shuddered, thinking about what the good people of the Midlands' lives were like now.

"We need to band together with the Wild Courts and present a united front." His words echoed throughout the gilded chamber. "Gideon will not stop until he has conquered the sylph lands."

Laughter erupted from the dais. Lord Cindron of the Court of Ashes hung his wiry arm over the edge of the podium. "A human army has never beaten a sylph army, let alone conquered a kingdom in the history of Moriana. Many have tried and failed. This king will be no different. The Wild Courts wanted to be separate from us. I say, let them fight their own battles. This is nothing we need to be concerned with."

"Maybe if they weren't so concerned with their parties, they would have seen this coming," a representative from the Court of Honey adorned in gold with honeycombs embroidered on her dress chimed in. Bees buzzed around her flower crown.

The council murmured in agreement.

Caiden swallowed his anger. He wanted to scream at all of them, but such an outburst would not do him any good. "Do you think the Highlands won't come for the Council Courts next? You hide here, deep inside council territory, but what of the courts bordering the Highlands? The Court of Scales could be next."

Lord Daynaris held up a gilded hand. "And should that time

come, we will be ready. But for now, I propose we send troops to the bordering courts. That should be enough to ward off any unwanted advances."

The council grumbled to themselves.

Hoping to call the court to order, Lord Daynaris slammed his gavel on the podium.

The members of the council quieted.

"Here is my ruling. Young Caiden will go on a fact-finding mission to the Highlands to infiltrate their court and see what he can learn. He will return when he has evidence we can use."

Caiden's heart sank. The Woodland's emissary deflated into the chair next to him as the members of the council filed out of the room.

"What now?" she asked in an exasperated tone.

Caiden rubbed his temples, hoping to quell his aching head. "Now, I find my Master of Shadows, Lucius, and make a plan to infiltrate the one place we swore we'd never return."

"I need to tell the Alder King about this," she said, jotting down something in a notebook. "Maybe he can help."

"Of course."

The emissary headed back to the Woodlands. "Thank you for everything," she yelled as she rode off.

Caiden made his way back to his parents' townhome on the upper east side of the city. They made the move permanent when his older brother, Aryn, came of age. His father opted to keep the title of High Lord in name only to focus on his council duties, leaving Caiden and his brother to run the Court of Storms.

Roderick and Lucius were seated at the large kitchen table, chatting with his mother, Tempestia. Her black ringlet curls flowed like water over her tanned skin. Her hazel eyes sparked with love at the sight of her youngest son.

"How did it go?" Setting her teacup down, she embraced her son.

The familiar scent of rosewater filled Caiden with nostalgia.

He hugged his mother tightly. "They want me to go on a reconnaissance mission to the Highlands to bring back proof Gideon plans to attack more courts."

Lucius laughed. "Us almost dying wasn't enough for them?"

"Apparently not," he said, taking the cup of hot marrow root tea his mother offered, and settled into one of the antique chairs at the dining table.

Lucius sighed. "I will draw up a plan and bring it to you tomorrow. We should leave as soon as possible."

"Agreed." Caiden sipped his tea.

Roderick fidgeted with his fingers. "I, uh, have something to ask you and your father."

Caiden raised an eyebrow. "What is it?"

"With your permission, I'd like to marry Amolie in a hand-binding ceremony in the temple of Illya in the Stormlands."

Tempestia's face brightened. "Oh, how wonderful! A wedding. We need some cheer."

A smile cut across Caiden's chiseled face. "Of course. I am happy to sanction it. Although you know you will have to ask Aryn. He handles domestic matters."

"I will go ask him now. I'd like to perform the ceremony as soon as possible. We've waited long enough." Roderick left with a skip in his step.

Caiden called after him, "And tell Amolie hello for me as well!"

Roderick smiled, his bright white teeth blinding against his umber skin. "Thank you."

Lucius came back, holding one of Caiden's mother's rose cakes. "I guess it's just you and me on the mission to the Highlands." Crumbs dotted his black attire after having enjoyed the treat. He brushed them away before heading out into the night.

Tempestia reached across the table, taking her son's hands in hers. "Please be careful, Son. I don't want to lose you again."

Caiden rubbed his thumbs in circles on his mother's tan skin. "It'll be fine, Mother. It's just an information-gathering mission. Nothing more."

She gazed upon her son with soft concern. "I will pray to Illya for your safe return."

The city sparkled for the Yuletide. Topiaries lined the cobblestone streets decorated with ribbons and small lanterns hung in bundles along the sidewalk.

Caiden's thoughts drifted to his wife. His heart yearned for her touch.

As a child, he envisioned a life of service to his kingdom, to the sylph. He wanted to be a soldier since the day he could hold a sword, but life had other plans.

Cassandra gave him purpose. He loved being her husband. His thoughts drifted to the sunny days when she worked in the gardens while he whittled toys for their future children. Her golden hair blowing in the summer breeze, her hands covered in dirt. A tear trickled down his cheek as he walked the snowy streets of Vantris.

He chucked a stone into the nearby river. Gideon would pay for what he did to his wife. He would make sure of that, with or without the sanction of the council.

As he returned to his parents' home, something gnawed at him. Something he couldn't quite place, like an itch he couldn't reach. Had he forgotten something?

A pain crept up his arm. He pulled back his sleeve, hoping to find the source, but he found nothing.

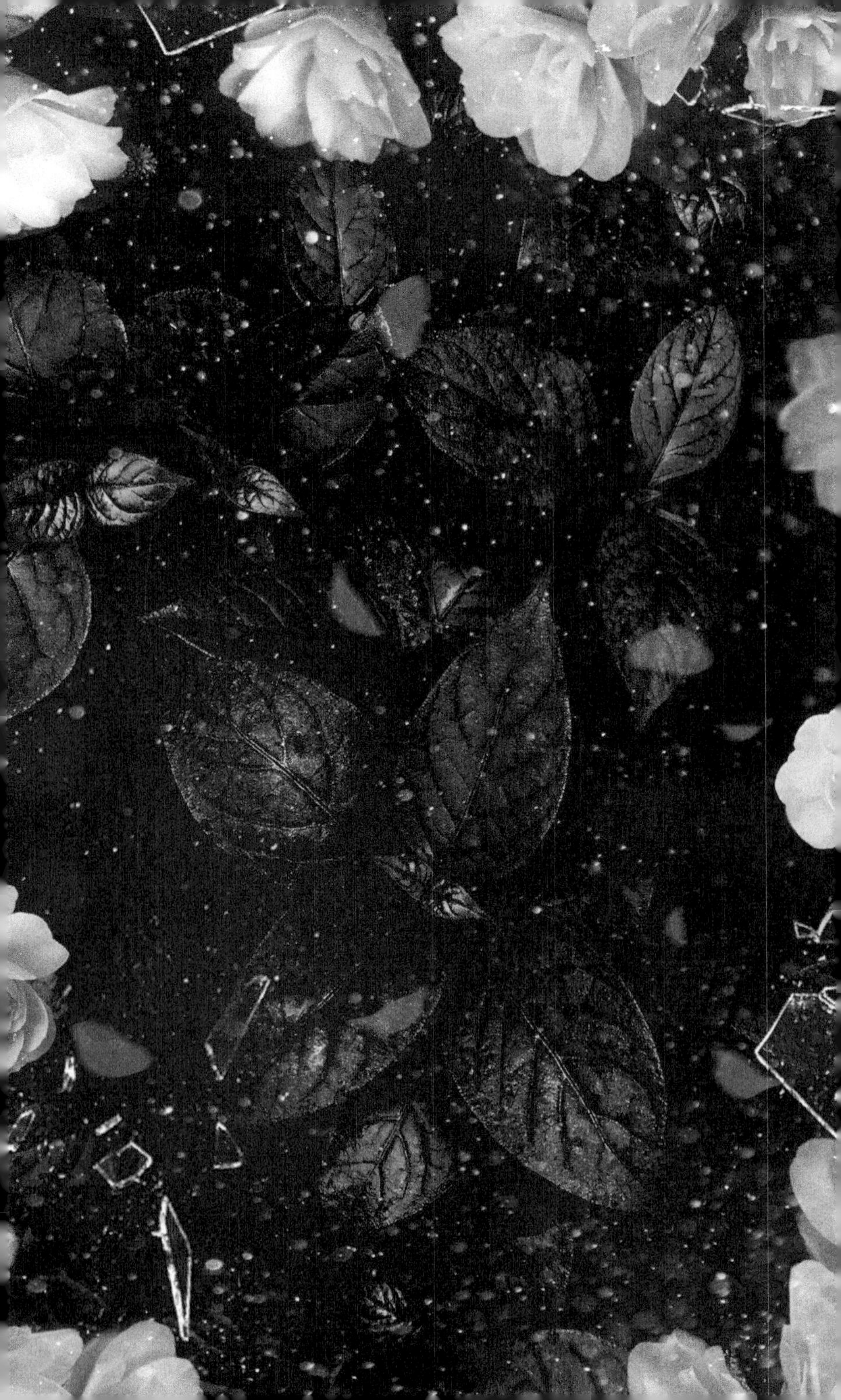

39 AELIA

Amolie woke me at dawn's first light. "Time to go."

Rubbing the sleep from my eyes, I let out a yawn. She shoved a mug of coffee into my hand. I sipped it, letting the warm liquid fill the hole in my chest. Utterly exposed, I would have to confront my fears without Caiden and without the numbness of dust.

The candle I lit the day before still burned beside Baylis's bed. Its little light fighting the fleeting darkness.

Amolie pulled a needle from her thick wool skirt. "Send some calming pictures into her mind."

Holding Baylis's hand, I tethered our minds together, trying my best not to trigger whatever I had before. I summoned a field of wildflowers, projecting a memory of us making daisy crowns, pretending to rule over a make-believe kingdom. Simpler times when we could be children. Before the darkness seeped into our home and into the kingdom.

I wanted to hug the little girls playing before me—protect them from the harsh future awaiting them.

Amolie touched my hand, signaling she had gotten enough blood.

I tucked Baylis's golden hair behind her ear. "I will come back for you," I whispered as we crept out of the room.

Amolie handed me the vial of Baylis's blood. "Keep it safe."

"Thank you, Amolie, for everything. I don't know what I'd do without you."

She squeezed my arm lovingly. "That's what friends are for."

I headed to my room to gather my things and change into peasant clothes. The Scepter of the Dead lay silent on the desk.

'You will need me before this is all over,' the Morrigan's voice hissed in my ear.

Begrudgingly, I packed it away in my sack.

Tharan waited outside with Arion tethered to a plain cart. He handed me a twine ring enchanted by Elrida with the glamour.

"Are you ready?" he asked, buttoning the simple cotton shirt, his toned arms gleaming beneath.

I sighed. "As I'll ever be, I suppose."

Tharan slipped on his twine ring. The glamour did little to hide his beauty.

I would not have such luck. Slipping on the ring, my skin became dull, and the shadows under my eyes returned.

Tharan patted the simple wooden seat next to him on the cart. "Got a seat waiting for you here."

I smiled and climbed in, trying to kill every butterfly dancing around my stomach.

"Let's get this over with," I said under my breath.

Tharan squeezed my gloved hand. "It'll be alright; we'll be in and out. I won't let anything happen to you."

I winced at the words. "You can't promise that. You do not control the lands of men."

He hooked a gloved finger under my chin, lifting my face, forcing our eyes to meet. "I swear I will do everything in my power to protect you, Aelia Springborn."

I noticed the glamour concealed his scar and turned his eyes a dull green. Still, they caused thoughts to empty from my head.

"I'll hold you to that."

He gave me a smile and flicked the reins. Arion sauntered forward.

"Good luck!" Amolie called after us. Frost and Winter whined at her side.

The trip to the Ryft took several weeks, through the Woodland Realm, across a slim bit of elven territory to the Stone Kingdom, where we'd cross the Ryft.

I fiddled with the ring, pulling it off and putting it back on. My skin glowed and dulled with its presence.

"You don't have to be human yet," I said, looking at Tharan, sporting lackluster auburn hair and pale, freckled skin.

He shrugged. "It's nice to be unknown in my kingdom. It's interesting."

Humans were weak and sickly compared to the magus. As much as I loathed my transformation at times, being part sylph had its benefits.

The hard wooden seat dug into my back as we traversed the snow-laden path. With little to nothing to preoccupy my time, my thoughts drifted to Ryft's Edge. Chest tight, I dug my fingers into the shoddy wooden seat, trying to ease the pressure rising in my veins.

We stopped to rest on the border of the Woodland Realm and elven realms.

While Tharan hunted for dinner, I built a fire, trying to quell the unease growing in my stomach. I had tried to forget Ryft's Edge, but every time I closed my eyes, there it returned.

Tharan entered the firelight holding a brace of rabbits and two large wild carrots he found. "How's this for dinner?"

"Lovely. Care to use some of your magic and conjure us some herbs?"

Tharan waved his hand over a bit of earth. Shrubs of thyme and rosemary burst from the ground. "How's that?" he asked, giving me a wry smile.

"Impressive," I said, picking the herbs and throwing them into the pan.

The forest lay eerily silent as we ate our dinner. Lights of the elven city across the border flickered through the trees.

"They call it Stealle. City of Stars," Tharan said, scraping his tin plate with his fork. The elves thought they were above all others and named their cities accordingly.

"City of Stars, what a bunch of horseshit." I took a swig of ale.

Tharan chuckled. "When you're immortal, you pick names you think will stand the test of time."

I rolled my eyes. "How boring."

Tharan nodded. "It is true. Everything is more beautiful, more precious when you know it's fleeting."

A question floated into my mind and out of my mouth, "Since you're half-elf, will you still live forever?"

Tharan shook his head, the fires golden light playing across his face, illuminating his green eyes. "I will live thousands of years, but my life will end. There was one other half-elf, half-sylph born before the ban, and we all know how he died."

I gave him a puzzled look.

He blinked at me. "Crom Cruach."

I gave him a startled look.

"Few people know that," he said, taking my empty plate.

"Is that why the mixing of elves and sylphs is forbidden?"

"Part of it." He held the plates under a trickle of water

spouting from a stone wall. "Both the sylph and elves are proud of their heritage and want to ensure each race survives. Some believe the magic will wane if the blood is not pure. Although it's the sylph's dirty secret, they use human females to strengthen the bloodlines. I suspect the elves do the same."

"I thought those were just stories," I said, remembering the stories of changelings we were told as children.

Tharan repacked the cart. "The sylph and elves like to look down upon humans when, in reality, they depend on them to ensure the survival of their respective species."

I strapped a feedbag onto Arion's mouth. "Is that why I could absorb the powers of a sylph? Is my blood a conduit for magic?"

Tharan rubbed his chin. "But you weren't human to begin with. Your mother is a Fate, which makes her a goddess. There's no telling how much of her magic runs through you."

I petted Arion as he munched happily on his dinner. "I never showed signs of powers before…"

Tharan threw me a blanket. "Perhaps it is hidden inside of you. There are ways of binding or hiding magic. Your mother would know how to do such a spell."

"Wouldn't I have sensed it before?" I threw the blanket over Arion.

Tharan rummaged around the wagon. "I could help you find it if you'd like."

"Mm… Let's concentrate on surviving the Highlands. We can leave my powers for later."

"Fair enough," Tharan said as he stood over the back of the wagon. Waving his hands, the bed filled with a thick layer of pine needles. "These will be softer than the ground for you." He placed another blanket on top of the needles.

I swallowed hard. "Where are you going to sleep?"

"The ground will be fine for me." He patted the soft pines.

Wrapping the blanket tighter around myself, I hesitated before laying in the makeshift bed. "Please come and lie next to me so I don't feel bad for making you sleep in the dirt. You are a king, and I am nothing."

Tharan smiled as he filled Arion's water. "I've slept in worse places." He patted the black stallion before removing his feedbag.

"You weren't a king then." My teeth chattered from the cold.

He sighed before reluctantly climbing into the wagon with me. "It only seems right for me to keep you warm."

His body radiated heat as we lay silent, listening to the sounds of the forest. It took everything in my power not to curl my body into his.

I rolled onto my back, staring up at the stars. "One last question."

"You're inquisitive tonight." His hand brushed mine gently, making my heart flutter.

"If you're a half-elf, can you transfer your immortality through the breath like full elves?"

"Do you want to find out?" Our eyes locked on one another. Electricity crackling between us.

Neither of us dared to make the first move.

A twig cracked in the forest, breaking our trance. He held his finger to his mouth before pointing at the ridge above us.

My eyes adjusted to the darkness as a blinding white light crept through the trees. I blinked, unable to comprehend what I saw. The creature came into focus, quickening my pulse.

A unicorn.

The majestic creature moved with an unnatural grace as it weaved in between the trees. Hunted to near extinction, unicorns were rare. So rare few believed they still existed.

"Would you like to pet her?" he asked.

"Are you serious?" I tried to hide my excitement, keeping my voice to a whisper.

Tharan smiled, whistling a beautiful melody.

The mare raised her head and came trotting down the path into the ravine where we lay. Arion whinnied in excitement.

Tharan sat at the edge of the cart, holding out a carrot.

She hesitated, but Tharan said in a calming voice, "She is a friend." The mare gently took the carrot from his hand. "You can pet her now if you'd like."

I slid the glove off my hand and ran it down her long, muscular neck. Soft as a baby bunny, her fur, almost translucent, glowed a radiant shade of white.

Tharan cooed over the mare, petting her gently on the neck. "I call her Aurora, for she is the dawn of a new age for the unicorns."

Tears welled in my eyes. "She's pregnant?" I asked.

"She is," Tharan said, rubbing the mare on the head. "I have been running a breeding program in secret for a decade." He gave the mare another carrot. "Magic makes the blood thin, so I've had to mix them with regular horses. The process is not exact, resulting in a unicorn a quarter of the time. It's a slow process, but my herd has grown from ten to nearly thirty."

Arion whinnied at the mare. "It seems like Arion has taken a shine to Aurora," I said. "Maybe you could breed him into your line."

"I think that could be arranged." Aurora trotted over to Arion, the two nuzzled each other.

My heart filled with love. "I can't wait to tell Amolie about this. She's not going to believe it."

We laid back down in the wagon bed watching the clouds sail over the stars. My heart torn in two. I could not deny my feelings for Tharan, but I also felt like I was betraying Caiden.

Tharan clicked his tongue. "Care to share what you're ruminating on?"

"How do you know I'm thinking about anything?" I scoffed.

"I can feel your thoughts turning over in your mind like

you're trying to put a puzzle together." His hand brushed mine again.

I hesitated, unsure of how vulnerable I wanted to be with him.

"You can trust me, Aelia." His hand squeezed mine.

I exhaled slowly. "I've fallen in love with every man who's ever shown me the slightest bit of attention. It's as if I'm a desert thirsting for a single drop of rain. I felt that way with Caiden and Gideon, and now I'm experiencing those same emotions with you. I feel guilty, as if I'm betraying Caiden, even though he doesn't know who I am. But I remember. I remember everything. Part of me doesn't want to let him go, but I know I must. I need to move on. And then there's you. You're so perfect and understanding, and you make my knees go weak, but I'm worried I'll never be enough—"

Tharan cut my rant short by pressing his lips to mine.

The breath left my lungs as arousal grew within me. We kissed as though we had known each other for years, each one anticipating the other's movements. I didn't want to stop, but I knew we had to.

"I've thought about our kiss every day since that night in the Court of Sorrows." He ran his thumb along my cheek.

Words escaped me. I pressed my lips to his once more, letting his heat consume me.

"We shouldn't," I whispered.

His eyes searched mine for answers. "Why not? We're both adults."

Twirling a piece of his auburn hair around my finger, I tried to find the right words. "I must protect my heart. You are the Alder King. You will marry a highborn magus woman. This will only end in heartache for me."

Tharan's gaze softened. "I can marry whomever I choose."

He leaned in for a kiss, but I stopped him before our lips could touch. "Don't be foolish. We both know how this ends."

He pulled me into his warm embrace. "I know you've been through a lot. We can take it slow if you'd like. Be friends for now. It's clear by the way you kissed me you want this too. Let me show you who I am."

Emotions knotted themselves in my chest. I could not deny my attraction to Tharan.

I nestled my head into his broad chest. I felt safe with him. In my heart, I knew I should let Caiden go. I had no loyalty to him. Tharan was real. Tharan was security and safety—something I hadn't had in years. In Tharan's arms, I didn't feel like prey waiting to be pounced on. He faced his demons. I wouldn't have to fix him—wouldn't have to empty myself to make him whole.

"Alright," I said after an awkward amount of silence. "We can take it slow. I want to get to know the real Tharan. I want you to woo me. Like a real princess."

Tharan laughed. "Oh, I know how to woo with the best of them."

"Judging by the way you kissed me, I'd say you've had a lot of practice," I joked, trying to hide my smile.

He leaned in and pressed his lips against mine, sending electricity through my veins. "Practice makes perfect."

This taking-it-slow thing would be harder than I thought. "Friends don't kiss."

He raised an eyebrow seductively. "Some friends do."

I shook my head, trying not to blush. "No, they don't."

He nibbled my lip.

A moan grew in my throat. My fingers ached to touch him—to rake my nails down his back while he plunged himself deep inside me. A slickness grew between my legs. I wanted him. No—needed him.

Get it together, Aelia.

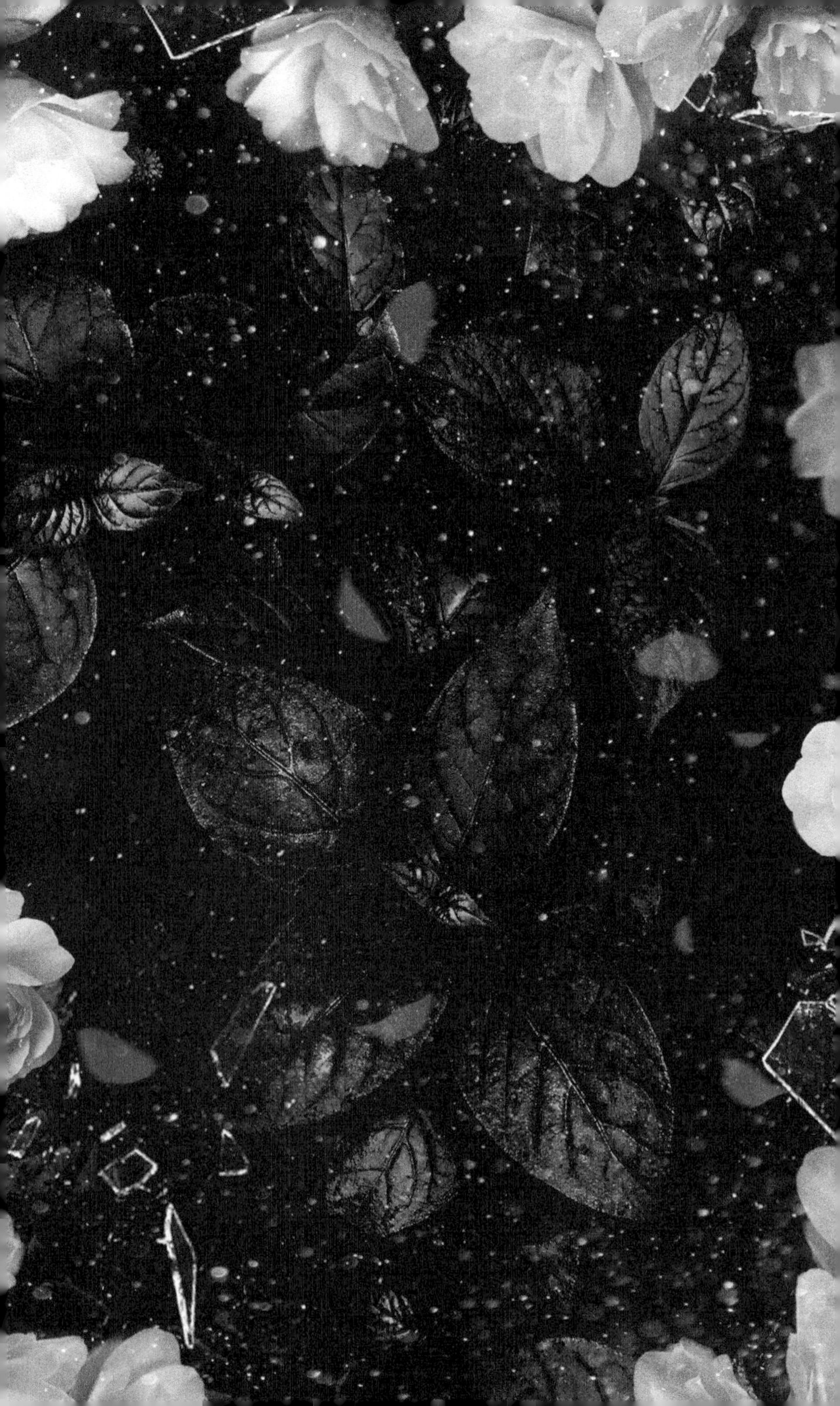

40 AELIA

Rising at dawn, we packed the little wagon and headed toward the elven territory. Neither of us said anything about the night before. Tharan made me a breakfast of rabbits with thyme and rosemary. Being with him was effortless.

The juices from the rabbit danced on my tongue, making me moan with delight.

"When you're at war, you learn how to cook for yourself," he said, handing me a slice of cheese and an apple. "Eat up. We are not stopping in elven territory."

Relief washed over me.

Tharan took off the twine ring, letting his true self shine through. The unforgettable scar snaked across his face, his skin glowing like dew catching the sun's first light.

"They won't bother us if they see it's me, but keep your hood up. We don't need word getting around we're traveling together."

I scrunched my nose at him. "Whatever you say, my king."

He rolled his eyes at me. "Get in the cart. The sooner we leave here, the sooner we make it to the Stone Kingdom. I do *not* want to get caught in the mountains at night. Harpies lurk there."

"Oh, is the Alder King afraid of a little bat?"

"They are not bats. They are terrible creatures sent by Hades to punish humans and magus alike."

I threw him a side-eye. "You fucked one, didn't you? And then she tried to kill you." Harpies were known for their ability to appear as beautiful young women to lure men back to their nests. Where they transformed into hideous beasts, tearing their unsuspecting victims to shreds.

He held his head high in the air. "I don't want to talk about it."

"He-he, harpy fucker," I said, jabbing him in the ribs with my elbow.

He scoffed. "I'm trying not to be that person, remember? I'm trying to show you I'm different, and fucking a harpy is not a great way to do that."

I waved him off. "It's fine. We both have pasts. No one can use them to hurt us if we laugh at them."

Tharan clasped a gloved hand around mine. "You're right."

Arion breezed down the freshly plowed streets, whinnying with delight as we traversed the elven kingdom.

Two colossal statues of halflings dressed in battle armor guarded the entrance of the Stone Kingdom. Over their heads, an inscription read: *We are the wielders of Mylar's ax. Let no rock break us. Let no stone disobey us.*

"The halflings of the Stone Kingdom are a proud race," Tharan said, urging Arion forward.

The primary city within the Stone Kingdom went by the name of Mineralia. A towering metropolis constructed into the side of the Cheyne Mountains, an impressive engineering accomplishment for any species, let alone one of such diminutive stature.

Here, halflings and humans mingled freely, linked by a treaty forged ages ago determining the stewardship of the mountain. At the city's heart lay a vast lake formed before any creature set foot on Moriana. Some believed the Trinity themselves shaped it.

Humans and magus gathered at its shores, drawn by its renowned healing properties. Vendors peddled an array of products crafted from its healing waters, such as curative elixirs and cleansing soaps.

Tharan gave me a nudge. "Cover up. You never know who's lurking here. Someone may recognize you."

We slipped on our enchanted rings before entering the city, but as a precaution, I covered my face with my hood.

Tharan stopped in front of a small inn. No grandeur for us tonight. Two human farmers who were selling their wares wouldn't have the money. Tharan enchanted a pile of leaves to look like apples.

I waited outside with Arion while Tharan secured us a room, keeping an eye out for any Highland soldiers.

A bell chimed, signaling the end of the workday. Children played and laughed in the streets as their parents returned from a long day in the mines. Their faces covered in black ash from the day's work. In the Stone Kingdom, even women mined. They spent years learning about rocks and geology. Only the most skilled halflings were chosen. Women's petite bodies made them ideal for mining smaller caverns.

One child ran into her mother's outstretched arms, something I remembered from my childhood. I missed my mother. The mother I had then, not the conniving lying one who lived in the Tower of Fates. I thought of the conversation I had with Amolie. Maybe I had judged my mother too harshly. I never had time to find out her true motivations. Perhaps I would pay her a visit if I made it out of here alive.

Our modest room was furnished with one medium bed, a dresser, and a small tub.

A wind whipped through the open window, looking out at a dirty alleyway. I shivered as Tharan lit a fire in the small woodstove in the corner.

"It should be warm in just a minute," he said, feeding logs into the hearth.

I shut the window then pulled the blankets tight around myself.

Once the fire was lit, Tharan plopped down on the bed next to me, propping himself up on an elbow.

"Nervous?" he asked.

I ran my hands through my hair. "About tomorrow? Who wouldn't be a little anxious about returning to a place where you were tortured and turned into a magical creature who can read minds?"

"I'll be with you the whole time, Aelia." He placed a reassuring hand on my thigh.

I rubbed my palm with my thumb. "I hoped I'd never have to return to the Highlands. A fool's hope."

"You don't have to do this if you don't want to. I can take the blood. You can tell me where to go telepathically."

I held the vial of Baylis's blood, rubbing my fingers over the smooth glass. "No, I need to do this. For Baylis. And besides, my telepathy doesn't reach that far."

Tharan brushed a lock of hair out of my face. "Your bravery is admirable."

"Yeah, well, I've got a lot of cowardice I need to make amends for."

Part of me had died in Ryft's Edge. I didn't notice it at first, but over time it became clearer. Emotions were muted. The beauty of the world had faded. I wanted the piece Gideon took from me back, and if that meant spilling blood, then I would drain every living soul in the Highlands.

"Don't do it," Tharan said as if reading my mind.

I gave him an innocent look. "What?"

"Don't even think about killing Gideon."

My mouth fell open. "How did you—"

"You forget—I once murdered my lover in cold blood in front of the entire court of the Woodland Realm. It will not give you the peace you seek." He placed his hand over his heart. "Peace is here. Within yourself."

Chewing on the inside of my mouth, I contemplated his words. "I want him to hurt the way I did."

"He can't, Aelia. He is a creature who cannot feel the way you and I do. His heart is a shriveled piece of rotten fruit hanging on by a thread."

I smirked. "I know, but my innate need for justice gets the better of me."

"I know who he is. Maybe he was born bad, or perhaps the world turned him that way, but either way, there is nothing you can do to hurt him in the same way he hurt you. And besides, only we know he was behind the attack at the Court of Sorrows. I have no doubt he's concocted some lie justifying his attack on the Woodland Realm."

My eyes trailed to the floor. My mind flashed back to the time I tried to hurt him—one of my lowest points. I had seduced one of Gideon's guards into taking me to bed. I wanted Gideon to know my pain. He'd had many lovers since we wed. Each one a slice to my heart, causing me to bleed to death from the inside out. I wanted him to see I, too, could take a lover. That I could hurt him in all the ways he had hurt me, but it ended in my shame.

His words still echoed in my head. "*You think you can hurt me?*"

I squirmed underneath his iron grip.

"Well, you can't. You can't hurt me because you mean nothing to me."

My chest tightened as he pinned me against the wall.

Gideon's advisors looked on as he humiliated me.

Tears streaming down my face, I retreated inside myself. He couldn't hurt me if I felt nothing.

I burned the faces of Gideon's inner circle into my mind as they looked on and did nothing. Each one would meet a fate worse than death for their complicity.

Leaving my victimhood behind, I honed my new telepathy skills to take from Gideon the one thing he loved more than anything else: his kingdom.

"Fine, I won't kill him. However, we should look for evidence of what he's planning while we're in the castle."

"I was thinking the same thing." The little fire gilded his features. For a moment, neither of us spoke. Staring into each other's eyes, the fire between us building to a roar. My lips yearned to feel the pressure of his on mine, to taste him on my tongue.

He cleared his throat. "I think I'll go grab us some food."

My cheeks flushed. "Sounds like a good idea," I said, sitting on the edge of the bed, straightening my ill-fitting clothes.

I let out the breath I had been holding in. At the very least, he provided a welcome distraction from the impending nightmare across the Ryft.

Tharan returned thirty minutes later, carrying two roast chicken and potato platters.

We sat cross-legged on the floor, eating dinner in front of the little stove. The smell of herbs and cooked meats filled the room.

After dinner, Tharan suggested we take a stroll around the lake. Despite the cover of night, I still took precautions, purchasing a thick scarf to hide my face.

Colorful fish swam beneath the surface of the crystal-clear

lake. Out of the corner of my eye, I could've sworn I caught the jeweled tones of a mermaid tale. My thoughts drifted to Ursula. I hoped she made it out of the Alder Palace.

Mer stuck to their own, rarely involving themselves with the dealings of land dwellers. They even worshiped an ancient god, Manannan.

"Beautiful night," I said, hoping Tharan would take my hand.

"Not as beautiful as you, my dear," he said with a mischievous grin.

"Your charms won't work on me." A lie.

Shrugging, he wrapped his arm around me. "Well, a king can try."

"He sure can." I gave him a warm smile. A fuzzy feeling bubbled in my chest.

As we rounded the lake, two humans and a halfling dressed in shabby clothing jumped out from behind a pair of bushes, brandishing knives.

"What do we have here?" a human said, his face pocked from years of picking. Bags hung low beneath his eyes, and his fingers twitched in a familiar manner. Dust addicts. Judging by the marks on their faces and their pale gray skin, they'd been using for a long time. The dust took its toll on them. Desperate for coins to pay for the drug.

A hand clenched my heart at the sight. I could've been one of them.

"Give us your gold, and we'll be on our way," the halfling said.

Tharan stepped between us. "Back away. No one needs to get hurt here."

A human with a knobby nose and a missing ear pointed a finger at Tharan's chest. "And who are you?"

Tharan's fingers twitched.

My breath came faster. Tharan couldn't use his magic here. We had to act human.

Glancing around for onlookers, I launched into the halfling's mind while Tharan took on the other two.

Do not be afraid. Let me help you.

'*Who or what are you?*'

I am a telepath and can help ease your suffering if you wish. You need to heal the parts making you seek dust, but I can remove the craving.

'*And what if I don't want to? Without it, I have nothing.*'

Then, I will ease your pain in another way. I am already in your mind. All I have to do is light a match.

His psyche tensed.

'*But I'm not ready.*'

Choose now, my voice thundered inside his head.

The halfling's pulse quickened. '*Fine, Fine, I'll do it. I want to live.*'

Very well.

Diving deep into his psyche, I found the area where the craving lived, plucking it like rotten fruit. The lust for the drug would regrow if the halfling did not clear the tree entirely, but at least I bought him some time to heal whatever haunted him.

Shaking my head, I tried to rid my mind of the hopelessness seeping in, grinding grit between my teeth. Traces of people's psyches lingered like they wanted to go with you.

The halfling lay unconscious on the side of the path next to his friends.

"Let me help them too," I said before I dove into their minds, easing their pain as best as I could. We pulled the sleeping bodies into nearby bushes. They would awake cold and hungover, but at least they wouldn't be dead.

"What did you do to the men back there?" Tharan asked, taking off his green cloak, and hanging it neatly on the wall of our room.

I bit my lip. "I took away their lust for dust."

Tharan raised an eyebrow.

"It's not permanent, but it'll ease their suffering for a bit."

Tharan ran a thumb over his lip in contemplation. "That was kind of you."

Leaning back on the bed, I sighed. "I'm trying to be a better person. And part of that is helping others. I didn't cure them but set them on the right path." The burden I carried felt a little lighter.

Tharan took my face in his hands. My skin tingled at his caress. The light of the fire danced across his face.

"I want to kiss you, Aelia. I would've killed every one of those men tonight if it meant you were safe."

Caiden would have, too.

My heart beat faster. I leaned in, touching my lips to his, our bodies pressing against one another. He gripped my thighs, hoisting me into the air, pinning me against the wall as our mouths consumed one another. Primal urges begged to taste him.

"I want you," he whispered in my ear as teeth nibbled my neck. "I want you more every day."

My breath caught in my throat. "I want you too."

A low growl came from Tharan. His arousal grew as his tongue found its way to my ear.

I moaned with pleasure. "But not yet."

"Aelia, please." His breaths ragged with lust.

Keep your head on straight, Aelia.

"I can't, Tharan."

He lowered me to the ground, giving me sad puppy dog eyes.

I ran a hand down his angular jaw. "It's not that I don't want to, but I want to take it slow."

"You're right, I'm sorry." His eyes sank to the floor.

"I let it go too far." I pressed a kiss to his cheek before climbing into bed.

Tharan laid down next to me, pulling me in close, letting his heat wash over me like a wave upon the shore. With Tharan by my side, I could face whatever awaited me in the Highlands.

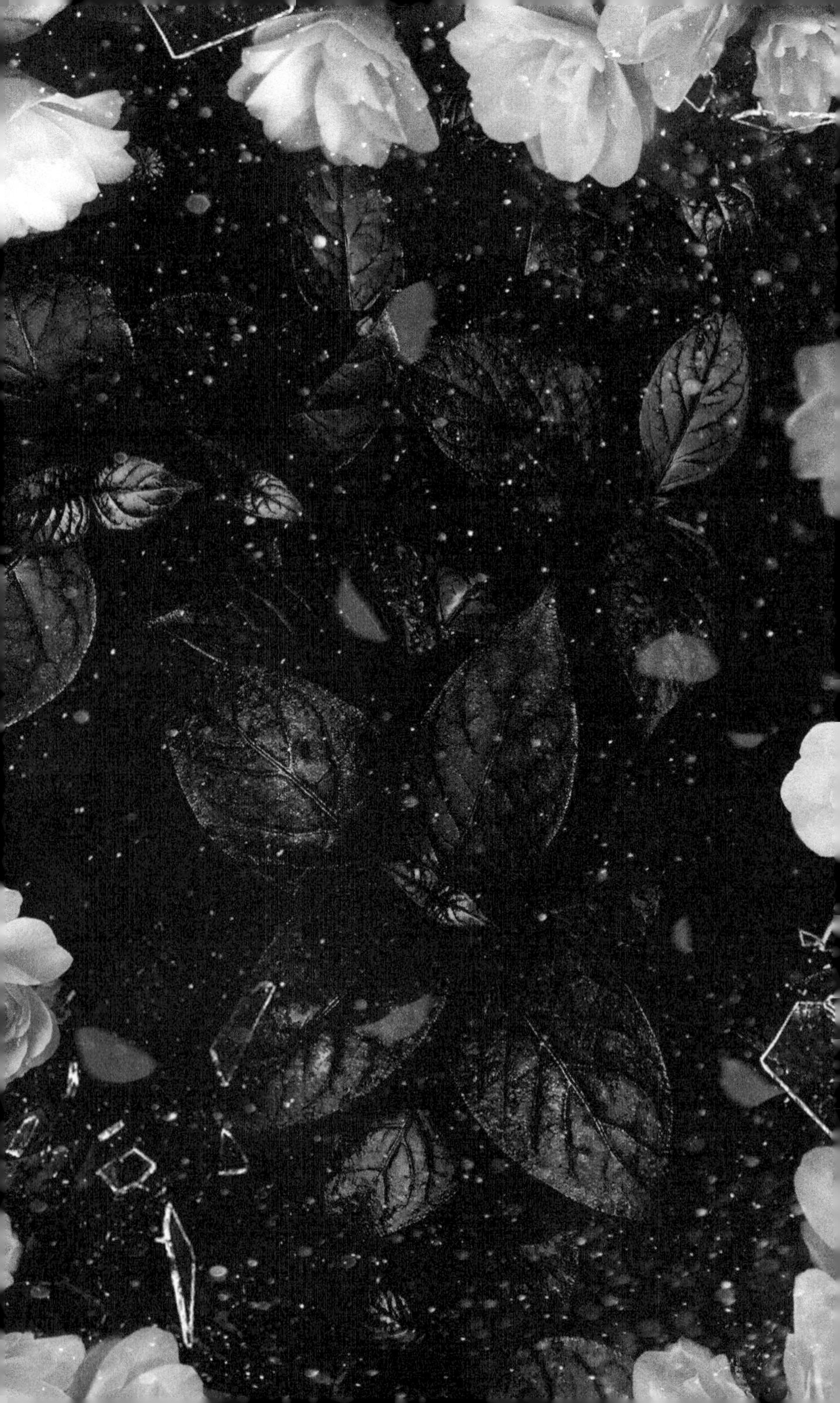

41 AELIA

Rolling over, I found only hollowness next to me. A note next to the bed read:

Went to get breakfast. Be back soon.

I sighed, pulling the covers tighter around myself. The fire died during the night, and cold crept in through every crevasse.

The steps outside our door groaned as Tharan made his way up.

Wrenching myself from the warmth of the bed, I pulled on a warm knitted sweater with wooden buttons over a thick wool skirt. I looked drab and human.

Tharan pushed open the door and handed me a plate of oatmeal with apples and cinnamon.

"It was all they had," he said, sitting on the edge of the bed next to me. He donned a plain knitted sweater paired with well-worn trousers and knee-high boots.

Finishing his breakfast, he set it back on the little tray. "Are you ready to go? I overheard some humans talking in the pub. Gideon added more checkpoints along the Ryft after the attack on the Woodlands, which he claimed was in relation to a sylph prince stealing his wife."

I raised an eyebrow. "I wonder if he meant you or Caiden?"

Tharan threw up his hands. "Does it matter? He's planting seeds to justify a war. If his allies believe him, his actions would be justified. He's already proved himself a hero in the Court of Sorrows."

My breath hitched in my throat. Of course, Gideon would use me as an excuse to wage war on Moriana.

Tharan put his hand on mine. "It'll be okay. We will free Baylis's soul, and then we will deal with Gideon's lies."

I tightened my mouth into a straight line. "You're right. We need to focus on the task at hand."

Tharan squeezed my hand, pulling me off the bed. "That's the spirit."

The trip across the Ryft took the better part of a day.

The first half would be easy. Gnomes didn't care who crossed. They needed the trade.

Meanwhile, the Highlands strictly controlled who entered and exited their half of the Ryft. Gideon monitored how many magi were in the Highlands—any magus needed documentation on the reason for their visit, signed by a magistrate of their kingdom. I prayed we looked human enough to pass, and I wouldn't have to use my telepathy. Using magic made humans taste copper. They would know we were magus.

I sharpened my blade as Arion trotted along the snow-covered path.

"Where did you get that dagger?" Tharan eyed the iridescent blade.

I hid the blade, realizing it might make Tharan uncomfortable.

"It's okay," he said, laying a hand on my arm. "The blade nor the wielder are the true cause of my father's death."

I turned the dagger over in my hands. Its iridescent hilt sparkled in the sunlight. "Caiden gave it to me as an Ostara gift. He said it would keep me safe."

"Such an item would cost a fortune. Dragons haven't existed in Moriana for hundreds of years."

I ran my finger over the smooth blade. "He loved me."

Silence filled the space between us.

The highway bustled with activity as numerous magi and humans traversed it in both directions.

"Not far until we hit the midway point." Tharan nodded to the path ahead.

A skeletal hand clutched my heart, and my body went stiff just thinking about seeing the soldiers again. *Everything will be fine; you will be fine.*

"It'll be fine," Tharan said, echoing my thoughts and giving my leg a comforting pat. "I'll be with you the entire time."

I ran my hands nervously over my skirt. "Let's get this over with."

At the first checkpoint, soldiers inspected our goods. Four guards stood around a fire waiting while two others checked the carts. Tharan maneuvered Arion into the inspection line.

Eying the soldiers around the fire, I looked for anyone I recognized. All fresh-faced—Ryft duty was reserved for the green and gray.

The weight perched on my chest lifted a little. These boys wouldn't know my face.

"State your business," the young officer said, not looking up from his list.

Tharan cleared his throat. "We are humble farmers traveling from Applewood to sell our delicious apples."

The soldier lifted his head; we piqued his interest. "Applewood? I have a cousin who lives there. Do you know Shelby Thomas?"

My heart leapt into my throat.

Tharan gave the man a rakish grin. "No, my boy, but we live far from town on a small farm."

"Really? I thought everyone knew him. His family owns the largest apple farm in the region."

Shit.

The boy examined us, tapping his quill on the parchment. "Do you have papers?"

Fuck. I panicked and launched into the boy's mind before Tharan could pull the papers, blasting through his mental door.

We are farmers. Your cousin knows us. Let us pass.

"You are farmers. My cousin knows you. Please, go ahead," he said in a monotone voice. The officer waved us on, and Tharan clicked his tongue at Arion to move him forward. The wagon crunched over the freshly fallen snow. I leaned back and let out a sigh of relief.

"Thank the Trinity," I said, stretching my legs over the cart's edge.

"I had papers made. You didn't need to do that." Tharan gave me a scolding look.

I bit at my cuticles, making little dots of blood form around my nails. "I panicked. I'm sorry."

He rubbed my shoulders, trying his best to soothe me. "I think there's one more before we enter Ryft's Edge. So, we should be at the inn in no time."

"Great, I'm going to shut my eyes for a bit. Wake me up if any harpies come wanting my dregs."

Tharan let out a warm laugh. "Technically, you're getting her dregs."

"I don't want to think about that." Pulling my hood over my eyes, I drifted off to sleep.

Two soldiers stood at the end of the Ryft. Beyond, the bronze spires of the castle rose out of the land, reaching into the heavens. I swallowed hard, bracing myself for the inevitable.

"Farmers?" an older officer said, looking at the apples in the back of our wagon.

"Yes, sir, the finest apples in all of Moriana." A lie. Tharan had enchanted a pile of leaves, but they'd never know.

"Mind if I have one?" the guard said, reaching into the back of the cart.

Gripping the seat tightly, I tried to calm my nerves.

Tharan caught his hand before he touched the apples. "Here, have mine. I was saving it because it was the best of the bunch. But a hardworking officer like yourself deserves it more than I do."

The graying guard took the apple from Tharan's hand, giving him a nod of thanks.

"Greenseed, the name's Greenseed. For your list."

The old guard waved us off. "Keeping track of humans is useless. It's the magus the king cares about. Be on your way."

I gave the old man the best smile I could conjure. "Have a good day!" I called as we passed into the Highlands.

The old guard raised his apple in a salute.

Our journey to cross the Ryft consumed the entire day, leaving me famished and my nerves frayed.

The castle towered above us, a haunting presence reminiscent of a scorned lover. My stomach churned with unease, a strong urge to flee tugging at me. I had grown stronger and wiser since my first arrival here. Yet, as I gazed up at the castle's bronze roof,

I couldn't shake the feeling of being a lamb awaiting its impending slaughter.

I took a shaky breath, grabbing Tharan's hand to keep myself from bolting.

Think of Baylis. You are doing this for Baylis. I repeated those words over and over as we neared the entrance to the city.

The wealthy lived in beautiful townhomes and lavish estates, while the working class and the poor lived on the city's outskirts. Pedestrians walked cobblestone streets buying their dinner without a care in the world.

Memories lingering like ghouls in the shadows haunted me as we trotted through the bustling city. My senses clawed at my skin, begging to be released from this torture. Taking a deep breath, I channeled my nerves into something more productive—thoughts of revenge.

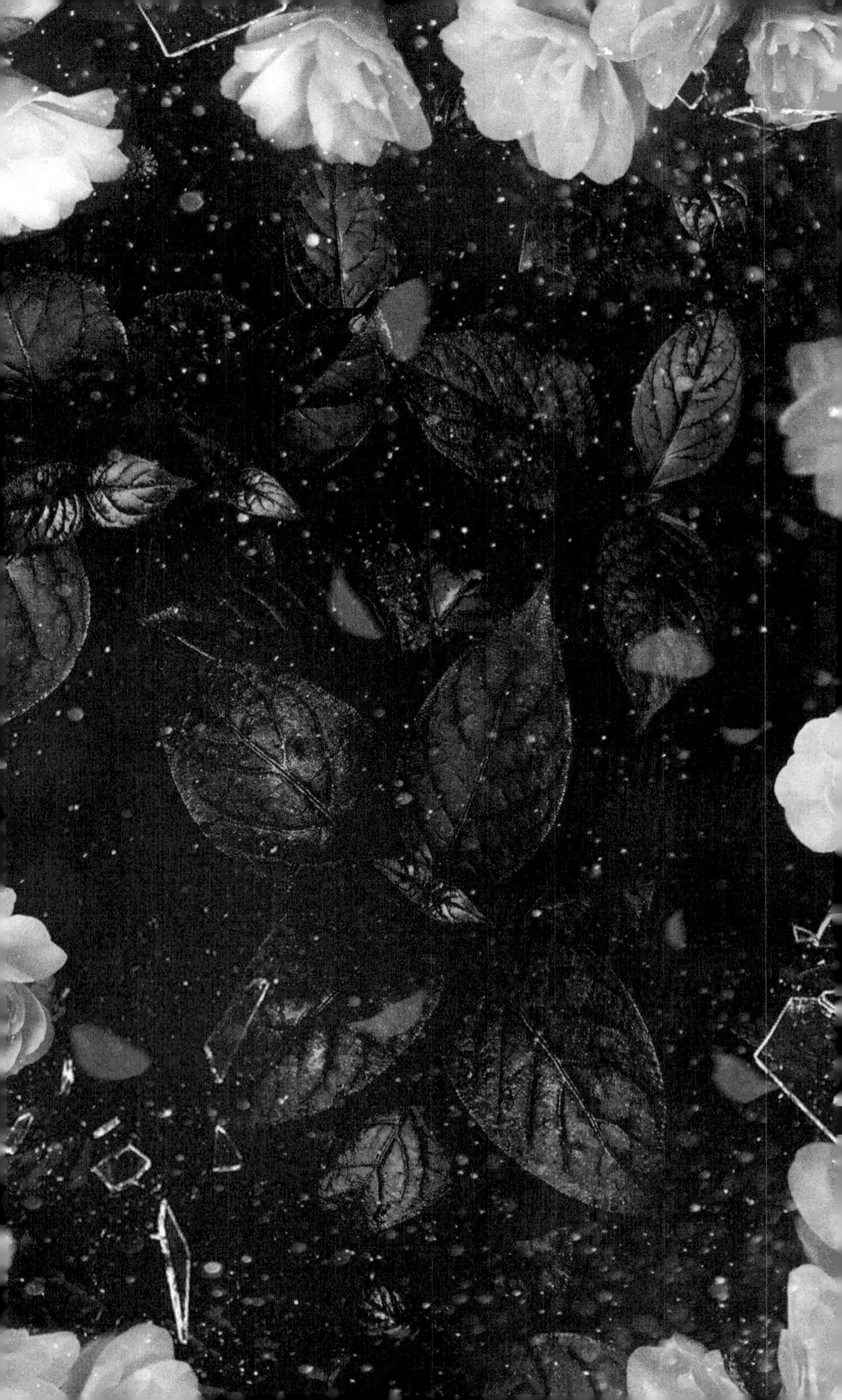

42 AELIA

The cottage Tharan arranged for us exuded coziness, furnished with well-worn pieces, a crackling fire, and candles flickering in the windows.

Tharan laid the castle map onto the little oak table. Cigarette in hand, his toe tapped the floor nervously.

I examined the servants' clothes—a simple white linen smock with a thick collar made of solid gold.

"What are you doing?" Tharan asked, an eyebrow raised.

"These are too clean. Servants wear the same frock until it rips from the collar." Taking soot from the fire, I smudged it on the uniforms. "There, that's better. They still look new, but at least they look a little more lived in."

"Smart," Tharan said, rubbing his chin with his hand.

"Not just a pretty face." I gave him a girlish smile.

"No, you certainly are not." Tharan's eyes raked over my body.

"I don't know what you're imagining, but you better get your head out of the gutter until we finish the task ahead."

"Oh, you do not want to know what I am thinking."

Heat bloomed in my chest, and pink dappled my cheeks. "You

men are all the same. Whether magus or human. You all think about one thing."

"It's hard not to when you're dressed so... seductively."

I looked down at the thick knitted sweater and skirt, making me look like a box. "Shut up."

A freezing rain pelted the little cabin with all the might the Trinity had given it. Tharan held me close as we listened to the hail hammer above.

"Do you think this roof will hold?" I asked, pulling Tharan's heavy arms tighter around me.

"It'll be fine," he murmured in his sleep.

"Glad someone can sleep tonight." In Tharan's comforting embrace, I found solace and safety. Nothing could touch me here.

Tomorrow would be a different story. Tomorrow, I would face my fears and enter the domain of my mortal enemy. The thought of facing Gideon, of seeing my gilded prison, made my brain scream for dust, but I would not feed it. I was stronger than my demons now.

Releasing a long breath, I reached for the clove cigarettes next to the bed.

Letting the smoke calm my nerves, I imagined a life where Tharan and I lived in this tiny cottage, selling apples for a living. What must it be like to live such a simple life?

'*Are you going to take me tomorrow?*' the voice of the Morrigan whispered in my ear.

"Oh, you again? When are you going to leave me alone?" I whispered into the night.

'*When you prick your finger and take control of my legions.*'

I blew out a smoke ring. "How many times do I have to tell you? I don't want my life force sucked out of me."

'*You are immortal. There is unlimited life to suck.*'

"I'm half sylph, and even full sylphs don't live forever."

'*Oh, you are much more, my dear. I know what power lies inside you. It is primordial, as mine is.*'

"I'm not risking it."

'*Tomorrow, you will enter the domain of the one they call Erissa. Long ago, I knew her by another name.*'

"She's ancient. Of course, you knew her by another name."

'*Wouldn't you like to know who she was before she came to the Highlands? An elven mage would never deign to serve a human king unless...*'

"Unless what?"

'*Unless she was running from something.*'

I arched my brow. "Alright, I'm intrigued. Go on."

The Morrigan clicked her ghostly tongue at me. '*Not until you prick your finger.*'

"I'll think about it." I took another puff from the cigarette.

The Morrigan did not respond.

"Goodnight," I said into the darkness.

The next morning, we explored the city, finding the sewer entrance.

"We'll go in here. Then we'll make our way into the castle."

Tharan nodded. "Can't wait. If my subjects could see me now, crawling through the mud, invading a human castle."

"Don't forget the shit. There's shit in the sewers too."

"Lovely. Let's eat before I lose my appetite."

We made our way to the market district, where farmers, like the ones we were pretending to be, sold their goods and where my favorite tavern happened to be located. The Drunken Pug, so named for the pugs Gideon's mother kept, provided drinks and food for commoners and travelers alike. Dark corners and hidden alcoves made the tavern a haven for those seeking discretion.

We took a seat at a secluded booth in the back. The old barmaid, Berta, greeted us. Her hair was more silver than I remembered. The effects of a hard life etched across her harsh face.

"Be right there!" she said in a gritty voice.

"Charming little spot," Tharan said, eying the cobwebs and layer of grease on the table.

Rubbing my hands on the worn wooden table, I felt safe here. "This is where queens go when they don't want to be spotted. The best shepherd's pie in Ryft's Edge."

Berta came over, greeting us with a cold smile. "What'll it be?"

"Two shepherd's pies and two ciders, please," I said, slapping two silver coins on the table.

Without so much as a glance at us, Berta collected the coins, nodding as she returned to the bar. "I'll get the ciders."

"So, this is the kind of place you haunt?" Tharan asked after Berta left.

"A far cry from the hallowed halls of the Alder Palace, I know." I surveyed my old haunt, the dingy mirrors, the cobwebbed corners—not much had changed in five years. The smell of stale ale and baking bread overwhelmed my senses. "Taverns like this are where I learned how the world worked. I'd listen for conversations I could use to my advantage."

"Using your…" He tapped his head.

I shrugged. "You'd be amazed at how much information people give away freely."

Berta arrived with the ciders. We thanked her and clinked our glasses together.

"To friendship," Tharan said with a wink.

I pushed my mug into his. "To friendship."

The sound of the bell on the door rang, breaking my nostalgic moment. Two large figures entered, taking seats at the bar.

I froze.

Tharan sat up straight. "What is it?"

I tapped my head and opened a line of communication between us.

Remus and Ramus. The Twins. My tormentors. They work for Erissa.

'*Is there a way out of here without them seeing you?*'

Maybe through the kitchen?

My heart pounded in my chest. Any second, they could turn around and see me.

'*I'll distract them. You run out of the kitchen.*'

Tharan chugged his cider, making sure to spill some on himself, and stumbled over to where the twins sat at the bar drinking their ale. I crouched low in the dark.

Tharan swung his arms around the men's broad shoulders. "Hello, boys. How about a ride on my cock? Or perhaps I could take a ride on yours?"

"What did you say to us?" The twins' beady eyes turned red.

Tharan seductively brushed his hair out of his face. "I said, do you want to fuck me?"

The scraping of stools on wood rang in my ears as I made my way through a maze of chairs toward the light of the kitchen, trying my best to walk on air.

"Look, we ain't like that." Remus's northern accent made it nearly impossible to decipher his words.

"Aww, but you two would be so much fun to play with." A mischievous twinkle glimmered in Tharan's eyes. "You know what they say. Two is better than one." A sly smile crossed his face just as Remus swung at him.

I ducked into the kitchen, surprising the cook, who almost dropped a soup pot on my head.

"Sorry." I gave him a genuine smile. "Exit?"

The cook nodded to the door behind him, and I ran for it.

A crowd formed around the tavern as Tharan and the twins brawled.

Berta's booming voice bellowed over the noise, "Enough! All of you... *out!*"

Tharan flew out the front door, landing in a snowbank near a farmer selling hogs.

The twins stumbled out after him, Remus holding his hand to his eye, Ramus limping.

I bit my lip as Tharan got to his feet, slinking away from the scene. Waiting until the twins were out of sight, I dashed through the alley after him.

"Are you alright?" I asked, pulling his arm over my shoulder. I wouldn't be of much help, but I could try.

Tharan gave me a wink, a smirk tugging at one corner of his mouth.

"Faker," I said, pushing his chest.

"Ow, I'm hurt, and this is how you treat me?" He couldn't hide his smile.

I shook my head. "You'll be the death of me."

He shook his head. "It's the other way 'round. *You* will be the death of me."

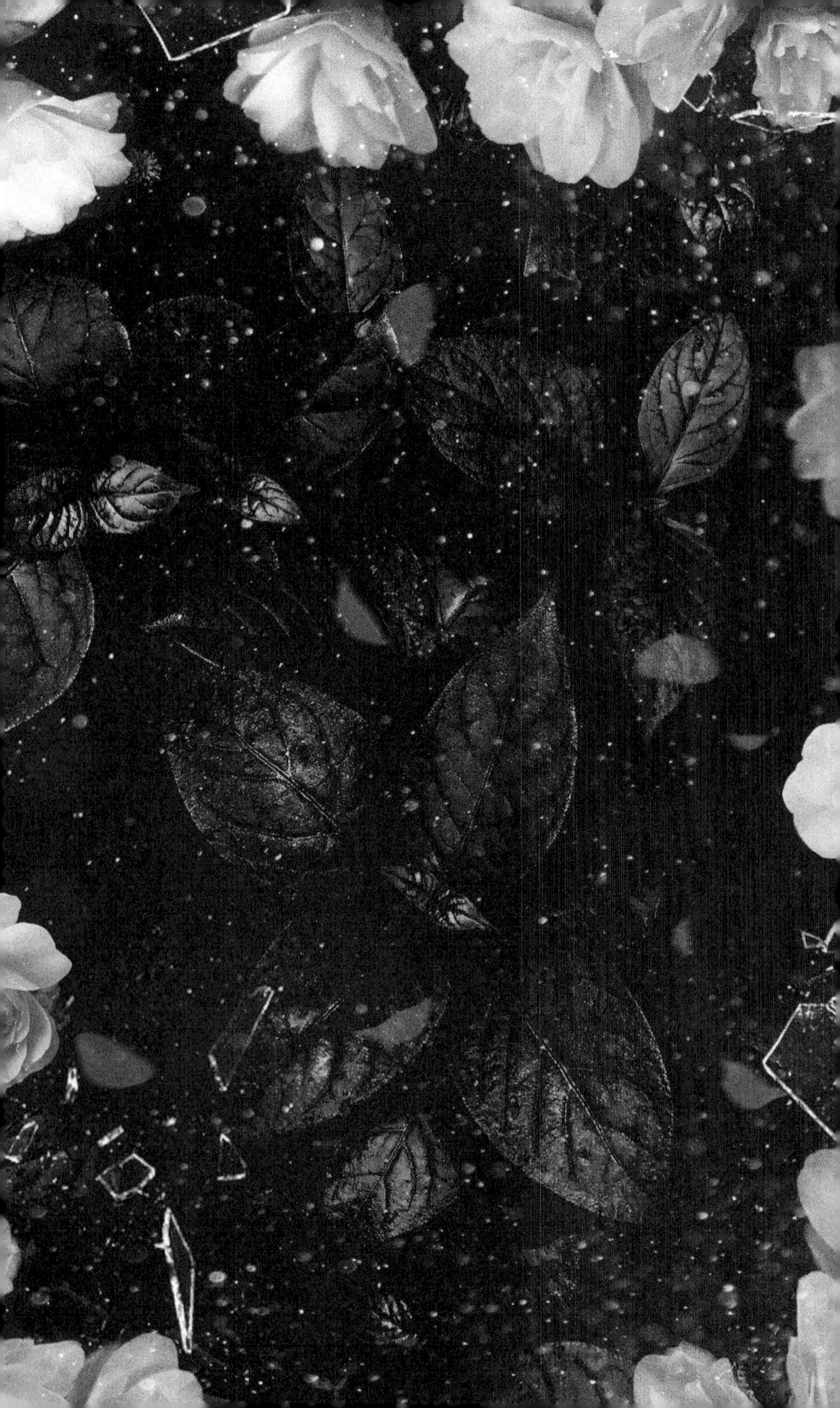

43 AELIA

I shivered as we walked to the entrance of the sewers, our uniforms providing little in the way of warmth.

The door groaned as Tharan pried it open. His expression darkened. The stench of piss and shit radiated from below, bringing bile to my throat.

"After you, my lady." He motioned for me to enter.

Feces squished between my toes as my feet tramped through the damp tunnel. Nauseated, I pushed forward. This place would not take anything else from me.

Tharan vomited as soon as his feet hit the sludge. "It's so much worse than I thought," he said, gagging.

I handed him two eucalyptus leaves. "Stick these up your nose. They will help."

Shaking, he took the leaves. Deep feces-filled muck sucked in our steps. Even rats did not dare to tread here.

Blinded by darkness, I ran my fingers along the wall, searching for indicators I carved long ago. "Ah ha! A pyramid means we're halfway."

"Great," Tharan said unenthusiastically.

We tramped through the tunnels, trying our best to hold our breath. The light of a single torch was our only guide.

The sound of rushing water filled the chamber. A marvel of modern invention, the Highlands diverted a river to run underneath the city, providing fresh water for the citizens.

Submerging his legs into the icy water, Tharan groaned with relief.

"Don't get too wet. We need to look like we have been working," I said, scrubbing the shit off my feet and ankles as best I could.

"Oh, c'mon. Have some fun." He splashed me playfully.

I slapped water back at him. "We can laugh later. This is serious."

"Fine." He pouted.

I cracked my neck, trying to adjust the invisible tension constantly pressing in on me at all times.

Only a few sleepy-eyed workers lingered in the servants' passageway, finishing the last-minute tasks. Concentrating on their work, they paid us no mind.

Dirt stuck to our feet as we padded through the dimly lit hallways. During the day, this would be a booming thoroughfare of servants, bustling about vendors selling their goods and services —a city beneath a city. Now, only the sound of our footsteps filled the plaster-lined halls.

"I've never seen anything like this before," Tharan said, staring into a tailor's window, where a little old man with thick spectacles worked on mending a dress for a highborn lady. "Sylphs don't have slaves."

That is what they were. Sure, they could hide behind the title of *servant*, but in reality, the servants—the backbone of the Highlands—were slaves, born and bred.

"Sylphs *were* slaves," Tharan said as I dragged him away.

Tharan might have been a slave. He fought in the sylph and

elven wars. I swallowed the lump of anxiety bulging in my throat. "Were you a…"

He held up his hand. "No. My father did not attend the celebration after Crom Cruach was defeated. Therefore, his kingdom remained untouched by the elves." He bit his lip, kicking a rock lazily.

Placing a hand on his arm, I wanted to say something, but what could you say to someone whose people had been enslaved for millennia?

"I wanted to free them, you know. Before I left. I wanted to free all the servants, but there were so many, and only one of me." Silver ringed my eyes.

Tharan rubbed my hand. "You were in a terrible place. You couldn't have helped them."

Lowering my eyes, I desperately searched for the right words but found none.

We walked silently along the deserted underground passage until we came to a winding stone staircase.

"This will take us to the royal suites," I said, staring up at the steep steps leading high into the palace.

My thighs burned as we climbed higher and higher into the tower.

"We should murder Gideon and Erissa for making us climb these," Tharan said, gasping for air.

"Just a little further." I could see the golden handle leading into the royal wing. "I'm going to connect our minds, so we don't have to speak to one another."

Reaching out, I linked our minds. A pain tickled the back of my throat at the memory of the last time I invaded his psyche.

Testing.

'I'm here.'

The door silently opened into a foyer housing a massive marble statue of Ammena holding her magical apple.

The hallway split into three directions—one to the north, one to the east, and one to the west. Ornate tapestry depicting the Highlands' many victories hung on the walls, while beautiful red and gold carpets covered the black-and-white tiled floors.

Erissa's room is just to the left of the statue.

A hawk and serpent locked in combat marked Erissa's chambers from the rest. Extending my power, I probed for any presence inside. Erissa took lovers, but never in her chamber. My magic sensed nothing. Gripping the handle, I attempted to enter the room. My heart sank when it stubbornly jammed.

Locked.

'*What do you mean, it's locked? Let me try.*' The golden swirled doorknob twitched again under Tharan's hand but did not open.

'*What are we going to do now? We don't have a key.*'

Her laboratory. She keeps a desk in it.

'*Where is it?*'

I'll get it. You stay here.

'*Alright, be careful.*'

I descended the colossal marble stairs, winding like a serpent circling its prey. Avoiding the guards was easy. I knew their routes, their shifts. Nothing changed in five years. Gideon thought he was untouchable.

Erissa's laboratory connected to the dungeons, providing her with an endless supply of test subjects.

A vivid pink glow emanated from within the lab.

Peering into the room, my eyes fell upon a glass beaker brimming with luminescent liquid, boiling despite the lack of flame beneath it.

Erissa must have been working late. The door to her office stood ajar as if she left in a hurry.

In the heart of the room rested a substantial maple desk. An array of skulls varied in size from large to small upon its surface.

Each skull cradled a candle, casting an eerie radiance illuminating their eyes.

I sifted through the desk, tossing papers everywhere.

Erissa researched everything from toadstools to curses. The key had to be here somewhere. I knocked on the desk, hoping to reveal a secret compartment, but found nothing. My pulse raced through my veins. She could come back at any moment.

Sifting through one last pile of folders, my eyes widened as they befell a diagram of my body annotated with clinical notes.

Subject losing weight: Appetite enhancer added to food.
Subject still resisting: Will try adding valerian root to tea.
Subject still fertile. Still bleeds monthly.
Still no sign of her mother's gifts.

I fell to my knees, clutching the chart. Rage ran hot in my veins. How long had she known of my mother's identity? Had Erissa been the one to broker the marriage arrangement?

Questions piled in my head like rubble after a battle as I flipped through the thick stack of parchment with my name and routine. My movements and eating patterns were noted, even when Gideon and I made love.

The door to the laboratory slammed shut, sending a shiver down my spine. *Fuck.*

Holding my ear to the door, I listened for the sound of Erissa's soft, elven footsteps as she padded around the laboratory. I prayed she would not find me.

Tucking myself under her desk, I called my dagger to my hand and waited.

Erissa hummed to herself as she tended to her potions. Popping and fizzing sounded from the room beyond.

I held my breath, searching the room for any way out. No other doors or windows lined the walls. I'd have to wait her out.

Crouching low, I settled in once more, my fist wrapped tight around my dagger.

Tick, tock, tick, tock. The clock on the wall mocked. If I didn't get back soon, Tharan would come looking for me.

Tick, tock, tick, tock. I matched my heartbeat to the sound of the clock.

Erissa continued her experiments. The smell of sulfur wafted through the cracks in the door.

Come on, I need to get out of here. My knee bounced on the wooden desk.

Finally, the door to the laboratory shut.

I wedged myself from under the desk, scanning the room beyond for signs of life.

Nothing.

I fled through the open door, through the lab where potions glowed, casting shadows onto the wood-paneled walls.

"Looking for this?" A voice like honeyed wine turned my blood cold. Dangling a key from her elegant fingers, Erissa let out a devious laugh. "You won't find what you're looking for in my chambers."

She glided toward me on light feet—a wicked grin cutting her elegant face in two.

Firm hands grasped my shoulders, throwing me into a shelf of old books.

"Tsk, tsk, Now, now, boys, we want her intact."

Her voice faded away as darkness crept in.

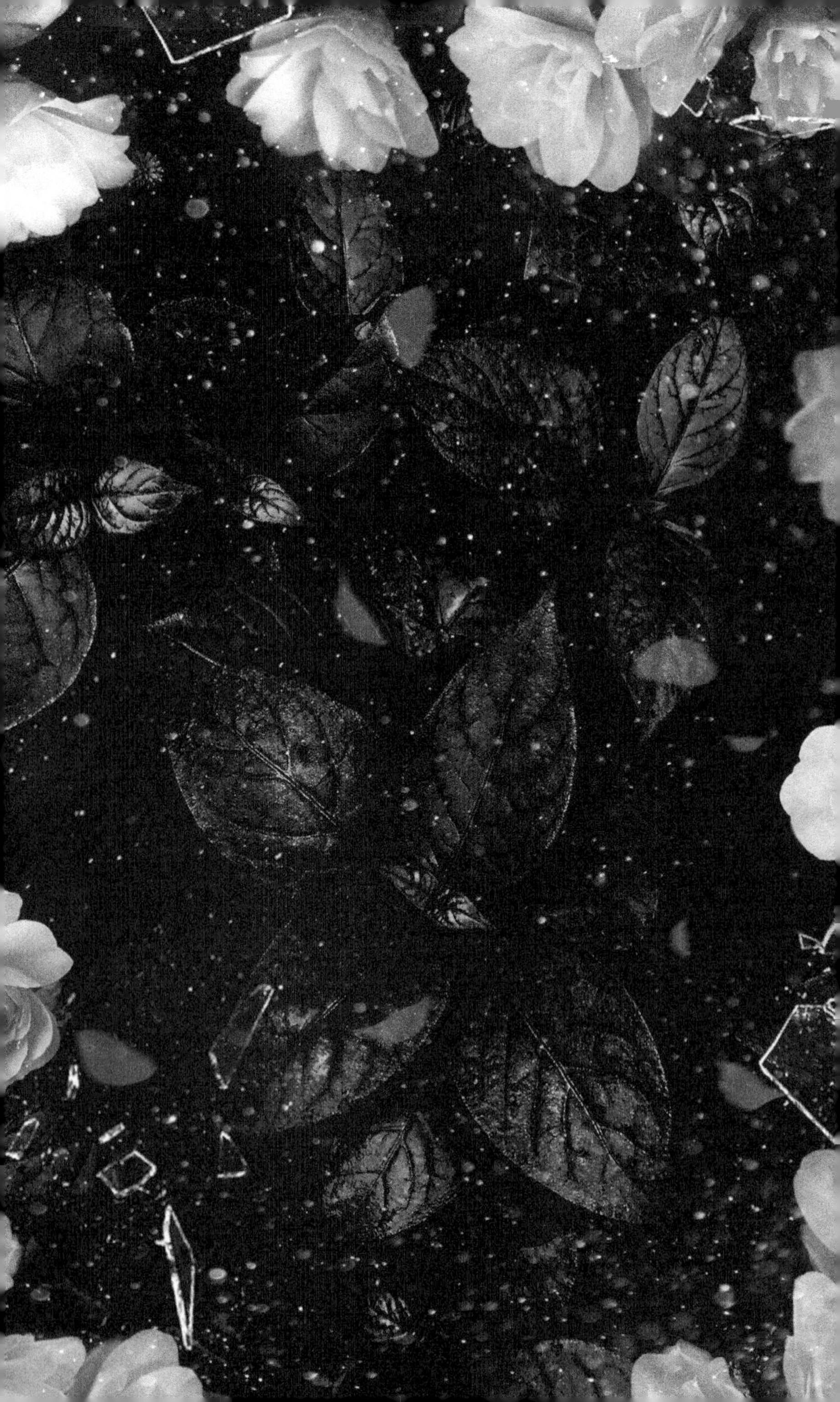

44 CAIDEN

"Trinity, I hate this place," Lucius said as they rode into Ryft's Edge under the cover of darkness. Tying their horses to a tree, they gazed upon the castle looming menacingly overhead.

"Let's get in and get out," Caiden said, taking a transfiguration potion from his pocket and handing it to Lucius.

Caiden grimaced as he slugged back the foul-smelling liquid. Skin bubbling, he transformed into a standard-issue Highlands soldier with dark hair and eyes.

"Trinity be..." Lucius said, looking down at his now human form. "Being human must be awful. They are so ugly."

Caiden rolled his eyes. Besides their elongated incisors, sylph and humans looked identical. "Let's go before the tonic wears off."

Two soldiers nodded their heads in acknowledgment as they passed through the stone archway leading to the royal residences.

Upon entering the marble castle, they parted ways. Lucius headed into the dungeons to Sir Brutus's chambers while Caiden headed up to the tower to search Gideon's study. The castle dripped with opulence—plush crimson rugs accented by lavish gold detailing graced the floors. Velvet curtains framed the windows. Paintings by some of the world's most revered artists hung on the walls.

Shrill sounds of fornication emanated from Gideon's room as Caiden passed, rolling his eyes at the attending guards.

Following the map in his mind, he climbed the winding staircase up to Gideon's study. Perched atop the highest tower, Gideon spent many days gazing out over his kingdom.

A locked door greeted Caiden at the entrance. Running his hands over the carved wood, he looked for a possible release button.

Nothing.

Charging his power, he sent a small bolt into the lock. With a puff of smoke, the door unlocked.

A green rug embroidered with fine gold accents led to an opulent parlor lined with rows of unread books. In the corner, a fire fought off winter's chill. A steaming mug of cardamom tea filled the room with a warm aroma.

Mangled papers piled high on Gideon's desk.

Rummaging through the ravings of a madman, Caiden searched frantically for Gideon's diary.

"There you are," he said proudly to an empty room. His fingers gripping a leatherbound book with the word *Ironheart* engraved on the cover.

With another tiny bolt of lightning, the little lock guarding Gideon's secrets clicked open. The journal brimmed with Gideon's most private thoughts, including observations on everyone he interacted with, from the servants to Erissa to the queen:

Aelia is nothing to me. Nothing but a useful pawn in a political game. I do not love her, although I cannot stand to be without her. I take her to bed because it is my duty. Soon, she will be beyond her child-bearing years, and I will dispose of her. At least she was useful in securing the Midlands.

The queen's name stuck out to him for reasons he could not comprehend. *Aelia.* His senses screamed at him to remember, but nothing came to mind.

He scanned the page, detailing Gideon's debaucherous sexual fantasies. His stomach turned at the unmasked depravity within.

The room went dark.

A wicked cackle filled the space, opening a pit in his stomach.

In the fireplace, a flame sprung to life, taking the form of a female body, twisting and turning until Erissa came into focus.

"Hello, prince. Did you think this disguise would fool me?" She snapped her fingers, and her magic enveloped him, revealing his true form, like ripping a shell off a hard-boiled egg.

"There you are. Still as handsome as ever." An evil smile was plastered on her face. Her long crimson hair spilled over her white satin robes. An amulet of red encased in gold hung around her neck.

"Hello, Erissa, always a pleasure," Caiden said as he fired a bolt of lightning at her. His hopes crumbled when it passed through her, leaving her unscathed.

Another devious cackle. "You didn't think I'd actually show up here in person, did you?" Her voice echoed through the room.

Iron shackles clasped around Caiden's wrists. Gideon stood in front of him, wicked as ever. Chaos danced in his dark eyes. Caiden's heart twisted in fear at the sight of Gideon's long incisors glinting in the flames. More sylph than man, the blood binding transformed him into a monster.

Iron seared into Caiden's skin as Gideon led him away.

"Come with me, prince. Someone is waiting for you." He yanked on the chains.

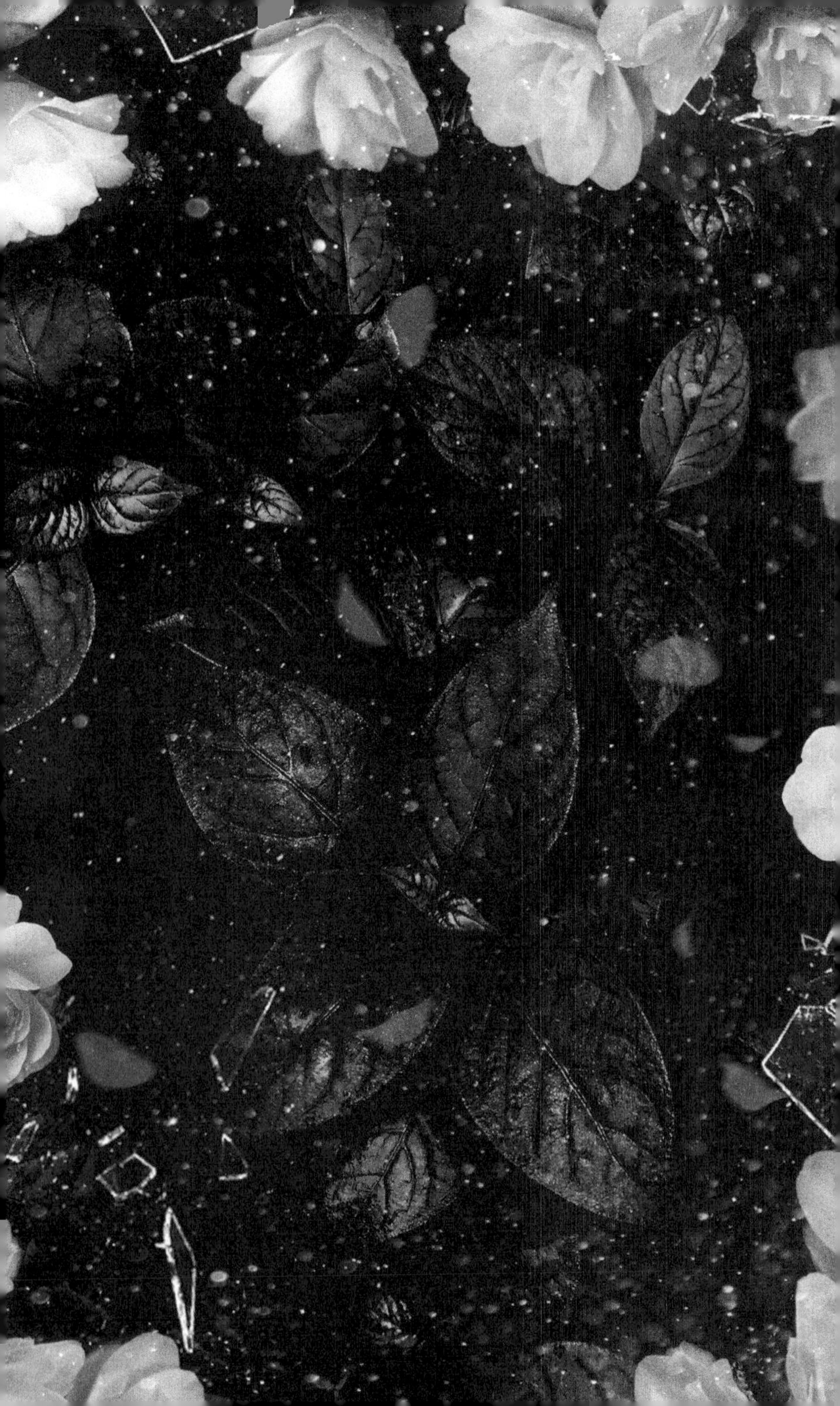

45 THARAN

Tharan's senses screamed at him to go after Aelia, but their efforts were better spent apart. He hurried up the stairs, hoping the invisibility potion lasted long enough for him to find something and return before Aelia did.

Hundreds of candles, all burning low, lit the study with an eerie glow. In the center, a desk made of mirrors sat decked with tomes and scrolls.

Tharan rifled furiously through the papers, covering the history of magic in Moriana.

Why did Erissa require all of this? What relevance did it hold in relation to Gideon's insatiable thirst for power?

A red leather journal lay hidden in one of the mirrored drawers. Flipping through the pages, a map with an 'x' caught his eye. A note next to it read:

Trinity Well?

Tharan racked his mind for the stories he'd heard as a child. Stories of the magical wells formed by each sister of the Trinity in secret. Wells of immense power. Power to raise the dead, power to set the sea ablaze. Tharan swallowed hard. Power to turn a man into a god.

Erissa had been a follower of Crom Cruach. He obsessed over the origins of magic.

The pieces of the puzzle placed themselves in Tharan's mind.

Erissa attacked the Court of Sorrows to gain possession of the Army of the Dead. With an army of that size and ability, she could trample over Moriana until she found the magic she needed. Gideon was a pawn in her game. He could play as conqueror while she amassed her desired power.

Tharan's breath caught in his throat at the thought of Erissa wielding the power of the Army of the Dead. She hadn't found the scepter, for she would have used it against the Woodland Realm. If she didn't have it, then who did? Maybe no one. Maybe it was still in the Court of Sorrows waiting to be found.

He needed to return to the ruins of the Court of Sorrows and search for the scepter, but that would have to wait.

Tucking the dairy into his smock, he headed for the door, only to run face-first into an invisible barrier.

"Going somewhere, King?" a voice as smooth as butter whispered in his ear.

Behind him, a gust of air whirled, revealing a female form.

"Erissa," Tharan spat the name out.

"I am surprised you remember me. The last time we met, you were nothing but a twig. You have grown…"

"I was a child, and you took advantage of me." A muscle ticked in his jaw at the thought of what occurred long ago.

"You were seventeen. Marriage age in the human lands. There is nothing wrong with an older female teaching a young male the ways of love." She ran a slender finger down his neck.

Tharan gritted his teeth in disgust. "Do not speak to me of love. For you know nothing of it."

An urgent tug pulled at his heartstrings. *Aelia*. "Where is she?" he growled.

"I guess you'll have to come find her." Disappearing into a cloud of smoke, Erissa's cackle shook the room.

Something hard thwacked his skull.

The world went dark.

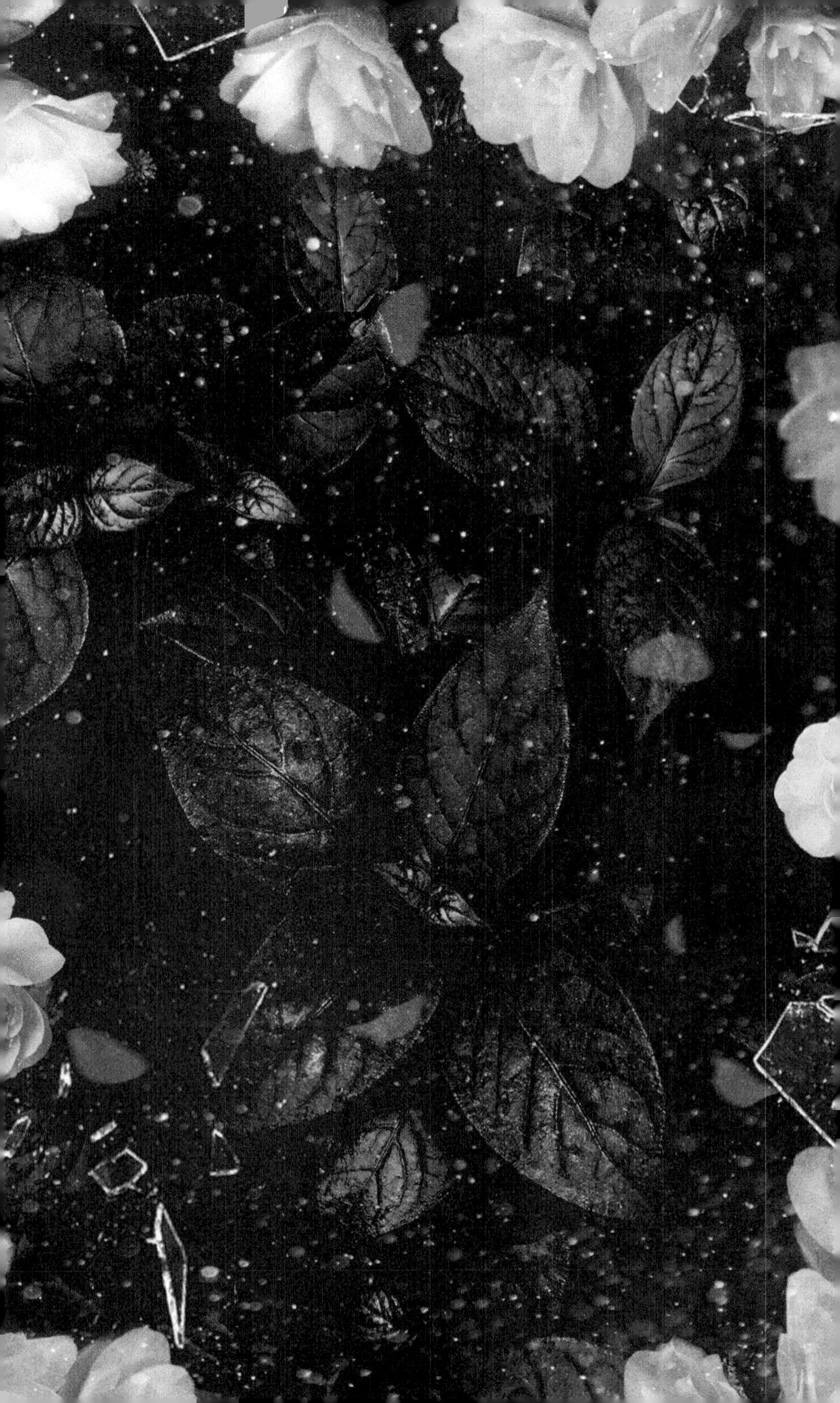

46 AELIA

I tugged at the enchanted iron shackles binding me to the table. The magic-laced iron burned my skin and blocked my powers. I recognized this scene, this table, these shackles. This is where Erissa made me the monster I am today.

She clicked her tongue at me. "Now, now, you know you can't escape these."

"What do you want from me?" My voice shook with rage.

From between her spindled fingers dangled a ruby encased in gold. "Is this what you were looking for?" The pendant sparkled. An engraving I couldn't make out carved on its glassy surface.

Pulling against my restraints, I howled in pain. "Just let my sister go! Why do you want her in the first place?"

"I don't. I needed you, and I knew you would come for her." Erissa twirled the pendant as she paced the room.

"For what?" I shook the shackles around my wrists, earning me a punch to the face from Ramus, splitting my lip. The taste of metallic blood filled my mouth.

"You do not question Mother," he said, stepping back into the shadows.

Tightness consumed my chest at the familiarity of it all.

"Thank you, Ramus." Erissa pulled a beaker containing a bright pink liquid from its burner and set it down on a little table next to me, then she uttered an ancient language.

The mixture swirled like a dervish before taking the shape of a scorpion.

My stomach turned sour as the creature sprung to life, crawling up Erissa's pale arm.

Stroking its back, she whispered something to the creature.

Suddenly the door behind me swung open, and Gideon entered, leading Caiden in chains. My heart stopped at the sight of him.

Caiden's head hung low.

"Excellent, our first guest of honor is here," Erissa said, motioning for Caiden to take a seat on a bench.

"What is this all about, Erissa? Who is this?" He nodded his head in my direction.

Caiden's indifference to me cut like a knife. I bit my lip to distract myself.

I hoped Tharan did the smart thing and headed back to the Woodlands.

My hopes were trampled a few moments later as Remus led in a bloody-faced Tharan.

"Found this one in the study. Just like you said, Mother."

"Excellent." Erissa clapped her hands with delight as Tharan took a seat next to Caiden.

Gideon ran a finger down my jaw. "Not so tough without your dagger, are you?"

My skin crawled at the sense of his touch, but I could not escape. Pooling blood into my mouth, I spat it at him.

Blood dripped down his muscled jaw. "You're feistier than you were when we were together." He wiped his face. "I like this Aelia better." He pressed his lips to mine in a sign of dominance.

I futilely pulled at my chains, trying to push him away.

"Does someone want to tell me who this is and what is going on here?" Caiden said.

Erissa scoffed at the question. "Oh, Prince, do not act dumb. Everyone knows you and Aelia shared a bed for years."

I closed my eyes. Nothing like having your romantic history laid bare in front of your current lover, your husband, and your ex-lover, whose mind you erased.

"He's telling the truth, Erissa."

The mage cocked her head to the side.

"I erased myself from his memory."

Blinking, Caiden stared at me, his mouth twisting as he searched his mind for me.

A light brightened in her eyes. "You have become powerful since we last met. How fortunate for me." She stroked the scorpion perched on her left shoulder.

"What do you want from us, Erissa?" Tharan asked as blood snaked its way down his face.

"Glad you asked, Alder King." She nodded to Remus and Ramus, who placed an iron collar around my neck, holding my shoulders down.

Panic ran through my veins.

"Each of you has original blood in your veins. Meaning the magic flowing through you is older than time itself. Caiden, your bloodline is as close as we can get to the original sylphs. Tharan, you possess both elf and sylph originals in your bloodline, so you will make up for whatever Caiden lacks, and Aelia…" She turned to me, a wicked gleam in her eye. "Aelia has the blood of Fate running through her."

"Why do you need originals?" Tharan asked.

Erissa laughed as if the answer was plain as day. "To unlock Trinity Wells. Where the ancient magic of Moriana is stored, of course."

Tharan tugged at his chains. "Those are a myth, Erissa." Fire burned in his verdant eyes. "What are you going to do? Pull the magic from our veins?"

"Precisely, my fair king." Erissa held out her arm, urging the scorpion toward me.

A scream built in my throat as the insect crept closer. Its legs like tiny needles on my skin. Powerless, I could not stop the creature. Screams burned my lungs as I looked on in horror.

The door to the lab swung open, and two crossbow bolts flew through the darkness, hitting Remus and Ramus. They released my arm and howled in pain. Blood gushed from their necks.

I wiggled as best I could, trying to throw the scorpion off its course.

Reaching my elbow, the creature dug its tail deep into my artery, ripping my magic from me.

I screamed as pain spread through me like fire through a dry brush. Every nerve firing, overloading my system.

Time slowed.

I floated above my body, watching a fight break out below. Lucius freed Tharan and Caiden, and now all three battled Gideon, the twins, and Erissa.

Caiden's lightning lit the room while Tharan unleashed a deluge of thorns onto Gideon and Erissa.

Blocking the thorns, Gideon fired his own dark magic back.

Erissa stared at the insect with its stinger in my skin. Whispering something, the scorpion returned to her hand.

A sharp sting hit my forearm as Tharan crushed the bug under his grip. I returned to my body.

"No!" Erissa shouted, reaching her hand out for the dead insect. "You will pay for that." Magic sparked at her fingertips.

Vines appeared through the cracks in the floor, splitting the granite, creating a wall between Erissa and us. Tharan tore the shackles from my body, crumpling the iron like old pieces of parchment.

Flames appeared in Erissa's hand.

"You'll take this castle down with flames like that," Gideon said, deflecting a shot of lightning from Caiden.

"So be it," Erissa said, hurling a ball of fire at me.

Blasting me into the wall, the flames threatened to engulf me, but they could not penetrate my skin.

My breath hitched in my throat as pain seared up my back. The room spun. I touched my hand to my head. Blood coated my fingertips as a muted battle raged around me.

"I can still collect your blood if you're dead." Erissa stalked toward me.

"You can have all the blood you want if you free Baylis," I said, frantically looking for anything to grab onto.

Erissa opened her mouth to speak, only to be cut short by a deluge of lightning slamming her into a shelf of potions.

The glass vials shattered, covering her in different mixtures. Erissa cried out in agony as her skin shriveled and died, leaving her face a mess of mangled tissue and bone.

Caiden's eyes hungered for revenge as he approached the mage. "This is for my wife." He plunged the blade through Erissa's clavicle and into her heart.

A high-pitched screech pierced my eardrums, making the world go hazy again.

Tharan ran to my side, helping me up. "We have to go now," he said, shooting another poisonous thorn at the twins.

"I want the twins," I said, my eyes locked on Ramus. "I will spare Gideon, but give me them."

Tharan nodded, focusing his vines on Ramus.

"What's happening?" the big man shouted as the vines snaked their way up his torso and around his limbs.

Remus hacked at the vines imprisoning his brother. The blades dulled with each strike.

Summoning every ounce of strength left in me, I got to my feet. "Let me go, Tharan."

He did as I commanded.

I narrowed my gaze at Remus, who tore at the vines with his hands. So distracted, he did not notice as I hobbled closer, using the nightmares they inflicted upon me to fuel my feet. The smell of Remus's desperation tasted sweet on my tongue.

Calling my dagger to my hand, I gripped the hilt tight before plunging it into Remus's thick neck.

"Who's the little bird now?" I whispered into his ear.

The three men looked on in awe as I became what nightmares were made of.

"Lucius, your sword." I held out my hand.

He offered me the hilt.

Taking the weapon, I lifted it above my head, letting my rage fuel me.

"No!" Ramus called as I brought the sword down on Remus's neck, severing his head from his body. Blood pooled at my feet as Remus's head rolled away.

A guttural scream rattled my lungs.

Gideon ran to Erissa, who lay slumped against a cabinet. "We have to go," he said, hoisting her to her feet. Through trembling hands, she conjured the last bit of her power. Snapping her fingers, they disappeared into a cloud of smoke.

The flames spread, crawling up the walls of the laboratory like spiders.

"What are we going to do with him?" Caiden asked, examining Ramus, who squirmed on his cross.

"He's mine," I said as Tharan helped me over to where Ramus hung. "Do not resist me." Reaching out my magic, I linked our minds. Inside sat a small boy with a head of curls, warming himself by a fire, surrounded by stars.

"*Hello*," he said in a cheerful but guarded voice.

A CURSE OF BREATH AND BLOOD

"*Hello,*" I replied.

Standing, the boy dusted the dirt from his pants. "*I know why you're here.*"

I gave him a reassuring smile. "*Why don't you show me where you keep your memories?*"

"*This way,*" he said, the fire gilding his features, making him look innocent.

Smoke formed a door. Taking a key from his pocket, the little boy led me through.

The inside of the room resembled a library, but instead of books, memories lined the shelves. In the center of the room sat a small bed with the sheets down-turned, waiting for him.

"*Why don't you hop in?*" I said, helping him into the bed and tucking him in tight.

"*Will it hurt?*" he asked.

"*No.*" I brushed the dark hair from his eyes. "*Now go to sleep.*"

He gave me a little smile, then drifted off to sleep.

Lighting a match, I touched the flame to every memory.

The bookshelves burned, but still, the little boy slumbered. I took the memory of Remus dying and set it on a loop in the little boy's mind before locking the door behind me.

When I opened my eyes, Ramus sat drooling in front of me.

"Let him rot here," I said, collapsing into Tharan's arms.

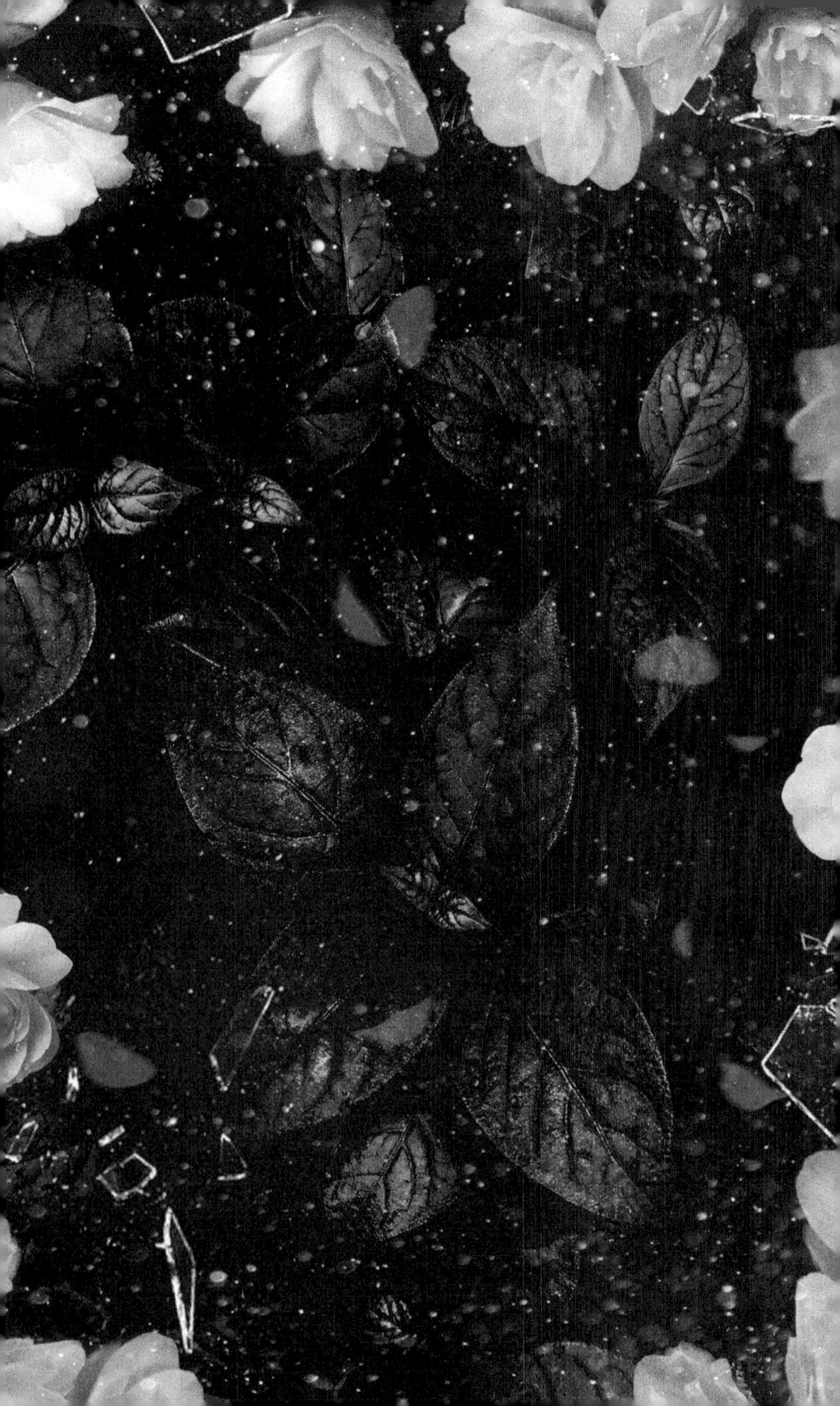

47 AELIA

"We need to get out of here," Lucius said as fire engulfed the room.

Part of me wanted to grab the notes Erissa had kept on me, and another part wanted them to burn—to let the fire cleanse what Erissa had sullied.

"I need you to carry me," I said to Tharan. A blinding pain ripped through my back. "I can't walk."

Caiden squinted at me as the flames grew, trying to decipher my face.

I wanted to shake him, to tell him everything we shared, but those memories were gone forever. My heart ached at the sight of his confusion.

"We can talk about it later," I said as Tharan scooped me up in his powerful arms.

"Follow us," Tharan said as we headed for the door.

Taking one last look around, I tried to find the amulet, but thick smoke blotted my vision.

I buried my head in Tharan's neck, trying not to cry. I fucked up—sentenced Baylis to an eternity of slumber.

Gideon's words echoed in my head. *You are nothing. You are useless. Weak, pathetic whore.*

Our footsteps echoed through the halls as we ran for the sewers.

"Halt! In the name of the king," soldiers called after us.

Using two coats of armor as conduits, Caiden made a wall of lightning, blocking their path.

"It won't hold forever, but it'll give us more time to escape," he said. His face strained as he concentrated on the magic.

Another troop of soldiers came bounding up the stairs. Lucius fired his crossbow into them, hitting the lead man and knocking the rest back.

The entrance to the tunnels were just ahead. The sewers meant safety.

A plume of thick, black smoke snaked its way across the ceiling, landing before us, revealing Gideon in all his dark glory. An evil smile marred his handsome face.

"Leaving so soon?" He cocked his head to the side. A strand of black hair fell in front of his eye. "I was just getting started." He called upon some unholy power, a ball of magical light forming in the palm of his hand.

I narrowed my eyes upon him, summing every ounce of courage left in me. "Let us go, Gideon."

Gideon shook his head, laughing to himself. "Oh, you know I can't do that, sweetheart. Two high lords trespassed in my kingdom. I cannot let that go unpunished. And besides, you heard Erissa, we need your blood."

My chest tightened at the look of pure chaos in his eyes. He would not let me slip through his fingers again.

"Set me down."

Tharan lowered me to the ground, propping me up against the marble wall. Pain, like a hot knife seared into my back.

I motioned for Gideon to come near to me.

"What do you want? Do you think you can get back into my good graces?" He let out a devious laugh. "That ship has sailed, sweetie."

While Gideon approached me, I sent a message to Tharan.

I'm going to distract him. Do not waste these moments.

Gideon saw my eyes glaze over. "You better be telling your dogs to back off."

I gave him a half smile. "You know me so well."

A bolt of lightning tore through him. He shook uncontrollably. Energy pulsed through him, and the smell of burning flesh filled the corridor.

Time slowed. His eyes burst from their sockets. His blood coursed with a multitude of potions and fresh sylph blood. He would not die.

Still, I felt vindicated.

Tharan lifted me back into his arms, but I could not tear my eyes from Gideon's mangled remains. He was everything I hated about myself. Every dark thought laid bare for the world to see. I despised the person I became when I was with him, yet a small part of me still longed for his validation. He sowed a seed of doubt that grew into a towering tree. I perpetually felt "inferior," and he affirmed it.

Gideon's men fled at the sight of their charred king.

Reaching the little cabin, Tharan laid me on the sofa as Caiden and Lucius barricaded the door.

"We don't have time," I said, propping myself up on my elbows as I sucked in shallow breaths. "Go into the bedroom and get my pack. Gideon's soldiers will be here soon."

Caiden and Lucius stood guard at the door while Tharan went

to fetch my satchel. Caiden shook his head as if trying to free a stuck memory.

Tharan emerged moments later, holding my leather bag. "Is this it?"

"Yes, bring it here." I rummaged through it, looking for the one thing that could save us from the horde of soldiers descending upon the tiny cabin.

My pulse raced with anticipation as I pulled the Scepter of the Dead from the bag.

'*It is time,*' the Morrigan's voice hissed in my head. '*Bind your blood to me and let me unleash my army upon these mortals.*' Excitement radiated through her ancient voice.

Calling Little Death to my hand, I pricked my finger. A drop of blood pooled on its tip.

"Tell your soldiers no innocents are to be harmed. Only soldiers and royalty."

'*Once you touch your blood to my scepter, the army is yours to command.*'

"What are you doing?" Tharan said, his face a mix of confusion and horror.

The sound of soldiers rattled the cabin as they encircled us.

"Come out! By order of the king. We may let you live."

I looked at Lucius.

A single tear fell down his pale cheek.

The sound of the soldiers banging their weapons against the stone cabin rang in my ears.

I looked around at the men. Just a few months ago, they were strangers to me. A pressure built behind my eyes. I knew what I had to do—the only way to save the ones I loved. I failed them so many times before. My father, my sister, Caiden; I would not fail them again.

My eyes flicked to where Caiden stood, bracing himself against the door, fighting the exhaustion.

I swallowed hard. It was time for me to leave the Traitorous Queen behind and become the Queen of the Dead.

Setting torches to the tin roof, the soldiers hoped to burn us alive. Thick black smoke blotted out the light from the candles and filled our lungs.

Rubbing my bloodied finger on the scepter, I brought the goddess to life.

'*Release me,*' the Morrigan cried. A blast of cold air flooded through the windows and doors, extinguishing the flames.

"Save us!" I yelled. "I release you. Come to my aid."

Gripping the scepter tightly, the magic seeped into my bones, binding itself to me. I gasped for air. A chill gripped my body, slowly growing more intense with each passing moment. I tried to scream, but no sound came out. The color drained from my skin as my bones became brittle.

Phantom soldiers rose from the floor, creating a barrier between the cabin and the Highland army.

Tharan scooped me up, carrying me out the front door, where Brutus Strong paced on his dappled gray gelding. His men stared dead-eyed at the ghost army before them.

"We aren't afraid of ghosts. Are we men?"

The men beat their chests with their fists in a sign of courage.

"Let us go, and none of your men will die," I said in a voice conjured by the Morrigan herself. Once again, I found my body being controlled by someone else. At least this time, it was my decision. My choice.

Brutus only laughed harder. "You think these apparitions will protect you? You and your friends are nothing but ants waiting to be squashed." He narrowed his eyes at me. "Kill them, and let's be done with it."

Plumes of black smoke rose with the red dawn as the castle burned behind us.

This would not be my ending.

As the soldiers moved closer, I raised the scepter high above my head. "Destroy them."

The scepter took its payment. I gasped for air as life seeped out of me and into the relic.

Lowering their spears, the ghost army charged, impaling the Highland guards. Screams rang out across the snowy fields, as one by one, Highlanders fell to their knees. Their blood stained the fresh snow red.

As chaos ensued, Tharan moved me toward the pen, where Arion ran in anxious circles. Raising a calming hand, he subdued the stallion enough for me to climb on.

"You're going to have to ride with me," I said, slumping onto Arion's neck. "I can't hold myself up."

Without hesitation, Tharan heaved himself onto Arion's back. "You are both welcome in the Woodlands."

Caiden and Lucius stood by the fence, taking in the carnage before them.

Lucius slid a bit into Arion's mouth. "We will meet you there." He handed the reins to Tharan.

They nodded at us and headed for the royal stables.

I prayed to Ammena for their safety.

Tharan clicked his heels, and Arion bolted into a full gallop. As we fled, I watched the Morrigan's army—*my army*—slaughter Gideon's men. A pang of guilt rang through my heart. They were so young. They did not deserve an ending like this. I tried to remind myself they were glamoured to feel no pain. At least Gideon gave them that.

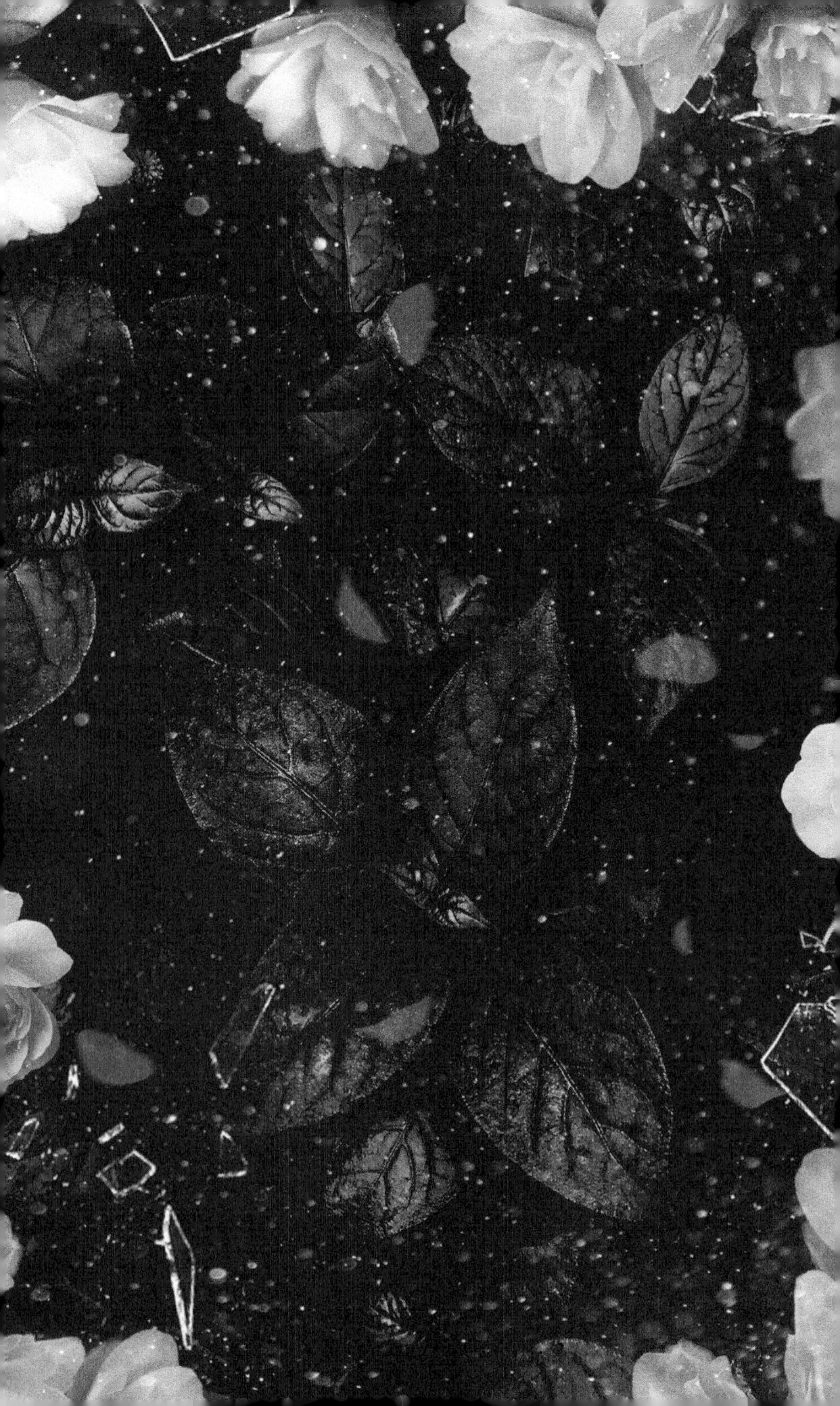

48   AELIA

EVERY STEP ARION TOOK SENT A BLINDING PAIN UP MY SPINE, BUT we could not stop. I braced myself against Tharan's hard body, seeking any sort of relief.

We rode until we reached the peak of the Ryft. Tharan turned Arion to face the city. Huge plumes of smoke rose like dragons in the morning light.

In the face of defeat, Gideon would be spurred to assert himself. He loathed appearing vulnerable, and this setback wounded his pride. There would be no refuge for me in this world now. Gideon wanted my head and my army.

Tharan looped an arm around my waist, pulling me in closer. "Are you okay? What happened back there? How long have you had the Scepter of the Dead? And why didn't you tell me?"

I blew out my breath. "It's a long story." A soreness resonated in the back of my throat. "I wasn't sure I could trust you." I motioned to the burning castle. "You've seen my experience with men."

"I'm taking you to Mineralia."

I nodded in agreement as Tharan turned Arion toward the

Stone Kingdom. "You better call the army back into the scepter, or they'll wander around looking for a battle."

I held the scepter as high as I could manage. "Return to me." The scepter glowed green with magic, and the battle ceased in the city below. As soon as the scepter went silent, life returned to my bones.

I almost fell off Arion when we stopped for the night. The streets of Mineralia were quiet. Either word of the attack hadn't reached them, or they were indifferent to it.

Tharan carried me to a room at the inn.

"Hold on a little longer. I called for a healer," Tharan said. Urgency filled his voice.

Wrapping me in a fur-lined blanket, he went to stoke the fire.

A stark departure from the inn we had lodged in earlier, ornate gold leaf wallpaper lined the walls, and a crystal chandelier dangled from the ceiling. A room fit for a queen.

Removing the ring, Tharan returned to his god-like splendor. The scar cutting his face a welcome sight.

"Do you need anything?" he asked, taking a seat next to the bed. His red hair pulled back into a low ponytail, eyes searching for a way to ease my pain.

"Just some water," I said, not wanting to be a burden.

Tharan handed me a glass of ice-cold water. "It has healing powers."

"Let's hope." I raised the glass to my lips.

"After the healer comes, I plan to take a bath, and then, if you'd like, I could help you."

My cheeks flushed. I wasn't ready to show Tharan my scars. "You don't have to."

Tharan pushed a dark lock behind my ear. "I promise I won't look if you'd prefer."

Swallowing the lump in my throat, I stared into his deep green eyes. Our faces nearly touching.

A knock at the door broke our trance.

The healer, a small, halfling woman with silver hair and umber skin, entered. She wore a green utilitarian dress full of pockets and thick-rimmed glasses.

"I hear someone has a broken back," she said, mixing something at the table in the room. "Here, drink this."

I grimaced as she handed me a tincture with the consistency of mud.

"It's wormwood, yarrow root, and the mud from my homelands far across the sea. It will help to mend your bones." She guided the glass to my lips.

I choked on the mixture.

She gently patted the bottom of the cup. "Drink up. In a few days, you'll be good as new."

Finishing the mixture. I wiped my mouth on my sleeve. "Thank you."

The old halfling turned to Tharan. "Take good care of her. She's special."

"I will," Tharan said, escorting the old woman out.

The elixir snaked its way through my wounded body, heating as it found bones to mend. I clenched my jaw, arching my back in agony.

Tharan heaped pillows behind me, allowing me to sit up.

"How about a story?" he asked, glancing at a bookshelf lining the wall.

My heart skipped at the simple act overflowing with kindness I was unaccustomed to. "That would be lovely."

Shirtsleeves rolled, he held his hands behind his back as she surveyed the books. A golden tattoo snaked its way up his forearm. Had I missed that before, or was the healing potion making me delirious?

Tharan grabbed a book and took a seat beside me. "This is good," he said, flipping to the first page.

My eyelids heavy, I fought to stay awake. "Don't you want to talk about the fact that I conjured an Army of the Dead?"

He looked at me through lowered lashes. "Yes, I have many questions, but seeing as we went through an ordeal... I'd like to enjoy this moment of peace. We can figure everything out once you're healed." He licked his finger, using it to separate the pages. The sight of his sensuous mouth made me swallow hard.

I let out a sigh, needing to focus on my healing. Tribulations pawed at my door like lost puppies, but they could wait a little longer.

I let the sound of Tharan's calming voice drift me off into a deep and dreamless sleep.

A searing pain woke me a few hours later. Tharan lay asleep in the chair next to my bed. The book he had been reading lay open on his chest.

I reached for the pain tonic, but my clumsy fingers knocked over the water glass instead.

The sound of shattering glass jolted him awake.

"Are you okay?" he asked, scooping the broken shards of glass into his hand.

Heat flushed my cheeks. "I didn't mean to wake you. I just wanted to take some pain elixir, but I couldn't reach it."

"It's okay." He poured the honey-flavored tincture into a glass and handed it to me. "You could have woken me up. I would have gotten it for you."

"You've done too much," I said, swigging back the viscous liquid.

Tharan grimaced.

"What?" I shrugged.

He pinched his nose. "You need a bath."

"No." I crossed my arms over my chest.

"Let me help you, you stubborn woman. It's not like I haven't seen a naked body before."

The smell of acrid feces rose from underneath the blankets, stinging my nostrils. "Fine."

Tharan called for attendants who carried in buckets of hot water and scented the bath with rose petals.

My skin prickled with anticipation. Tharan would see my scars. I hesitated, uncertain if I was prepared to be this vulnerable with him.

"It's ready," Tharan said, standing in the doorway. The light from the bathing room created a halo behind him.

"Okay." I held my arms as high as they could go.

Tharan lifted the servant's smock over my head, exposing my naked body. Instinctively, I covered my breasts.

Tharan's eyes did not leave mine.

"You are beautiful," he said, slipping his arms underneath me, lifting my broken body into the air.

Hundreds of candles illuminated the bathing chamber, casting the room in a warm glow.

Sucking in a breath, I winced as Tharan lowered me into the warm water. The pain subsided to a dull ache, resembling a bruise rather than a raging river of fire. Illya's gift, coupled with the healing elixir, accelerated my recuperation.

Tharan dipped a sponge into the water before carefully lifting my arm to scrub away the mud. Washing me like I was a prized piece of art to be restored, I quivered at his touch.

I bit the inside of my cheek, knowing he saw my shame. "Aren't you going to ask about my scars?"

Tharan continued scrubbing. "I would ask who did this to you, but I think I know."

I closed my eyes, remembering the tips of the whips shredding the flesh.

I lowered my head in shame. "I am damaged, Tharan. And I may never be whole again."

Tharan lifted my chin so our eyes met.

He set the sponge down before taking my face into his hands. "You are beautiful to me, Aelia Springborn. Your scars are a testament to your strength. Wear them with pride."

Tears welled in my eyes. "There's something else." With shaking fingers, I unscrewed the golden stud in my ear. A jagged scar appeared across the side of my face where a blade slit me from mouth to ear. "This is who I am."

My heart raced. My scars laid bare.

For a moment, Tharan stared at pink flesh.

"Say something," I said as tears trickled down my cheeks.

Tharan leaned in, kissing my scarred cheek.

My stone heart cracked.

"You are the most exquisite creature I have ever laid eyes on." He pulled me in for a passionate kiss. Our mouths consumed one another. Any pain I felt diminished by the arousal growing inside of me.

Tharan lifted me from the bath. The cold air pebbled my nipples. Laying me down on the bed, he looked at me lovingly while his thumb rubbed my cheek. "You need to rest, Aelia."

I didn't want to rest. I wanted to kiss Tharan until the sun came up.

"No, it doesn't hurt that much." My voice cracked with desperation, but I didn't care. I wanted him.

Tharan pushed my hair behind my ear. "There will be plenty of time for kissing when you are healed." His lips touched my forehead. "Sleep now, my Traitorous Queen, my King Killer."

"You forgot my new title, Queen of the Dead." A smirk crossed my face.

Tharan shook his head. "You need your rest." He kissed my forehead again. "I will be right here next to you." He motioned to a little bed he had made on the floor. "I promise I won't leave you."

"Okay," I said, shutting my eyes. Sleep took me before Tharan could blow out the light.

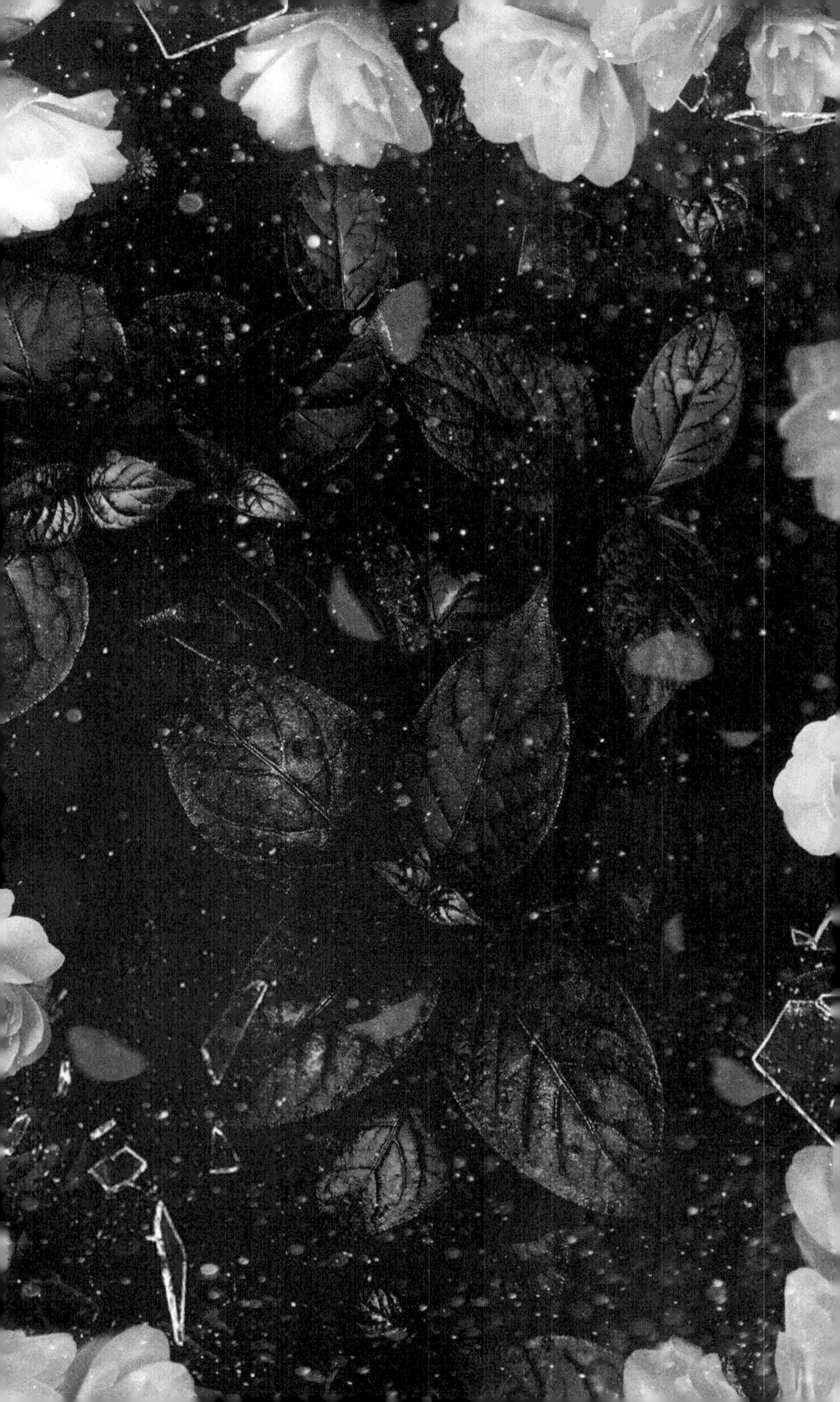

49 THARAN

Tharan watched Aelia sleep, running his hand through her hair, listening as she made little murmuring sounds. He couldn't explain how he'd became so enamored by such a woman. For once, he didn't need to pretend to be anything other than himself.

Reluctantly, he pulled himself away from her. The Scepter of the Dead lay quiet on the polished oak table. "Morrigan, show yourself. Bow before the Alder King."

The scepter sprung to life. From the mouth of the bird, a thick black smoke poured onto the floor, taking the shape of a woman warrior.

"My king," the Morrigan said, bowing low. The fair-haired maiden possessed both striking beauty and a fierce spirit, her azure eyes piercing and her complexion as fair as fresh milk. "You are not the Alder King."

"My father is dead. Killed at the hands of the kingdom your army massacred." A knife sliced through his heart at the thought of his father's untimely death.

The ghostly figure of the deity took a seat at the table. "It was glorious. My army has not shed blood for an age."

Tharan waved her off. "That's not why I summoned you."

The Morrigan cocked her head. "Then why, my king, did you summon me, if not to gloat over your victory?" She turned to look at Aelia, who still slept silently in the next room. "I have been waiting for one like her, you know. One which has the power to unleash me."

"I know what the scepter does to the wielder. It sucks their life force until there is nothing left of them but a dried husk."

"A small price to pay for the power the wielder gains." She tapped her fingers on the table rhythmically. "She is no normal magus. There is a great power trapped inside her."

Tharan raised an eyebrow at her. "She is made of that which came before."

"Before?" The Morrigan's brows knitted in confusion.

"Before the Trinity. Her mother is a Fate."

"So, she is a goddess?" The Morrigan leaned back in her chair, crossing her hands over her chest.

"We are all ancient in our own ways. My father was born from the trees themselves. I'm guessing you knew him." He fought back the tears welling behind his eyes.

A smile tugged at the corner of her lush lips. "Yes, I knew him before they called him king. When they called him by his name, Eoghan." She leaned in close to Tharan. The smell of death lingered on her skin. "I loved your father for many centuries. Before the Trinity culled the land, we slaughtered creatures, both magus and humans, together. But he never returned my feelings." She ran a ghostly finger over his scar. "How did you get this, fair king?" Sadness and longing flickered behind her ghoulish eyes.

Tharan lowered his eyes. "I loved the wrong woman."

"Shame. You have your father's eyes."

Clearing his throat, he glanced toward Aelia.

The Morrigan caught his glance, pouncing like a cat on a mouse.

"You care for her, don't you?" She sat back in the leather chair. "You called me to make a bargain for her life."

Tharan's body went rigid. "And what if I did?"

The Morrigan twirled her white hair lazily around her finger. "I'd say, once the blood is bound, there is no going back."

Tharan's heart blazed with what could be described as love for this woman he barely knew. "Take me. Bind me to your army."

The Morrigan chuckled. "Oh, but I would, my fair king. Too bad the blood has already been bound. There is no reversing it until the wielder is dead."

He clenched his jaw. "If you take too much from her, I will kill you, Morrigan."

"I am already dead, my king, but you can try. Besides, I think you'll come to find you will need me before too long."

Tharan raised his chin, studying the Morrigan and how confidently she sat there. "Go on."

"I know little more. I do not venture where the darkness lingers. But there are those who travel to the land of shadow, and they say those who live there are biding their time, waiting for an opportunity to escape into the land of living again and reclaim what they lost."

Tharan tucked the information away for later. "Thank you, Morrigan."

She nodded.

"One last thing before you return to the world beyond."

The Morrigan held him with an inquisitive stare.

"Don't kill her before I make her mine."

She gave him a small smirk. "Perhaps when I am free, I will call you mine. You never know."

"Be gone." He waved her off, and she disappeared the way she had come—into a cloud of smoke.

Aelia slept silently as Tharan climbed into bed next to her.

Intertwining his hand with hers, he replayed the fight in the castle in his mind, guilt plaguing him for not doing more to protect her.

Aelia flinched in her sleep. Her eyes fluttered open, a slight smile tugging at the corners of her pink lips. She opened her mouth as if to speak, but instead, she nuzzled her face into his chest. "Thank you for taking care of me, Tharan."

He ran his fingers through her ebony hair. "You're welcome," he said, kissing the top of her head as she slept. "I promise I will not fail you again."

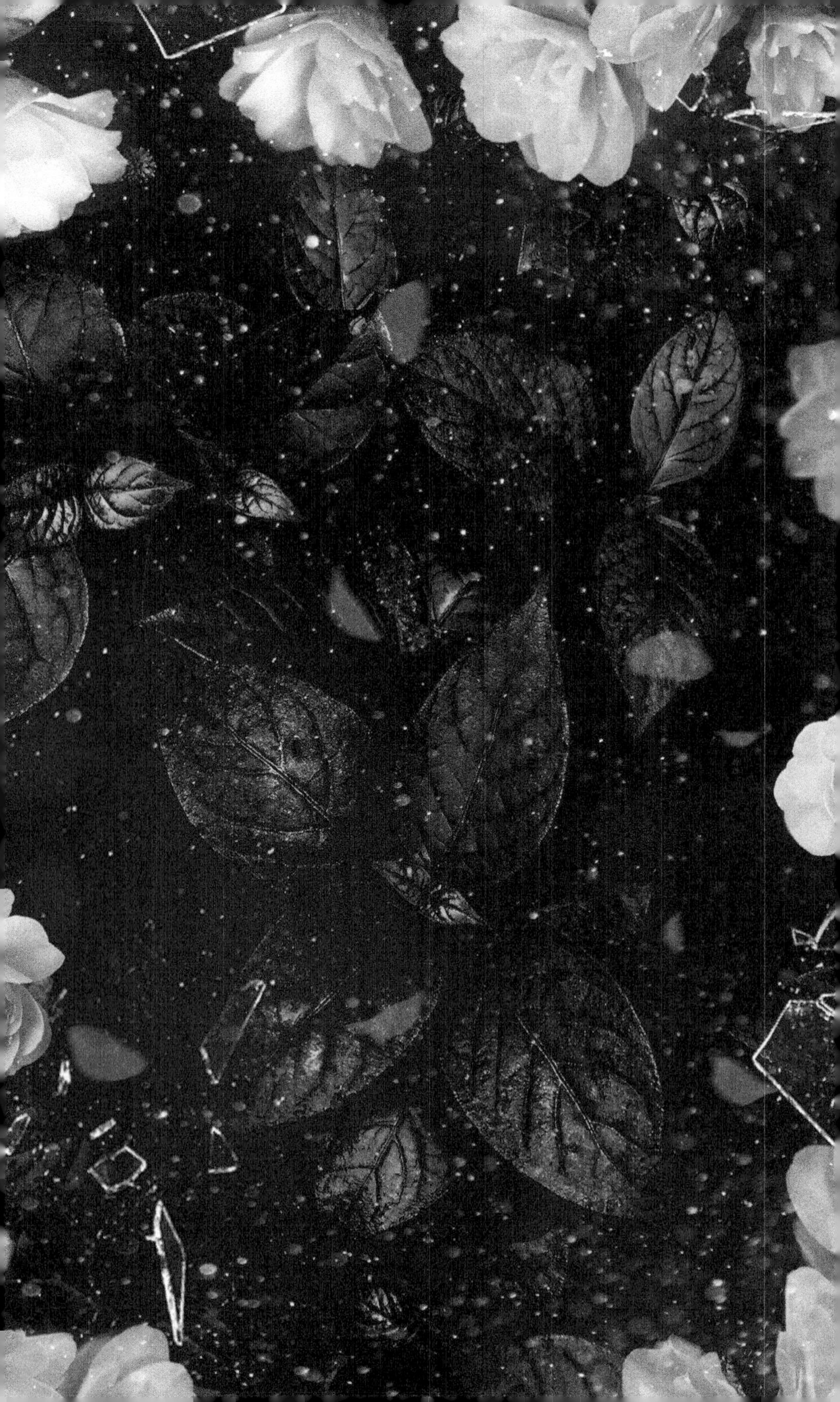

50 AELIA

THARAN TENDED TO ME AS I HEALED, DELIVERING SOUP FOR nourishment and assisting with mundane tasks. Far from my most glamorous moment, but if Tharan found it repulsive, he didn't reveal it.

He slept next to me at night, allowing me to rest my head on his chest. The powerful sedative the healer had given me provided me a brief respite from my nightmares.

Once I regained my strength, we headed back to the Woodland Realm. Arion bobbed his head contently as Tharan led him through the snow-slicked streets.

I cleared my throat nervously. "So, uh, do you want to talk about the whole me conjuring an Army of the Dead? Or are we just going to act like it didn't happen?"

He gave me a sideways glance. "I was wondering when you would bring it up."

I tossed my head. "Yes, well, I sort of made a deal with an ancient goddess."

Tharan didn't say anything, so I continued.

"I knew I needed a backup plan, and well… if I'm being honest… I had nothing to lose."

"Nothing to lose?" Hurt flooded his voice. "You had everything to lose. You had your sister, your freedom, m—" He stopped himself from saying what we both knew he wanted to say.

"I'm sorry, I wasn't thinking," I blurted out.

Tharan brought Arion to a halt. "Perhaps I was not clear about my intentions, Aelia."

My chest tightened.

His expression softened. "I'm falling for you. I want you to be mine forever. So, if you're planning on making a deal with an ancient deity... at least tell me first."

I let out a breath of relief. Years of being reprimanded for the slightest indiscretion set me on edge. Gideon burst into a rage anytime he perceived my actions as a threat. After a while, I stopped telling him things. I'd been on my own for so long that I didn't know how to have a partner. "I'm sorry. I'm not used to being part of a team."

He kissed my gloved hand. "You are not alone anymore, Aelia."

A bittersweet taste filled my mouth. I wanted to trust Tharan, but I had been let down so many times before. "Do not make promises you cannot keep, King."

Amolie and Roderick were waiting for us when we arrived at the Alder Palace, accompanied by Frost and Winter, who came bounding out of the foyer, licking Tharan's face.

"Well, it's nice to see you, too," he said as the pups whined for attention.

A solemn look crossed Amolie's round face. "Since Baylis is still asleep, I'm assuming you didn't get the amulet?"

I looked at my feet. "It's a long story, but we didn't."

A CURSE OF BREATH AND BLOOD

Amolie bit her lower lip. "I don't know how much longer I can keep her in her current state. We may not be able to pull her out." She ran a hand nervously through her wild curls.

I wrung my hands. "I should not have asked you to do this, Amolie. This must be taking a toll on you."

Amolie straightened. "I will do it for as long as possible, but I am not as skilled as others in my order. I may need to send for help."

I nodded. "Thank you for everything."

My heart ached at the thought of my sister wasting away in a bed for the rest of her life.

Tharan put a reassuring hand on my shoulder. "We'll figure something out."

Roderick cleared his throat. "Uh, there's something else."

"What?" I shot Amolie a panicked look.

"Caiden is here," she whispered, taking my hand in hers.

Caiden emerged from the shadows, the winter sun illuminating his cold blue eyes.

A rope knotted itself around my heart. Words eluded me. What do you say to someone who has no recollection of your history?

"I'm Caiden Stormweaver. I don't believe we've been formally introduced." He held out his hand in a sign of greeting.

My heart sank as the shred of hope I held onto disintegrated into nothing. Clearing my throat, I took his hand. "Aelia."

He gave me a devilish smile, making butterflies dance in my stomach. "Excuse me for saying this, but I can't help but feel we've met before."

A knife twisted in my heart. I pushed back hot tears. "Perhaps when you came to visit my sister, Baylis, in the Midlands."

"Oh, you're Baylis's sister. That makes sense now. I'd love to chat more about the Highlands and Gideon. You were impressive back there."

A sob built in my chest, and I nodded. "I'd like that too." My words, a whisper.

"I'll see you at dinner." He headed back into the castle.

A single tear snaked its way down my cheek.

We recapped our adventure in the Highlands over a dinner of roasted lamb stew.

"What about Gideon and Erissa? They still need to stand trial," Roderick asked.

"Scattered to the wind, laying low, biding their time," Caiden replied.

Roderick slurped his soup. "What of the Highlands?"

"Ashes, I assume. We may have made them martyrs in the eyes of some. The continent will divide further. But I still need to find them. They need to stand trial." Tharan took a sip of wine before motioning to Hopper to come closer. "Call the Phantom."

Hopper nodded and left the room.

I couldn't look at Caiden or Tharan, so I focused on Amolie.

"So, what's the plan?" Amolie said, dipping her crusty bread into her stew.

My eyes fell to the floor. "For once, I have nothing. Baylis will need to be sedated for the long-term…"

Underneath the table, Tharan placed a reassuring hand on my knee.

"Is there a chance Erissa still has the amulet?" Amolie asked.

"I think I can be of help in that regard," Caiden said, pulling something gold from his pocket. Laying the amulet on the table, its weight *thunked* against the hardwood.

The knot in my chest unbound. "Where… how?"

Caiden shrugged. "I saw her dangling it in front of your face when you were strapped to the table and figured it must be important." He slid the amulet across the table. "So, when I stabbed Erissa, I grabbed it."

I held the amulet to my chest. "Thank you, Caiden. You do not know what this means to me."

He nodded like the soldier he was. "Glad I could be of service."

Amolie's eyes darted between us. "Well, we better go try to wake the sleeping beauty up, don't you think?" She pushed her chair back from the table with a screech.

I followed suit, and we headed to Baylis's chamber together, leaving the men on their own.

Once we were out of earshot, Amolie said, "Well, that was awkward."

I gave her a knowing glance. "You're telling me."

"So, who are you going to choose?"

I shrugged. "I don't know."

Amolie pulled her dark curls back into a bun. "You and Caiden have a long history together."

"One filled with heartache and regret," I said, placing my hand on the door to Baylis's chamber. "Let's get Baylis back, and then we can focus on the mess that is my love life."

Amolie shook her head, a grin lighting her face. "Life is never dull being your friend."

Baylis lay perfectly still in her extended slumber.

I held my breath as Amolie pulled the blood from her veins.

The amulet weighed heavy in my outstretched hand. The rune engraved on the stone glowed as Amolie brought the blood nearer.

"Well, this is either a grand sign or a terrible one," she said, tapping her finger on the needle.

The amulet absorbed the drop.

Amolie and I exchanged hesitant looks. I took Baylis's hand in mine, praying to Ammena, one last time.

Baylis shook.

"Quickly, put something in her mouth so she does not bite off her tongue," Amolie cried as we tried to pin Baylis down.

Baylis's frigid, gray eyes remained open as if she were witnessing some dreadful spectacle only visible to her. Her body convulsed, and then, there was stillness. Once more, she lay motionless, her eyes closed as if in slumber.

Slamming my fist onto the side table, I let out a primal scream. "Damn you, Erissa. Damn, you, Trinity. I swear, I will have my vengeance on all of you."

I buried my head in the mattress, hiding my tears. "Please come back to me, Baylis. I need you. I can't do this alone."

The amulet burned hot in my hand, pulling it away, the jewel clunked onto the floor. "What the?"

Soft fingers touched my hair.

"Aelia?"

Baylis stared at me, her gray eyes full of life.

"Baylis?" I asked, unable to believe my eyes.

"Where am I?" She looked around the stark room.

A wave of relief washed over me. "You're in the Alder Palace."

Her eyes blinked rapidly. "Where?"

"It's a long story. I'll explain it later. For now, let's get you something to eat. You must be starving." Tears streamed down my face. For the first time in a long time, my body felt light.

"I was having the most terrifying dream," she said, taking my hand in hers.

"It's alright, I'm here now," I said, sliding into bed next to her.

She laid her head on my chest like she did when we were young.

Two satyrs brought in silver trays filled with food. The aromatic scent of stew wafted through the air. Caiden, Roderick, and Lucius lingered in the doorway.

"Caiden!" Baylis's face lit up at the sight of the Lord of Lightning.

"Baylis! I'm glad to see you're feeling better," Caiden said, embracing my sister.

A piece of my heart cracked.

Seeing my pain, Lucius returned a knowing glance.

"Please, all of you, join us." Baylis sat up, making room for the three large men on the bed.

"Leave room for me," Amolie said, climbing into the bed. "Eat, everyone, before it gets cold."

We did as we were told. Looking around at my friends, laughing and drinking, I could not believe my luck. A couple of months ago, I was a lone mercenary at the edge of the world, running from my past, slowly killing my future. Somehow, I still felt incomplete.

"There's something I need to do," I said, jumping off the bed, sending some of the rolls flying into the air.

"Where are you going?" Baylis shouted after me.

"I'll be back shortly. There's something I need to do."

My heart beat wildly in my chest as I climbed the stairs to Tharan's study. Each step brought me closer to something I had been afraid to admit. Tharan helped me. He saw me for the person I was without the titles forced upon me.

Heaving open the heavy doors to the study, I found Tharan sitting cross-legged on the floor with his two pups. Their tails thumped on the floor wildly at the sight of me.

"This isn't what it looks like," Tharan said, getting to his feet. "I wasn't cuddling them."

"Yes, you were, but that's not why I'm here." I rested my hands on my hips.

He cocked his head in concern. "Is something wrong with Baylis?"

"No, she's fine. Well... she seems to be." I moved closer to him. The scent of the forest radiated from his glowing skin. "I need to tell you something."

"Oh?" He swallowed hard.

I gazed into his green eyes, searching for any hint of deceit, but found only love reflected back at me. "I think I'm in love with you, too."

His angular face lit up with delight as he pulled me in for the first kiss of many.

Our lips explored one another. No longer holding back the passion we both felt. Tharan's hands caressed the curves of my body.

I deserved this. I deserved the love of a man like Tharan. We were good together. I would not deny myself happiness any longer.

Tharan pulled away, taking my face into his hands. "You are everything I dreamed of," he said before kissing me on the forehead. "Now, shall I meet your sister?"

I unscrewed the gold earring once more, letting my scar show. "Yes, I think that seems fitting, seeing as you saved her life."

Taking my hand in his, we made our way to Baylis's chambers.

I don't know what the future holds for us, but with Tharan by my side, I know I am on the right path.

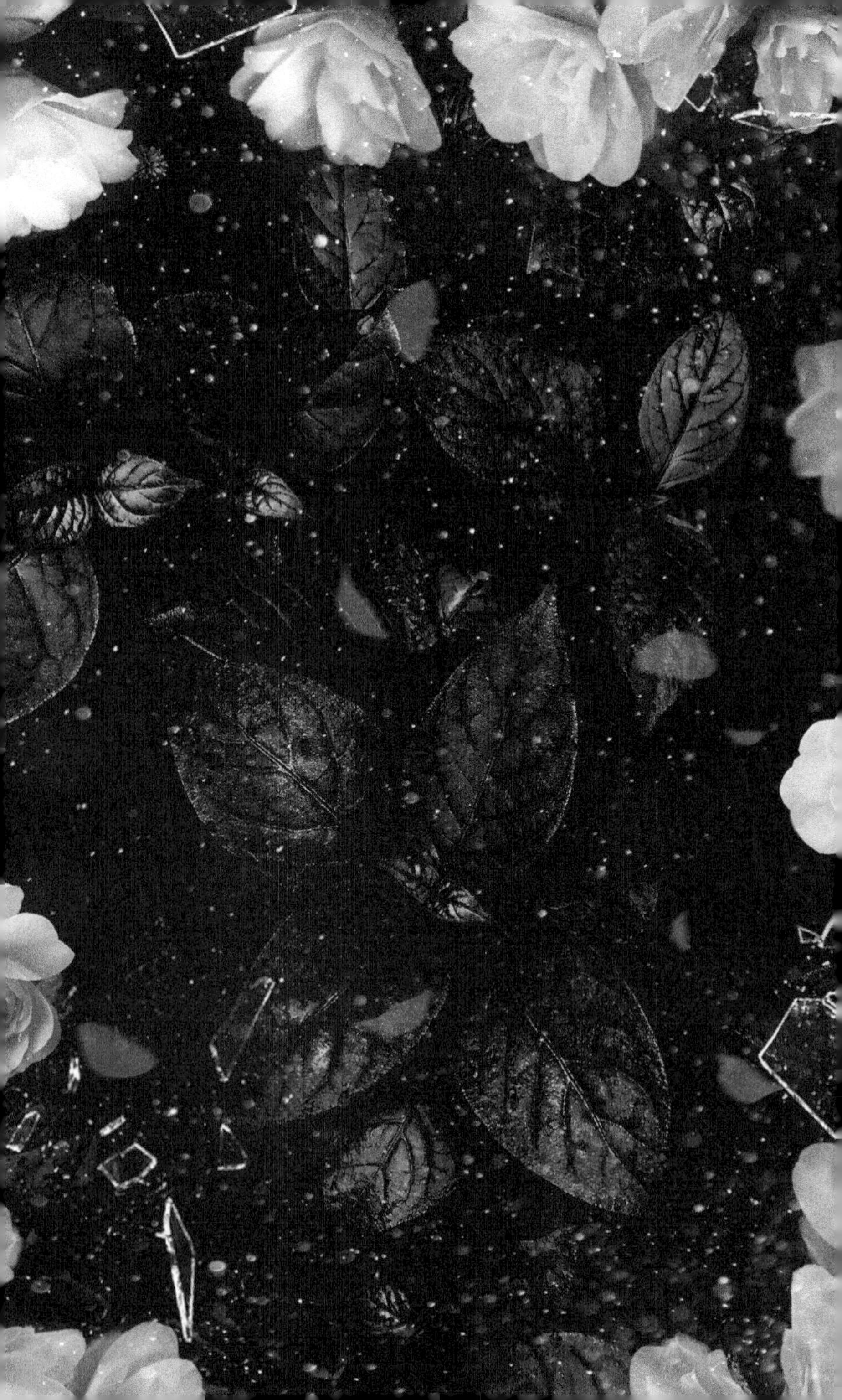

EPILOGUE

Gideon's freshly shined boots clicked against the stone floor as he paced back and forth.

"Are you sure you're ready, my love?"

Baylis sat on his bed, wrapped in a fur-lined blanket, her blonde hair cascading over her bare shoulders. "Yes."

"It will not be easy. Your sister is… difficult." He ran a hand down her jaw and over her shoulders, making her blush.

"She deserves whatever is coming to her." Her gray eyes held his.

Gideon smirked. "Good."

"But what about your kingdom?"

"Oh, my sweet love." He cupped her angelic face in his hands. "Sometimes we must destroy the things that we love to build anew. Like a phoenix rising from the ashes."

Baylis nodded.

"Should this plan succeed, you and I will be separated for a long time. I want you to know that I love you." He kissed her forehead gently. "But I need you on the inside, to relay information to me. You're the only one she'll trust."

"Yes, of course. I know how to play that part well."

Pushing her golden hair behind her ears, Gideon examined Baylis. "I have no doubt you will make me proud."

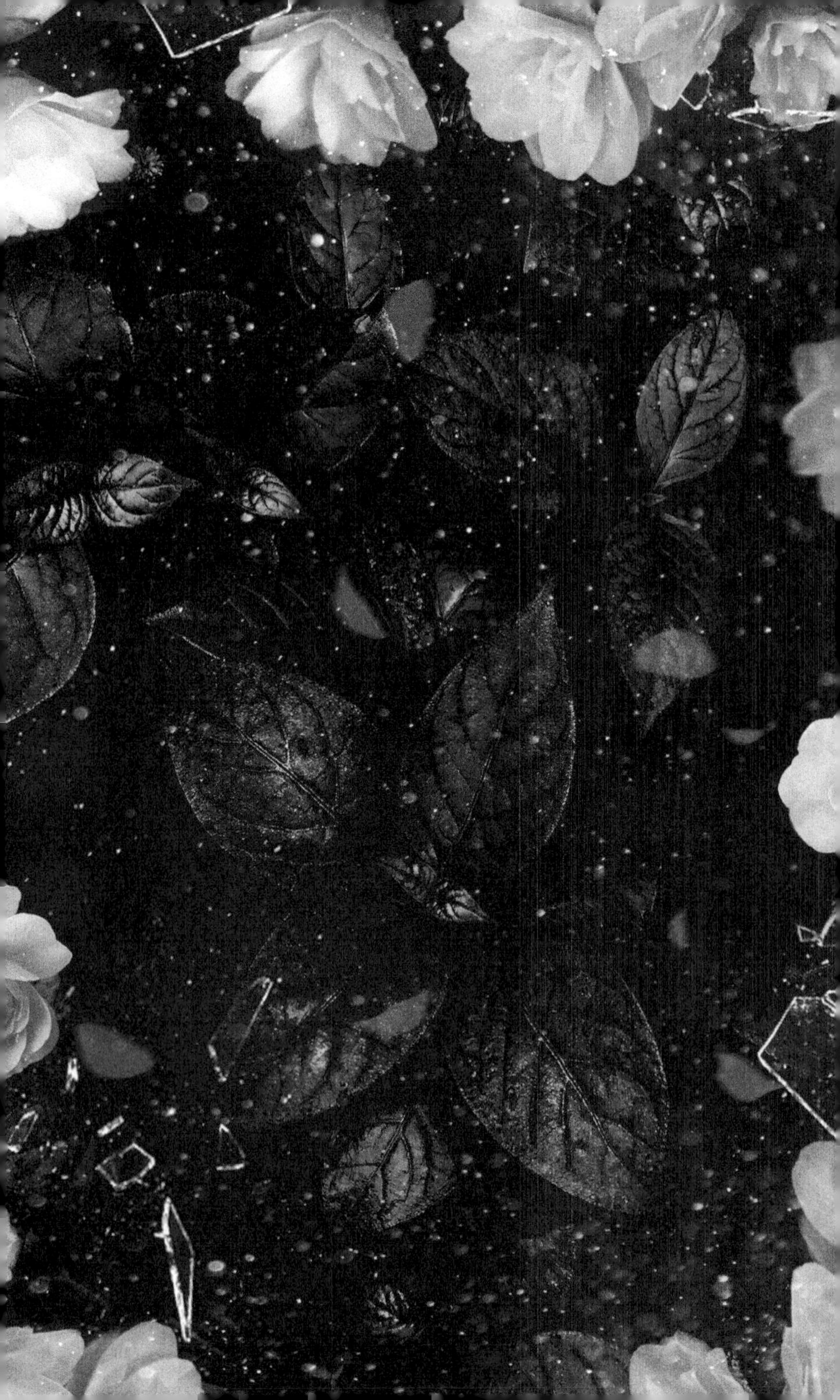

THANK YOU FOR READING A CURSE OF BREATH AND BLOOD!

We hope you enjoyed it as much as we enjoyed bringing it to you. We just wanted to take a moment to encourage you to review the book. Follow this link: A Curse of Breath and Blood to be directed to the book's Amazon product page to leave your review.

Every review helps further the author's reach and, ultimately, helps them continue writing fantastic books for us all to enjoy.

Also in series:
A Curse of Breath and Blood

Want to discuss our books with other readers and even the authors? Join our Discord server today and be a part of the Aethon community.

Facebook | Instagram | Twitter | Website

Join our non-spam mailing list by visiting www.subscribepage.com/aethonreadersgroup_romantasy and never miss future releases.

Looking for more great Romantasy?

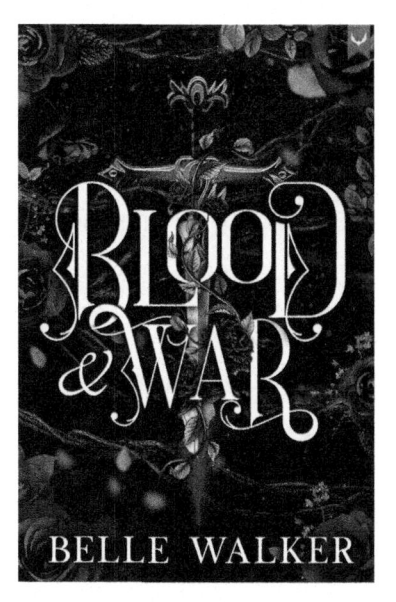

Loyalty and love can ruin you. But hope is the deadliest of all. For ten years Demitria Collins has fought the creatures of nightmares to protect the one person she has left. With a rising string of demon attacks on the forefront, she knows it's only a matter of time until they're next. But when a routine patrol goes awry, and Demitria has a fated encounter with the legendary Horsemen known as War, everything she fought for is threatened. Including her life. Kellan, one of the Four Horsemen of the Apocalypse, has been sent to Earth by the High Council of Eden to restore the balance with his siblings. Dispatched on their newest assignment, he expected the task to be simple. Not for his charge to be human. When a split second decision leaves even more blood on his hands, Kellan has questions for the council– Ones they won't answer. The warrior should embody everything Demitria hates, but a growing darkness forces them into an unlikely allegiance to uncover a deadly truth. When an inexplicable pull complicates matters even worse, and that unyielding hostility turns into something beautiful and fiery that breaks through every belief they've ever had, both know the consequences will be deadly. But together, they might stand a chance to restore order before the ultimate destruction of a planet that she, and the High Council, hold dear.

Get Blood & War Now!

A shattered life. A dormant power. An arms race between realms—for her. When twenty-one-year-old Nyleeria met King Thaddeus for the first time outside her family's rickety cabin, she had no idea how irrevocably her life would change. The Spark. Magic. Spellcraft. Fae. The Great War. All elements wiped from human memory and written histories—an ignorance Nyleeria would have gladly maintained. But fate had other plans when it shattered her world with the disappearance of her siblings and the brutal murder of her parents all because of a latent power she unwittingly possessed. The primordial Spark lying dormant within her was coveted by two opposing realms who would unquestionably use its force to extinguish the other. In a war she never knew existed, where the veil between human and fae realms is becoming dangerously thin, Nyleeria finds herself in possession of the very magic that can alter the fabric of her world. **Don't miss this captivating adult Fantasy Romance by debut author CC Hartly. With its intricate magic systems, believable characters, and richly developed world-building, it's sure to delight romantasy and epic fantasy readers everywhere!**

Get Mythic Spark Now!

For all our Romantasy books, visit our website.

ACKNOWLEDGMENTS

I'd first like to thank my husband. Without his love and support, this book would've never been possible. Not only because he's my biggest fan but because without him, this book could never have been written. He is my light in the darkness, my knight in shining armor, and my best friend.

Speaking of best friends, I also have to thank my dogs, Duke and Zeus, who happily let me walk them ten miles a day while I worked out the plot and characters of these books.

Thank you to my family, who have always supported every endeavor I embark on. I love you more than you know. Especially my mom and sister– we've walked through the fire together and come out clean on the other side. I love you to the moon and back.

This book would not be what or where it is today without the help of my writing group, who helped me craft the query that got this book its deal and helped me improve my writing and listen to my bitching.

Thank you to Crystal Lynn, who ripped this book apart and sewed it back together.

And thank you to Arzu and Nicole for always letting me vent.

Thank you to my beta readers, especially Ally, Rusty, Sage, and Kyle, who gave me excellent feedback and continued to cheer me on through my querying journey.

ABOUT THE AUTHOR

K.W. Foster is the author of deliciously haunting and spicy fantasy romances featuring morally grey women and the men (and women) who love them. Originally from the Midwest, she now resides in the Mid-Atlantic with her husband and two big fluffy dogs. Follow her on Instagram @authorkwfoster, and on TikTok @kwfosterwrites

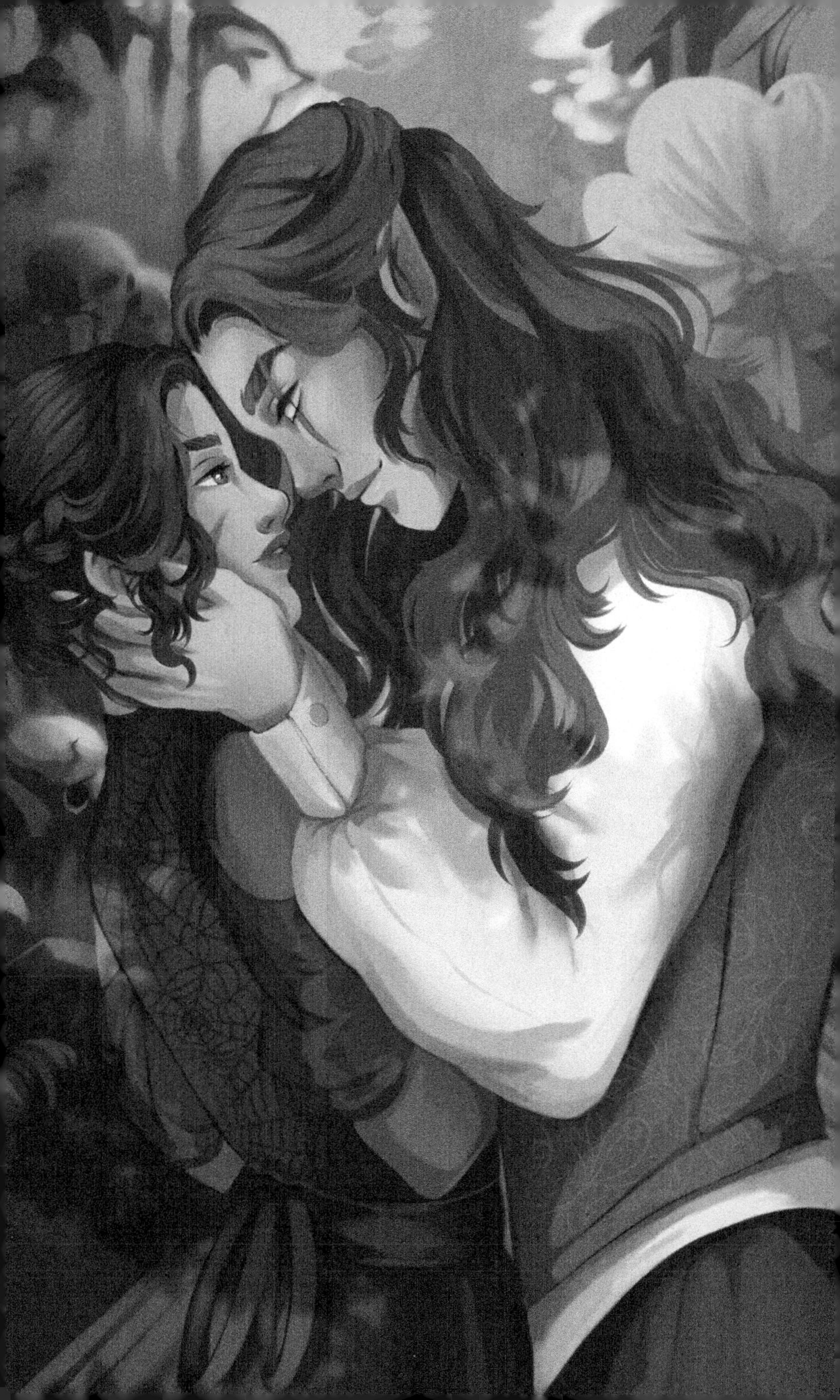